About the Author

Jennifer Gladwell is the pen name of freelance editor and writer, Genevieve Herr. She has previously written romantic fiction such as *A Gift in December* and *This Year, Maybe* but has always loved the Golden Age of crime fiction. Gen lives in Scotland with her family.

The
BOOKSHOP
MURDERS

JENNIFER GLADWELL

HODDER &
STOUGHTON

First published in Great Britain in 2025 by Hodder & Stoughton Limited
An Hachette UK company

This paperback edition published in 2025

The authorised representative in the EEA is Hachette Ireland, 8 Castlecourt
Centre, Dublin 15, D15 XTP3, Ireland (email: info@hbgi.ie)

1

A CIP catalogue record for this title is available from the British Library

Paperback ISBN 978 1 399 70428 1
ebook ISBN 978 1 399 70426 7

Typeset in Sabon MT by Hewer Text UK Ltd, Edinburgh
Printed and bound in Great Britain by Clays Ltd, Elcograf S.p.A.

Hodder & Stoughton policy is to use papers that are natural, renewable
and recyclable products and made from wood grown in sustainable
forests. The logging and manufacturing processes are expected to
conform to the environmental regulations of the country of origin.

Hodder & Stoughton Limited
Carmelite House
50 Victoria Embankment
London EC4Y 0DZ

www.hodder.co.uk

For Alex, Florence and Theodore, with love

'Vengeance and retribution require a long time; it is the rule.'

– Charles Dickens, *A Tale of Two Cities*

Prologue

he streets of Bloomsbury were wet with spring rain, gleaming in the lamplight. A figure moved quietly through the shadows towards Cecil Court. He paused for a moment, listening. A cat brushed against his ankles, startling him, and he let out a low breath of a laugh.

'Hello,' he murmured. 'Fancy seeing you here.'

He stooped to pet it for a time, then straightened, pulling his collar close. A perfectly ordinary man on a perfectly ordinary night. But for him, tonight was a long time in the making.

So much careful thought, preparation and planning, all coming down to this.

He reached into his coat pocket, felt the light weight of the knife. A delicate blade, designed for quite a different task. And yet it would suit his purpose. The night was fraught with danger and difficulty, he understood that, he was no fool. Confidence surged through him – the confidence of a man who has patiently waited, biding his time for this very moment.

He glanced at his watch, tilting the face to see the time. He was early. In only a few short moments, everything would change. There would be no going back. He almost felt sorry for what he was about to do; he deplored pain and violence and this country had already seen too much of it. But he had no choice.

Footsteps approached, hesitant, uncertain. The man found himself smiling in the dark. How long ago had his victim's fate been sealed? What terrible thread had led him here? At last, after years of waiting, Fate had handed him the means to enact justice.

Tonight, he would act at last.

Tonight, the first blow would fall.

PART ONE

DAILY MIRROR

Mummy Reaches Our Shores!
But does it bring a deadly curse?

Tragedy swiftly followed triumph. Within minutes of the historic discovery and opening of the tomb by the Egyptian Society, Sir Archibald Drake, funder of the expedition, was dead. Heart failure, the doctor said. But, this reporter asks, was it? For the expedition has since been beset by misfortune. Maybe, this reporter wonders, the Egyptian king's resting place should never have been disturbed . . .

Speaking exclusively to Max Bird at the *Daily Mirror*, the expedition's leader, Dr Gordon Lyle, spoke of his regret that the discovery had been overshadowed by tragedy. He did not, however, deny rumours of a curse. 'I am a man of science. And yet,' he told this paper, 'the past holds untold mysteries. Who can say what power this mummy possesses?'

And now, the mummy has reached our British shores. And many fear that Sir Archibald Drake's death may just be the beginning.

Chapter 1

T he man speaking at the lecture podium was handsome, famous, widely celebrated – and Lucy Darkwether disliked him on sight.

Dr Lyle was the leader of the famous expedition and tomb discovery in Egypt. He wore his shirt sleeves rolled up to reveal tanned forearms, his fair hair was artfully rumpled and he had intensely blue eyes. He might have been standing on a rocky outcrop in Persia instead of on-stage in the British Museum's elegant reading room, opened that night especially for the occasion – his lecture on the discovery of the mummy.

'Look at him,' Lucy murmured. 'He's central casting for dashing explorer. A bit too good to be true, don't you think, Professor?'

'It would seem he can do no wrong,' said her friend and colleague Mr Tollesbury, his pale-blue eyes crinkling in a smile. 'The golden boy of archaeology. But rumour has it the man never lets the facts get in the way of a good story.'

Lucy had never seen Dr Lyle before that night, but she'd heard plenty about him. Most people had – Dr Lyle was famous up and down the country. The leader of many an expedition to the Middle East, he had most recently headed up the Egyptian Society's expedition to the pyramids of Giza. The expedition had also been funded in part by the wealthy American heiress Mrs Moira van Buren, and Sir Archibald Drake, an elderly peer whose family fortune had long benefitted the Society. The press and public, their interest whetted by the notorious opening of Tutankhamun's tomb five years earlier by Lord Carnarvon, had all avidly followed the story. After all, Lord Carnarvon had died, suddenly and mysteriously, only a few months after the tomb opening. That had been all that was needed to seed sensationalist newspaper reports of the cursed tomb. The public were avidly awaiting something equally thrilling.

So far, this had surpassed expectations.

First, an actual burial chamber of a king had been discovered by the motley crew on the expedition. Rumours of vast piles of gold and jewels swirled in the press. Public imagination had then reached fever pitch when Sir Archibald Drake had suddenly died on the very day the tomb was opened. As soon as the press got hold of the news, they had only fanned the flames: now anyone who was anyone in London believed there was a curse bestowed upon the tomb.

Now plucked from Egypt and brought to British shores – such was the expedition's 'Finders Keepers' attitude – the tomb was set to be put out on display somewhere in London over the next few days and excitement levels throughout the city were through the roof.

It was the mummy itself, of course, that would draw the crowd, and Lucy had been waiting with interest to see where it would be exhibited in London ever since she'd heard the news. She had a keen interest in Ancient Egypt herself, having studied Ancient History at Oxford. When she heard that the museum was looking for a more intimate venue, rather than its own vast rooms, to place the body, she even wrote to them to suggest her own bookshop in Cecil Court. She had heard nothing back.

Although she had never *really* expected that they would take her up on her suggestion, her excitement turned to irritation when she discovered that the valuable exhibition was in fact being housed a mere few metres away from her shop at Dakin & Co Rare Books, owned by her most disliked neighbour.

'Mr Dakin,' Lucy had fumed to whoever was around her when she'd heard the news, 'is a charlatan who knows as much about the Ancient Egyptian period as I do about – about fishing.' She had to admit her dislike of Mr Dakin was partly to do with his uncanny ability to always be in the right place at the right time. He had large premises and his bookshop was the first port of call for the great and good of society. Next to them, Lucy's own bookshop was something of an underdog. Snaring the mummy was a coup by Dakin. Just that morning, Lucy had been forced to watch as the precious mummy was transported into the space, with him issuing anxious instructions.

Despite her fury, Lucy had been curious enough to attend the lecture tonight at the famous British Museum with her old college professor. Although there was no mummy to catch a glimpse of, Lucy was nevertheless excited to watch Dr Lyle speak here tonight. Or rather, she had been before she arrived – desperate simply to hear the secrets that had led them to their discovery. What she hadn't anticipated was how galling it would be to watch Dakin smirking in the wings as Dr Lyle held forth. Dakin was a short man with lavishly pomaded hair and an expression Lucy could only describe as smug. Close to the podium, the rest of the Egyptian Society were seated – Mrs van Buren herself, a tall, elegant woman with a striking grey streak in her dark hair; Sir Hector Derwent, a red-faced peer who had backed the expedition, and a bearded man who Lucy didn't recognise, who kept glancing at the clock, looking rather bored with the lecture.

It was so crowded in the auditorium that many were standing. Lucy found herself crammed at the very back, along with Mr Tollesbury and a cleaner clutching a broom.

'Sorry you lost out on getting the mummy in the shop, Lucy,' said Mr Tollesbury. He had always possessed an uncanny knack for knowing exactly what Lucy was thinking, even now, as Lucy pretended to pay attention to what Dr Lyle was saying.

'Dakin does have more room than us,' Lucy replied, practically. 'We'd have to move all of your first editions.'

Mr Tollesbury shuddered. 'Over my dead body. One day those will be worth a lot of money.'

They fell silent as Dr Lyle concluded the thrilling tale of the discovery of the tomb, culminating in bandits attacking the camp and storms battling the ship on their return voyage.

'And now,' Dr Lyle said, beaming out at the audience, 'you've humoured me long enough. I wish only to thank you for coming tonight.' His eyes twinkled. 'Many of you will have read the lurid tales of an ancient curse and might be surprised to see myself and the other members of the expedition still standing – and yet we remain well, my friends.'

Sir Hector, down in the front row, mimed mopping his brow, while Mrs van Buren smiled faintly. The bored-looking bearded man craned his neck to look again at the clock.

'I only hope my words have been helpful in satisfying your curiosity regarding this extraordinary discovery – for we can't all travel to Egypt, can we?' There was a murmur of laughter. 'And I am delighted that you will all be able to visit the exhibition at none other than Dakin's Rare Books in Cecil Court tomorrow night, before the mummy is removed for study at the museum.'

Mr Dakin gave a small bow to the audience's applause.

'Now, before we step into the hall outside to raise a glass or two to the historic discovery, are there any questions?' asked Dr Lyle, smiling out at his rapt audience.

A man near the front raised his hand. 'Do *you* believe you've unleashed the mummy's curse?' he asked.

Dr Lyle shook his head. 'Sir Archibald Drake's death was indeed tragic, but there was no supernatural force at work. He had a long-term heart condition, exacerbated by the heat. The doctor present – Mr Ahmed here – is certain he died of a heart attack.' The bored-looking man to his left inclined his head slightly – *the expedition doctor*, Lucy thought. Not a member of the Egyptian Society, but still in attendance when the tomb was opened.

'And yet you disrespected the king's soul by disturbing his resting place!' called a woman.

'We undertook this expedition in pursuit of public knowledge,' said Dr Lyle, unfazed. 'We are men of science, not superstition.' He nodded at Mrs van Buren. 'And women, of course,' he added quickly.

'Because the Ancient Egyptians knew nothing of science,' Mr Tollesbury murmured to Lucy.

'I suppose it suits the Society to have the public half-believing in a curse,' Lucy said, looking around at the rapt audience. 'It's why most of them are here, let's be honest. The potential for gossip and death is more exciting to them than Ancient Egypt, unfortunately. Lyle certainly knows how to pack a lecture hall.'

Dr Lyle continued to field questions with ease and charm, then held out his hands for quiet. 'I will be happy to answer any more questions outside,' he said. 'But before we leave, I would like to thank the rest of the team, without whom the exhibition would never have been possible. To our patrons, our sadly departed Sir Archibald Drake, and to Mrs van Buren, without whose generosity the Society would never have made the strides it has done. To Sir Hector, our long-standing patron and the founder of the Society. To my dear Mr Dakin, who will be giving my humble discovery a safe home for one evening only. Thank you, each and every one of you—'

'What about *me*?' cried a shrill voice from the crowd. 'Leaving me out, are you Lyle?'

Dr Lyle paused and peered out at the crowd, still smiling. 'What was that?' he said. 'Not the voice of an Ancient Egyptian king I hope!'

There was a ripple of laughter, and then a scuffle as a dishevelled man in a crumpled suit and unkempt hair shouldered his way through the crowd. He looked to be about thirty and was trembling with rage.

'Leaving me out, are you?' he demanded again, more forcibly. He was unshaven and his eyes were wild. 'I'd like to know, who raised the possibility of a tomb in the first place? Who spent the last five years uncovering its location? Who pinpointed the co-ordinates? Who—'

There were murmurs and gasps from the crowd, and a scattering of shocked laughter. Dr Lyle shook his head, still smiling, although Lucy thought his expression was a little fixed. 'I don't know what you mean.' His eyes moved over the man's head and Lucy noticed a security guard lay a hand on his arm.

'Come with us, sir,' the security guard said reassuringly. 'This isn't the place. If you've something to discuss with Dr Lyle, then you can do it after. You can have a nice chat.'

'Something to discuss!' cried the man with a high-pitched laugh. 'A nice chat! Lyle stole my life's work! He's standing there holding forth about the expedition that made him famous and I, who discovered the tomb, have nothing! I've lost my job, my reputation! I have a wife and child! I—'

'My dear Dr Curry!' cut in Dr Lyle sharply. 'You are confused.'
So, Dr Lyle clearly knows the intruder, thought Lucy.

'Confused,' shrieked the man bitterly. 'Confused am I, Dr Lyle? I have evidence, you know! Evidence that this tomb was found because of research by *me*, Dr W. Curry, that you stole.' He appealed to the gathered audience. 'I was out there in Egypt with them! I led them to the spot. The tomb would never have been opened without me!' He gave a loud and nasty laugh. 'Sir Hector, Dr Lyle, Mrs van Buren – the esteemed Society, ladies and gentlemen! And yet I know their secrets. I could ruin each and every one of—'

'Enough!' snapped Sir Hector sharply, half-rising and nodding at the security guard. 'Remove him, if you please.'

Another man took hold of Dr Curry's other arm.

'I *will* have revenge on the Society!' the man cried, as he was urged backwards. 'I'll bring down the whole rotten lot of you!'

'Oh dear,' murmured Lucy.

The man wasn't going without a fight: he aimed a vicious kick at one of the guards, who yelped and bent over. By this point, the guards had managed to drag him to the back of the room to be level with where Lucy and Mr Tollesbury were standing.

Mr Tollesbury sighed. 'I think I'm needed,' he said nobly.

'Professor, remember your blood pressure,' Lucy said, as he squared his shoulders and entered the fray. For a man in his sixties, the professor was surprisingly wiry, and together he and the two security guards managed to wrestle the struggling man out of the door. 'There, there,' Mr Tollesbury could be heard saying. 'Come and get some fresh air and cool off a bit.'

'He's lying – why won't anyone listen – I have *proof*—'

The heavy door closed behind Dr Curry's faint protests. The cleaner beside Lucy, a stooped man with a drooping moustache, sighed. 'If this overruns, I'll miss the bus,' he muttered, to no one in particular. 'Got to wait to clear up after.' Lucy took in his dejected air, before snapping back to the front as Dr Lyle once again spoke.

'Apologies, ladies and gentlemen.' He smoothed a lock of fair hair off his forehead as he did, and Lucy caught a sheen of perspiration in the lights. In spite of his wide smile, she thought he looked shaken. 'These expeditions catch the public fancy, and that can attract some interesting types. Unlike your good selves, of course!' Polite laughter broke out. 'Now, shall we continue this conversation over some drinks?'

The audience filtered out into the atrium, where certain objects from the tomb were displayed, leaving museum staff to stack chairs and sweep up. In the atrium, waiters circled with trays of champagne. Dr Lyle took up a position in front of an iron dagger and was immediately surrounded by a crowd of audience members, brandishing their programmes and asking more questions.

Mr Tollesbury came back in after a short while, straightening his tie as he approached Lucy again.

'Are you all right?' Lucy asked.

'He was perfectly meek once we got him outside. I put him in a taxi and he promised to go home quietly,' the professor said. 'I think he scared himself. All bark and no bite.'

'Well done,' said Lucy, selecting a stuffed mushroom from a silver tray. 'Lyle didn't like the interruption, did he? I wonder who that man was – a Dr W. Curry, he said.'

'Exhibitions like this *can* attract a strange crowd,' said Mr Tollesbury philosophically. 'Frustrated academics and historians and all sorts of hangers-on – I should know.' He shuddered, clearly thinking of his long and somewhat dull tenure at Oxford as professor of Ancient History, punctuated by the occasional dispiriting dig in the English countryside. 'I'm glad to be out of that game. It's thankless work for the most part, so everyone wants a piece of the glory when they finally strike gold. Dr Lyle will go down in history for this discovery.'

'Speaking of which, shall we introduce ourselves to the man of the hour?' said Lucy, nodding at Dr Lyle, who was standing with the rest of the Society and the expedition doctor, Mr Ahmed. 'I'm curious to meet him.'

They joined the admiring group around Dr Lyle, who was mid-anecdote, flushed and beaming, a drink in his hand. A lock of his golden hair had fallen rakishly over one eye. 'Yes, yes dear lady – there were indeed bandits at the tomb! A whole horde of them. And that is why I always carry a revolver,' he finished triumphantly, patting his breast pocket. 'You never know when the locals might turn nasty.'

'It does sound terribly dangerous,' said a woman, clutching her furs to her fearfully. 'Bandits – and heart attacks – and then storms at sea . . .'

'All in the pursuit of knowledge, dear lady,' said Dr Lyle. He took a large swallow of champagne. 'Although not *every* incident was archaeology related.' He nudged Sir Hector, who was standing next to him. 'Remember that married woman outside of Port Said?'

'A misunderstanding,' said Sir Hector coldly. 'When it comes to the dig itself,' he assured the animated crowd, 'we of course ensure a level of protection. The natives *can* be unfriendly.'

The exhibition doctor, Mr Ahmed, shifted and Lucy turned to study him. He was a tall man with grizzled hair at the temples and wire-rimmed glasses. He turned his champagne glass in long fingers. 'People don't want their dead disturbed,' he said, his calm voice carrying above the chatter. 'I should think you'd get the same response if you started digging up Westminster Cathedral.'

'Oh quite, quite,' said Dr Lyle, with a grin, his mind clearly still running along coarser channels. His handsome face was ruddy, his voice was slightly slurred, and Lucy was beginning to wonder if he'd had too much champagne, or was simply intoxicated by his triumph. He lowered his voice, although it still carried. 'This country can be as prickly. My first ever dig in the Dales, sleepy little place and not a decent-looking girl in it – I was there for the Victoria Caves, I remember – and I still found myself in hot water with a local girl. Couldn't pack fast enough. Why, she had a club foot and a squint eye.'

The mood in the surrounding area turned cooler. 'Well!' murmured the woman in furs, in a scandalised voice. Beside Lucy, Mr Tollesbury flinched and Sir Hector scowled. Mr Ahmed set down his drink. Lyle beamed at them all, unconscious of any offence.

'I think I'll be off now,' said Mr Ahmed. 'I'm in surgery first thing tomorrow.' He nodded to them all and left.

'But those days are done, eh,' said Sir Hector, shooting a dark look at Dr Lyle.

'Absolutely! I am a happily married man now!' Dr Lyle exclaimed, gesturing to a woman sitting in the corner, resplendent in purple velvet, who was immersed in a paperback. 'Married to a wonderful woman.'

Married to a wonderfully rich woman, Lucy thought. Mrs Lyle had been Lady Dartington before she married and had funded her husband's expeditions from then on, alongside Sir Archibald. Although, Lucy recalled, not the last one. The Society had needed funding for that urgently – it was only thanks to Mrs van Buren stepping in that they had been able to go.

'Congratulations,' Lucy said now, taking control of the conversation and pushing through the group to get closer to Dr Lyle to shake his hand. 'My name is Miss Darkwether – my shop is just next door to where the mummy will be housed tomorrow night. I can think about nothing else.'

'Wonderful,' said Dr Lyle, beaming at her. He took another large swallow of champagne. 'You will have to come along for the unveiling.' He winked. 'If you're not too scared, of course, my dear.'

'I'm not scared,' Lucy said. 'I studied Ancient History at Oxford, with Mr Tollesbury here and I know better than to believe in sensationalist stories. I'm more than familiar with—'

Mr Tollesbury put out his hand and shook Lyle's. 'Quite a wonderful discovery,' he said warmly. 'Really, I must congratulate you, Lyle. I have long admired the research that led you to the tomb. I am in the field myself, you know.'

'Really,' said Dr Lyle, casting a disparaging glance at Mr Tollesbury, in his worn but neatly darned tweed suit. 'I don't think our paths have ever crossed.'

'Probably not,' agreed Mr Tollesbury. 'You move in more prestigious circles – I'm only a humble, retired professor. Lucy, I see our neighbour Mr Dakin over there – we must congratulate him too.' He bowed to Dr Lyle. 'Goodnight.'

'What a nightmare of a man,' Lucy said, refreshing herself with another sip of champagne after they moved away. 'Not what I expected. How strange to have such a brilliant mind – and yet be so – so coarse, to use one of my mother's favourite words.'

'Indeed – very coarse. I don't approve of those sorts of stories or behaviour,' Mr Tollesbury said severely. 'Why, that story about the girl – I should have been ashamed to act like that as a young man. I dare say I'm awfully old-fashioned. There's Dakin. I suppose he can't resist gloating.'

'Miss Darkwether. Professor.'

Lucy turned to see Dakin, pale gooseberry eyes protruding with his own importance. 'My neighbours from Cecil Court! How nice of you to join us. I came to offer you two invitations to my little exhibition tomorrow night.' He pressed two embossed cards into Lucy's hand. 'It's completely sold out! I heard you applied to host it yourself, my dear lady. I can understand the museum's reasoning though – I must say, such a precious artefact needs *expert* handling and care.'

'I imagine you've created quite the spectacle,' said Mr Tollesbury, before Lucy could retort. 'Expectations are high. London can talk of nothing but the mummy – and tomorrow night they will lay eyes on it. What an occasion! A great deal of responsibility for you, of course.'

'Indeed,' said Mr Dakin. A look of faint concern crossed his face. 'It *is* a great deal of responsibility. I want the exhibition to be a *triumph*.'

'Let's hope the mummy's curse doesn't mess it up,' said Lucy bluntly.

Mr Dakin wagged a finger at her. 'You've been reading the *Mirror*, my dear! That rag of Max Bird's. I hope you aren't nervy about such things.'

'Aren't *you* nervy?' said Lucy, widening her eyes, hoping to frighten him a bit. 'Why, within moments of the tomb opening, Sir Archibald was dead. As though we were being warned.'

'Nonsense,' Mr Dakin said loftily. 'I reject superstition!'

'Superstition is not to be dismissed lightly,' said Mr Tollesbury, his tone serious. 'It has a great power.' He gestured at the crowd clustered around Dr Lyle. 'You can see it tonight, can't you? All these rational people, educated people, under the spell of an ancient curse. Wiser men than me acknowledge the dead should not be disturbed. Many papers have been written about it, especially recently.'

'Nonsense,' Mr Dakin said again, although more uncertainly. 'Utter nonsense. Now, Mr Tollesbury, a small favour – as the expert in Egyptology, I wondered if I could ask you about the leaflet I have written to accompany the exhibition . . .' He led the professor off, Mr Tollesbury casting a desperate look over his shoulder at Lucy.

Shame there isn't really a curse, Lucy thought gloomily. Dakin deserved one. She knew he would pump the professor for his knowledge so he could look good in front of the audience tomorrow night, and never credit him. She would wait five minutes, then rescue the professor and they would leave. She went to put on her gloves, then realised she must have left them in the reading room, where the earlier talk had been held.

She hurried back inside, where the cleaner from earlier was sweeping the polished floor. 'Excuse me,' called Lucy, her voice echoing in the space, 'I've misplaced a pair of gloves.'

The cleaner didn't pause. 'I haven't seen any gloves,' he said. 'I found a cigarette case and eleven programmes.'

'Unfortunately, I'm only in the market for gloves. I'll have a look,' said Lucy, walking briskly over to the window ledge where she had been standing. 'What did you make of the lecture? I was standing with you at the back. You said you had a bus to catch.'

The man snorted, still sweeping. 'That Dr Lyle? He doesn't know the first thing about the Armana period,' he said.

'Do you think?' asked Lucy, rifling through a pile of discarded programmes. 'The British Museum would seem to disagree. He did lead the expedition. Gave this whole talk.'

'Talking's one thing,' the man said, pausing and leaning against his broom. 'Lyle doesn't *know* anything. I saw it tonight. Man's a charlatan.'

'Do you know, you're the first person I've ever heard question Dr Lyle's credentials,' said Lucy. 'I suppose he attracts publicity and secures the funding – why, there they are!' She scooped up the cream leather gloves, which were lying crumpled on a shelf. 'Thanks awfully. I hope you make the bus.'

'Missed it twenty minutes ago,' said the man glumly, returning to his sweeping. 'Should think I'll get the next one.'

Lucy found Mr Tollesbury by the door, still pinned by Mr Dakin. He shot Lucy another pleading look. *Save me*, he mouthed over Dakin's head.

'It should be all about atmosphere,' Dakin was saying. 'We should feel as though Egypt has *arrived* in London. We should—'

'Professor, we must go,' said Lucy briskly. She'd had altogether enough of Mr Dakin for one night. 'I do hope your final touches go well, Mr Dakin.'

He spared her the briefest glance. 'Thank you, my dear.' He patted his pockets fretfully. 'It's very annoying – I seem to have misplaced the keys to the shop. I do hope they turn up tonight or I shall have to call a locksmith in the morning . . . I need to get into the shop *first thing* to see to the arrangements, I'm due at the museum at eleven, more publicity for the mummy you know.' He furrowed his brow and dug through his pockets. 'Most strange. They were just here.'

'Let's hope it's not the curse at work already,' Lucy said gaily. 'Goodnight, Mr Dakin!'

They left him tutting and patting his pockets. As she and the professor headed gratefully into the cool spring night, Lucy said, 'This exhibition may only be for one night—'

'But Dakin is going to crow over us for eternity,' finished Mr Tollesbury, grinning. 'Shall we repair to the shop for a nice cup of tea?'

Chapter 2

'Hallo,' said Felix, the bookseller at Cecil Court Books, as Lucy and Mr Tollesbury walked through the door half an hour later. He was sticking stamps to several parcels alongside Susan Barrow, Lucy's bookkeeper. Their bookbinding assistant, Toby, was nowhere to be seen. 'You're both late – Toby's gone to the pictures,' Felix continued, apparently reading Lucy's mind. 'I was just about to lock up myself. How was the lecture?'

'The *lecture* was lots of Dr Lyle showing off and then Dakin was predictably awful about getting the goods. Couldn't stop gloating over his coup.'

'I'm sorry about that,' said Felix sympathetically. He was a tall, willowy man, always immaculate in a grey suit and crisp white shirt. He had a sharp eye for literary trends, pouncing on little-known novels that would become bestsellers, always knew the latest society gossip and managed to get on with everyone and anyone, chatting as easily to a passing duke as he did the postman. His success in sales lay in the fact it never seemed to occur to him he might be rebuffed.

Lucy slumped into an armchair. 'Oh, it's all right Felix. How were sales this evening?'

'Susan will have to give us the bottom line, but I think we did nicely. People can't get enough of Jerome K. Jerome.'

'They like a bit of comedy right now.' Lucy looked round with pleasure at the cosy surroundings of her shop. Cecil Court Books, which had originally been an antiquarian and rare bookshop, now consisted of three rooms – a room for regular fiction, a historical section, and a bookbinding area. There was also a small stock room and a gas ring for making hot drinks and two rooms above the shops, taken by Mr Tollesbury and Toby. There were low lights and cosy armchairs and china cups scattered about. Lucy had intended it to feel comforting and peaceful – a haven for those who loved books as much as she did.

* * *

As a bright young socialite, Lucy had, at the age of nineteen, shocked her social circle and horrified her impoverished family by breaking off a promising engagement to a wealthy and handsome young man she had known since childhood, insisting that she would be attending the University of Oxford instead. She had persuaded her father, in spite of their straightened circumstances, to agree to at least the first year's tuition. 'You'll get bored, Lucy,' her father had told her. 'This is just another fad.'

'She always did have her head in a book as a child,' her mother had said mournfully. 'I suppose we have that to blame.'

Lucy, who had indeed always loved reading and stories, had intended to study English, only to discover that the course had its quota of female students. Undeterred, she had settled on Ancient History and, after the first year, had prised the remainder of the tuition from her father, on the promise that she would graduate with a brilliant degree.

'We'll see how long it lasts,' her mother had told her friends. 'She'll come to her senses and marry Edward once she gets sick of all those dull books.'

Lucy had not come to her senses; rather, she had loved every minute of her years at Oxford. She became best of friends with her roommate, a girl called Susan, and adored her professor, Mr Tollesbury. She had relished the opportunity to test her sharp mind. Upon graduating from Oxford – women had only recently been allowed to receive a degree – Lucy had, however, realised fairly swiftly that her options as a highly qualified, independently minded woman were limited. How far, she wondered, would a degree in Ancient History get her? Women professors were scarce and a qualification would require years of expensive study. She could attend archaeological digs in the capacity of patron – but she hadn't the funds. Or as the wife or secretary of one of the members – but contemplating either left her feeling queasy.

So, Lucy had spent the summer after her graduation anxiously drifting around her parents' large, increasingly dilapidated old house in North London, writing letters begging Susan to move to the city, and spending her evenings with her old London crowd, who told her fondly that they were glad she was over her blue-stocking phase. Sometimes a letter from her ex-fiancé, Edward Vyse, would arrive from the Argentine, where he had moved to take up farming, urging her to reconsider his proposal.

Lucy began taking long walks around London. She found herself drawn, as she had been as a child, to books – to the book-shops of the city where she could read for hours, losing herself in the stories and adventures of people with lives far richer and more thrilling than her own. In particular, she would return often to quiet, cloistered Cecil Court in Bloomsbury, where she would take refuge in Cecil Court Books. She would enter the cool dark of this particular shop and let the door close behind her, losing herself in the clutter and dust of the past.

When the manager, Mr Burnside, had announced he was giving up the lease, Lucy had been shocked.

'I can't afford the lease by myself anymore,' he had told her sadly. 'Not much of a market for all these old texts. People like to look but they don't buy much.'

Lucy had felt guilty – she had herself spent many hours reading books she had no intention of buying. She had also felt bereft. Where, she thought, am I to go now?

It had been the end of the year and London was decked with Christmas finery. She had walked out into the chill air and imagined for a wild moment that *she* could take possession of Cecil Court Books, make it her own. She knew instinctively that she could make a success of the shop. She would strip out the old stock and fill the shelves with new fiction. She could bring the dusty old shop into the modern age. And why not? She had always been persuasive – she could surely persuade people to buy books.

Lucy hadn't waited to think twice. She had marched home to her parents, and argued that, since she wasn't planning on getting married, they should give her the money saved for her wedding as a deposit so she could lease the shop.

'Oh, darling. That's all gone,' Mrs Darkwether had said. 'We thought Edward's family would perhaps . . .'

'I'm not marrying Edward or anyone,' Lucy had insisted. 'Is there really no money?'

Her father had shaken his head sadly. 'Our investments were hit hard by the war,' he had told her. Lucy had sighed. She would have to find another way.

She had spent the night writing a business plan and had approached her father's bank in the morning, only to be swiftly turned down. Undeterred, she had tried three more banks, only to be rejected each time.

It had so happened that one afternoon that week, in the aftermath of another rejection, her beloved tutor, Mr Tollesbury, had invited her to a lecture in London. He had taken her for tea afterwards, where Lucy had complained bitterly about the situation.

'It's not fair,' she'd told him. 'Because I'm a woman, they think I can't run a business. I'd do a sight better than Mr Burnside at any rate. How hard can it be to sell people books?'

'I suppose people who have never run a bookshop before might think that,' Mr Tollesbury had said slyly.

She had rolled her eyes at him. 'I could do this, Professor. I'm no good at figures, but Susan from college could handle my accounts, she's kicking about without a job while she waits for her Masters to start. And I really do love books.' She'd leant forwards, fixing him with a firm gaze. 'Remember when you were trying to raise money for the field trip to Newstead? Well, who got the most cash out of the donors? Who persuaded the board to let us go? *And* throw in a welcome dinner?'

'It was you, my dear,' the professor said placidly.

'And do you remember what you said afterwards?'

'Well . . .'

'Because *I* do. You said I could sell anyone anything. Selling books is what I'm meant to do with my life, I know it is. Or at least,' she had concluded, 'it's what I'm meant to be doing for the next few years.'

There was a pause while Mr Tollesbury had considered. 'You're clever, Lucy, but you're flighty,' he had said at last. 'I can see you getting bored of this and then where will you be? Lumbered with a shop and a pile of debt.'

'I'm twenty-two. I'm meant to be flighty.' She had angrily drained her cup of tea. 'You'd rather I get married, I suppose.'

'Goodness, no. Not *that*,' Mr Tollesbury had said, smiling.

Lucy had moodily eaten a scone while Mr Tollesbury had thought some more. 'If you're really set on this bookshop idea, you'll need a silent partner,' he said finally. 'A respectable man, with a decent lump sum to add to your deposit, to reassure the bank and the landlord.' His slow smile had spread across his face, crinkling his eyes. 'Myself, in other words.'

'You!' Lucy had stared. 'But surely . . .'

But surely, Lucy had thought, the professor was broke. In all the years she had known him, Mr Tollesbury had been neatly but modestly dressed, darned his shirts, and cycled everywhere on a battered upright bicycle; he loved his work, his extensive stamp collection, a few treasured relics from his digs and forensically dissecting a student's poorly constructed essay. As far as she could see, his only extravagance was ordering packets of tea from Fortnum's and buying rare stamps.

'Do you *have* a decent lump sum, Professor?' Lucy had asked, trying to be polite.

'I have amassed a modest amount over the years,' he had explained. 'I live very frugally, my dear. I should like it to go to good use. But there is one condition – I would like you to offer me a job in your shop.' When she had stared at him, he had laughed. 'I'm too old for teaching now,' he had told her. 'The college has been keen for me to retire for some time. But I'll need something to do. Yes, I should like to take up bookbinding. And I'll need space for my stamp collection, of course.'

'It's your life savings,' Lucy had said uncertainly. 'You clearly don't think a bookshop is a good investment, any more than the bank does. And you've no experience of working in a shop.'

He had poured her another cup of tea. 'Have I ever told you what I did before I became a professor, my dear?'

'No,' Lucy had said. She hadn't thought much about Professor Tollesbury's origins. He had surely emerged at birth, grey haired and kindly, dressed in tweed, wearing horn-rimmed spectacles.

'I did plenty of things – plumber, electrician, a bit of manual labour. But I also ran a shop,' he had said. 'A tobacconist's shop. Sold it for a tidy sum when I took the job at Oxford. The Dean had no idea!' He had winked at Lucy. 'It doesn't do any harm to have a few practical skills up your sleeve in life, Lucy.'

Lucy had considered him. It made sense somehow that Professor Tollesbury had seen more of the world than most of the dons, cloistered in their pristine quads: there was a mischief to him, a sense that he cared less for convention than his colleagues. It was why they got along so well.

'The thing is,' she had said, recalling an aphorism of her father's, 'money and friends shouldn't mix.'

'What else should I do with the money?' he had asked mildly. 'I have no wife or children to leave it to – not anymore. I shan't interfere, if that's what you're worried about.'

Indeed, once the loan had been approved and the lease transferred, Mr Tollesbury had never mentioned the money again. Instead, the two of them had spent a pleasant first few weeks sorting and selling off old stock and, as they wiled away the hours in the shop together, Lucy had been shocked to find she got to know him even better than she had at Oxford.

Once, when Lucy had been alone in the shop with Mr Tollesbury one night after closing, she had even felt bold enough to ask about his family. He had said nothing for a moment, then, quietly, 'I don't speak of it often. The great Spanish flu epidemic took both my wife and my girl Rosie. It only took a few weeks to lose them both.'

'How dreadful,' Lucy had said, feeling horribly inadequate.

'Dreadful indeed – Rose was sixteen, had her whole life ahead of her. Although there's a sort of beauty in grief, Lucy, if you look hard enough. When you lose everything, you do see the world afresh, in a terrible sort of way.' His expression had become distant. 'My girl was peaceful when she died.'

Lucy had shivered at the look in Mr Tollesbury's eyes – an expression of such loneliness and desolation. Her own father had the same sadness in his eyes when he spoke about the Great War and the friends he had lost. She hoped she never had to see the world in that way.

A few weeks later, when the shop was largely clear of old stock, Lucy had put out adverts in the trade press for a bookseller. Her first hire had been Felix Fletcher, bookseller, who had breezed into the shop, cast a professional eye around, and said, 'You'll have to rely on character my dear. That's about all this place has going for it. Luckily, I'm a terrific salesperson.' Lucy had loved him immediately.

'Do you have references?' Lucy had asked, dimly aware that this was something she should ask for.

'I've worked in all sorts of places,' he'd told her airily, throwing himself into a chair. 'Big business. You wouldn't believe me if I told you.'

'Maybe I wouldn't,' Lucy had said suspiciously. 'What makes you want a job in a bookshop if all these grand places want you?'

'The world of business is awfully dull,' he had said, crossing one elegant leg over the other at the ankle and avoiding her gaze. 'I miss people, you know. And books. Books are my *passion*.'

'Name one,' Lucy had said, narrowing her eyes. 'Name *one* book you've read recently.'

Felix had eyed the shelves behind her. 'Well, none of these,' he had said, smirking. 'They look horribly dull. I understand people. I know what public want and it isn't . . .' he squinted, '*The Origins of Sumerian Language*.'

'We're still going through the old stock,' Lucy had said defensively.

'Of course, darling. But let me sell some good, racy fiction alongside and this place might have a hope of staying in business.'

Lucy didn't entirely trust Felix Fletcher – the references she wrote to never replied – but she was charmed and had hired him for a trial two-week period. Soon people from all walks of life came into the shop, drawn gradually by Lucy and Felix's more canny purchases – thrillers, gossipy memoirs and romances that society ladies smuggled out in plain brown paper.

And Lucy's own instincts had been right. She did have a knack for bookselling. In this little corner of the world, snug in its narrow alley between the bustle of Tottenham Court Road and Gower Street, she had created her own world, with fires flickering, cups of tea, and the chatter of happy customers. The shop – instead of her parents' house – with its faded grandeur, formality and parade of society visitors, truly felt like home. She had the knack of conversation and she could get customers to open up to her, revealing truths much like the pages of her beloved books. Soon she was earning enough that she could rent her own flat and hire a house-keeper, saying goodbye to the faded grandeur and stuffiness of her parents' house.

In an astonishing coup, Felix had blithely announced one May morning that Eleanor Valentine, the esteemed and scandalous stage actress, would be happy to launch her memoir – a thinly disguised exposé of her affairs – at the shop.

'But we haven't the money to host a launch!' Lucy had said.

'That lot don't need much – put out some ashtrays and sand-wiches, they'll think it's all literary atmosphere,' Felix had said, and he had turned out to be right. The great and good of theatre-land attended in droves, with Eleanor languidly smoking by the antiquarian section and photographers waiting outside. One young actor was thrown out and another ended up in jail for the night after punching a third – it was, the papers declared, an aptly dramatic and thrilling evening. It had put Cecil Court Books decidedly on the map and business had taken off from there.

Lucy's next hire had been her old friend Susan Barrow, who had come to London to specialise in psychiatry. 'Please be my numbers woman,' Lucy had begged her. 'Just while I get started. The hours are good, you'll have plenty of time for studying.'

And then one day Mr Tollesbury had announced he'd found an apprentice – a thin, blond, freckled boy of nineteen called Toby Calvert who had travelled from a village near Leeds a few months earlier to look for work in the city. He seemed painfully shy, turn-ing red whenever he was spoken to. In the first week, Lucy wasn't sure he had ever said a full three words together. He had a scar stretching from above his right eye from a childhood injury and wore his cap down low to cover it.

'He's awfully quiet,' Lucy had whispered critically. 'Are you sure he won't go scurrying back to Yorkshire?'

'Give him a chance,' Mr Tollesbury had said, watching Toby's bent head as he worked. 'He'll make a first-rate bookbinder yet.

Very precise. Never seen anyone with such a knack for illustration too – almost perfect recall.'

Lucy had agreed to a trial and to let Toby live in one of the two rooms above the shop, which he quickly papered with posters of film stars and filled with stacks of detective stories. The professor, who kept a flat in Bermondsey, decided to take the other at the same time. 'Think of me as a sort of caretaker,' he had said, as he had unpacked his small suitcase. 'This way I won't be late for work.'

'All right,' Lucy had told him, thinking that the professor, who was half-deaf and had just turned seventy, would make a poor caretaker. 'But no pets.'

In truth, the sparseness of the professor's worldly possessions tugged at her heart – a few worn books, his suits, neatly pressed, his shining brogues, a photograph of his dead wife and child in an ornate silver frame. The relics from his academic career – clay pots and statues, fragments from when he had once attended local digs.

It had been the five of them ever since then, and Lucy wouldn't have had it any other way.

* * *

The professor set a cup of steaming jasmine tea before Lucy in his best rosebud china. She took a fragrant sip, groaned and glanced at her watch. 'I should leave in a minute. It's John's engagement party tonight, I need to go home and change. Mother has instructed me not to be late, upon pain of death.'

Her younger brother John, who had missed the war by a hair's breadth, had been a wild youth, given to fast cars and gambling. When he had been packed off to New York two years ago with the vague idea of 'getting into business' it had been generally assumed he would plunge further into dissolution. Instead, he had announced last month that he had proposed to a girl he had met out there – a Maggie Potts, of Potts Iron Girders. His telegram had been short and buoyant, declaring that Maggie's father owned the company and had offered him a job, so there was the bonus of a promotion. *At least one of the siblings was doing the right thing*, Lucy imagined her parents thinking. They had indulged her attending Oxford, but running a shop was taking things too far.

'It's not something a girl of our class does,' her father would say. 'It's embarrassing.'

And, 'You will never find a husband, holed up in that dusty old shop,' her mother would moan. 'Boys will think you're dreadfully odd, Lucy.'

'Lucy,' said Felix now, rapidly writing down quantities in the order book, 'you need to order some more of that Western series. I thought cowboys wouldn't sell, but you were right and I was wrong.'

'People still want escapism, Felix, I told you. That's why they're so hot for this ridiculous mummy story. Susan, can I persuade you to come along tonight?' Lucy asked. 'My parents love you.' That wasn't entirely true; her parents regarded Susan – with her outspoken, 'modern' attitudes – with mild suspicion, but Lucy wanted company tonight. She'd heard a rumour that her ex-fiancé, Edward, was in London for a short stay and, knowing her mother, would likely have been invited to the party.

'I've got the women's education reform meeting,' said Susan. She was angular, with red hair, spectacles and an alert expression. The political movement for equal voting rights was the latest recipient of her ferocious energies, which included life drawing and the psychic world, along with her psychiatry degree. 'Remind me who the lucky girl is?'

'An heiress called Margaret Potts *and* she has pots of money. John has landed on his feet.' She drained her teacup. 'By the way, you missed a drama tonight at the lecture. A man called Dr Curry burst in and accused the famous Dr Lyle of stealing his research. The professor had to help manhandle him out.'

'I didn't manhandle anyone, Lucy,' the professor said mildly. 'I just asked him nicely.'

'Delusions of grandeur,' said Susan. 'A classic case. He projects Lyle's dashing exploits onto his own frustrated ambition. Don't you think, Mr T?'

'You're the expert on psychology my dear,' said Mr Tollesbury, looking amused. '*I* thought Dr Curry seemed convinced that he was right.' He took a bite out of a chocolate biscuit and winced.

'Your tooth again?' said Lucy sternly. 'You must book a dentist's appointment.'

'I will,' he said with a groan. 'But every time I go, he finds another problem.'

'That's what delusion will do,' said Susan. 'Convince a man he's the King of England sometimes.' She glanced at her dainty mother-of-pearl watch. 'I'll walk out with you, Lucy – I've got a political meeting. Leave Felix to finish closing up and get yourself home. Any mail today, Felix?'

Felix yawned. 'Nothing again. These postal strikes are a frightful pain. And I'm meant to be taking possession of a rather special delivery.' He nudged Lucy. 'Remember, darling?'

'Oh yes,' said Lucy, sitting up. 'Our latest racy novel. You'll be discreet, won't you, Felix? I don't want this getting back to my mother.'

'I have confidence it will sell like hot cakes,' said Felix. Under his breath, he muttered, 'So long as the police don't get wind of it.'

'The police?' said Mr Tollesbury, blinking nervously. 'What are you two young people up to?'

'Don't you worry about it,' said Felix soothingly. 'Trust me, this will do our accounts the world of good. Lucy, if this pays off I'd like to discuss a raise. My rent is going up – the landlord is a criminal. At this rate, I'll have to move.'

'Let me think about it,' said Lucy.

'Come on.' Susan stood and buttoned her coat. 'We'll both be late at this rate. And you're on pain of death! There's meant to be a thunderstorm later.'

They opened the door to pouring March rain and Lucy groaned at the sight of a large poster adorning the outside of Dakin's shop.

'See The Cursed King . . . If You Dare' it cried, in large, blood-red font. A crack of lightning lit the sky, illuminating the sombre image of the mummy's death mask.

Lucy scowled. 'I hope there *is* a mummy's curse,' she said. 'And I hope it takes out Mr Dakin!'

Chapter 3

The rain, though fierce, eased quickly. Lucy walked Susan to her meeting, then carried on briskly and alone, her stout boots striking loudly against the cobbled streets of Covent Garden, past the bustle of flower sellers and coffee houses towards Seven Dials, then up towards the elegant squares and townhouses of Bloomsbury.

She entered her mansion block, walked up one carpeted flight, then paused outside her flat, where she lived alone except for her housekeeper Mrs Thorpe, key in hand. She was preparing to leave the world of the shop and step into her parents'. As though she were taking off one dress – made of thick, sturdy fabric – and stepping into another, made of gauze and silk. She liked them both, but, increasingly, her society gauze did not sit comfortably.

'Hurry up!' called Mrs Thorpe, flinging open the front door. She was a tall woman, with a tough, weather-worn face and grizzled hair. 'You don't have long.'

'I'll be fashionably late,' said Lucy, wriggling out of her coat.

'That you won't be, because your mother's sending a car,' said Mrs Thorpe, ushering Lucy down the corridor. 'Said she wasn't having any excuses this evening.'

They went into Lucy's bedroom, beautifully decorated in pinks, peach, champagne and eau de nil shades, with perfume bottles, silk shawls and decanters brushing up against dusty books on Egyptology and academic papers and fountain pens. There was a gramophone and scattered records lying about and photographs of her family in silver frames, the dainty jewelled dagger she had bought at a market stall to the most recent monograph on preserving clay figurines. A diaphanous heap of whites, pale greens and pinks lay tumbled on the bed.

'I wasn't sure what you'd be wearing,' said Mrs Thorpe. 'I didn't realise you'd be cutting it so fine. Now, I gather Mr Vyse is going to be there. Your mother said on the phone he was back in the country and you should look nice.'

'Well, I'm glad you've both discussed it,' muttered Lucy, who never ceased to be amazed at how her mother could control her even when they didn't live in the same place. 'Although what Edward has to do with what I wear—'

'In that case I'd wear the pink,' said Mrs Thorpe, gathering up the other dresses and bustling out of the room, through the adjoining door into the smaller room that she used. 'I'll just stitch up that frill where you tore it dancing last week.'

Lucy sighed and began to unbutton her dress. 'I don't know why people keep mentioning Edward,' she called through the open door. 'We ended things so long ago.'

'You mean, when you called the engagement off, went to Oxford, and caused a scandal?' said Mrs Thorpe, returning with a needle and thread. 'And he went to the Argentine to nurse his broken heart?'

'Well, yes,' said Lucy, watching her housekeeper's fingers fly as she sewed the flimsy material. 'He'll have moved on by now though.' Mrs Thorpe held out the dress and Lucy ducked her head, letting the silks slither over her shoulders and back.

'Beautiful,' said Mrs Thorpe, as Lucy emerged from the cloud of fabric. 'Pink really is your colour. I don't hold with all this black the girls are wearing now. Look like they're forever in mourning.'

Mrs Thorpe herself only wore black, in mourning for her son who had died in the war and a husband who had died shortly after. She began to pin back Lucy's dark curls with deft fingers. 'I wasn't so sure when you got this crop,' she said, twisting a jewelled pin into the waves, 'but it does suit you, Lucy, and it's less bother washing it.'

'It's all right,' said Lucy, eyeing herself critically. 'I need lipstick, I look positively ill.' She tucked a stray curl behind her ear and Mrs Thorpe batted her hand away.

'No time for that. The car will be here any minute.'

As if on cue, the headlights of her parents' massive, yet battered, Bentley swept into the square. Lucy caught up her velvet clutch, gave herself a spritz of perfume, and tugged on her silk shoes.

'Goodnight, Mrs Thorpe!' she cried, 'Don't wait up, will you?'

And with a wave, she vanished into the night.

* * *

Her parents' home in Hampstead was a large, white-fronted townhouse, and the hallway was beautifully panelled, with a shabby old-world air and soft, diffused lighting from the elegant art nouveau glass lamps that dotted the hall. As Lucy walked through the house towards the upper floor – and the buzz of laughter and chatter – she passed a dining room, with a long, polished table set with candles, bowls of pink roses, and their best silverware.

Mrs Darkwether, as she would tell anyone who would listen, loved throwing parties. After the war and a series of unfortunate investments on Mr Darkwether's part, she could rarely justify the expense, so tonight her excitement was palpable.

Upstairs, Lucy stepped into a fug of cigarette smoke, laughter and music.

'Lucy, darling!' Her mother enveloped her in a hug and Lucy breathed her in. Her mother always smelt delicious, of amber spices. As usual she was beautifully dressed in a simple and presumably eye-wateringly expensive grey silk that Lucy was sure had been bought on credit. She and Lucy had the same cloud of dark curls and large, seemingly innocent brown eyes. She veered from being infuriatingly vague to devastatingly practical, sometimes within a single conversation.

'Thank goodness you're here, darling,' she said. 'I was worried you'd get absorbed in those dull books and forget all about us.'

'Not for the world. It looks lovely in here, Mother.'

Her mother looked around, her mouth curving in a satisfied smile. 'It does, doesn't it?' Her eyes narrowed. 'Is that girl Susan not with you?'

'She might pop in later. She's at a political meeting.'

'You girls,' said her mother, sounding half-amused and half-despairing. 'All your serious meetings.' She leaned closer and said in hushed tones, 'Edward's coming tonight.'

'Mother, you don't need to be so dramatic. I heard he was back in England. And we ended things five years ago.'

'You don't fool *me*, Lucy Darkwether,' her mother said. 'He's proposed to you countless times since hasn't he?'

Lucy was silent for a moment. Then she burst out, 'Well, what on earth made you ask him?'

'I didn't darling, he wrote to say he was in London and could he come. I couldn't say no – it's *Edward*. I've known his mother since school. Why, you grew up together.'

'So, you're not trying to trick me into anything?'

'Darling, would I?' Her mother squeezed her elbow, leading her through the throng. 'It wouldn't hurt to be nice to him, though – you might have second thoughts. And there is someone else you might like to meet – in your line of work. He owns that bookshop on Charing Cross Road where everyone goes nowadays. They call him the PT Barnum of bookselling, as if that's a good thing. Lots of stunts, and he is fearfully handsome – apparently he was brave during the war too. Won a medal.'

'Not Bryan Campbell?' said Lucy, craning her neck. 'That *is* exciting.'

Campbell's Books, established by the brother and sister team of Bryan and Chessie Campbell, was the first purpose-built and the largest bookshop the city of London had ever seen, more like the American-style bookshops that Lucy had read about in magazines. Apparently, there were grand plans for expansion and events in the works. Chessie and Bryan Campbell were revolutionising bookselling. Lucy couldn't help but be intrigued – and a little jealous.

Her mother nodded in the direction of a throng of people at a tall man with his back to them. 'He's just there – what a crush, I'm sure *I* didn't invite all these people – I'll introduce you. Bryan!'

The man, who had been taking a cocktail from a waiter, turned. He was tall and broad shouldered. Even in his evening dress, there was a power and grace to him.

'Bryan,' said Mrs Darkwether, holding out her hand. 'Come and meet my daughter, will you, I can see Lady Fortescue.' She breezed off in a cloud of Chanel, calling out to the next newly arrived guest.

Bryan Campbell bent over Lucy's hand. It was an attractive face – a determined chin, guileless blue eyes that looked straight at her. 'Miss Darkwether,' he said, smiling down at her. 'I understand that we are business rivals.'

She smiled back at him. 'Not rivals – my shop wouldn't occupy one floor of yours. But I confess I have been desperate to hear more about your expansion plans. I heard you intend to buy the building next door, is that really true? How many books can you be selling?'

'You should speak to my sister, Chessie. She's the brains behind all of that, I just write the cheques,' he said, with a boyish bashfulness that Lucy instantly took with a pinch of salt. 'But yes, we are looking to expand. Our literary luncheons have been a great success. I could share some of my insider knowledge, such as it is.' His smile widened. 'Over a cocktail perhaps?'

'Perhaps,' said Lucy demurely. Bryan Campbell was very handsome but she had the strongest sense she couldn't trust him an inch. Then she yelped as someone flung their arms around her from behind. 'John!'

She turned and embraced her brother warmly. He was round-faced, pleasant, rather vacuous looking, with a toothbrush moustache that never quite took off. 'Luce,' he said, taking her by the wrist and leading her towards a cluster of people, 'I need to introduce you to Maggie, your new sister-to-be.'

Lucy had seen photos in the society pages of Maggie Potts but nothing could have prepared her for the real thing. It was easy to see why the heiress had taken London society by storm. In the flesh, her sister-in-law was a good half a head taller than Lucy, with high colouring and freckles, and a string of emeralds round her neck. She wore an expensive-looking black velvet gown and was talking to a short man and drawing rapidly on a cigarette when John tapped her on the shoulder.

'Darling, I want you to meet my sister, Lucy.'

Maggie swung round and pressed a warm hand into Lucy's. Her eyes were green – the first time Lucy had ever seen truly green eyes – and fringed with copper lashes: even standing still she had an almost electric energy. 'Great to finally meet you,' she said in a low, hoarse voice with a New York twang, squeezing Lucy's hand with surprising strength. 'John's told me all about you. Always saying how smart you are. Cambridge, wasn't it?'

'Oxford,' said Lucy. 'They don't like to hand out degrees to *undergraduettes* in the Fens. Not yet, anyway.'

Maggie blew out cigarette smoke. 'Opposite to me – haven't a brain in my head.'

'But you're so beautifully decorative it doesn't matter,' said John, squeezing her arm. 'Besides, you have *street* smarts. Maggie was quite a New York broad, Lucy – before her father became respectable.'

Maggie winked at him. 'It's a wonder we met at all,' she said. 'Given *you're* so respectable and haven't a dime, and my father is in steel girders. Making money, how coarse.'

John beamed back at her. 'Isn't she something, Luce? Darling, Lucy's shop is next to where Lyle's mummy will be shown tomorrow night.'

'Oh yes, I've heard all about the cursed mummy,' said Maggie. 'One of the funders is an old family friend – a Mrs van Buren, you know her?' She turned back to Lucy as she said this.

'She stepped in and saved the expedition,' said Lucy, recalling the handsome woman at Lyle's shoulder. 'Yes, she was at a talk I attended just this afternoon in fact. She actually *went* to Egypt,' she added enviously.

'Well,' Maggie said with a drawl, 'she *is* one of the wealthiest women in the country and she funded the *whole* thing, so I guess they had to let her come along. Her husband was a gangster, pretty much – that's what my pa always said. He died a few years back and left her an absolute fortune. Rumour is she and Dr Lyle are *very* close.'

'Really!' said Lucy, fascinated. 'An affair?'

'That's what people are saying, although Moira is so serious, I can't imagine it. But they brought back the goods, didn't they? There's going to be queues round the block to see that mummy, it's saying in the papers. How much did the expedition team get for it, do you know?'

'I don't think you can put a figure on something so precious,' said Lucy. 'The mummy is priceless.'

Maggie gave her a shrewd look. 'You can always put a price on something,' she said.

'Well, I don't like you being so close to it,' chimed in her mother, joining them with a glass of champagne. 'What about the curse? Poor Sir Archibald Drake – healthy one minute and dead the next, on the very day the tomb was opened. All those other disasters, bandits and things. And now the mummy *here*, in London, right next to your shop, Lucy – who knows what will happen?'

'That's rot, Mother, forgive me for saying so,' Lucy told her. 'The papers are just drumming up interest – there's no curse.'

Her mother lifted her chin obstinately. 'Tell that to Sir Archibald.'

'He was eighty,' said Lucy. 'I doubt a curse had anything to do with his heart failure.'

Maggie gave an elaborate shudder. 'Well, you couldn't pay *me* to go see it,' she said. 'Awful smelly old thing.'

Her voice grated. Lucy was suddenly aware of a strong urge to leave. The room was hot and stuffy now, and the champagne was sitting uncomfortably in her stomach. She wanted to go home.

'I have the most awful headache,' she said. 'It's been hovering all day and I think the heat is making it worse. I'm sorry, Mother – I might need to go home and lie down.'

'It's not like you to leave a party,' John protested. 'I don't get engaged every day.'

'Yes, it's early yet,' her mother protested over her glass.

'I have to work tomorrow,' Lucy said apologetically. 'I'm sorry, Maggie – I'll visit soon.'

'That dreadful shop,' her mother said sadly. 'Well, goodnight, dear.'

Feeling guilty, Lucy began to pick her way through the crowd to the door. Her mother really had invited too many people. As she pushed through the crowds, someone stumbled into her and she in turn fell into a tall, distinguished dark-haired man standing by the open doorway.

'Lucy!' She'd recognise that voice anywhere.

'Edward?'

Dear Edward, Lucy thought, her heart thudding unexpectedly in her chest as he took her hand. He looked exactly the same – perhaps a little more lived in, a line or two creasing at the corners of his eyes, leaner, a tan from his years in Argentina. It suited him, she thought – if anything he was even more handsome than she remembered. But still the same crisply curling dark hair, the same angular face, still the same boy she had grown up with.

'How are you?' he said, gripping her hand. 'We have so much to catch up on.'

'I know, so much – but I was actually just leaving,' Lucy said, apologetically.

'I hope not because of me,' Edward said gravely, still holding her hand. 'Surely we can attend the same party – in spite of our past?'

'Oh, no – I was going anyway,' said Lucy, flushing, and he laughed.

'I was only teasing, Lucy. That was five years ago!'

Had Edward developed a sense of humour in the Argentine? 'Walk with me for a bit, would you?' she said impulsively. 'I'd love to hear what you've been up to all this time.'

He smiled down at her. 'All right. I mostly came to see you anyway.'

* * *

They walked out into the moonlit night, away from the fug of the crowd. It had rained again since she had gone in, and Lucy took in deep breaths of the cool air. 'Mother can be insufferable,' she said. 'Honestly, she scrimps and saves all year and then goes and spends the money on this ridiculous party full of people she hardly knows, flowers and cases of champagne. You could barely move in there. All to impress some heiress. And then she'll spend the next six months worrying about paying for the roof.'

'She likes to enjoy herself,' said Edward. 'Doesn't get to that often these days, I suppose. She says you're still working in that shop.'

'I still am,' said Lucy, bridling slightly. 'In Cecil Court. And I don't just *work* there. I own it.'

'Cecil Court? Not really – are *you* the shop who is exhibiting the mummy tomorrow?' Edward asked, sounding half-impressed, half-scandalised. 'Goodness, it's all over the papers. I was reading about it at the club.'

'Oh, no,' said Lucy, deflating. Not this again. 'That's not us.'

They walked in silence for a few minutes.

'How is the Argentine?' Lucy asked, feeling oddly awkward: she and Edward had always spoken so easily to each other. 'Is it still frightfully exciting and romantic? Your last letter made it sound wonderful.'

'It's going well,' he said. 'Although, to tell the truth Lucy, I'm not sure I'm cut out to be a farmer.'

Lucy repressed a smile. Edward had never been practical and had grown up with a doting mother and plenty of servants; it was hard to imagine him wrangling cattle and worrying over the cost of livestock and grain.

As though reading her mind, he added, 'I lost a fair bit of money last year, between us.' Then he brightened. 'I'm sure it will turn around though, once I get a handle on things. I've got a new, er, business partner who seems to know their stuff. You'd like it out there, you know. The ranch, all the space. Horses. You should consider a visit, Lucy.'

'Maybe I will,' said Lucy. For a moment, she imagined it – hot Argentine sun, dry grass stretching out forever, Edward, riding beside her.

They chatted about Argentinian ponies and the food he missed from England and the weather and how much land the ranch had. When at last they turned into her street, they fell silent.

'What is it, Edward?' said Lucy.

'What do you mean?'

'Something is bothering you. You've smoked three cigarettes since we left, even though you don't smoke.'

He gave a nervous smile. 'How do you know I haven't taken it up while I've been away?'

'You're a creature of habit. That's why I was so surprised when you left England.'

'I had to get over you, Lucy.'

Lucy glanced up at him. His dark gaze was on hers, intent and full of meaning. Lucy's heart quickened once more and she felt her pulse begin to flutter, partly with longing – she had *almost* forgotten how handsome Edward was – and partly with dread.

'Let's not go over it all again,' she said hurriedly. 'We agreed we didn't suit, and we could be good friends instead. You said it yourself – it's been five years. Please don't let's talk about it—'

Edward said gently, 'I was going to tell you that I'm engaged.'

A long silence stretched out. Then Lucy gave a laugh, which sounded brittle even to her own ears. 'Goodness. Engaged! Well, I look a bit of a fool, don't I?'

'Not at all,' he said politely.

Lucy collected herself. She was happy for Edward; she had wanted him to move on for years. It was just a shock, that was all. 'Congratulations, Edward, and thank you for telling me. I hope that you and . . .'

'Helen.'

'I hope that you and Helen will be very happy.'

'Thanks,' Edward said. 'She's an awfully jolly girl. Thinks she can turn the ranch around. She's from a ranching family and has got a real head for that sort of thing – numbers, you know, and how to vaccinate cattle against sickness and what the market price is.' He hesitated. 'We've set the date for next year in Cambridge. She wants to come over and see England.' In a flatter voice, he added, 'I imagine you and your family will want to come.'

'I imagine so,' Lucy said lightly, feeling stung. Did he not *want* her at the wedding? 'Mother never passes up a chance to buy a new hat.'

They walked on a little way until they reached her door.

'Well, this is my stop,' Lucy said cheerfully.

'Is this it?' He looked up at the mansion block. An expression of disapproval passed faintly over his face. 'You live here alone?'

'Not at all. I have a housekeeper, Mrs Thorpe.'

Edward ignored the idea of Mrs Thorpe. 'You really are an independent woman, aren't you? University and the shop and now this. I just hope . . .'

'What?' asked Lucy.

His brow remained furrowed. 'You don't need to prove anything, you know. I think you made your point already when you threw me over to go to Oxford.'

Lucy could feel familiar irritation rising within her. 'Do you think I went to university to *make a point*?'

'Perhaps,' said Edward, an amused smile playing on his mouth. 'It would be very like you.' He gestured up at the mansion block. 'Is all this what you want, Lucy? The shop, this flat? It seems so . . . lonely.'

Lucy followed his gaze up to the second floor. Mrs Thorpe had left the lights on and, despite Lucy telling her not to, would probably be waiting up for her. She would make Lucy a mug of cocoa. There would be a novel open by the bed, one she could happily have curled up with all evening. It looked warm and cosy and inviting in there – *exactly* how Lucy wanted it. When had Edward become so pompous and small-minded?

'It's what I want,' she said crisply. 'Independence suits me down to the ground.'

He stretched out a conciliatory hand. 'Then I believe you. Let's not quarrel,' he said.

Lucy hesitated, irritation wrestling with her old affection. 'We never fight,' she said at last, forcing a smile. 'I'm just tired.' She stretched up and gave him a kiss on the cheek, smelling the same citrus cologne he had always worn, familiar after all these years. 'Goodnight, Edward – and congratulations again.'

Chapter 4

Did the dress go down well?' asked Mrs Thorpe as she bustled about the room, gathering up Lucy's things from last night.

'Everyone seemed to like it,' said Lucy, taking a sip of a strong morning coffee. She was lying in bed, surrounded by the day's papers. The headlines were all about the exhibition that night.

Will the Mummy's Curse Strike Again?
The Tomb's Secrets Revealed Tonight.

She turned the page to read about the recurring postal strikes instead. Her room was in its usual state of pleasant disorder. Weak, early morning sunshine streamed through her patterned curtains, glittering through the perfume bottles. A half-eaten piece of buttered toast lay on a willow-patterned plate on her breakfast tray.

Edward didn't know what he was talking about, she thought. Her life wasn't only good – it was wonderful. Exactly how she wanted it.

'Edward is engaged, by the way,' she added, her eyes fixed on the paper. 'So, there's no need for you and Mother to worry about him any longer. Consider his heart thoroughly mended.'

'Really?' said Mrs Thorpe. She poured herself a cup of coffee and took a sip, eyeing Lucy speculatively over the rim. 'Nice to see him then?'

'Very nice,' said Lucy, turning the page, and resolutely offering no further information.

The phone rang and Mrs Thorpe picked it up.

'Morning,' she said. 'Oh, hello dear, how are you? You're at the shop early. Yes, she's right here.' She handed the receiver to Lucy.

'Lucy,' said Felix's voice. His voice was high and excited. 'Listen, the you-know-what has arrived. The special delivery.'

'Oh, yes?' said Lucy. She was looking down at the society page. There was John and Maggie, arms wrapped around each other in a haze of cigarette smoke, emeralds at Maggie's throat, Lucy's mother beaming in the background. 'It's arrived safely then?'

'Yes, only – well, I need to show you. Come right away, will you? I don't care how hungover you are. And you have to promise me you won't get angry.'

'Felix!' said Lucy. She flung off the bedcovers. 'Give me half an hour. I have a bad feeling about this.'

* * *

In the small backroom of the shop Lucy stared speechlessly at the large crate of books.

'Have you bought the entire print run?' she said. 'We said twenty copies! There must be at least a hundred here.'

Felix flushed. 'I might have got a bit carried away. I said I'd take what they had. It started innocently enough, Lucy – Lady Melford heard about it when she was in Paris over Christmas, asked me if I could find her a copy. And then I kept hearing whispers. There's clearly a market.'

Lucy picked up the slim volume, with its innocuous cover. 'But Felix, this is *smut*. I've been reading about it in the *Times*.'

'It's *literary* smut, darling, which is completely different. On the continent this is considered art. And they'll sell like hot cakes, I know they will. You can only get copies in France and Italy. Ever since it was banned, it's been the talk of London. We're the only place – that I've heard of, and I've heard of them all – selling copies here in London. Lady Sutcliffe has put her name down for five copies. Cash in an envelope.'

'Well, I think it's a scandal waiting to happen,' muttered Lucy anxiously.

Mr Tollesbury came in with his morning cup of tea. 'You're both in early,' he said. 'It's not yet eight. I thought you and Susan had that meeting with the wholesalers this morning, Lucy.'

'I had to come in and deal with *this* first,' Lucy said severely. 'I don't care what they're doing in France and Italy, Felix. What if someone gets wind of them here *in London*? We can't exactly hide this lot! The Met are taking this seriously now by all accounts. We could go to jail for this, at the very least it would be in the papers – and my mother will *not* be pleased. I should drop them all in the river and write this off as a poor business decision on the part of my so-called expert bookseller.'

'Give me a month,' Felix said insistently. 'A month and you'll see. The cash will come rolling in and – what is it, Toby?'

The bookbinding assistant had wandered in and was pulling drawers open. As usual, his response was a shrug, but Lucy had learnt to be patient. 'Lost something?' she prompted.

'Bookbinding knife,' he muttered, his fair hair falling over his eyes as he dug through the drawer.

'The new one with your initials in the handle?' said Lucy sympathetically. He jerked his head in assent. Mr Tollesbury had bought it for Toby when he had passed his probation and he looked after it carefully, packing it neatly away every night. 'When did you last have it?'

'Last night. It was here when I finished up, before I went to the pictures.'

'Have you tried retracing your steps like they do in detective stories?'

Toby nodded. 'I did all that. S'nowhere.'

Felix coughed pointedly and Lucy turned her attention back to him. 'Oh, all right – a month. Put them behind all the encyclopaedias for now. And get them shifted, fast—' She broke off at the sound of loud banging. 'What is that infernal racket?'

'I think,' said Mr Tollesbury with a smile, 'that Dakin is getting ready for his exhibition. He's been here since the crack of dawn.'

Lucy marched through the shop and out into the street, where Mr Dakin was supervising as two burly men hammered a post to the brick wall of Cecil Court Books itself. Attached to it was another enormous billboard showing a mummy, bandages unravelling to reveal glowing red eyes. 'Enter – if you dare!' it read in large letters across the top. Susan, who had just arrived, was staring up at the banner critically. 'I think it's crooked.'

'Mr Dakin,' snapped Lucy. 'What do you think you're doing?'

'Marketing, my dear!' he said, clapping his hands. 'A little to the left – that's enough. Yes, that's nice and eye-catching.'

'It obscures *half of my shop*,' said Lucy. 'We can hardly see out of the window.'

'I suppose it could come up a bit higher,' said Mr Dakin, eyeing it critically. 'More impact that way.'

'I think you should remove it all together,' said Lucy.

'Oh, you can't begrudge me a little fanfare, Miss Darkwether!' cried Mr Dakin. 'Wait until you see the shop. Why, you'll feel like you are *in* Egypt! Imagine a tomb, the floor worn by ancient footsteps, the smell of sanctified death—'

'You managed to get inside then,' said Lucy sourly.

'Yes, my keys, ah, turned up,' he said, flushing a little. 'Don't mention that to the Society, will you? No harm done – everything is in shipshape order. Now, I must be off, my dear – a busy day at the museum! A lecture, then a lunch – quite a celebration!'

'Mr Dakin!' cried Lucy. 'This monstrosity of a poster needs to be moved to *your* shop immediately! This is a commercial premises!'

'No sour grapes now, it's only for tonight,' he said. 'It'll be gone by tomorrow and then *all* your customers,' he repressed a snort, 'can see inside your little shop again. I look forward to seeing you later! Come nice and early, if you want to get a good spot. It's going to be heaving.'

Lucy watched him go and then turned to the workmen. 'Shift it,' she snapped. 'My father is best friends with the chief of police and you're trespassing. Defacing property. Mr Dakin is too stupid to know that, but I hope you're not.'

'All right,' said one of the workmen. 'It's not worth getting in trouble.' He looked up at the grim face above them. 'Dead creepy isn't it? This is about as close to the mummy as I want to get.'

* * *

The rest of the day passed peacefully. Lucy and Susan returned from their sales meeting around lunchtime, to find Mr Tollesbury and Toby working quietly in the back room. Felix was occupied in the front with sales. When the door rang at almost closing time, Lucy, who was up a stepladder reshelving the mythology section, barely glanced up.

'Well, well,' came a low drawl. 'So, this is where the competition is.'

Lucy looked down to see Bryan Campbell standing in the doorway, his bulk blocking out the daylight. She grinned at him and began to clamber down. 'So, you found us,' she said. 'I thought we might be *so* small you overlooked us entirely.'

He held out his hand to her and she hopped the last few steps off the ladder and took it. The shop seemed even more diminutive with him in it.

'I just looked for the signs to the mummy and found you.'

'Are you here for the exhibition, then?' Lucy asked.

'Thought I might as well see it. Quite a crowd out there already. And my sister spent the morning telling me how I absolutely *had* to visit your shop. She was awfully impressed you managed to get

Eleanor Valentine to speak about her memoir,' said Bryan Campbell. 'She tried for six months, but no cigar.'

'I can't take any credit for that,' Lucy said. 'That was all Felix. He's got his finger on the pulse. Felix!' Her bookseller came out of the stock room, shirt sleeves rolled up. 'This is Mr Bryan Campbell of Campbell's Books. He wants to congratulate you on snaring Eleanor Valentine.'

'Five hours I sat with her in a terrible little bar in Soho, listening to her complain about her love life,' Felix said. 'But it paid off, in the end.'

The bell above the door sounded again and Lucy recognised a customer. 'I'll be right back,' she said, hurrying over.

When Lucy returned, Bryan Campbell was regaling Felix with gossip about a famous author and Felix was giggling appreciatively. Lucy was sure she noticed a white slip of card disappear into Felix's sleeve as she approached. A business card. Her eyes narrowed. She was reminded of her first instinct upon meeting Mr Campbell – that he was entirely untrustworthy.

'Well, this has been swell,' said Bryan Campbell. 'I'd better go along to the exhibition now – I'm meeting Chessie there. I was wondering whether I might take you for dinner some evening, Miss Darkwether.' He smiled, showing white, even teeth, his eyes crinkling attractively. 'I could impress you with my business acumen.'

'I'd like nothing more,' Lucy said demurely. 'Just call me up. I'll see you inside.'

He tipped his hat, walked out and the door clanged behind him. Lucy and Felix watched the tall figure disappear down the cobbled alley towards Dakin's shop.

'Do you know, Lucy,' said Felix conversationally, 'I wouldn't trust that man if I were you.'

'I think you're right, Felix,' she murmured. 'Good looking though, isn't he?'

'Frightfully,' said Felix cheerfully, busying himself with his stocklist. But Lucy couldn't shake the sight of the business card disappearing up his sleeve.

'Are you ready, Lucy, or are you too busy ogling men?' called Susan. She was buttoning her jacket.

'Ready for what?' said Lucy.

'It's ten to six – Dakin's exhibition will start in a minute. Can't you hear them?' Sure enough, Lucy could hear the chatter of an excited crowd filling the court. 'We don't want to miss the grand reveal, and it will be crowded as it is. Got the invites?'

'I've half a mind to give it a miss,' said Lucy. 'It'll just be Dakin crowing.'

'And miss seeing the mummy itself?' said Mr Tollesbury, rising and stretching. 'Don't cut off your nose to spite your face my dear, as my mother would say.'

'Are you sure you don't mind me taking your ticket, Professor?' asked Susan.

Mr Tollesbury shook his head. 'No, my dear – I shall stay in with Toby and Felix and listen to the wireless. I'll rely on you to tell me all about it.'

As Lucy and Susan stepped out into the street, the door opened again behind them. 'Wait, Lucy,' cried Felix, sticking his head round, 'the post came this morning and there's a letter for you, marked urgent. I forgot to tell you earlier!'

'I'll open it later,' said Lucy, already hurrying down the alley. 'It'll only be another bill.'

* * *

The crowd outside Dakin's Rare Books was large enough to fill the alley and spill out onto the street beyond. A hum of excited chatter filled the air. The little man himself was dressed to the nines, beaming and welcoming the visitors – each one a potential customer, Lucy thought bitterly. She saw Dr Lyle, shaking hands complacently, Sir Hector Derwent holding court, and Mrs van Buren

53

talking to a group of serious-looking men. Mr Ahmed stood apart, huddled in his great coat, looking at his watch. *He hates all this*, Lucy thought; I wonder why he's bothering. She had read up on the expedition doctor since the lecture and discovered that he was a well-known surgeon.

Through the crowd, she saw Bryan Campbell, with a tall, sensibly dressed woman who must be his sister, Chessie. He waved to Lucy, then bent and spoke to his sister. She shot Lucy a look that seemed thoughtful – almost calculating. I don't think I'll trust *either* of the Campbells, Lucy thought.

'Miss Darkwether! Welcome, welcome,' Mr Dakin said, clasping her hand and preening. 'I can't wait to see your face when you go in. You'll have quite the surprise, Miss Darkwether. Quite the surprise!'

'I can't wait either,' Lucy said, forcing a smile.

'I think that's all we can fit tonight,' Dakin said. 'They'll have to come back tomorrow. We might need to extend the exhibition by another few nights, eh Lyle?'

'Perhaps, perhaps,' said Lyle, taking in the crowd and smiling expansively. Lucy could practically see him calculating the money the night had raked in.

'Ladies and gentlemen!' called Dakin and the crowd fell silent, 'we shall shortly enter my humble shop, and then the exhibition space where the mummy now sits.' He lowered his voice ominously. 'I must ask those of a nervous disposition to think twice before entering this hallowed place . . .'

There was an anxious shifting from the crowd.

'Please,' said Mr Dakin, 'form an orderly queue. No pushing! Let's not annoy our royal guest!' He gave a happy little laugh.

'How ridiculous,' said Susan, eyeing a woman who was nervously clutching her friend's arm. 'Do they think the mummy is going to get out and walk around?'

Lucy scowled. 'I wouldn't put it past Dakin to have organised something of the sort. One of the most important finds of this century and he's reduced it to this – this *sideshow*!'

'Then why are you here?' asked Susan, as they queued up behind a woman wearing gold scarab-shaped earrings.

'The professor persuaded me to come,' said Lucy. 'How was the meeting last night? I've barely had a quiet moment all day to ask you.'

'It was wonderful,' said Susan, her eyes shining. 'There's talk of an Equal Franchise Act. It's not the end of the struggle, but it might be the *beginning* of the end . . . Sorry I didn't show at the engagement shindig. How was it?'

They stepped inside. The visitors were being held in the outer room, while the inner door remained shut, the exhibition presumably inside. Mr Dakin had turned off the electric lights, opting for a queasy yellow lamplight. Waiters shuffled around in sandals and white smocks, gold jewellery jangling.

'Juice?' one asked. 'Ancient Egyptian honey cake?'

Lucy refused a piece of the stale-looking cake. 'It was fine,' she said. 'The fiancée is dripping in diamonds.' She took a deep breath. 'And I saw Edward, who is . . . engaged.'

'Engaged,' breathed Susan. 'I didn't think he had it in him. Part of me thought this whole charade in the Argentine was just a play to—'

There was a mournful, booming sound and they turned to see Mr Dakin solemnly striking a brass gong with a golden rod. Dr Lyle stood behind him, arms clasped behind his back.

'Ladies and gentlemen!' called Mr Dakin. 'I must ask you for quiet.' A hush fell and every eye was fixed on Mr Dakin and Dr Lyle, standing by the doors to the exhibition. 'I thank you for braving the journey here – and bravery may yet be the operative word, for you are about to see something which will test your nerves.' There was a pleasurable flutter of anticipation in the crowd. 'I welcome esteemed Egyptologist Dr Lyle, who led the expedition and discovered the tomb itself, to tell us why we are all here this evening.'

There was a pause, in which the anticipation built.

'It is with great pleasure,' said Dr Lyle, his rich voice resonating in the close room, 'to introduce you, on this grey London night, to a long-dead Egyptian king, from a land of sun and heat. Who knows what secrets he holds? Who knows what sort of violent life he lived – or what sort of death befell him? Those mysteries are not easily surrendered – but tonight, you will discover them for yourself.'

The audience were silent now, rapt. 'Goodness,' murmured Susan. 'He's really going for it isn't he?'

But Lucy was also immediately uncomfortable. There was an apprehensive air in the room. *I don't like this*, she thought suddenly.

'Let us tread quietly into the chamber within,' continued Dr Lyle. 'For this king has travelled many miles, across sun-bleached lands and azure seas. Prepare yourselves, ladies and gentlemen, for the extraordinary.' He nodded at Mr Dakin, whose eyes were glittering in the half-darkness.

'Enter, esteemed guests,' said Mr Dakin. 'Behold, the ancient king.' He turned and flung open the heavy door.

And screamed.

Chapter 5

T he figure was curled on the floor, facing the wall, wrapped in strips of linen. It was such an odd, unnatural pose that Lucy did not at first notice the blood.

It was wrapped in bandages, which hung loosely, as though they had not been properly fixed, and the lower half was covered in what looked like pelts. The bandages were spotted with blood, except for at the throat, where they were thick with it, forming a heavy, crimson collar.

As her eyes adjusted to the gloom, Lucy recognised that Dakin had fashioned the room into an approximation of an Ancient Egyptian burial chamber. The walls had been painted a sandy colour, presumably to mirror the inside of the original chamber, and there was blood spattered up them where the figure lay. Squinting into the gloom, Lucy could also make out some sort of dark mass near the figure – an animal pelt, it looked like. The electric light bulbs had been covered in fabric, creating a reddish hue and the room smelled of spices. Hieroglyphs had been crudely sketched on the wall – a set of scales, the eye of Horus. Dakin had managed, with limited time and resources, to create an effective scene – hammy as anything, but that was Dakin all over. The centrepiece of the room – the sarcophagus and mummy – were almost an afterthought. The sarcophagus, ornately carved and gilded, stood upright on a black marble pedestal draped in rich crimson velvet. The gold leaf glimmered faintly in the low light.

The entire scene spoke of mystery – the mystery of the dead king, who lay within.

The bloodstained figure, though, Lucy thought, was taking it rather too far.

The crowd of guests alternately laughed, shrieked or whispered. Someone giggled and someone else called out that Dakin should be ashamed of himself, frightening the ladies like that. The famed sarcophagus itself, in the middle of the room, containing the mummified ancient king, seemed a positive afterthought.

Honestly, thought Lucy, *Dakin really was the pits*. Only he could transform a discovery so extraordinary, so fascinating, so historically important, into a tacky theatrical. But when she looked at Mr Dakin, she saw to her surprise that he was ghostly white, eyes staring at the scene before him. His mouth opened, but no words came out.

'What is this?' said Dr Lyle, pushing his way to the front of the crowd. His usually unctuous voice was rough and angry. 'Dakin, what *is* all this?'

Dakin only gasped and stared, his jaw slack.

The guests began to shift uneasily. There was a murmur of disapproval. If this was a joke, the collective thought ran, it was in poor taste.

Susan gripped Lucy's elbow. 'What is going on?'

'I think,' said Lucy, eyeing the scene with apprehension, 'that we should take a closer look at that figure.'

Cautiously, she took a step forward, edging towards entering the tomb. As though released from a spell, Dakin cried out, 'Who did this? What's happening?'

Lucy ignored him and walked over to the figure, curled in that unnatural pose. She stretched out a hand and touched the still shoulder. A strip of linen came loose and Lucy could see pale flesh beneath.

That decided Lucy. 'Everyone out, now,' she said loudly, in her most autocratic voice. 'Don't touch anything. And Mr Dakin – call the police.'

Mr Dakin began to shriek at everyone to leave and the crowd streamed back through the doors, leaving Lucy and Susan unnoticed and alone with the body in the semi-darkness, lit by the flickering lamps.

'This is a crime scene,' whispered Lucy, taking another small step closer to the body. 'No one can be in here.'

'Shouldn't that include us?' asked Susan, while also edging closer. She peered at the floor through the dim light, where a rusty substance was spread. 'Is that more blood?'

Lucy crouched and touched the substance on the floor with her gloved fingertips. 'It's not blood,' she said, looking at her fingers. 'It's powder. Dust.' She stood and tiptoed closer to the body. 'There are furs here too. The Ancient Egyptians may have believed they kept a person warm in the afterlife. And this . . .'

A small wooden figurine lay next to the body, only a few inches long. She picked it up. It was crude, hastily made and roughly done, but she knew exactly what it was.

'I've read enough Sayers to know you're not meant to touch things at a murder scene,' said Susan sternly. 'What about fingerprints?'

'I'm wearing gloves. This is a shabti,' said Lucy. 'The Ancient Egyptians often put them in their tombs.' She turned it over. There was a gash at its throat. She laid the figure down gently where she had found it and stepped closer still to the body. Carefully, she peeled back the wide strip of rough linen which hid the face. Her stomach lurched.

'Susan,' she whispered. 'I know who that is.'

*   *   *

The scream of sirens could be heard as Lucy and Susan made an unobtrusive exit, along with the other frightened guests piling out into Cecil Court. It was easy to slip back to the shop, where they found Felix, Toby and Mr Tollesbury standing in the window, peering out in bewilderment and some excitement at the activity before them.

'What,' said Felix, 'on *earth* happened at Mr Dakin's exhibition opening?'

'Lucy,' said Mr Tollesbury, sternly. 'I hope this has nothing to do with you. Professional jealousy is one thing, but—'

'It was nothing to do with me,' said Lucy. 'There was a *body*. As in, a murdered one, next to the sarcophagus.'

'That's right,' gasped Susan, hurrying inside and joining them at the window. 'The Body in the Tomb. How's that for a book title?'

'A body!' cried Mr Tollesbury. 'Surely not. Mr Dakin was planning some sort of theatricals, wasn't he? Isn't this circus all part of it?'

Lucy shook her head. 'I thought so at first, but no,' she said. 'It really was a dead body.'

'Well!' said Mr Tollesbury, drawing a long breath. 'How – entirely – unexpected. I think I had better make some tea.'

Lucy and Susan sank into chairs. Toby, silent and wide-eyed, and Felix, clearly bursting with questions, sat opposite. Mr Tollesbury laid a delicate china cup in front of Lucy.

'Thank you, Professor,' said Lucy. She breathed in the fragrant steam. 'You do make the best cup of tea.'

He placed his worn hand briefly on hers. 'My dear, what a terrible shock,' he said quietly.

'I can't believe it!' exclaimed Susan, who was sitting wreathed in cigarette smoke, chin in her hands, under one of the green lights. 'A real dead body, in the middle of Mr Dakin's shop!'

'And I know who he was,' said Lucy hoarsely. 'I recognised him.'

Four pairs of eyes turned to her.

'It was Dr Curry,' she said. 'Dr W. Curry, who disturbed Dr Lyle's lecture last night.'

'Dr Curry?' said Mr Tollesbury slowly. 'That man who accused Lyle of stealing his research. Are you *sure*?'

'Absolutely. I recognised him, even though he was all pale and . . .' She broke off with a shudder.

'And are you sure he was, ah, dead?' asked Mr Tollesbury, his brow furrowed. 'Only I still wonder whether it might have been some sort of stunt. I wouldn't put much past Dakin. He said he wanted to get people talking, didn't he?'

'He's certainly done that. Dr Curry was very definitely dead,' said Lucy firmly. Her stomach lurched again as she recalled the pallor of Dr Curry's skin against that terrible encrusted blood. 'A few hours I should say. The blood was all dry and . . .' She broke off and took a swallow of tea.

'That poor man,' said Susan. She lit another cigarette with a shaking hand. 'He wanted to expose Dr Lyle, you said. He seemed determined to get people to notice him. Could this have been a bid for attention gone wrong?'

'Hard to see how he could have inflicted that wound on himself,' said Lucy.

'That tomb should never have been opened,' Mr Tollesbury said, almost to himself.

Lucy gave a weak laugh. 'Professor! Honestly. Please tell me you don't think this was the work of the curse. You sound like my mother.'

He shook his head. 'It should never have been opened,' he repeated.

'Lucy,' whispered Felix. 'I need to show you something.'

Lucy groaned. 'If this is about those bloody books, Felix—'

'No.' He was holding a white envelope in his hand and looked uncharacteristically grave. 'I think you should see this.'

Lucy took the envelope. It was stiff paper, clearly good quality, addressed to her in typeface, and neatly slit open at the top. 'Felix!' cried Lucy accusingly. 'You've been opening my mail.'

'I tried to give it to you earlier! You said it was just a bill,' he said indignantly. 'You know you never remember to open them and then I'm the one who has to deal with the tradespeople. They all came at once because of the postal strike. I opened it after you left – assumed it was some sort of joke. But now . . . well, look at it.'

Lucy drew out the contents. Inside was a piece of white card, with typed words.

> *Their greed will be their undoing. First, the fool, in Egypt.*
> *Tonight, the architect, in London. All who desecrated the*
> *tomb will be soon punished by my hand.*
> *I hope you're ready, Miss Darkwether.*

And then, in black ink, a series of symbols neatly blotted. Lucy felt her hands grow cold. Whoever had sent this knew her name.

'What are those?' said Susan, nodding to the symbols. 'Are they hieroglyphs?'

'Approximations of, I think. This is a figure – a man with his hands bound,' said Lucy. She passed her tongue over lips that were suddenly dry, the image of Dr Curry's bound and helpless figure rising before her eyes. 'What do you think, Professor?'

Mr Tollesbury glanced over her shoulder. 'Like he's being punished – research suggests a thief might have been punished that way. And this symbol here means two.' His eyes scanned the card. 'This here, that looks like an arch – it's ten – two tens.'

'Some sort of code?' said Susan.

Lucy laid the card down gingerly and examined the envelope. Her name was also neatly printed. *Miss Lucy Darkwether.* 'When did this arrive, Felix?'

'It arrived in that big pile yesterday. You don't think – you don't think that it came from the killer?'

Mr Tollesbury was now examining the note. 'These exhibitions attract cranks,' he said reassuringly. 'It's a coincidence.'

'But the mummy is next door. Why is it addressed to *me*?' said Lucy.

'Should we tell the police?' asked Susan. She rose and looked through the window. 'They're there now, I can see them. I wonder how they'll get an ambulance into the court, it's awfully small.'

Lucy took another large swallow of tea. 'I'm sure they'll be along to interview us any minute. We can show them the note then.'

She saw Toby stiffen. 'The police will come here?' he asked, his expression alert. 'Tonight? Why?'

'Susan and I were witnesses. And they'll want to speak to us all, find out if we saw any suspicious characters sniffing around Cecil Court today. The victim and the murderer must have got into Mr Dakin's shop at some point.'

'But Lucy,' hissed Felix, 'this is awful!'

'I know,' said Lucy. 'The poor man – frightful. A horrible thing to happen.'

Felix hopped from foot to foot. 'Yes of course, horrible – but damnit, Lucy, I don't mean the murder. Have you forgotten what's currently stashed in our back room?'

Lucy groaned. 'Those awful books!' She pressed her fingers to her forehead. 'We'll just have to keep the crate covered up and hope the police don't go sniffing around. Surely they've got more important things to worry about. Put some other books on top, something innocuous – some Agatha Christies, or some gardening books.' She stood and gripped his shoulders. 'Stay calm Felix.'

'If you say so,' said Felix, casting a hunted glance out of the window. 'Do you really think they'll come here?'

As though answering his question, there was a sharp knock at the door. Felix let out a cry of panic and Susan jumped. Toby stood and wiped his palms on his trousers. Mr Tollesbury looked only slightly less composed than usual.

'I'll let them in,' he said, rising. 'It's an awful night – they'll want a cup of tea.'

'Just stay calm,' Lucy murmured, to herself as much as anyone. She stood and smoothed down her dress. 'The police have bigger fish to fry. They'll only want to ask us a few routine questions. Got it?'

'Got it,' her staff murmured.

Mr Tollesbury opened the door to a tall, fair man in a suit and greatcoat, and another man behind him, with curly brown hair and a round, innocent face.

'Officers,' Lucy said. She was pleased with how steady her voice sounded. 'Come in. Would you like a tea or coffee?'

'No thanks.' The fair man had a clipped voice with an East End accent. 'Inspector Hayes. Mr Dakin told us where to find you. This is Sergeant West.'

'Lucy Darkwether,' said Lucy. 'Please, take a seat.' She ushered them into the bookshop as she spoke.

'S'cuse me,' Toby muttered, moving out of the way for the inspector. He took up a position in the gloom and the inspector's eyes lingered thoughtfully on him for a moment.

The inspector sat, folding his long legs, on one of the reading chairs. Beside him, Felix fidgeted uneasily and darted a glance towards the back office. Lucy kicked him stealthily under the table.

'Let me introduce you to everyone,' Lucy said, keeping her voice steady. 'This is Mr Felix Fletcher, my bookseller, Mr Tollesbury and Tobias Calvert who do bookbinding, and Susan Barrow, accounts.'

The inspector took out a notebook. His voice was low and unemotional. 'I understand you were present when the body was discovered, Miss Darkwether. You and your friend, Miss . . .'

'Barrow,' said Susan. She stubbed out her cigarette. 'Susan Barrow.'

'Mr Dakin says you both remained for some minutes in the room after he and the other guests left. Why did you do that?'

Lucy cursed Mr Dakin, who even in his shock and fright had remained sharp-eyed. 'I thought someone should stay with that poor man,' she said innocently. She felt somewhat nervous under the inspector's dispassionate gaze. 'He *is* dead, isn't he?'

'Yes, he's dead. And we know who he is. Mr Dakin, Sir Derwent, Dr Lyle, Mrs van Buren and Mr Ahmed all concur that the body is that of a Dr William Curry, a former colleague. The last time they saw him was last night, at a lecture at the British Museum.'

'He interrupted the lecture,' Lucy said. 'He created an awful fuss, said that Dr Lyle had stolen his research, that he had evidence to prove it. Said he knew secrets about each member of the Society and wasn't afraid to tell them. Did they tell you *that*?'

The inspector nodded. 'A version of it.'

'I bet they underplayed it,' said Lucy. 'We can tell you what *really* happened. Mr Tollesbury was there also.'

The inspector glanced at Mr Tollesbury. 'We would be interested in your version of events. And we'd like to get your opinion on a few interesting aspects of the crime scene too, if that's all right?'

'Why don't you ask Mr Dakin?' Lucy couldn't help asking. 'It is his bookshop after all.'

'Mr Dakin is still . . . recovering from the dramatic curtailing of his exhibition,' the inspector explained.

'All right,' said Lucy. 'He's hysterical, I understand. I'll fill you in. You want to know all about the red ochre, don't you? And the shabti doll. And the bandages. Did I miss anything?'

The inspector consulted his notes. 'This . . . what did you call it? The red powder.'

'Red ochre,' said Lucy. 'If it's a reference to the original tomb. Isn't that right, Professor?'

'Technically it would be iron oxide,' said Mr Tollesbury. 'Associated with the cave paintings of Lascaux and has been mentioned in monographs about Persian burial sites, for instance, Tepe Yaha.'

'In short?' said the inspector, pencil poised.

'In short,' said the professor, 'believed to be an ancient symbolic method of purifying the body to allow it to enter paradise.' He leaned forward. 'Which fits with the linens that were used – rough linens as befits someone of a lower class. The wooden figurine. Someone was preparing the body for the life *after* death.'

'The question is,' Lucy said thoughtfully, 'was all that stuff there before? Or was it staged after Mr Dakin left the mummy?'

The sergeant flipped a page of his notebook. 'Mr Dakin says he painted the tomb and drew hieroglyphs on the walls, set up some lighting. But the ochre, furs and this, er . . .'

'Shabti,' supplied Lucy.

'Yes, these were all new additions.'

'So, whoever murdered Dr Curry was someone familiar with the Ancient Egyptian burial rites?' murmured Susan. 'That's interesting, isn't it Lucy, given the press coverage—'

'Now hang on,' said the inspector. 'I'm asking the questions.'

'I think, given all the press coverage as you say, whoever did this wouldn't have needed to be *much* of an expert,' Lucy continued, ignoring him. 'Inspector, I'm assuming you've been following the doomed expedition to Giza, the tomb opening and the death of Sir Archibald Drake? The disasters which befell the expedition on its return voyage?'

The inspector stared at her for a moment, then laughed. 'Oh, I've seen it all right. The Curse of Tutankhamun: The Sequel? Tomb robbers cursed to death. Ridiculous stuff.'

'Then perhaps you should also see this note. It arrived this morning.' Lucy handed the inspector the envelope with a gloved hand.

The inspector read aloud. 'Their greed will be their undoing.' He tapped the hieroglyphs. 'What are these?'

'I believe it's some sort of code.'

'Possible code,' the sergeant murmured excitedly, scribbling in his notebook.

The inspector shot him a look. 'The architect?'

'Well, if Dr Curry *was* the one who actually located the tomb rather than Dr Lyle, as he claimed, then I suppose he was really the *architect* of the whole thing.'

The inspector frowned and dropped the note back across the table. 'I understand the expedition has created a great deal of press,' he said. 'Sir Archibald's sudden death, a series of disasters – I suppose people can't resist. But Dr Curry was murdered by a human hand. I am not inclined to believe in a supernatural angle, Miss Darkwether.'

'Neither am I,' said Lucy, irritably. 'Much like Lord Carnarvon probably died of blood poisoning not Tutankhamun's curse several years ago, I imagine Sir Archibald died of heart failure, just like the doctor said. But I do think this note is interesting. It foretold the death of Dr Curry and reached me long before anyone else knew he was dead. Which rather implies that the note-writer knows exactly what he's talking about.'

There was a silence, during which the inspector stared at Lucy and the sergeant stared at the envelope nervously.

Mr Tollesbury, who had been sitting so quietly they had almost forgotten he was there, said, 'Leaving the supernatural out of it, I don't like this note either, Inspector. The Ancient Egyptians may not have believed in vengeance from beyond the grave, but they did believe that mummification enabled their souls to live on in the afterlife. It gave them a link to their ancestors. Desecrating a tomb, as Dr Lyle and the others did, is a terrible thing – so *someone* might think. Someone who was willing to take matters into their own hands to avenge a dead king.'

The inspector sighed and nodded at the sergeant, who reverently placed the note into a folder. 'I'll take the note back to the station and have my men take a look. Now,' he swept on, before Lucy could interrupt, 'Sergeant West here would like to speak to you all individually, to ascertain your whereabouts today. Are you all happy with that?' His tone brooked no disagreement.

'Why *us*?' asked Felix sharply. 'We weren't there, except for

Lucy and Susan. Couldn't care less about a mummy or this Curry fellow. We were in the shop all day, minding our own business. We weren't hanging around waiting to murder anyone. We can vouch for each other.'

'Routine, sir,' said the sergeant soothingly. 'Got to follow proper procedure after a violent death. It'll only take a few minutes of your time.'

'Oh, longer than that,' said Susan pleadingly. She laid a hand on the sergeant's arm and he blinked. 'I insist on a proper grilling. It's fascinating – I've always wanted to meet a real-life police officer. You must know so much of the psychology of a killer, the criminal mind—'

'I'm not sure about that,' said the sergeant doubtfully, withdrawing his sleeve and looking rather pink. 'I'll probably just ask where you were today, miss, at the time we think the murder was committed. It seems it would have been around eleven this morning, although the coroner will confirm.'

'That would make sense,' Lucy said thoughtfully. 'The blood was all dried. You will look at the note seriously, won't you, Inspector? Only let's say it's not a coincidence. Let's say the killer is communicating using these notes and—'

'Like I said, we will have it examined back at the station,' he said. He raised his voice. 'A word of warning,' he said, 'and I shall say this only once. The last thing the police need in a case like this, that's already going to get attention, is a lot of unnecessary public hysteria and baseless theories. *That's* how we get timewasters, calling us up, saying they've seen the ghost of Isis outside their house.'

The sergeant nodded sadly. 'I can see that happening in this case, sir. Curses bring out those types. Meddlers too, thinking they can do better than us.'

'I know the type,' said the inspector, his eyes landing again on Lucy. 'Now, you'll get a lot of press buzzing around over the next few days. For now, all they need to know is that a man was found dead. We don't want them getting hold of the Ancient Egyptian burial angle just yet. We don't want any wild theories.' He met and held Lucy's gaze. 'Which means no mention of this note, Miss Darkwether, are we agreed? And no meddling.'

There was a pause, in which Lucy's dark, defiant eyes met the inspector's inflexible grey ones. 'Is that an official police warning?' she asked.

'A suggestion,' he said quietly. 'For your own safety.'

Lucy gave him a sweet smile. 'Of course, Inspector,' she said meekly. 'No meddling. I wouldn't dream of it.'

THE EVENING MIRROR

**Letter From A Killer?
Mummy's curse claims second victim.**

What the Police don't want you to know . . .

The *Evening Mirror* has received exclusive details on the shocking murder of Dr Curry in Cecil Court tonight. They are almost too horrible to describe, but he was arranged in the tomb in the manner of one entering the underworld. And, as the *Mirror* has discovered, the killer sent a terrible warning only hours before . . .

Chapter 6

The inspector and sergeant were sitting in the station across the desk from each other, running through the details of the day. A small coal stove hummed quietly. The inspector's desk was strewn with papers and telegrams and they could hear the muted sound of typewriters in the distance. The air was thick with cigarette smoke.

The inspector tossed over the evening edition of the paper. 'The girl didn't listen,' he muttered. 'Went straight to the press.'

'They never do,' said the sergeant. 'Meddlers will meddle, sir. Sir Marcus isn't going to like this, is he? A lot of big names associated with this case. His own brother, Sir Hector, one of the Society. If it's in the *Evening Mirror* it'll be everywhere in the morning.'

Sir Marcus Derwent was the chief of police. He was less than a month away from retirement and had made no secret of his annoyance at the arrival of such an attention-grabbing case in what should have been his final, peaceful weeks – a case that involved his younger brother, no less. In fact, the inspector had only an hour ago received a brusque call from his superior urging him to *get on with it*.

'Any hope we have of keeping the crime scene details quiet is shot to pieces now. And no, the chief is not going to be happy.' Inspector Hayes went to his office door and called out to another sergeant. 'Send some more men down to Cecil Court, will you? The press will be swarming all over the place tonight.'

When he came back to the desk, the sergeant was studying the note. 'What d'you think of this, sir?'

The divisional surgeon had been in to examine the body, the photographer had done his work, the fingerprint expert had dusted the scene. Dr Curry's body had been removed. And so had the mummy, returned to the British Museum, where it might be more safely stored.

'I think nothing of it,' said Inspector Hayes tersely. 'Some crackpot latching onto this mummy's curse story and it coincides with a brutal murder. Sir Marcus is . . . very keen that this be a suicide.'

The sergeant snorted. 'Be a contortionist for that to be the case, I should think. Have to wonder how many crime scenes our chief of police has actually attended,' he said.

'Quite. We should wait for the inquest, but I picked the coroner's brain. He said it's *just* about possible to cut your own throat, although stressed it was highly unlikely. There are usually hesitation marks, for one. Given the young man's state of mind, though, one *could* make a case for an elaborate suicide. Perhaps this Dr Curry wanted to punish this Dr Lyle by publicly humiliating him. Set this whole thing up himself.'

The sergeant drank some more tea. 'Weird way to kill yourself,' he said. 'By reenacting the mummification process.'

'That's true,' agreed the inspector, with the ghost of a smile. 'I have to say, West, it seems highly unlikely to me, even if it *is* physically possible. Besides, no weapon was found at the scene. What have we got so far?'

The sergeant flipped open his notebook. 'Coroner places time of death at around eleven o'clock that morning. Victim is a Dr William Curry, 32 years of age, born in Dublin, living in Shoreditch. Leaves behind a wife and child. Robinson spoke to the wife briefly – terribly upset she was, sir. He slept downstairs since their baby was born but she last saw him about ten-thirty last night when they went to bed. There's no record of him after that. No one saw him go into Dakin's Rare Books.'

The inspector nodded. 'So, between ten-thirty last night and around eleven this morning he must have somehow got inside. And the shop was definitely locked?'

'Mr Dakin is sure of that, sir. He did lose his keys last night—'

'Ah!'

'It doesn't help us, sir. He was fretting about getting a locksmith in, very worried about security with the mummy inside – Miss Darkwether and Mr Tollesbury say he mentioned it to them, among others. I don't think the Society would have been too impressed if someone had broken in and taken this precious mummy. He was so worried that he was at the shop first thing, around seven, where he found them on the mat. He went into the exhibition space and found it all as he had left it. He quickly painted the walls and put some red scarves over the lights. Then went out around eight-thirty to the museum, where he attended a lecture that Lyle was giving. He had lunch with the Society board, little celebration they all had at Claridge's. He didn't return until four, when he was letting the caterers in, giving interviews to the press. Doesn't think he went back into the exhibition space – he was busy and he knew it was all set up.'

'What's the lock to the shop like?'

'A night lock, sir, so it locks behind him. But he says he closed the door firmly and had the keys on him all day.'

'Hm. Let's put our esteemed boss's theory to one side. What if what Dr Curry said last night was true – he had evidence to show that Dr Lyle stole his research and the Society hushed it up. That wouldn't look good for the Society, would it?'

'It wouldn't,' said the sergeant, his eyes gleaming. 'A good motive there. They'd lose all the glory of the expedition.'

'Not to mention funding for future expeditions. Their reputations would be on the line. This Society,' said the inspector. 'Run through 'em will you?'

His sergeant, while possessed of a round, baby-faced, disingenuous air, was sharply perceptive when it came to dramatis personae of a case, and an excellent judge of character.

'A Dr Gordon Lyle, who led the expedition in Egypt; a Mrs van Buren, one of the funders; and Sir Hector Derwent, from the British Museum, who established the Society over a decade ago. Not a member but in attendance in Egypt was a Mr Omar Ahmed.'

'I'll need a bit more meat on the bones there, West.'

'Well, Dr Lyle is a celebrity. Good-looking, confident, pleased with himself, I'd say. Mrs van Buren is a wealthy widow, elegant lady, seems intelligent. Her husband was a nasty piece of work – you'll know *him*, sir.'

The inspector snapped his fingers. 'Lucas van Buren. The gangster.'

'As crooked as they come. Made a fortune in the war. He died a few years ago and it all went to his widow – she stepped in with the expedition when they were struggling with funding. Sir Hector, founder of the Society.' The sergeant hesitated. 'And, as you say, the brother of . . .'

'Yes, I know. It won't make interviewing him easy, but we'll have to do our best. Go on.'

'Mr Ahmed, moved here from Egypt when he was a boy and attended Eton. Senior consulting surgeon at Imperial Hospital. Interesting choice to moonlight as an expedition doctor, he says he was curious about the tomb and fancied a holiday.' The sergeant wrinkled his nose. 'Some holiday.'

'What about this Dakin chap whose shop it is?'

'Mr Dakin . . .' Sergeant West gave a sigh. 'Hard to say what he's like as he's so upset. Furious his big moment was ruined. Blaming everyone he can think of for it.'

The inspector tapped his cigarette over the ashtray. 'And he only admits to painting the walls?'

'A bit of set decoration – the walls, he lit some incense, organised the lighting. Everything else is our murderer gilding the lily.' The sergeant thought for a minute. 'He had the best opportunity for murder. Would have been easy for him. Invited Dr Curry round,

74

lured him into the tomb and slit his throat, shut the door and pretend to be as shocked as the rest. But it's hard to see *why*. This has cost him his chance to exhibit the famous mummy.'

'Did you ask him about this note Miss Darkwether got?'

'I did, went back and spoke to him about it. Just looked blank, said he knew nothing about it. I believed him, sir.'

There was a moment of silence, during which the inspector smoked and the sergeant looked over his notes. The inspector stubbed out his cigarette suddenly.

'I agree – opportunity but no motive that I can see. Go on – what about the others, do they have an alibi for eleven AM?'

'Dr Lyle was giving a lecture at the museum that started at ten and then he was lunching afterwards with the Society at Claridge's. We've spoken to the taxi driver who picked him up in Chiswick and he made no detour to Cecil Court. After the celebration lunch, he went directly home and worked some more until gone five. Annoyed his wife with his typing.' He flipped a page. 'Onto the rest, sir?'

'Yes, go on.'

'Mrs van Buren was meant to attend Dr Lyle's lecture, but she was suffering from a migraine and was late – got there about eleven thirty. Says she just walked around in the fresh air outside. After the Society lunch, she went home to change. Mr Ahmed was at Imperial Hospital in Charing Cross until lunch, as vouched for by his surgical team, and only stayed at Claridge's for an hour. He was in surgery until 4:57 and barely made the exhibition. Sir Hector—'

'I very much hope the chief's brother has an alibi,' muttered the inspector. 'Because he's got the same motive as the others. To shut Dr Curry up before he exposed a scandal.'

'I think it's worth noting that he has even *more* motive than the others. The Society is his baby, he started it from scratch, put everything into it. But yes, a rock-solid alibi, sir. He was at the lecture, then lunch, then his club – White's – he had a big row about politics in the smoking room, a few heard him. He joined the rest of the Society at the exhibition.' He leaned forward. 'Unless they *all* did it, sir, pretending to be at this lunch. Gave each other an alibi. I read something like that in a book.'

The inspector gave one of his rare smiles. 'I forgot you were such an avid reader, Sergeant. No, I don't think they were all working together – for one, the lunch itself certainly went ahead, the waiting staff confirm it. But they all have a motive to shut Curry up.'

The sergeant shrugged. 'We'll have to tread carefully. A lot of gentry in this case, sir.'

'Tell me about it,' muttered the inspector grimly. 'Let's hear about the neighbours. The other folk of Cecil Court.'

'There are three shops on the north side of Cecil Court. The first is Dakin's Rare Books. The second belongs to an art dealer who is away for the winter. Which leaves the inhabitants of Cecil Court Books. Can't imagine *they* had anything to do with it.' He paused and eyed the inspector, who said nothing. 'All the same, I took statements like you wanted. They open at ten on a Friday. Two staff members have rooms above the shop – one is a Mr Tollesbury, retired Oxford don, works in the bookbinding department – bit doddery and vague-seeming but sharp underneath it, I reckon. Says he woke early *as was his wont* – that's how he put it. The other lodger is Toby Calvert, apprentice bookbinder. They were just unlocking the shop when Mr Fletcher and then the owner, Miss Darkwether arrived, just after eight. Then Miss Darkwether and Miss Barrow, accounts, were at a presentation in Covent Garden till lunchtime. Mr Fletcher, the bookseller. Doesn't live at the shop like the others, but certainly spends a good deal of time there. He was selling books in the front room – plenty of customers can vouch for that – and Mr Tollesbury and Mr Calvert were working in the backroom all morning. There's a back door to the alley but neither went in or out for more than a minute or two.'

The inspector thought of the quiet boy at the shop, who had

remained resolutely in the shadows. 'What's this Calvert like? Seems familiar for some reason.'

'Doesn't say more than he has to and that's an understatement. Can't see how he would have a motive for murder though.' The sergeant hesitated, then went on, 'There is one other thing to add, sir, but it's only nonsense.'

'Go on.'

'Mr Dakin is convinced *Miss Darkwether* is responsible for the murder. Says she's jealous he got hold of this mummy and wanted to ruin him.' The inspector was silent and the sergeant went on. 'Little thing like her, murdering a man – arranging him like that – like I said, nonsense.'

The inspector frowned. 'That *little thing* looks like trouble to me, sergeant. Although I agree it would be physically difficult. Maybe Miss Darkwether had help from her friends in the shop.'

The sergeant stared. 'Are you teasing, sir?'

'Partly – but I've got an odd feeling about Cecil Court Books.'

'Some sort of revenge scheme gone wrong?' asked the sergeant doubtfully. 'Quite dramatically wrong, if so.'

'Run their alibis through the usual checks, will you?' said the inspector. 'I want to be sure we're not missing anything. Speak to everyone in the local area – someone must have seen something, someone going in or out of Cecil Court who didn't have a reason to be there. For goodness sake, it was the middle of the day.' He yawned and stretched. 'Bed now, sergeant. Our first move tomorrow is to speak to Dr Curry's widow. I want to find out if he was telling the truth about the esteemed Dr Lyle stealing his work. And where this evidence he talked about might be.'

'Yes, sir.' The sergeant hesitated, then said, 'And the note, sir? The mummy's curse?'

Emphatically, the inspector pushed back his chair and stood. 'Forget the curse,' he said.

Chapter 7

After the inspector and sergeant had left the shop, Lucy and her staff conducted their own post-mortem over a bottle of good single malt that Mr Tollesbury had brought back from a trip to the Highlands, while making a pilgrimage to a particularly interesting set of ancient Celtic crosses. A ginger cat, who seemed to be of no fixed abode but would sometimes appear at Cecil Court looking for food, was curled up on a chair, snoring quietly. All were sitting around the table, except for Felix who was still groaning over an enormous pile of post.

'The note said it all,' said Lucy. '*More will die*.' She groaned and reached behind her for the *Mirror* and the front page by Max Bird. 'This Mr Bird seems awfully keen to keep the public imagination stoked and someone played into his hands by telling him the contents of the note. I wonder who went to the press with it? We're the only ones who knew.' She frowned at Felix. 'It wasn't you, was it? All publicity is good publicity and all that?'

Felix held up his hands. 'Innocent, I swear,' he said. 'I wouldn't disobey that stern inspector.'

Lucy raked Toby and Susan with her gaze and they both shook their heads. 'Not us, guv,' Susan said.

Toby said, 'Maybe one of the police blabbed . . . you can't trust a copper, miss.'

Lucy sighed. 'It's a mystery,' she said. 'Speaking of mysteries, I wish I knew why the note was addressed to me.'

'Tell me what happened again tonight, Lucy,' said Mr Tollesbury. 'Right from the beginning.'

Lucy cast her mind back to the terrible event. 'Susan and I got there just before six, we were in the queue. We all got herded into the shop. It was frightfully hot and the mummy had attracted the exact crowd you can imagine and Dakin had sold too many tickets for it to be comfortable. There were waiters in costume, that sort of rubbish. Mr Dakin introduced Dr Lyle in the most sycophantic way – and Dr Lyle made the most awfully compelling speech, like a showman.'

'He does know how to create an atmosphere,' admitted Susan.

'Then Mr Dakin opened the door . . .'

'And he *screamed*,' said Susan, with relish. 'We saw this awful scene, the body wrapped in bandages. For a minute I think we all thought it was part of the show. The Society were all shocked, I could tell.'

'Perhaps they're good actors,' said Felix. 'Murderers often are. They each had a reason to get rid of Dr Curry, didn't they? If this evidence of his had materialised . . . Well, that would have spelled the end of the Society. What's that you're drawing, Toby?'

Toby, who had been scribbling away on a piece of paper, now looked up, and pushed it across the table. 'I was trying to remember the note the inspector took away,' he explained. Sure enough, Lucy saw that the hieroglyphs were elegantly drawn and the note copied exactly as she remembered it. 'That's extraordinary,' she murmured, and he shrugged.

'Got that sort of memory,' he explained. 'I see it once and it's in there. So, you think it's some sort of code? Not these . . . what did you call it before, Professor?'

'Hieroglyphic writing,' Mr Tollesbury said. 'A system which evolved throughout the Egyptian Ages and centuries. Late hieroglyphic use was found well into the Persian and Ptolemaic Periods and indeed the Roman . . .'

'Right,' said Toby, blinking.

Mr Tollesbury grinned. 'But yes, Toby, I think this is a crude code, alluding to the hieroglyphic system. The bound man, I should think, stands for poor Dr Curry, a thief to be punished by death . . . then, we have the sarcophagus, relating to the sacred tomb furniture. And then we have two cobbles, or tens, giving us the number twenty.'

'Twenty,' said Toby. 'And it's the twentieth of March today.'

Susan shivered. 'You're all acting like the killer definitely sent this.'

'Remember what you always used to tell us, Mr T – in archaeology, you're allowed one coincidence,' Lucy said. 'This note might have nothing to do with the crime at all.'

Mr Tollesbury nodded, looking rather grim. 'That's true, my dear. I'll allow a coincidence in any archaeological investigation. But it does seem *unlikely*. The note says there will be more deaths. Hoax or not – I suppose we'll find out one way or another.'

Lucy rose angrily. 'You mean sit around and wait for someone else to die! Not likely. I bet the inspector hasn't even dusted it for fingerprints, or whatever they're meant to do.' Lucy prowled up and down the shop. 'If the killer intends to avenge the king, then all those who were in Egypt are in danger – Dr Lyle, Mrs van Buren, Sir Hector, Mr Ahmed. I'm tempted to take matters into my own hands and do some digging myself—'

The shrill sound of the telephone made them all jump.

'I told you to leave the phone off the hook, Felix,' said Lucy, nerves making her snap.

'I thought the reporters would have eased off and the customers might come pouring in. I'll get it,' said Felix. He answered, listened, then waved to Lucy. 'It's a man, for you. A Mr Vyse.'

Lucy took the receiver, while the rest of the staff went back to their whisky. 'Edward.'

'Lucy!' Edward's voice was full of barely concealed strain. 'I've been trying you all day at home, at your parents, at your shop. Bloody phone kept ringing out. We're all worried. Mrs Thorpe said she hadn't heard anything. Your parents are frantic – your mother keeps calling me. How are you?'

'I'm all right,' Lucy said. 'It was rather horrible. Susan and I were there, you see. Can you let Mother know I'm alive?'

'Of course. Listen, why don't I come and pick you up and drive you home – to your parents, I mean.'

'There's no need,' said Lucy, 'I can't think of anything worse than dealing with Mother right now. And everyone is here.'

'Who is everyone?' asked Edward. 'Will someone see you home?'

'Of course. Edward, don't fret. I doubt the killer is still lurking in Cecil Court.' A gust of wind rattled the window and Lucy shivered. Suddenly she *could* imagine the killer lurking in the dark.

There was a pause and then Edward said, in a gentler voice, 'I don't like how we left things the other night, Lucy. We're old friends, aren't we?'

'Absolutely.' Lucy was suddenly aware that her friends had gone quiet and might be listening.

'Well, can we have dinner – next week perhaps? I rather sprang the news of my engagement on you. I'd like to talk to you properly about it.'

'Dinner would be lovely.' Lucy bit back a yawn; perhaps now the shock was finally wearing off, exhaustion was setting in. 'I'll ring you up and arrange it this week. Good night, Edward, and please don't worry.' She went back to the table.

'I wish I could like whisky,' said Susan was saying, sadly, as she sat back down. 'My mouth just tastes of bonfire.'

'You don't appreciate the finer things,' said Felix. 'Toby doesn't either.'

'It's all right,' said Toby, pulling a face. 'I'd prefer a beer.'

'I think we should all go home and get some rest,' said Mr Tollesbury. 'Lucy, I'll call you a taxi.'

Lucy shook her head. 'I'd rather stay here tonight, Professor,' she said. She felt an obscure need to barricade herself inside the shop, rather than venture out into the wind and dark.

Giving sombre goodnights, Felix and Susan headed into the night and Toby retired to bed.

Mr Tollesbury hesitated in the doorway. 'You mustn't take this too personally, my dear,' he said gently.

'How can I not?' she demanded. 'The killer wrote to *me*. Professor. If I had only opened the letter sooner, I might have been able to save Dr Curry. I should like to speak to his widow.'

Her old teacher looked startled. 'Why on earth?'

'To offer my condolences – no, really – but also, I want to ask her some questions,' she said. 'I can't *not* take this personally. And you wouldn't be able to either, if the note had come to you.'

'Perhaps,' he admitted. 'See how you feel in the morning, my dear. I'll make up the day bed for you in the stockroom and let Mrs Thorpe know. Toby and I are just upstairs if you need us.'

But Lucy did not go to the day bed. She stayed at the table long after the professor had gone upstairs, gazing at Toby's copy of the note until the hieroglyphs swam before her eyes.

All who desecrated the tomb will be soon punished by my hand.

Lucy was determined not to let that happen.

Chapter 8

The next day was a Saturday.

When Lucy awoke to pale sunlight, stiff and uncomfortable, she found that Mr Tollesbury had put a blanket around her shoulders and there was a steaming cup of tea at her elbow, and a slip of paper with an address in the East End written in his careful hand, the same hand which had once upon a time ruthlessly yet politely torn her essays to shreds.

I've gone for a walk. This is Dr Curry's home address.
One of those reporters let it slip for a pound. If you must
meddle, be careful.

Lucy smiled. Her old teacher knew her well. She washed her face in the sink at the back, tidied her hair, drank her tea and ate a piece of bread and butter, then buttoned her coat. She could hear Toby's wireless playing upstairs as she set off.

In the morning light, Cecil Court, with its shuttered shops and a sheet of newspaper blowing across the cobbles, felt quite ordinary. Last night, with its atmosphere of fetid horror, seemed almost unbelievable. Surely such a thing couldn't have happened, only metres away from Lucy's beloved shop.

But it did *happen*, thought Lucy. *And I'm going to find out why*.

As if to emphasise the fact, the sheet of newspaper caught on a railing and she saw the headline: 'Bookshop at Centre of Curse Killing.'

There was police tape outside Mr Dakin's shop, but the reporters had gone for now. The only other person in Cecil Court was Mr Dakin, who was standing in the alley, gazing out at the street beyond and moodily sipping a cup of coffee, a folded paper under his arm. He shot Lucy a look of such malevolence that startled her.

'Good morning, Mr Dakin,' she said, edging past. He looked tired and dishevelled, unlike his usually neat appearance. 'Did you spend the night in the shop?'

'I did,' he said, eyeing her unpleasantly. 'Even though the inspector told me to go home. Wanted to make sure nothing else untoward happened. And I don't know how you can call it a *good morning*.' He flapped his newspaper angrily. 'Someone's been spreading rumours and I heard that's you. Some note you got, purporting to be from the killer! More deaths to come! Do you think I need any more bad publicity?'

'I only told the police, no one else,' Lucy protested.

'Well, it's been splashed all over this rag,' said Mr Dakin, waving his copy of the *Mirror*. 'The press will be back again today, shouldn't wonder.' He let out a wail of rage and frustration. 'This exhibition was going to make my name!' he cried. 'All anyone will remember is a *disaster*. And now – now the museum have taken him away!'

'Him?' said Lucy, marvelling at Dakin's self-centredness.

'The mummy,' he sighed. 'I had hoped to persuade the Society to let me open for another night, but they arranged for him to be removed. Said he wasn't safe here, that the security was better at the museum.' He seemed to recall the subject of his ire and shot Lucy another filthy look. 'I imagine you're pleased about that, aren't you? You never hid the fact *you* wanted the mummy.'

'Not enough to murder a man, if that's what you're thinking,' snapped Lucy, who was tiring of Mr Dakin's grievances. 'Do you honestly believe I snuck in, killed Dr Curry and arranged him in your bookshop, all while you were having lunch?'

Lost for words, Mr Dakin simply glowered at her.

'You misplaced your keys the night before the murder,' said Lucy, taking advantage of his temporary silence. 'I would have thought you'd have been more careful with the precious mummy inside your shop. I hope you told the police that?'

Mr Dakin flushed. 'I found them again early the next morning,' he said. 'And I was inside that morning and there was no body! None of that red dust and stuff. Oh, but it doesn't make any sense! Why was this Dr Curry, whoever he was, in my shop at all?'

'I'm working on that one. Whose idea was it to organise the shop as an Egyptian tomb?' asked Lucy.

'It was mine,' said Mr Dakin, a shred of pride in his voice. 'I'd been trying to decide how to make the exhibition special and then I realised at Dr Lyle's lecture what it needed. The audience would step into the *tomb itself*.' He scowled. 'Fat lot of good it did me in the end. I've lost *everything*.'

Lucy took a deep breath and adjusted her hat. 'Not nearly as much as Dr Curry has lost. Now, if you'll excuse me,' she said, pushing past him into the street, 'I have an appointment.'

＊　＊　＊

She did not, of course, have an appointment, but she did hope she could speak to Mrs Curry. She felt for the young widow, so recently and shockingly bereaved, with all the attendant media attention – and she was intensely curious about Dr Curry and his accusation that Dr Lyle had stolen his work. Underneath the hysteria, his words had rung with truth. Lucy had believed him, and she wondered whether others might have too. Then there was the evidence that Dr Curry had spoken of . . . could that be somewhere in his home? Might his widow know where it was?

A tube journey and a bus later, Lucy reached Shoreditch, a quiet area with modest terraced houses and neat front gardens, a few small shops, a newsagent selling cigarettes, magazines and sweets.

Children played out in the street and neighbours talked over walls, voices low. It was entirely ordinary and yet, as she walked, Lucy could not shake a subtle sense of dread. As though, just out of the corner of her eye, menace was lurking.

Not you too, Lucy told herself severely. There's no such thing as a curse; but there is a murder to solve.

Lucy spotted the house from a distance by the plain clothes officer waiting outside. She stopped, pretending to tie her shoe, then turned and doubled back, skirting the row of houses, walking quickly down a back alley, passing a surprised cat, until she reached the kitchen door, which, when she tried it gently, she found to be open.

Lucy knocked softly, receiving no answer. She knocked again. Then she opened the door quietly, stepping into a kitchen with a sink full of baby bottles.

I'll leave a note, she decided, drawing her card out of her bag. But then she heard the sound of weeping, broken by a cold, male voice, and she stiffened. A journalist or police officer, she thought, come to bully Mrs Curry into an interview when the widow was too grief-stricken to protest. Lucy felt obscurely protective of the widow. She would listen and see if everything was all right.

Lucy walked down a narrow corridor, followed by the cat, reaching a shut door, from which low voices could be heard, broken by more sobbing. All sounded calm: she would leave and return later. As she turned, though, she accidentally trod on the cat's tail, causing it to shriek and her to collide with a small occasional table and bang her knee. When she looked up, the door was open and a startled face looked out at her.

'Mrs Curry, I presume,' said Lucy. 'Sorry for barging in like this. I – I wasn't sure whether anyone was home.'

The woman hesitated. A lock of dark hair hung over one temple. She wore a faded print robe and looked utterly exhausted, blue circles like bruises under her eyes.

'I believed him,' Lucy whispered. 'I believed your husband's story.'

'You did?' Mrs Curry said. 'I'm not sure *I* did, half the time.'

'Is that Miss Darkwether?' came a familiar, sardonic voice from inside the sitting room. 'Tell her to come on in. I'd quite like a word with her myself.'

Lucy gave an internal groan. She recognised that voice now and knew that she had been caught in the very act of meddling. But she couldn't leave now: Mrs Curry was ushering her inside a small sitting room where none other than Inspector Hayes himself stood, looking tall and incongruous amongst the chintz. The room smelt musty, and the net curtains were drawn. In the corner was a roll-top desk, with neat stacks of paper, notebooks, and freshly sharpened pencils, rolled maps and plans.

'You should introduce yourself properly, Miss Darkwether,' said the inspector. Lucy couldn't tell how annoyed he was; his expression was irritatingly impassive. 'She owns the shop opposite Dakin's Rare Books, where your husband died, Mrs Curry. She's also a meddler of the first order, but I didn't think she'd stoop to doorstepping.'

Lucy hung her head. 'I wasn't doorstepping – but I do apologise, Mrs Curry.'

'Like those reporters,' said Mrs Curry. She seemed almost too exhausted to be angry, pleating her handkerchief in her lap. 'They've been knocking every five minutes, shouting about an Ancient Egyptian curse or some rubbish. *Who's next*, that's what one said.' She drew a shaky breath. 'William would have hated for me to be bothered like this.'

'We've put a man outside now,' said Inspector Hayes. 'He should fend the press off till they get bored. Although it seems Miss Darkwether managed to elude him.'

'I wanted to give my condolences,' Lucy said. 'It must have been a terrible shock.'

Mrs Curry wiped her eyes, which were red with weeping. She seemed dazed. 'The baby will be up soon,' she said. 'I still can't believe it. That their daddy – that William won't be coming home.'

'I'm sorry for your loss,' said Inspector Hayes quietly. 'It's a cruel thing.'

'Cruel is right,' said Mrs Curry fiercely.

'Your husband attended a lecture at the British Museum the night before last,' said Inspector Hayes. 'Did you see him after that?' Lucy stayed very still in the doorway and held her breath, hoping he might forget she was there.

'Yes, he came back all steamed up and angry. He went to the door after dinner and when he came back, he said he'd had a message. He seemed much more cheerful. Said he'd found a way out of all this, that's what he said. He slept on the sofa like he always did – the baby keeps him up otherwise. And then when I came down yesterday morning, he was already gone. Unusual for him to be up that early, since his contract was terminated. That was the last I saw of him.'

The inspector nodded and cast a quick glance at Lucy. 'You can draw breath, Miss Darkwether – I wouldn't want you to expire in the doorway. In fact, why don't you sit down.' Lucy scurried to an armchair and sat. The cat jumped into her lap. 'Losing his job – that must have been difficult,' the inspector continued, turning back to Mrs Curry.

Mrs Curry nodded eagerly. 'It was very hard for him, sir. William liked keeping busy. He was away for months at a time when he was on a dig, in all kinds of far-off countries, and when he got back he'd be researching the next one. He was so excited for the latest expedition in Egypt, I can't tell you. Been dreaming about it for years, planning this tomb discovery. He was honoured to be chosen by Dr Lyle. Thought he'd be out there a good month or so – but he was back after only a few weeks. He'd been let go, he said.'

'He blamed Dr Lyle for that, didn't he?' said the inspector.

The woman looked embarrassed. 'Yes, sir. He thought that Dr Lyle had taken his research for his own and sacked him to get him out the way. Conspired with the Society – that's what he said, *conspired*. He thought they were discrediting him on purpose so that no one would take his claims seriously. He had a lot of wild stories about everyone in the Society.'

'And what did *you* think?' asked the inspector.

'I couldn't believe it of Dr Lyle,' murmured the widow. 'He's such a clever gentleman – and so nicely spoken and well respected. And Mrs van Buren, Sir Hector . . . I couldn't believe it.'

'What sort of stories?' asked the inspector curiously.

'I don't remember,' the widow admitted. 'William seemed to be saying any old thing, he was so angry. I told him to let it lie. Did it matter who found the mummy?'

'It seems to have mattered to your husband.'

'His reputation was ruined, he said. And there was the money. He was worried about paying our rent, and we had the baby. I told him to look for something else, but he wouldn't. Said he wasn't going to let Dr Lyle get away with it. That he'd make him pay.'

'Were you worried he meant to hurt himself?'

'Oh no, sir,' she said. 'That didn't occur to me, not for a second. I was worried he might have meant to hurt Dr Lyle.'

'Then the night before last he told you he'd *found a way out of this*. What did you think he meant by that?' asked the inspector.

Mrs Curry considered for a moment. 'I thought he'd decided to see sense and get another job. He seemed sort of excited, keyed up. But when I woke up and he was gone, I wasn't sure. I was so worried all day – and then – and then . . .' She buried her face in her handkerchief. Lucy and the inspector were silent for a moment while Mrs Curry composed herself.

At last, the inspector said, 'Did he have any enemies, aside from the expedition members and Dr Lyle? Anyone he might have fought with in the past?'

'He was prickly, William,' admitted Mrs Curry. 'Bit of a chip on his shoulder about not having gone to a smart university like the others in his field. Wasn't above complaining if he thought some-one had taken one of his ideas without citation. But nothing that would have made anyone want to kill him.'

'He went a bit further with Dr Lyle though, didn't he?' said the inspector, pushing her to give him more answers. 'Threatened him. Said he had *evidence* that Dr Lyle had robbed him. I wonder how seriously Dr Lyle took that threat.'

And what he might have done to stop it, Lucy thought, filling in the rest of the inspector's sentence that seemed to hang in the air between them.

The widow blanched. 'Dr Lyle seems like a nice man – I'm sure he – he wouldn't have . . .' She trailed off, shaking her head. 'This feels like a bad dream,' she said.

The inspector made a note. 'Did your husband have a will?'

'A life insurance policy. He had it made up before he went to Egypt this last time. He told me about tomb openings being cursed, Tutankhamun and all that – said he might as well, in case some ancient plague got him. It was a joke really, but then that old man died – and then . . .'

And then so did Dr Curry, thought Lucy.

The three of them were silent for a long minute. Somewhere in the back room a baby started crying. The woman roused herself and frowned at Lucy, seeming to see her for the first time. 'What did you say you'd come for again, miss?'

'An excellent question,' said the inspector. 'Perhaps you might wait outside, Miss Darkwether. I'd like to have a little chat with you when I finish up here.'

* * *

Lucy couldn't help feeling as though she were waiting outside the headmistress's office as she stood on the step in the cold air for another fifteen minutes, smoking with the sergeant. The neigh-bourhood was quiet, respectable, children being called in for their lunch. It seemed far too ordinary a background for such tragedy to be unfolding.

As Lucy chatted distractedly and heard about the sergeant's plans for the vegetable garden that spring, she was making some notes of her own in her head.

Dr Curry had returned from the lecture upset – then a message had come for him. He had returned cheerful, happy. But why?

Where had he gone when he left his house?

What were the wild stories Dr Curry knew about the other members of the Society?

Had Dr Lyle really stolen Dr Curry's research, then had him fired?

Did Dr Curry have evidence to that effect?

And was that evidence enough to push Dr Lyle to murder?

Eventually, the inspector emerged.

'If you see this one here again,' he told Sergeant West, nodding at Lucy, 'escort her from the premises immediately.'

'Yes, sir,' said the sergeant, grinning at Lucy.

The inspector started down the steps and Lucy fell in beside him.

'You didn't seem surprised to see me here today,' she said. 'Annoyed, maybe, but not surprised.'

'I'm not,' the inspector said curtly. 'Something told me you'd be a meddling sort. Although I had hoped you had better manners than to force yourself into a grieving widow's home. Or more consideration, perhaps.'

'I really did want to give my condolences,' Lucy said. 'And I'll admit, I wanted to strike while the iron is hot.'

The inspector set a brisk pace and Lucy followed 'Did you learn anything in there after I left?' She was determined not to be deterred, and to find out as much about this investigation as she possibly could.

'Nothing I'm willing to share.'

'Well *I* was wondering what was in that message that cheered him up. Did you find a note in the house?'

'No, we didn't.'

'She said Dr Curry seemed excited on his last night. Keyed up, she said. That's interesting, don't you think? He was so angry at the lecture.'

'What was *interesting* is that your precious anonymous letter is all over the papers,' Inspector Hayes said, turning his collar up against the cold. 'Which is what I wanted to discuss, since you're here. I told you not to tell a soul about it. I've no doubt it'll be recycled for the evening headlines. The *Mirror* also seemed to have an in-depth knowledge of the crime scene, down to the arrangement of the body, the furs and the red ochre. Could you not keep quiet, Miss Darkwether?'

'I *did* keep quiet,' said Lucy, with spirit. 'It wasn't me who told the press anything!!' She was indignant. Not only was the inspector refusing to answer her questions, he was also accusing her of something she had played no part in. 'But I have a suspicion as to who did.'

The inspector turned to look at her, seemingly finally intrigued by something she had to say. 'Who?'

'Mr Dakin,' said Lucy promptly.

'Nonsense,' exclaimed the inspector. 'This scandal ruined his exhibition. He was furious. Why would he want to attract more notoriety?'

'At *first* he was furious, maybe,' said Lucy. 'But maybe that's all an act. Once he'd had some time to think, he realised the publicity the crime would bring in, especially if he could tie it to the tomb openings. He's lost his precious mummy – why shouldn't he capitalise on the sensationalist aspects of the crime? Get more customers through his now-famous door.' She shook her head. 'The man is a ghoul, but he's a good businessman.'

'He didn't know you'd received an anonymous note,' the inspector pointed out.

'You didn't mention it in questioning him?' The inspector hesitated, then nodded slowly. 'Well, I thought so,' Lucy continued. 'He's sharp. He doesn't miss a trick, and he wouldn't scruple to turn a tragedy to his advantage. Now, as to the curse . . .'

The inspector stopped in the street and wheeled round.

'Ah, the curse. Let me guess,' he said 'A vengeful Ancient Egyptian king is picking off members of the expedition – rather obligingly, they're letting us know in advance with typewritten letters. Tell me, Miss Darkwether – were the Ancient Egyptians a vengeful lot? And do they tend to carry typewriters with them while travelling?'

'No,' Lucy replied with composure. 'As it happens, I gather that vengeance was contrary to all Egyptian belief and thought. But it *is* possible that someone believes themselves to be acting *for* the king, whose sacred tomb was disturbed for monetary gain.'

Inspector Hayes snorted. 'You'd be surprised how many anonymous threatening notes we get in the force, Miss Darkwether. If we paid attention to every single one, we wouldn't get much work done.'

'And how many corpses do you get that are surrounded by furs and red dust?' Lucy asked. He remained silent. 'How much do you know about archaeological theory, Inspector?' she pressed on instead.

'Not an awful lot,' he said, his mouth twitching in a smile. 'I'm sure you'll enlighten me.'

Lucy took a deep breath and summoned her best, Finals-rehearsed answer. 'There are two schools of archaeological theory. The first is that you can develop accurate information about the past by using the scientific method. The facts and just the facts. The second argues that all archaeological data is tainted by human interpretation. Any interpretation is therefore subjective.'

Inspector Hayes looked at her thoughtfully. 'And which one are we talking here?'

'The second,' Lucy said promptly. 'The facts only go so far. We need imagination to fill in the gaps.'

'Imagination? I'm sure you have plenty of it. I'll tell my superior, Sir Marcus Derwent, that we're throwing out the facts and using imagination to solve the case then,' he said. 'I'm sure that will reassure him. I'm here to catch a killer, Miss Darkwether, not indulge in fanciful nonsense.'

'If it was as straightforward as all that,' Lucy said reasonably, 'you wouldn't be talking to me now.'

The inspector's lips twitched again, as though he were biting back a smile. They started walking again.

'Is the head of the Yard pushing for an arrest?' asked Lucy. Sir Marcus, the chief of police, was an old family friend of her father's, but she decided not to mention that; she didn't want to annoy Inspector Hayes any more than she already had.

'Pushing hard,' said the inspector frankly. 'His brother's Sir Hector, the founder of this ridiculous members of the Society, and he doesn't want to be involved in a scandal. For what it's worth, I mentioned your note to him. He said it's a lunatic at work and they should be easy enough to find.' He took a packet of cigarettes from his pocket and shook one out. 'If someone really wants the Society dead, why the elaborate charade?' he murmured, almost to himself. 'Why not just kill them all quietly?'

'Our murderer is a showman,' said Lucy. 'But – and I'm sure Sir Marcus won't like to hear this – the main suspects are surely the three members of the Society, who have everything to lose – the sarcophagus, their reputation, their funding. Dr Lyle, Mrs van Buren, Sir Hector Derwent. You need *them* under surveillance.'

The inspector's jaw hardened. 'I'm not stupid, Miss Darkwether. And yet I can't see my boss signing off surveillance on his own brother.'

'Well, I, in fact, hope it's one of them and not our letter-writer,' Lucy huffed. 'Because otherwise . . .'

'Otherwise?'

'Well, if the killer intends to punish the Society one by one, like the letter says . . . then it won't be long before there's another murder.'

The inspector swallowed down a sharp retort. 'No one else is going to be *punished*. I'm going to leave you here, Miss Darkwether. And I should ask you to stop feeding stories to the press and meddling in my investigation. Do you understand?'

'Of course,' she told him. 'At least, if I do, I'll be discreet.'

'Let's see how long that lasts,' Inspector Hayes muttered, turning on his heel, a flush of anger on his cheeks.

Lucy watched the inspector go. She had no intention of stopping her meddling – in fact she was just getting started.

Chapter 9

ucy walked back to the shop past newspaper billboards that were still screaming about the murder.

TERROR STRIKES IN LONDON

ANCIENT CURSE CLAIMS SECOND VICTIM

EXPLORATION SOCIETY IN GRIP OF FEAR

The *Daily Mirror*, as ever, shouted the loudest.

THE MUMMY'S CURSE KILLS AGAIN. WHO WILL BE NEXT?

Lucy bought a paper – she went for the *Mirror*, deciding they seemed to be the best informed, although who was tipping them off, she didn't know – and stopped to open it on the corner, stamping on the spot in the cold street. She turned to Max Bird's famous editorial, in which he laid out his own theory of the crime. To her dismay, she saw her own name on the page.

This paper has learned that the killer may be taunting the police by sending cryptic notes to a Miss Lucy Darkwether, of Cecil

Court Books, hinting through a series of fiendish clues who their next victim will be.

It is not yet known whether Miss Darkwether has received another note . . .

Lucy sighed and shut the paper. 'They say that all publicity is good publicity,' she told herself. 'Let's hope so.'

When Lucy arrived at the shop, there was a crowd of men jostling with notebooks outside. Dakin's Rare Books was shut up, still cordoned off with police tape, and it seemed that Cecil Court Books, where the warning note had been sent, was the next best thing. There was no sign of Mr Dakin.

'Excuse me,' she said, tapping one man in a raincoat on the shoulder. 'That's my shop, so I need to get past.'

The man turned and snapped to attention, eyes narrowing. 'Miss Darkwether?' he said keenly. 'The girl who got the note?'

'That's me,' said Lucy, sheepishly, quickly wriggling under his arm when he refused to move out the way.

'The girl who got the note!' cried another as Lucy fought her way past, batting away questions and cigarette smoke. She was used to photographers waiting outside nightclubs, hoping to catch a society scandal or two, but it seemed the crime scene hacks were made of tougher stuff. Then, strong fingers closed on her wrist and she was whisked into the doorway of the shop.

'I told you,' Felix addressed the crowd from the doorstep in a severe tone. 'You can come in *one at a time*. If you crowd us like this, I will renege on my offer.'

'What are you doing?' whispered Lucy.

'You can't fight the beast, Lucy – we may as well make friends with it,' he told her. 'Feed it a few crumbs.'

'I'm not talking to reporters! That inspector would murder me himself.'

'*You* won't talk to anybody. Just leave it to me,' said Felix. He pointed to the man nearest the door. 'Mr Banks, wasn't it? You can come in first as you've been waiting so nicely. Come in, come in.'

Mr Banks followed Felix and Lucy inside and licked his pencil. 'Is this where the note came?' he asked, looking around eagerly.

'It is,' said Felix. 'We thought it was a bill at first. Before we realised it was a – a missive of doom.'

Mr Banks scribbled urgently. 'Missive of doom, right. Can you describe the envelope? Was it typed or handwritten?'

'One of those,' said Felix, waving a hand. 'I can't be sure.'

'And what did it say exactly?'

'It was,' whispered Felix, leaning into the theatrics, 'a terrible warning – the exact wording escapes me. Are you a reader, Mr Banks?'

'Me? No. The missus, she likes a good thriller. I read the papers of course. Now—'

'You *must* read something beyond all that death and misery. Some fiction, perhaps. It's a window to the world. Let me show you something that I think would really take your fancy and your wife's perhaps, it's in the backroom – a necessary precaution, with all these police around – but you look like an open-minded man . . .'

Felix took Mr Banks' arm, leading him firmly into the back room and Lucy caught the soothing yet unstoppable murmur that she recognised as Felix in full sales mode. When the reporter emerged, bewildered, he was clutching a brown paper bag, while Felix put a few coins in the till.

'Thank you so much, Mr Banks,' he called after the reporter. 'I think you'll enjoy the novel. Sorry I couldn't tell you anything more about the note, but I hope this will be helpful for atmosphere. Do send your friends – discreetly, of course.' He shut the door.

'You don't miss a trick, Felix,' said Lucy.

'They're going to wheedle their way in somehow,' said Felix philosophically. 'They might as well buy something.'

'What if they go to the police about the book?'

'They won't risk their source,' Felix told her. 'They're all hoping we get another note and there's another death. Bloodthirsty lot.' The bell rang and he sprinted for the door.

It seemed that more reporters were keen to see the inside of Cecil Court Books, in the absence of Dakin's Rare Books being open to the public, and the little bell above the door rang all after-noon as various reporters tried their luck and left, most of them confusedly holding brown paper bags.

* * *

When the bell rang at four, Lucy barely looked up. 'Another customer for you, Felix,' she called.

'Actually,' a cheerful voice said, 'it was *you* I was hoping to speak to, Miss Darkwether. Although I do admire your entrepreneurship. Half my staff have come back with a novel that's banned in most of the continent. Goodness, what would the police think?'

Lucy looked up sharply to see a sturdy, genial man with greying hair at the temples. 'I hope they don't find out. Mr Bird, isn't it?'

Max Bird, the editor of the *Daily Mirror*. Lucy had seen him at various society parties and knew he had the country hanging off his every printed word.

'So, you're the one behind the stories. This so-called curse of the Egyptian tomb,' said Lucy. 'The man responsible for whipping the public into near-hysteria. I bet you're persona non grata with the police, not to mention Dr Lyle.'

Max Bird twinkled at her. 'Oh, Dr Lyle didn't mind. Whose idea do you think this curse business was?'

Lucy groaned. 'Of course,' she said. 'It was Dr Lyle's. The rumours started when Sir Archibald died, but someone on the inside had to have been feeding you the story.'

Max shrugged. 'Dr Lyle was kind enough to give us an interview.'

'Someone had to hammer home the Carnarvon link, tell every-one how fit and healthy Sir Archibald seemed before his unex-pected death,' Lucy went on. 'Practically spoon-fed you the story. He's sent the whole of London into a frenzy just for publicity for his exhibition. I didn't realise he was so cunning.'

'He has a knack for getting people talking, that one,' said Mr Bird. 'Of course, it's kicked off now that second poor gentlemen died. Maybe there was actually some truth in it,' he mused. Anyway, enough about Dr Lyle, Miss Darkwether. That's not why I came here today.'

'Why *did* you come here?' said Lucy suspiciously. 'I won't tell you anything about the note, you know.'

'Oh, I think you will,' said Max. 'You don't want me telling that Inspector Hayes about your backroom smut peddling do you?'

Lucy scowled. 'Fine, you can ask me one question. But let me ask you one first. Someone must have told you about the note I got. Who was it?'

There was the briefest glimmer of amusement on Max Bird's face and then it was gone. 'I can't give away my sources,' he said smoothly. 'Just like I won't give *you* away when you tell me – have you had another note?'

'No.'

'But you think you will?'

'I think it's likely.'

'And you'll call me up when you do?' Lucy opened her mouth to refuse when Max broke in. 'Those reprehensible books aren't all you don't want dug up I imagine. You wouldn't want reporters camped outside your shop for weeks, would you? Writing stories about you, the girl who got the note? We *could* mention your family's dwindling fortune – they wouldn't like that, would they, with your brother's big society wedding coming up?' He smiled a shark-like smile. 'I can be a good ally, Miss Darkwether, and a bad enemy. Just a tip off if another note comes, that's all I need.'

Lucy sighed. She knew when she was beaten and could see no

other option. 'All right. *If* another note arrives and *after* I call the police, I'll let you know. Now get out of here, will you?'

* * *

At last, at around five, the shop fell quiet, the fire crackling gently in the grate. No one was doing any work. Mr Tollesbury, who had spent the day in the bookbinding room, had retired behind his newspaper and Toby was reading a detective serial in the corner. Felix had gone out, armed with several brown paper parcels, off to deliver some merchandise to several ladies in Belgravia. All was peaceful, and yet Lucy felt uneasy. A dark shadow that had been cast by Dr Curry's murder – and, she felt, perhaps long before, in Egypt itself – seemed to hang over Cecil Court Books.

'What sort of person do you think the police will be looking for?' Lucy asked Susan as they sat with cups of tea and the end of a currant loaf. The ginger cat who frequented the shop in search of biscuits wound itself round Lucy's ankles.

'Hmm,' said Susan. Behind her glasses, in the pool of lamplight, her eyes gleamed. 'Let us assume that our killer and the note-writer are the same person. If so, our killer has a crusade. He believes that he is acting on behalf of a dead Egyptian king and must punish those who desecrated his tomb. And he likes codes and games – simple ones.'

'It was on nice paper too,' said Toby from the corner. 'Good stuff.'

'So, the police should be looking for a person with an interest in Egyptology and a passion for justice, fine stationery and childish games – and who carries a blade.' Lucy groaned. 'They could be anywhere. Where should they start?'

'I'd be looking at people who were tangentially connected to the expedition, to the Society or the British Museum – someone with enough knowledge to understand the implications of opening the tomb, but not important enough to participate in it. Someone who has perhaps felt sidelined and let down all their life, who now hopes to do something heroic and brave, by any means necessary. How's that for psychology?' Susan beamed and gave a bow.

Lucy began to clap. 'Impressive,' she said.

Behind his paper, Mr Tollesbury gave a small snort. 'You young people and your psychology,' he said indulgently.

'Oh, you can mock,' said Susan. 'But now Lucy, I think we're overlooking the *real* question here. Why send the note to *you*?'

'I don't know, and I don't like it.' Lucy took a fresh piece of paper and picked up her pen. 'Let's assume you're right – that our note-writer is also our killer. In which case, who is next on their hit list?' Lucy wrote her list of potential victims out and Susan leaned over her to take a look. 'Let's hope we don't have to start crossing them off, week by week, like crossword clues,' Lucy said as she did.

Sir Archibald Drake – funder, died 5 January 5, heart failure
Dr William Curry – researcher, died 22 March, stabbed
Dr Gordon Lyle – expedition leader
Mrs van Buren – funder
Sir Hector Derwent – head of the Society

The two of them stared at the list for a short while, but neither seemingly had any grand ideas of where to go next.

'Maybe we should go back to the beginning, with Sir Archibald Drake,' said Susan, eventually. 'The first victim of the curse, or so our killer tells us. Did they kill him too, somehow – all the way out there in Egypt?'

'We could interview the Society and Mr Ahmed about the circumstances of his death. Find out if there was anything unusual about it—'

'Lucy!' Mr Tollesbury set down his paper. His expression was uncharacteristically severe, and Lucy was reminded of his expression when she had missed a deadline. She hadn't even realised he was listening in. 'Lucy, I can accept a *degree* of meddling, but now I am drawing a line. This could be extremely dangerous.'

Lucy lifted her chin. 'The killer wrote the note to *me*. I'm involved, whether you like it or not.' *And I'm not your student now*, she added, in her mind.

She locked eyes with her old tutor and at last Mr Tollesbury looked away with a faint groan. 'I wish you wouldn't,' he said, less sternly. 'I should have known there would be no stopping you once you get an idea into your head. It's what made you such a good student.'

Toby tossed down his detective story and stood. 'Going to the pictures,' he muttered.

'Seeing anything good?' asked Lucy and was rewarded with a shrug. But at the door, Toby stopped.

'The professor's right – stay out of it, miss. There's a man out there with a blade and he's writing *you* notes. And it doesn't do anyone any good to get mixed up with the police.'

He left, shutting the door behind him.

'That,' said Felix, arriving in the doorway, 'is more words than Toby has said all at once in the last year. I'd listen to him if I were you, Lucy.'

'He's right,' agreed Susan. 'Besides, don't get delusions of grandeur, Lucy. Why would any of these potential victims speak to *you*?' She stretched out a hand for the ledger with the day's accounts and frowned. 'Blast, these figures can't be right – we're out again. Felix, have you miscounted?'

Felix shook his head. 'I wrote down every shilling and pence, honest.'

'Well, something is out.' Susan turned the pages, rubbing her forehead. 'Honestly, an MA in Mathematics but running this shop exhausts me.'

'You were late for work this morning, Felix,' Lucy said crossly. She knew she was taking out her worry on her bookseller, but she couldn't help herself.

'Have you *ever* been on time for work, Lucy?' he asked sweetly, sitting down and looking at her over his glasses.

'That's not the point . . .'

Susan finished her tea and glanced at her watch, interrupting Lucy as she did so. 'I'm off to a meeting – fancy coming along, Lucy? Nothing like discussing the Franchise Act to distract one from murder.'

'I can't,' Lucy said. 'I'm dining with Bryan Campbell tonight.'

Felix's hand slipped in the act of pouring a cup of tea and Lucy sighed. 'Felix! You've spilt tea all over my list of potential victims.'

'Sorry,' said Felix, grabbing a cloth and dabbing at the table. 'I – I forgot you were meeting Mr Campbell.'

Lucy shot him a searching look, remembering the white card disappearing into his sleeve the other day, but said nothing.

'Bryan Campbell, the roguishly handsome bookshop owner?' said Susan. 'Well, well. Can you be business rivals *and* lovers? Every romance novel would indicate a hearty *yes*.'

'It's not romance,' said Lucy. 'I'm hoping he's going to give me some business advice.'

'Observe the competition,' said Mr Tollesbury, removing his pipe. 'Very sensible, Lucy. We could learn a good deal from Campbells – an audacious business model. Noticed they've started selling stationery, too.'

She certainly did intend to observe the competition. But, Lucy thought to herself, she *would* wear her new dress.

Chapter 10

ryan Campbell had made a reservation at The Savoy which, with its glittering lights and merry chatter, offered a contrast from the oppression Lucy had felt since the night of Dr Curry's death. Bryan was smoking as Lucy approached the table, with its white linen cloth and chrysanthemums in a little vase, wearing a pale-green evening dress. His eyes widened admiringly.

'Sorry I'm late,' said Lucy, taking her seat opposite him, conscious of a glow of pleasure – both at the prospect of forgetting about murder and death for the night, and of being somewhere lovely with good food and a charming, entertaining dinner companion. Even if it *was* one whose motives she did not entirely trust.

Just observe the competition, she told herself.

'I'll have a martini,' Lucy said to the waiter at her elbow. 'Very dry, thank you.'

Within moments, the cocktails arrived along with a plate of oysters.

'I took the liberty of ordering food,' said Bryan Campbell. 'The waiter made some suggestions. Oysters followed by beef and champagne.'

Lucy took a sip of her drink. 'It sounds perfect,' she said, thinking that she would have rather had soup to start and then the sole.

'You're lovely,' Bryan Campbell said dreamily. 'Out of your shop-floor pinafore. The minute you walked in I thought you

109

looked like an elf, or do I mean a fairy? It's all that dark hair and your big eyes. Like ebony pools.'

Lucy laughed. 'They're plain brown. Please, Mr Campbell. I thought you were going to impress me with your business acumen.'

'Of course, the bookshop,' he said. 'I'll cut to the chase. There *is* something I should like you to consider,' he said. 'Chessie wanted me to talk to you about it. But I mean to ply you with champagne first.'

'Tell me now straight up, and I'll consider it,' said Lucy warily. 'I shan't relax with a proposal hanging over me. I've had dinners like this before and it's very off-putting.'

Bryan Campbell cleared his throat. His cheeks were flushed under his tan. 'My sister feels – and I do too of course – that we should like to . . . incorporate your shop under the Campbells umbrella.'

Lucy hid her surprise by eating an olive. 'Campbells would like to take over Cecil Court Books?'

'We would. Chessie doesn't mess about. We have made the owner a handsome offer for the lease. More than you can afford, I'm afraid. But we should like you to stay on and manage it.'

'How do you know what I pay for it?' Lucy asked, careful not to let her true feelings sneak into her voice. He smiled kindly and she groaned. 'Oh, you – or Chessie, I imagine – asked my landlord. Probably took *him* out for champagne. Is he delighted?'

'He is amenable to the offer,' Bryan said cautiously. 'Most amenable, in fact. But we don't just want the real estate. We should like to keep the name and – well – most things about it. With your permission of course.'

Lucy swallowed her ire and forced a smile. Dinner tonight had been a trap. 'This explains your appearance in the shop the other day. You can drop the bashful schoolboy act, Mr Campbell – you were casing the joint. Now why, I wonder, are the great and mighty Campbells so keen to take over insignificant little Cecil Court Books?'

'A few reasons,' he said, becoming businesslike. 'One, expansion. We had a good first year of trade, the market is booming, Chessie thinks we should strike while the iron is hot and expand. Cecil Court Books has a ready-made customer base. You've managed to grow it beyond whoever was buying those crumbly ancient texts and plenty of the society ladies have been going there. Location-wise it couldn't be better for us. And all that murder stuff only adds to the buzz. Two,' he pointed a finger at Lucy, 'character. You've made it a real sweet place haven't you, ginger cake and cups of tea – catering to the old guard.'

'Mr Tollesbury does all the baking,' said Lucy. 'He doesn't come with the shop.'

'We can outsource. Three, you've got quite a reputation, thanks to some smart book buying. Everywhere I go, people are talking about Cecil Court Books. It's got character.'

'So, you'd keep the, er, character?' Lucy asked sweetly. 'I'm so glad.'

'Well, we'd change things a bit,' conceded Bryan Campbell. 'Your stock has a few too many wild cards – all that modern stuff is a bit of an acquired taste, you need more safe bets. I like your bookseller though. Smart kid.'

The waiter took away the oyster plates and set down beef tournedos. Champagne was opened and poured. 'Why don't you poach Felix instead?' said Lucy. 'I know you've tried. He was late to work this morning and Felix is never late. I assume he was also being wined and dined by you, or perhaps breakfast rather than dinner.'

'Oh, that,' said Bryan Campbell. His teeth flashed in a grin. 'Yes, I met him for a coffee this morning and made him a handsome offer. Didn't think it could hurt. Turned me down, if it makes you feel better – for now, anyway. Consider it a compliment. But he'll come round eventually,' he went on complacently. 'They always do. You might as well join me, Miss Darkwether – or can I call you, Lucy? I could turn that little shop of yours into something really special.'

Lucy smiled back at him. Her friends would have recognised it as a dangerous smile. Two spots of colour had appeared on her cheeks. 'You're too kind – about my little shop. But I think we manage nicely on our own. We expect to turn a tidy profit at the end of year accounts.'

Bryan Campbell laughed and poured some more champagne. 'A *small* profit, perhaps.'

'Would you like to bet on it?' said Lucy, setting down her empty martini glass and taking a long drink of champagne.

'I should not like to take your money, Miss Darkwether,' Bryan said.

'I will bet you,' said Lucy recklessly, 'that not only will Cecil Court Books turn a profit by the time we close up for Christmas, but – but that, in the fiction section, our sales will surpass yours at Campbell's!'

Bryan Campbell stared at her, then began to laugh again. 'But you're joking. Why, our shop is three times the size of yours!'

'That's true,' said Lucy.

'Our stock must be at least double.'

'Indeed.'

He eyed her curiously. 'And you still want to place a bet?'

By now, Lucy was regretting her hasty words and would have given a lot to be able to take them back. But if she did, then Bryan would know she was weak. Her indecision must have shown on her face, because he patted her hand. 'Don't worry, Miss Darkwether,' he said kindly. 'I understand this was all just a little—'

'I still want to make the bet,' she broke in. 'You win, I concede. You and Chessie take Cecil Court Books and I won't stand in the way. And if *I* win, you tell my landlord the deal's off, apologise for doubting my business acumen and – and – and you stop trying to poach my staff.'

Bryan Campbell raised his eyebrows. 'You have a deal, Miss Darkwether. Now, shall we order another bottle of champagne?'

Chapter 11

L ucy slept poorly and awoke irritable, with a niggling headache. She was regretting both the champagne and her rash wager last night and wanted nothing more than to retire to the cosy warmth of the shop and enthuse with her customers about Virginia Woolf's new novel.

But she had something more important to do. She was going to stop another murder. The members of the Society were either each a potential murderer – or in danger of being killed themselves. Either way, Lucy was determined to meet with and warn each of them. In some way, this felt like her mess to solve. If she had opened that note sooner, then Dr Curry might still be alive. The killer was communicating through her – why, she wasn't sure – and as much as she disliked the fact, she had a responsibility to stop any more killings.

I'll begin with Gordon Lyle, she thought.

'Mrs Thorpe,' she called, pulling back the covers and standing, 'would you call Dr Lyle up for me and say I shall be with him at the British Museum in an hour?'

Her housekeeper stuck her head round the door. 'Expecting you, is he?'

Lucy paused with a stocking in her hand. 'Not exactly. I'm sure he'll agree to see me though – he'll be curious if nothing else. Call him up, will you?'

Mrs Thorpe didn't move from the doorway. 'Talking of curious, your friends have been calling. I've a lot of messages for you.'

Lucy began to brush her hair. 'I thought they might start sniffing around now I'm all over the papers. Read them out, please?'

'Your mother has rung twice,' Mrs Thorpe said, reading down her list. 'She says, *Darling I always knew the bookshop was dangerous. Don't forget tea on Sunday.* Then Freddie Carlton says, *I haven't been reading that rag of a* Mirror *of course but is it true you're being stalked by this killer? Come and stay this weekend darling you can tell us all about it.* And then someone called . . . Jonesy? Wants to tell you that she hasn't been reading the *Mirror* either but, *Is it true the shop was targeted by a cloud of scarab beetles.* And Mr Edward has rung three times trying to arrange dinner.'

Lucy grinned. 'Odd how none of them will admit to reading the *Mirror* and yet all of them are frightfully well informed. Although I don't think even Max Bird mentioned scarab beetles.'

'*I* would tell you to be careful too,' said Mrs Thorpe. 'If I thought there was any point.' She sighed. 'I'll ring up Dr Lyle.' She left and by the time she returned, Lucy was fully dressed and applying lipstick.

'Dr Lyle would be delighted for you to join him,' Mrs Thorpe said. 'And Mr Edward rang you up again.'

'I'll speak to him later,' said Lucy, shrugging on her coat. 'Just tell everyone "I can neither confirm nor deny", like they're the press.'

* * *

Lucy had visited the British Museum a great deal as a child, and to this day enjoyed walking up the enormous steps and into the grand, imposing building. It was like stepping into a Greek temple, with its elegant columns and pediment, dedicated to the pursuit of knowledge. It housed many treasures from all over the world, including some considered to be controversial items, such as the Elgin Marbles which had been removed from Greece by Thomas

Bruce. Many were full of admiration for this act; others had been critical and there had been requests for their return. Lucy had always turned a blind eye to where these objects had come from – now, she could feel the weight of all that history, a history that was not hers, pressing down on her. As though much here was far from its rightful home.

Or, she thought, this talk of a curse was getting to her.

A lady at the front desk pointed in the direction of the staff offices and told Lucy that Dr Lyle was expecting her.

The door to Dr Lyle's office was ajar and there was a voice coming from within. Lucy, pausing in the doorway, had the chance to listen.

'I told you,' Dr Lyle's voice hissed, 'enough of this now. It's causing too much damage.'

A pause, and then he broke out angrily. 'Well, then you must make it stop! Or else you won't get another thing out of me, do you understand! Or any of us!' He banged the receiver down and Lucy could hear him breathing heavily.

So, the poised Dr Lyle *could* lose control. Lucy wondered who he had been talking to as she studied him in the muted light. She still thought that Gordon Lyle was a handsome man – yet still, too, felt that instinctive dislike. With his curling blond hair, piercing blue eyes in a tanned face and his shirtsleeves rolled up, he looked every inch the intrepid explorer. It was a shallow sort of hand-someness, though, Lucy thought, like a mask. She cleared her throat and knocked gently on the door.

'Ah! Come in, Miss Darkwether,' Dr Lyle said expansively, his expression as jovial as ever. He rose to shake her hand, then sat again behind a large desk with a dim reading lamp, littered with papers. A delicate jewelled, carved dagger sat at his elbow which he had clearly been using to open letters and there was an ornate Chinese screen dividing the room.

'What a lot of interesting finds,' Lucy said, looking around with genuine admiration. 'From all your travels, I assume?'

He beamed at her. 'Indeed – a few spoils that I couldn't resist keeping. Most belong to the museum, of course. My work is dedicated to public knowledge.'

'I understand the mummy has been moved here,' said Lucy, taking a seat. 'A safer place for a king, perhaps – although some would say he should always have remained in Egypt.'

'But think of the cost to our field,' sighed Dr Lyle. He gestured to the corner, where an elegant blue and gold death mask rested, and Lucy's heart fluttered suddenly. 'A facsimile of the death mask has been made up for the public – we will install it this week. We met the other night, didn't we, at the lecture? You're Dakin's neighbour. What a shame that we are meeting again under such tragic circumstances.'

Lucy drew off her gloves. 'What I remember is Dr Curry interrupting your very interesting lecture that night.'

Dr Lyle nodded slowly. 'Ah yes. Most distressing,' he said, leaning back and regarding her over steepled fingers. 'I hope it didn't ruin the night for you. It was good of you to attend.'

'I wouldn't have missed it for the world, Dr Lyle,' said Lucy fervently. 'Your findings have changed the field of Egyptology for ever.' Even though she didn't trust the man, Lucy couldn't help but feel excited about his work.

'I try my poor best,' Dr Lyle said with a modest smile, although Lucy was sure even that was fake. His eyes raked over her form in a practised manner. 'And please, do call me Gordon. Unusual to find a young lady with such a keen interest in Egyptology – particularly, if you'll excuse me saying so, one as lovely as yourself.'

'Not merely a keen interest but a degree in Ancient History, Dr Lyle,' said Lucy. She pressed on. 'It was remarkable how you managed to so accurately pinpoint the location of the tomb so quickly. Many had tried and failed.'

'A flash of inspiration,' he told her. 'Sometimes research will only get you so far, my dear lady. Instinct, that's what matters.'

'And this flash of inspiration came to you out of the blue?' she inquired. 'Because Dr Curry seemed adamant that it was *his* research and – ah – flash of inspiration that led you all to the tomb.'

She thought she caught the flash of surprise in Dr Lyle's eyes, before the benign mask descended once more. He chuckled sadly. 'Poor man. Considered himself a scholar when his knowledge was superficial at best.'

'So, there is no truth to the accusations that you stole his research and had him fired from the expedition?' she asked, hoping to startle him into an honest response.

'Miss Darkwether!' Dr Lyle looked genuinely wounded. 'You cannot think I would do such a thing?'

'You *didn't* then?' she said, determined to get a straight answer.

His mouth tightened momentarily. 'Those are serious accusations, Miss Darkwether, which I absolutely refute. And I should be careful, if I were you. The Society will not take kindly to rumours like these. We have our reputation to protect, after all.'

'If they're only rumours,' Lucy said carefully, 'then you needn't worry. But I appreciate the warning. You had worked with Dr Curry for a while, then?'

'Yes – he joined the Egyptology research department a year ago. His theories were rather raw and undeveloped, but I took a chance on him – thought I might be able to cultivate his ideas. We agreed that he should travel out to Egypt with us. In the event, he did not take well to it. People have all sorts of romantic ideas of what an archaeological dig is like, and the reality is, it's hard work.' His blue eyes looked past Lucy, as though seeing tombs and rubble under a hot sun, squaring his jaw manfully. 'It's not for everyone. In the end the Society decided he had better return to London. I wanted to let him down gently.' He sighed. 'To be frank, Miss Darkwether, I was not in need of intellectual assistance from Dr Curry. And I was not the first public figure he had accused of some sort of intellectual theft.'

Lucy remembered what Mrs Curry had said about her husband writing angry notes to other academics who he believed had stolen his work. But had he been justified in this case?

'Can you think of anyone who would want to hurt Dr Curry?'

Dr Lyle shook his head. 'Between us, Miss Darkwether, I had wondered whether his injury might have been self-inflicted.'

'I think that would have been quite impossible,' said Lucy, shuddering at the memory of the bloody throat. 'What did you think when you first saw the body?'

Dr Lyle considered. 'When the door first opened, I initially assumed that Mr Dakin had . . . overegged the pudding, so to speak. He gets rather carried away.' He gave an embarrassed laugh. 'Making a theatre out of it and hiring an actor to – ah – play dead, as it were. Ridiculous, I know, but that's what I thought at first. Then I saw the blood and I realised the body was real.'

'Yes,' said Lucy quietly, recalling that pale figure, the bandages stiff with blood. 'It was real.'

'It was the most frightful shock,' said Dr Lyle earnestly. Shock and distaste played convincingly across his handsome features. 'I was horrified. I didn't know it was Dr Curry until the inspector told me afterwards.'

'Some believe he was the second victim of a curse.'

'Of course, the curse. The press do love that story,' Dr Lyle said, with an indulgent smile. 'The public lap it up. A tomb can never simply be a burial site – it has to also be the seat of a terrible curse! You and I know better, Miss Darkwether.'

'I thought so myself – but then I got this note.' She drew out Toby's copy of the anonymous note and handed it to Dr Lyle.

Mr Lyle scanned the paper, let out a bark of laughter and tossed it carelessly back to Lucy. 'The police showed me this. I've lost track of the number of warnings and ominous curses I've received in my time, some from Tutankhamun himself! Ignore it, Miss Darkwether.'

'It's interesting though, isn't it? It arrived the day of the murder – *before* the murder in fact – and seems to predict it. Describes Dr Curry's death as the *second*.'

'The second? Oh. You mean poor Sir Archibald. I can assure you that there was nothing supernatural about *that* death – I was there. The doctor in attendance, Mr Ahmed, recorded the death and diagnosed heart failure, exacerbated by the heat and strain of the expedition. Sir Archibald should never have attempted it, but he only agreed to fund the expedition on the condition that he attend.' Dr Lyle shrugged. 'We could not prevent him. It was his funeral, so to speak.'

'You were there, then, when he died?'

'It was the day we finally opened the tomb, a moment of great excitement. Suddenly Sir Archibald looked pale – the heat is no joke in the middle of the day, even at that time of year. He sat in the shade, in good spirits – chatting and calling out to us. Within minutes he was dead.'

'An entirely explicable death,' said Lucy thoughtfully. 'Were it not for Dr Curry dying a few weeks later.' She lifted the note and read aloud. '*All who desecrated the tomb will soon be punished by my hand.*'

'The ghost of a king guiding a killer's hand – you can't believe such nonsense.' She thought that Dr Lyle glanced rather nervously at the death mask in the corner.

Lucy left a pause, then tucked the note back into her handbag. 'I'm not saying I do believe that a ghost is doing this,' she said, considering him. He looked a little pale, she thought; it felt satisfying to at least slightly rattle the complacent Dr Lyle. 'But I *might* believe that a person *is* killing to avenge the desecration of the king's resting place.'

The man passed a tongue over his dry lips. 'Nonsense. As I said, my dear girl – this is someone trying to frighten and disturb you. Do not pay it a second's thought.'

But it was Gordon Lyle who looked disturbed, Lucy thought. There was a faint sheen of perspiration on his brow. This tale of the curse – and its attendant tragedies – had made an impression on at least one of the expedition party.

She drew on her gloves. 'I won't keep you Dr Lyle – I appreciate how busy you are. But do take care. Just in case there is something to this curse nonsense, after all.'

She left Dr Lyle sitting in his chair, looking rather more worried than when she had come in. The sightless eyes of the golden mask, a facsimile of the gilded original, followed her out of the room.

It seemed that Dr Lyle had a motive for murder. Reputation and glory; both would have been in tatters had Dr Curry lived to present his evidence. Lucy was sure that people had killed for far less.

And yet she could have sworn Dr Lyle's shock on discovering the body had been genuine. Was he simply a good actor? Or was the real killer someone else entirely?

* * *

Lucy passed a busy day in the shop. To her relief, given her foolish bet with Bryan Campbell, the customers were flooding in, whether to examine her stock or see the place the ominous note had been sent, she wasn't sure, and so it wasn't until the next morning that she embarked on a visit to the next potential victim on the list.

Ashbourne Square was the home of the wealthy widow and amateur Egyptologist, Mrs Moira van Buren. Her collection of antiquities was famous throughout the world, as was her generous patronage of the British Museum. Lucy had written to her the day before requesting an interview and she had replied with a brief note including only a time and the address. It was a large house near Russell Square, which had been divided into two flats, beautifully proportioned, with a vast entrance hall and a sweeping staircase leading to the upper apartment. The late Mr van Buren might have been a criminal, but he had excellent taste in houses.

'Will you come this way, miss?'

A butler led her to an elegant sitting room, where spring sunshine streamed in through huge windows. It was an stylish room full of the evidence of restrained wealth – elegant brocades, modern paintings, bowls of fresh flowers, a grand piano and some clay shabti in a case.

'Miss Darkwether?' A woman came forward.

'Mrs van Buren,' said Lucy, holding out a hand. 'Thank you for seeing me. Your house is lovely.'

'It's divided into flats now,' said Mrs van Buren. She looked tired, Lucy thought. 'I remodelled it after my husband died, so that my sister could have the downstairs one. Amelia insisted on moving in with me to support me in my grief – and I haven't been able to get rid of her since,' she paused looking around the room, before seemingly remembering that can't have been what Lucy came here for. 'What can I do for you, Miss Darkwether?'

'It's a pleasure to see you again, although I wish the circumstances were better,' began Lucy hesitantly.

The woman considered her with sharp eyes. 'You'll have to refresh my memory, I'm afraid. When did we meet?'

'It was only briefly,' lied Lucy. 'At Dr Lyle's lecture. And again, at Mr Dakin's exhibition, where . . .' She let her voice trail off.

'Oh yes,' said Mrs van Buren, her gaze drifting over Lucy's shoulder to the window, as though recalling. 'Lucy Darkwether – the girl with the bookshop. Mr Dakin pointed you out to me, said you were something of a bluestocking. Jealous of him for snaring the mummy, he said.'

Lucy chose to ignore the slight. 'I was terribly excited to see it for myself in Mr Dakin's bookshop. He kindly gave me a ticket.'

Mrs van Buren nodded. 'A moment of triumph for Dr Lyle. For all of us who were on the expedition. It should have been a wonderful night, a celebration of scholarship and progress . . .'

'And it ended in murder,' said Lucy. 'The second in the chain of tragic events.'

Mrs van Buren frowned. 'The second?'

Lucy perched on a pale-yellow silk sofa. 'The police may have mentioned a note I received on the eve of Dr Curry's death.' She handed her copy over to Mrs van Buren, who read it with raised eyebrows, but said nothing.

'It implies that Dr Curry was the second victim of the curse, the first being Sir Archibald. *The first, a fool, died under the Egyptian sun.* You were there when Sir Archibald died, weren't you?'

Mrs van Buren gave a wry smile. 'I was – and if you, along with the gutter press, think he died by supernatural influence, you're wrong. He was a weak old man who had no business being out in the midday sun in such a climate. The doctor who attended said as much.'

'Do you really believe that, Mrs van Buren?' Lucy pressed. The widow hesitated. 'Can you explain Dr Curry's death so easily?'

Mrs van Buren shook her head. 'It seems utterly fantastic,' she said.

'*Did* Dr Lyle steal Dr Curry's research, as he claimed?' Lucy asked boldly. 'And did the Society cover it up?'

Mrs van Buren went very still, then smiled easily. 'Of course not, Miss Darkwether. The man was quite paranoid.'

'I shall tell you what *I* think is a possibility,' said Lucy, making a decision as she spoke to reveal her theories to Mrs van Buren, in case it garnered a response. She watched her closely as she spoke. 'What if Gordon Lyle was something of a charlatan? What if he lacked the knowledge, brains and persistence for such painstaking work? What if someone else was behind it entirely? Let's say it was Dr Curry's research, conducted over many years, which led you to the location of the tomb. Dr Curry was thrilled when he was asked to join the expedition, but you used him to discover the location and then orchestrated his dismissal. The entire board closed ranks against him and let Dr Lyle take the glory for Dr Curry's life's work.'

There was a long silence in which Lucy waited nervously, half expecting Mrs van Buren to insist she leave. At last, Mrs van Buren shrugged an elegant shoulder. 'All right, let's say for a second you are right. I shan't admit it outside this room, mind. But who is Dr Curry, when it comes to it? Dr Lyle . . . *he* is the face of the expedition. He gets funding both from his wife and private investors . . . or he *did* anyway, because his wife cut him off. The papers love him, so do the public. No one was going to take Dr Curry's side over his, least of all the Society. A hot-tempered and troublesome man, with a history of writing angry letters to academics who he felt had wronged him, while Dr Lyle was a hero.'

'Well,' breathed Lucy. 'I had no idea archaeology was such a cut-throat business – if you'll pardon the phrase.'

Mrs van Buren lifted delicate silver tongs and dropped a slice of lemon into her tea. An amused smile played about her lips, but Lucy was sure that her hand trembled slightly. 'I hope you aren't serious about a mummy's curse, killing all those who disturbed it.' She shook her head. 'There aren't many women in our field, Miss Darkwether – it would be a shame for someone with your privilege to also be silly.'

'I do not consider myself silly,' said Lucy, matching her tone. 'I discount a supernatural influence. But this note implies that someone wants you all dead – one by one. And I have another theory, an altogether less spiritual one – that Dr Curry was silenced to stop him revealing the scandal. If that's the case, the Society are all prime suspects. But you all seem to have convenient alibis.'

'We were at a lecture, then having lunch together when the so-called murder took place,' Mrs van Buren agreed. 'I joined a little late – a headache – but I wasn't busy killing anyone, I can assure you.'

It was certainly hard to imagine the elegant woman cutting anyone's throat, Lucy thought: but you never knew.

'Dr Curry said something the night before he died,' she said slowly. 'When he disturbed the lecture. He said that Dr Lyle *wasn't the only one with secrets*, that he knew what you had done and he would have no reservations about telling the world.'

'Did he?' said Mrs van Buren without interest. 'I don't recall.'

'He said that each and every one of you had a secret he could reveal,' Lucy said firmly. 'Do you have any idea what he meant?'

'None whatsoever,' Mrs van Buren said. 'He was trying to draw attention, that's all.'

Lucy said, 'I have heard rumours that – that you and Dr Lyle may have been closer than was professional.'

Mrs van Buren flushed tellingly. 'If you'll believe that, no wonder you believe in a curse, Miss Darkwether. Dr Lyle is a happily married man. Half of London academia has been gossiping about *that*. If you think I committed a murder to keep such a ridiculous story quiet, you are wrong. And I am not someone who is easily blackmailed.'

'Silly gossip I'm sure,' said Lucy lightly. 'Thank you for your time and for humouring me. And – I know you think me silly, but I really *would* be careful, you know. Curse or no curse, two people associated with the expedition have died.'

Mrs van Buren inclined her head, the picture of elegant grace once more. Nevertheless, Lucy was sure that she had rattled the widow.

The two women shook hands and Lucy went out of the room and down the stairs, into the street. The branches of the trees, still without leaves, stretched bare and skeletal into the pale sky. She shivered.

As she walked away, she glanced back over her shoulder, up at Ashbourne Square. Mrs van Buren was looking down at her from one of the tall windows. Her expression was no longer amused and ironic. Instead, she looked almost haunted.

Had Dr Curry discovered a secret about Mrs van Buren? And was it one she would have died to protect?

Chapter 12

Lucy's next meeting took place the next day in a bustling greasy spoon near Imperial Hospital in West London. It was busy and Lucy sat inconspicuously at a Formica table, while an espresso machine belched steam, white tiles damp with condensation. When a tall man in his mid-forties entered and looked curiously about, she stood.

'Mr Ahmed,' she said, holding out a hand. 'Thank you for meeting with me.'

She had failed to impress Dr Lyle and Mrs van Buren of the danger she believed they were in. Or, to scare them into a murder confession. She hoped to have better luck with the fifth member of the expedition and discover the circumstances of Sir Archibald's death at the same time. Her father's old schoolfriend, Sir Clyde, head of surgery at Imperial, had requested the meeting on her behalf, as she knew she'd never be able to reach Mr Ahmed herself.

The man shook her hand. Lucy had always heard that surgeons had delicate hands – Mr Ahmed's was fine boned and light in hers.

'Any friend of Sir Clyde's is a friend of mine – technically,' he told her. 'But I've only got ten minutes between surgeries. And I'll have to eat something. You can ask me questions while I do.'

He ordered eggs and a pot of coffee. The coffee arrived with a plate of buttered toast, which he began to eat rapidly. 'Go on then,' he said. 'Ask away. Questions about the expedition to the tomb, isn't it? You and half of London seem curious about it. That Max

Bird in the *Mirror* seems to enjoy stirring up trouble. What's your connection to it? Are you a journalist too?'

'Not a journalist, but I do have questions,' said Lucy. His brisk air was catching. 'First of all, I understand you attended the expedition in the capacity of a medical professional.'

'That's right,' the doctor said, around a mouthful of toast. 'Every expedition will have a doctor on board, you know. Helps if they have one who can speak the language, which I can.'

'You're a successful surgeon. You pioneered ground-breaking surgery in this country after the war. What made you take a job as expedition doctor?'

He gave her an amused smile. 'You've researched me, Miss Darkwether – I'm flattered. My motive is less interesting than it sounds, I'm afraid: I simply decided I should like a holiday in Egypt.'

'Then why not take one?' asked Lucy. 'You could have visited Egypt by cruise, attended digs with a guide. Why make it a busman's holiday?'

The surgeon took a large swallow of coffee and wiped his mouth. 'To be frank, it was curiosity, Miss Darkwether. British archaeologists have been raiding the country's religious artefacts for years in the name of research – I wanted to see exactly what they were digging up. I wanted to see what the Society were really like.'

'And what did you find out?' said Miss Darkwether curiously.

'The expedition only cemented what I have thought for a long time – that the Society are jackals fighting for scraps and the dead should remain buried and left in peace in their own country.' He gestured to the waitress for more coffee. 'I don't disapprove enough to kill, of course, if that's what you're thinking. I've heard about this anonymous letter nonsense.'

Lucy filed that away for later. The surgeon had evidently felt strongly enough to inveigle his way into the expedition. He had been on the site. Had he murdered Sir Archibald in an opportunistic fit of revenge, a killing which had only spurred him on to more? To frighten people away from future expeditions? But it was hard to imagine the business-like Mr Ahmed sitting down to write her a taunting note, or staging a theatrical murder scene.

'I was wondering about the circumstances of Sir Archibald's death actually,' Lucy said then. 'I understand it was recorded as a heart attack.'

'Because it was,' the surgeon said, receiving his plate of food from the waitress. 'He was just shy of eighty-one, you know, and in delicate health. It wasn't his first attack – he'd had another some eighteen months before. Not as exciting as a mummy's curse, I know, but the truth.'

Lucy grinned. 'I don't say I suspect a mummy's curse. But it would seem remiss not to look at Sir Archibald's death in a new light following the death of Dr Curry last week. One theory is that someone intends to pick off all the members of the exhibition.'

'I see. And yet I would stake my career on it being heart failure, not murder. Can I see this famous note?'

Lucy took out the slip of paper and slid it across the table to him.

'This is a copy. I received it the day Dr Curry was murdered, at Cecil Court. It names the architect as the second victim. Was that your impression of Dr Curry – that it was his brains that had led the Society to the tomb?'

'I was only tangentially involved in the conversations around the dig. They didn't bother to keep someone like *me* informed.' Lucy caught a faint eye roll. 'But I got the impression that Dr Curry knew his stuff all right. Dr Lyle may have taken the glory, but it wouldn't surprise me if Dr Curry was the true brains behind it all. Don't quote me on that, obviously.' The surgeon sat back and wiped his hands on a paper napkin. 'If someone is so considerately warning you by post before he kills, where was Sir Archibald's letter?'

Lucy sighed. 'Good point. I don't know. I certainly didn't receive one. Did *you* see such a note, in Egypt? Did Sir Archibald seem worried, shaken, on the day of his death, as though he might have had a warning?'

Mr Ahmed burst out laughing. 'The old goat, worried? No, he hadn't a care in the world.' He lit a cigarette. 'Two deaths then, within three weeks of opening the tomb. And you think there will be more. Well, the world won't be worse off without them. Dr Lyle – corrupt as they come. Mrs van Buren – rich as Croesus and fanatical about the expedition. Both of them having an affair, to add to the mix.' Lucy nearly gasped at this confirmation but managed to restrain herself. 'And as for Sir Hector, he's a thug in aristocratic clothing.' He drank the rest of his coffee rapidly. 'I have to go – I'm due back in surgery.'

'So, you discount the threat, then?' said Lucy glumly. 'Just like Dr Lyle and Mrs van Buren and the inspector. I can't get anyone to take it seriously.'

Mr Ahmed wrapped his scarf around his neck. 'This notion of vengeance beyond the grave is a Western construct. Popular in the imagination of the British public, but antithetical to most Ancient Egyptian beliefs.' He stood, looking down at Lucy. 'No,' he said slowly, 'No, I should say whoever is doing this has a very human face – and a very human motive.'

Chapter 13

ucy was growing weary and footsore. She was determined to speak with the fifth and final member of the expedition, Sir Hector Derwent, but she was nevertheless reluctant to go alone. Mr Ahmed had called Sir Hector a thug; she might need reinforcements. And, besides, she was getting hungry. She called up the shop from a payphone and met Susan at Wilton's, where they had omelettes, then the two women continued on together, Susan having been relatively easy to convince to join her on her expedition.

Sir Hector lived alone in a handsome house in Islington, although Lucy knew he had an estate outside of London near Oxford as well. As Lucy and Susan walked along the tree-lined street, Lucy noticed a familiar figure, sitting on the bench opposite the house, writing busily in a notebook.

'Down here,' she hissed. 'It's Inspector Hayes. He doesn't want me meddling. Let's go round the back and get the servants to let us in.'

The pair knocked meekly on the servants' entrance, and they were shown into a rather oppressive sitting room, filled with dark furniture. Crimson drapes shut out the weak winter light. It was all expensive, and very ugly, Lucy thought, as they peered up at an oil painting of a man in satin, holding a greyhound's leash.

'That's Sir Reginald Derwent – notoriously mean, hoarded a fortune but gave it all to the oldest brother,' she told Susan. 'Sir

Hector's a well-known patron of the arts and an esteemed member of the House of Lords. His brother, Sir Marcus, is the chief of police – he's an old friend of my father's, which I shall mention of course.'

'Miss Darkwether, Miss Barrow?' Sir Hector Derwent was a large, imposing man, with ruddy cheeks and a lot of dark hair. Hawkish eyes peered at Lucy under heavy brows. Like an aristocratic villain straight out of a melodrama, she thought.

'Thank you for seeing us,' Lucy said, holding out her hand. 'I know how busy you are.'

She gave the girlish smile she reserved for elderly members of the aristocracy, but Sir Hector remained unmoved. 'I *am* busy,' he said stiffly. 'Fending off the press, trying to keep the Society on track, trying to reassure our funders. And I've had that damn inspector pestering me all morning. His men rummaging through my things, looking for what, I don't know. Daring to ask *me* about my whereabouts on the morning that chap got killed. What can I do for you both?' He did not precisely add, 'you two silly girls, disturbing my peace,' but the sentiment hung in the air.

Susan folded her hands in her lap, assuming the expression of owlish detachment she bore around loud, angry men, while Lucy explained her errand and held out the note. Sir Hector's face grew ruddier by the second, and by the time she had finished he was an alarming shade of purple.

'This bloody note! I told that idiot of an inspector just now that it must be easy enough to trace it back – the fool has done nothing to apprehend this lunatic. I'll have words with my brother about it. Some crackpot decides to polish people off – in England for God's sake! – and the police do nothing!'

'The killer might not look like a lunatic,' Lucy said. 'He might look like – well, like you or me.'

But Sir Hector had moved on. 'This entire exhibition has been nothing but trouble,' he muttered, his dark brows lowering further.

'Wish I'd never agreed to the damn escapade. The expedition was the thing – no need to tout the mummy about London. First, Sir Archibald dies, then this idiot Curry. From now on, the mummy can stay in the museum where it belongs.'

'Some would argue it *belongs* back in Egypt,' said Lucy, unable to resist. 'And I heard the expedition was nearly called off – that Mrs Lyle withdrew funding.'

'Damn fool of a woman,' muttered Sir Hector. 'She'd got wind of some rumour about her husband and – well, it was ridiculous. Said she'd had enough. Years worth of work would have been for nothing.' He puffed out his chest. 'It would have been an embarrassment to the Society. Luckily, we found more funding.'

'Mrs van Buren,' Lucy said. 'She's very wealthy, isn't she?'

Sir Hector eyed her with dislike. 'She is,' he said shortly. 'Not precisely top drawer, you know. Her husband had some dirty dealings in the war.'

'All the same, you were happy to take her money,' Lucy mused. 'And then the expedition could go ahead. It must have been a tremendously exciting moment, when the tomb was finally located. Tell me, did you know at the time that Dr Lyle had pinched Dr Curry's research?' Lucy had decided to be more cut-throat this time and simply lead with the accusation. 'Or was it only afterwards that you realised?'

Sir Hector started. 'I – I know nothing of the sort! Lyle is – is—'

'The face of the Society, I know,' Lucy said. She heard Susan stifle a small chuckle beside her. 'But I'm starting to wonder if he wasn't also a thief. You know, Sir Hector, I have another theory about the murder.' She paused for dramatic effect, enjoying the role she was playing. 'That the motive was to silence Dr Curry.'

'Silence Dr Curry?' cried Sir Hector in apparent disbelief.

'Dr Lyle stole his research that guided him to the tomb and brought you all glory. Were you a part of that?'

Sir Hector stared at her. 'This is outrageous,' he said weakly. 'Slander. Lies. I – I barely had any idea who this Dr Curry was. I believed Lyle *implicitly*.'

'I wonder where that evidence is,' said Lucy thoughtfully, as though musing aloud to herself. 'The evidence that Dr Curry said he had, to prove that he was the brains behind the whole thing. Maybe the killer got hold of it. Or maybe it's out there, some-where. It wouldn't look good for the Society though, if Dr Curry was proved right.'

'I don't suppose you hold much with this curse nonsense,' said Susan suddenly. 'A man of science and all that.'

Sir Hector shook his head vehemently. A clock chimed some-where in the house, deep and solemn. 'Of course not. Utter rot, dreamed up by the papers. Only the gullible would believe such a thing.'

Lucy considered him and nodded. Sir Hector was not one to fear a conscience, or the shadows of his own mind. What he did fear, she thought, was likely to be far more prosaic. Blackmail, disgrace, loss of his precious Society – those were the things that troubled him. Did they preoccupy him enough to kill?

'The press do seem remarkably well informed,' Susan said. 'They knew everything about the expedition and when Sir Archibald died. Especially the *Mirror*.'

'Someone's been talking, obviously,' Sir Hector snapped. His eyes narrowed. 'And I mean to find out who. Now, if there's noth-ing else . . .'

Lucy stood. 'Nothing – thank you for your time. Good after-noon, Sir Hector. Come on, Susan.'

They left Sir Hector glaring after them, alone in his dark room.

* * *

Lucy and Susan snuck out the back door, past the bins and down the alley, emerging two doors down to find Inspector Hayes still sitting on a bench opposite the house. He had put away his note-book and was finishing a sandwich.

'I wondered when you two would emerge,' he said. 'You were trying so hard to be subtle.'

'You waited for us,' said Lucy. 'How nice of you. We wanted to warn Sir Derwent about the threat to his life, since the police aren't going to. If you saw us go in and didn't stop us, then I think you wanted us to do exactly that.'

The inspector nodded slowly. 'I did think it might be helpful for Sir Hector Derwent to be . . . made aware of the threat. He seems to believe himself out of danger. But suicide has now been thoroughly ruled out. We are looking for a killer.'

'What was your impression of Sir Hector?' asked Lucy curiously.

He gave her a quick smile. 'It wouldn't be professional of me to say.'

'Well, *I* was struck by how stupid he seemed,' said Lucy. 'One of those types who is so sure he knows best that he won't listen to reason. I'm delighted you're no longer working under the incorrect assumption that Dr Curry's wounds were self-inflicted, but, if the note-writer means to follow through, they will strike again. That's what the papers think, at any rate.'

'I'd give good money to find out who is tipping the papers off,' said the inspector. 'Could it be someone in your shop? Fletcher seems the sort who wouldn't be above taking a fiver to let slip some information.'

'I disagree,' said Lucy hotly. 'Felix is the soul of discretion.' Mentally, she glossed over the many times that Felix had been horribly indiscreet.

A car pulled up, with the sergeant at the wheel. The inspector stood. 'All very dramatic, isn't it? A curse and a long-dead King. Most crimes are committed for far simpler reasons. Money. Lust. Revenge. I wouldn't be surprised if that was the case here. All of our Society had pretty mundane reasons to kill, when you think about it. Good afternoon, both of you.'

'I'll see you at the inquest, Inspector,' Lucy called, as he walked to the car. 'I wish we could find this evidence that Dr Curry talked about, don't you? The research that he died for.'

'It's not in his house,' he called back over his shoulder. 'And it's not in Sir Hector's either. We searched it top to bottom. Goodbye, Miss Darkwether.'

Chapter 14

A s they drove away, the inspector looked over his shoulder at the two women.

'I should like her to leave this investigation alone,' he said. 'If it's the killer behind this note, then he has her name, her address. He has clearly been observing her closely.'

'Not sure she's one you can bully into giving anything up,' said the sergeant. 'She's stubborn, I can tell.'

The inspector's eyes followed Lucy's upright figure as she disappeared from view. 'I was afraid of that,' he said. 'Well, go on. What have you got for me?'

'Everyone's alibi checks out – except one. Mrs van Buren's maid let slip her mistress got a cab on the morning of the murder. Struck her as odd as she normally would walk to the museum, where she was heading for the lecture that morning – it's only a short distance. We got a hold of the cabbie and guess where he dropped her?'

'Cecil Court,' said the inspector. 'What time was this?'

'Around twenty past eleven, which puts it just in the window for the killing. That's where the trail goes dead, sir – no one at Cecil Court Books saw anything. Mr Calvert and Mr Tollesbury were in the back room, they can vouch for each other, and Fletcher was busy with customers. And Dakin had already left for the museum. But there's another thing about Mrs van Buren.'

'Go on.'

'She was alone with her husband when he died. He'd always been hard-living and they found cocaine and alcohol in his blood. His heart must have simply given out.'

'And Sir Archibald Drake *also* died of a heart attack. So that's two people who have died of heart attacks in the vicinity of Mrs van Buren,' said the inspector. 'I think we should have another conversation with her, don't you sergeant?'

Chapter 15

Lucy and Susan returned to the shop to pack up some orders before the day ended. Lucy was tying up the last of the parcels, when Susan appeared holding the accounts ledger.

'That ginger cat's still sniffing around the alley,' Lucy said absently, listening to its plaintive miaowing. 'Should one of us feed it, do you think?'

'He's just playing on your good nature – I bet a hundred people are feeding it.' Susan said briskly, clearly disinterested. 'Lucy, can I speak to you a sec?'

'Of course. Shoot.'

'In private,' said Susan, shooting a meaningful glance at Felix, who was chatting to a customer.

The two women crowded into the stock room at the back. 'I was checking the accounts,' Susan explained. 'Our numbers have spiked this last week, thanks to that racy number of Felix's.'

'It's making me nervous having it in the shop,' Lucy said. 'I think we're down to the last few copies and then it'll be gone, and I can finally breathe easy.'

'Don't worry, I chose a nice innocuous title – *Love in a Country Cottage*. Anyway, I was entering the latest figures in the ledger, when I found another discrepancy. I double and triple checked.' She wedged the accounts ledger on the shelf beside them. 'See? Small amounts have been going missing this last eight weeks or so.

A few shillings here and there. Nothing you would notice at first, really. But it's steady.'

Lucy followed Susan's finger as she pointed out several instances. She was right, it wasn't much – a few shillings here and there, siphoned off from the total – but the amounts were being taken increasingly often. Lucy's heart sank.

'You don't think . . .' said Susan, 'that someone in the shop . . .'

'Surely not,' said Lucy in dismay.

Susan studied her shoes. 'I heard Toby asking the professor for money the other week,' she said unwillingly. 'He said, *I've got myself in another fix, Professor*. Mr T gave him a five-pound note, told him not to worry about paying it back. I was watching through the door – and don't tell me not to snoop, because it's a good thing for you I do.'

'Right,' said Lucy. 'Well, that could have been about anything.'

'And Felix was worrying about paying his rent, remember?' said Susan.

The pair stood there in silence for a long minute, staring at the damning ledger. Then Lucy let out a great sigh.

'How on earth,' she said, 'do I ask my employees whether they've been stealing? Toby's knife went missing the other week too. Surely no one here would steal.' And yet she could not ignore this. Not only was it bad business, but Cecil Court needed every last pound, shilling and pence if she stood a chance of winning her bet against Bryan Campbell.

Susan shrugged. 'I don't know. But—'

The miaowing from the alley grew more insistent and Lucy open the back door with an impatient gesture. 'All right, you brute,' she called, going into the kitchen and rummaging in the drawers. 'I'm sure we must have a sardine or something in here.' She pulled out a tin and a key and went out into the alley.

'If you feed it, Lucy, it will never go away,' said Susan wisely, following her out. 'I'm telling you, it'll be getting fed all over the place. We had a cat growing up and they're opportunists.'

Lucy opened the can and looked down the alley to where the cat was obstinately pawing at a rotten plank that boarded up the side of Mr Dakin's basement. 'Cats are good news in Ancient Egyptian mythology,' she told Susan. 'Although poor Dr Curry had a cat – it didn't bring *him* much luck.' She held out the tin and the cat came over, sniffing it delicately, before wolfing down the fish.

'I told you,' said Susan. 'Opportunists.'

But Lucy had straightened up and was considering the rotten plank. She walked over, crouched down and examined it. The plank was loose, dislodged. She came out here often, to get away from customers or get some fresh air, and she'd not seen it before. With a sudden gesture, she ripped the plank away.

Behind her, Susan gasped. 'What are you doing? Dakin will be livid if you destroy his property. He hates us enough as it is.'

'This isn't normally here,' said Lucy, ignoring her friend and instead lying flat on her stomach on the cold ground. 'Get a flashlight, will you?' The more she squinted, the more she could see something in the gloom – a bundle of papers, it looked like.

Susan diligently returned with a torch – she knew better than to argue with her friend after all these years – and they peered into the dark hole. 'It'll be rats, making a nest,' she said anxiously.

'I'm wearing gloves,' said Lucy, stretching a hand into a gap. She reached in quickly and, forcing the gap wider, drew out a bundle, wrapped in oil cloth. She unfolded it gingerly to find a bundle of folders and old papers, tied together with string.

'Newspapers,' said Susan dismissively. 'Thank God. Given our run of luck, I was scared it was going to be a severed hand or—'

'It's not newspapers,' said Lucy, slowly turning over the pages. They were neatly collated, covered in precise handwriting. 'These are maps, detailed drawings, coordinates . . .' She looked up. 'Dr Curry *did* have evidence that it was his research that led the Society to the tomb. And I think this is it.'

Chapter 16

ucy arrived at her parents' only a few minutes after four, out of breath and dishevelled, having rushed there – only for her father to announce he was retiring to the library and her mother that she was going shopping to look at dresses for the wedding.

'Even though everyone knows the mother of the groom must be an awful frump in an ugly hat,' Mrs Darkwether said mournfully, fastening her coat in the hall. 'I should still like to have something pretty to wear.'

'You'll look lovely, Mother,' Lucy said dutifully, wondering where the money for a shopping trip was coming from. She was still clutching the folder of Dr Curry's research – she *would* take it to the police, she told herself, but she wanted to read through it first.

'John is probably the only one of my children who will get married, so I need to make the most of it.' Her mother eyed her daughter in the mirror. 'He and Maggie are having tea on the lawn. In March, can you believe it! John has moved bath chairs and a table outside. I said it was too cold, but they didn't listen. That girl will catch pneumonia before the wedding like this.' She nodded at a pile of parcels on the hall table. 'Take these out to them, will you? Engagement presents, I should think.'

Lucy went out onto the terrace and found that a table and chairs had indeed been moved to the lawn and the best silver tea set laid out. John and Maggie were bundled up, the sun teasing them by putting in an early appearance.

'Honestly, John,' said Lucy, setting down the parcels. She took a seat and buried her hands in her coat pockets. 'Tea outside, in March. What madness is this?'

'Maggie wants the full English afternoon tea experience,' said John, shooting his sister a warning look. 'Besides, it's practically spring.'

Lucy, who could feel the tip of her nose becoming numb, said nothing.

'It *is* nice, isn't it?' said Maggie, lifting her lovely face to the faint sun. She was wearing slacks and a canary-yellow jumper, and her glorious auburn hair was bundled under a headscarf. 'London isn't so bad after all. I feel nicely English here, with tea on the lawn and cucumber sandwiches and an elderly butler who looks at me with disapproval.'

John, who had stood up and was pouring tea, bent and kissed her forehead. 'We'll get you back to the States soon enough. Perhaps we should honeymoon there. Are those more engagement presents?' He asked, nodding at the pile Lucy had carried out with her.

'Oooh,' said Maggie, sitting up, removing her sunglasses and taking possession of several beribboned oval boxes. 'Chocolates, how lovely.'

'Are you all right, sis?' asked John, nudging Lucy. 'You're quiet. Have a sandwich, it'll perk you up. Not still brooding over that murder business, are you?'

'Not really,' Lucy lied, pushing back her hair. She absently ate the sandwich, which did make her feel better, and took another. 'Although Dr Curry's inquest is next week, which should be interesting.'

'Interesting! This isn't a game, Luce,' John said – rather sanctimoniously, Lucy thought. 'A man died and horribly. I read the papers, you know.'

'Congratulations,' said Lucy sweetly. 'You must keep it up, John – you might learn all sorts of things, like who our prime minister

is. Maggie,' she asked suddenly. 'Your family friend, van Buren –
do you think she *was* having an affair with Lyle?'

Maggie thought for a moment. 'Maybe. She's got rotten taste in
men. Her first husband was a real crook and dragged her into all
sorts of scandals. It's a good thing he died when he did, if you ask
me.'

'Really, Lucy,' said John, 'that's very rude of you to ask.'

Maggie, who was ripping off wrapping paper, said, 'She can ask
me anything. I'm not sensitive.'

'If I'd been receiving notes from a would-be serial killer,' continued John, 'then I should keep a low profile, rather than digging any
further.'

Maggie lifted the lid on another box. 'I don't know how you can
expect her to resist,' she said. 'A murder, on her doorstep! An
Ancient Egyptian curse! Anyone would be curious, even you John.'

His expression relaxed and he gave a rueful smile. 'Perhaps.
What else is on your mind, Lucy?'

Lucy reviewed her list of concerns, which ranged from the
murder next door to the accounts, to Toby's missing knife, to her
bet with Bryan Campbell. 'Do you remember Bryan Campbell? He
was at your engagement party. Big, handsome, runs a book shop.'

'Oh, *I* noticed him,' drawled Maggie.

'I don't want to know what you noticed, darling,' said John
with dignity. 'Yes, of course I know Campbell. He did well in the
war and now he's frightfully successful.'

'Well, he took me for dinner last week,' Lucy said through a
mouthful of fish paste, 'and he said Campbell's wanted to take
over my shop. I lost my temper, ended up making him the most
impossible bet. I can't see how I can win it – unless miracles *do*
happen.'

'I wouldn't gamble with him, Lucy – he's a serious businessman. What was the bet?'

'I bet him that our shop would overtake Campbell's profits-wise
in the fiction department by the end of the quarter,' said Lucy

gloomily. 'If he wins, he gets Cecil Court Books without me putting up a fight.'

John burst out laughing. 'Luce! Might have to eat humble pie there. He'll think you were joking. Bat your lashes at him and he'll forget all about it. But would it be so bad if Campbell's took over? They've done great things with their shop.'

Lucy watched as her sister-in-law's white teeth chomped vigorously on a chocolate. 'He made me angry,' she said inadequately. 'People always think the underdog can't win . . .'

'Usually because they can't,' said Maggie. 'Ugh, are these violet creams? Disgusting.' She shut the box and pushed it away. 'Take these back to your shop, darling, I don't want them.'

'How kind of you,' said Lucy with a sarcasm that was evidently lost on Maggie, who was opening a box of crystalised ginger. 'Is that the extent of your business advice? I was hoping for more, as the daughter of a steel magnate.'

'Iron girders,' Maggie corrected her. 'And I *do* know a bit about business, actually.' She wound a ribbon around one scarlet-tipped finger. 'My pa wasn't always the man he is today – for a long time, *he* was the underdog. What he always said is, you got to figure out what you can do that the other fellow can't. And then do it, fast.'

'Campbell's can do everything I can and better,' said Lucy, eating a violet cream.

'Can they?' said Maggie. 'Don't be defeatist. Usually there's *something* that gives the little fellow an edge, no matter how outlandish. So long as you don't mind not always playing by the rules.' She shrugged. 'But what do I know?'

An edge. Something outlandish, not playing by the rules . . . Lucy snapped her fingers. 'Actually, you've given me an idea, Maggie. Excuse me – I've got a call to make.'

Chapter 17

That Thursday was the inquest for Dr Curry's death. Lucy showed up inconspicuously dressed in a navy suit. Susan had needed little persuasion to accompany her again. On the way, they had seen various paper billboards, each plastered with headlines about the killings. London was being whipped into a feverish state of fear and excitement. They had even seen one vendor selling crude death masks. She glanced at Inspector Hayes as she went in and he gave her a brief nod. Lucy found herself shivering, perhaps with anticipation. It seemed the evidence that she and Susan had found and handed over to the police would indeed play a part today.

Unsurprisingly, for a case that had gripped the capital, a large crowd had gathered into the court. Lucy squeezed into a seat at the back, beside a woman in a tall hat whose nose was quivering with excitement and a man scribbling notes throughout, clearly from one of the papers.

It began quietly, seemingly a purely formal affair. Inspector Hayes was called to the stand to explain his arrival on the scene and what he had discovered. His sergeant stood near the back of the room. Dr Curry's wife, red-eyed and pale, came forward to identify her husband as the deceased and attest to his disturbed state of mind in the weeks before his death. She revealed nothing that Lucy had not already heard – that her husband had been in a surprisingly good mood the evening before his death, after weeks of upset and worry. That he believed he had at last found a way to improve their situation.

Sir Hector Derwent took the stand positively bursting with indignation, but the coroner, an elderly man with shrewd eyes, kept him firmly on track, asking him about his interactions with Dr Curry in Egypt.

'Barely met the chap,' muttered Sir Hector. 'I don't get involved with the day to day, you understand. Lyle hired him.'

'You were present during the lecture where he alleged that Mr Lyle stole his research – and that the Society covered it up?'

'I was. And it was a pack of lies. Dr Curry wanted to bring dishonour to the expedition and the Society, to drag our reputation through the mud!'

'So, there is no truth to the allegations,' said the coroner, looking at him over his spectacles.

'None,' said Sir Hector firmly, avoiding the coroner's gaze. 'None whatsoever. You need to be looking into whoever this letter-writer is. This killing is the work of a—'

'Thank you, sir,' said the coroner, cutting him off.

Mr Dakin was next. He bustled to the stand, light shining on his balding head, eyes glistening. Like Sir Hector, he clearly had things to say, but, again, the coroner kept him firmly on track.

'Prior to the discovery, when did you last go into the exhibition space where the victim was found?' asked the coroner.

'I went in that morning, early,' said Mr Dakin, perched on the edge of his seat. 'Before seven o'clock.'

'Why so early?' asked the coroner, fixing him with stern eyes.

'I – I wanted to check everything was in order.'

'It wasn't because you had lost your keys?'

Mr Dakin flushed. 'I – yes, all right, I had misplaced my keys the night before. I had spent all night searching at home and I was worried that the mummy might be unsafe, if someone had got hold of them. But when I got to the shop, I found them on the mat. And everything was exactly as I had left it inside.'

'So, then you prepared for the exhibition?'

'I wanted to add a few more details and I knew I shouldn't have any time later. I painted the walls, set up some special lights, burnt some incense for atmosphere, you see. Supervised some posters being put up outside. Then I left around nine for breakfast.'

'Locking up?'

'It's a night lock. But yes – the door was shut fast behind me, and I had the only key.'

'And did you see anything suspicious in Cecil Court when you left? Anyone hanging around?'

'Not at all,' said Mr Dakin. 'Miss Darkwether, who owns the shop next door, and I had a little chat about the position of my posters. That was all, I think. I wasn't paying much attention – I was in a hurry.'

'You returned at four. Were there any strangers in or around the shop during the day?'

'No!' he cried. 'Well, tradesfolk, you know, from various companies – bringing wine, cake, glassware. Some waiters I had hired. But no strangers and no one went into the room with the sarcophagus. I would never have let them. It might have been a journalist or someone hell-bent on destroying the exhibition. The tomb opening and the discovery of the mummy had already attracted all sorts of talk and excitement. And now people are asking for their money back – I have spoken to a solicitor to ascertain my legal position—'

'Can I ask whose idea it was to arrange the exhibition as a tomb?' The coroner said, unmoved by Mr Dakin's woes.

'I had been pondering it for weeks, how to make the expedition really *memorable*, you know. And then it came to me at Dr Lyle's lecture – we recreate the tomb itself.' He looked around defensively. 'Of course, I had no idea that it might suggest such dark intent to someone!'

The coroner shifted his glasses down his nose. 'Who knew what you had planned?'

Mr Dakin considered. 'We mentioned it in passing to the rest of the board at breakfast – Mrs van Buren, Sir Hector, Mr Ahmed.' His eyes narrowed. 'Miss Darkwether knew, I told *her* all about it when she complained about the posters outside that morning. Other than that, no one. And I didn't bring all those props – the dust and furs, the figurine. *That* was all the killer.'

'It seems like an extremely strange thing for the killer to do,' said the coroner disbelievingly. 'And what went through your mind when you saw the body?'

'I was shocked, angry – I thought someone had played some sort of joke. Dr Curry perhaps, causing a scene. Or Miss Darkwether and her friends, from next door. I didn't think for one moment that someone was really *dead*.'

The coroner said drily, 'It would have been quite an effort, for a malicious prank.'

'Oh, of course,' said Mr Dakin quickly. 'I'm not alleging that Miss Darkwether or her staff had anything to do with it. Just that it crossed my mind, at first.'

Lucy looked at the reporters scribbling and gritted her teeth. If her business survived a brutal murder next door, coverage in the papers, *and* Mr Dakin implicating her at the inquest, it would be a miracle. *All publicity is good publicity*, she chanted in her head.

Mrs van Buren took the stand next. She testified that Dr Curry had initially been enthusiastic about joining the party to Egypt, only to exhibit unbalanced behaviour on the dig itself.

'Did you think there was any weight to Dr Curry's accusations of intellectual theft?' the Coroner asked.

'None whatsoever,' she said calmly. 'As I said, he seemed an unbalanced man, given to greatly inflating his own contributions. Dr Lyle was the driving force of the expedition.'

Liar. And not just a liar but an accomplished one, thought Lucy. Anything to protect the Society and to secure future expeditions. For Mrs van Buren and Sir Hector, she suspected that was everything.

Mrs van Buren made a good witness: convincing, articulate and calm. The only brief hesitation came when she was asked about her whereabouts on the morning of the murder.

'Did you take a detour on your way to the museum?' asked the coroner.

'Absolutely not.'

'You didn't, for instance, take a taxi to Cecil Court Books before continuing on?'

Lucy nudged Susan meaningfully. So, Mrs van Buren had been on their doorstep on the morning of the murder.

Mrs van Buren's eyelids flickered ever so slightly. 'I went straight to the museum,' she said calmly. 'I walked around outside for a time – I had a headache. Dr Lyle saw me arrive.'

As she stepped off the stand and passed Dr Lyle on his way up, Lucy was sure they exchanged a brief glance and Mrs van Buren gave the faintest nod.

'Those two,' Susan whispered. 'Dr Lyle and Mrs van Buren. *Are* they having an affair?'

'Mr Ahmed says so,' Lucy whispered back. 'Or at least they *were*. But I think they're interested in one thing only – protecting the Society and covering up what they did to Dr Curry.'

Dr Lyle took the stand next. He cut an appealing figure, managing to convey both horror at what had happened and a faint distaste that he should be involved in such a sordid business.

'Can you think of anyone who would want to hurt Dr Curry?' asked the coroner.

Dr Lyle shook his head, looking honestly bewildered. 'Not at all,' he said. 'I must admit, suicide seemed far more likely for such an unhappy man. I really thought that *must* be it, when we saw the body. But I gather . . .' his eyes darted to the coroner, 'that is quite out of the question?'

'It is,' said the coroner sharply. 'Dr Curry accused you publicly of stealing his research. The night before he died.'

'A disturbed young man,' murmured Dr Lyle sadly.

'Hmm,' said the coroner. He laid his hand on the pile of tattered papers at his elbow, and Lucy felt a flutter of excitement. She nudged Susan again and sat up straight. She could tell the crowd, who had been growing bored, were also alert now to the possibility of drama – there were rustles, murmurs. 'Do you recognise these, Dr Lyle?'

A court assistant carried the papers over to where Dr Lyle was standing. Lucy noticed Mrs van Buren leaning forward, Sir Hector frowning. The doctor examined the papers, going pale as he did so.

'They seem to relate to the dig site,' he said shortly. 'Someone's notes.'

'The papers you are looking at comprise the research conducted by Dr William Curry. It's his handwriting and his research, signed by him, pinpointing the exact location of the tomb and expanding on its historical significance. Research which matches the reports you signed as your own. Research that has been published under your name as the man who discovered the hidden tomb.'

The excited murmuring of the crowd grew in volume.

Dr Lyle had gone white to the lips. 'Where did . . .' His voice trailed off. Forcing a smile, he went on. 'There is always an element of collaboration in research.'

Lucy looked eagerly at the rest of the Society. Sir Hector was purple up to his roots and Mrs van Buren was swallowing convulsively. They looked astonishingly guilty.

'I see,' said the coroner quietly. 'So, you do not admit to using Dr Curry's research under your own name, neglecting to credit him, and refusing to cite his contribution to the historical discovery?'

'I . . . No, of course I do not admit such a thing.' Dr Lyle's voice was more assured now, but his face was still ashen. Lucy could see court reporters scribbling fast. 'I deny it all.'

'I see,' murmured the coroner. He nodded to the court assistant. 'Have Dr Curry's research files entered as evidence.'

When Dr Lyle descended, he looked altogether less confident. His eyes were darting frantically and he was struggling to maintain his usual careless smile. Lucy was sure there was now an entirely different atmosphere in the room – as though the hero of the hour had been decidedly tarnished. The reporters were still scribbling and Sir Hector looked furious.

Mr Ahmed, lean and carelessly dressed, and looking as always like he was in a hurry, took the stand and explained that he had known Dr Curry only slightly, and that, in his opinion, he had been of sound mind, in Egypt at least. A police doctor explained that the wound could not have been self-inflicted.

The coroner then recorded a judgement of death by person or persons unknown. An investigation would be launched by Inspector Hayes of Scotland Yard.

'That's that,' said Lucy, standing with the rest. All around them, excited chatter had exploded, most of it centred on Lyle and his duplicity. 'Now the real detective work begins.' She nodded to where the inspector now stood, in the back of the room, his face cast into shadow. 'The inspector looks rather grim about it, doesn't he? I don't think his boss is happy the attention is all on the Society. Still, there's a good case against Lyle, surely. His reputation was on the line unless he could shut Curry up.'

Susan yawned. 'It's hot in here, isn't it? Shall we scram? I'm dying for some fresh air after all that talk of tombs and death.'

As they left the chamber, Lucy caught sight of a stooped figure who seemed vaguely familiar, walking ahead of them. 'Hold on a moment, will you?' she said to Susan. 'Wait for me outside.'

'I'll be on the corner, smoking a cigarette,' said Susan. 'As if we were in a detective novel, which this is starting to feel like.'

* * *

Lucy caught up with the man, who was edging along slowly with the crowd.

'Excuse me,' she said, laying a hand on his sleeve. 'I saw you at Dr Lyle's lecture at the British Museum. You were sweeping the floor – you missed your bus.'

'That's right,' said the man, looking at her curiously. He wore pale tan overalls under a dark jacket, and had an earnest, hesitant expression that was rather endearing – dog-like, Lucy thought. 'I remember you, miss – from the lecture. Lost your gloves, didn't you?'

'I lost them again on the way home,' said Lucy, grinning at him. 'You have a good memory.'

He returned a shy smile. 'I'm good with faces,' he said modestly. 'Got something of a photographic memory.'

'Listen, I hope you don't mind me introducing myself. My name is Miss Darkwether.'

He held out a hand. 'Mr Eastley.'

'What made you come along today to the inquest – rampant curiosity, like the rest of us?'

'I suppose so, miss. I was there when it all began, at the lecture. Although I suppose it started before that – in Egypt, when the first gentleman died.'

Lucy eyed him thoughtfully. 'Can I buy you a cup of tea now and ask you a few questions about that evening, when Dr Curry interrupted the lecture? I keep thinking I might have missed something important.' The man hesitated. 'There's a tea shop just around the corner,' she added persuasively.

'All right,' said Mr Eastley. 'But I need to be on my next shift at six.'

As they walked past Susan, Lucy gave her a wink and a subtle nod towards Mr Eastley. Susan sighed and buttoned her coat, turning to go back to the shop alone.

* * *

In the tearoom, they ordered a pot of tea and a plate of cakes. When the waitress had gone, Lucy said, 'I remember how you didn't think Lyle's lecture was up to much.'

The man gave a rather sweet, crooked smile. 'You're right – I didn't,' he said. 'Always had an interest in Egyptology and I listen to those lectures all the time, while I'm cleaning up. Lyle made small mistakes – dates and places that weren't quite right. Now it turns out he might have nicked that other chap's research after all.'

'You seemed to know an awful lot about it. Did you read history?'

The man's face, which had been alight with interest, fell again. 'No, miss. Only what I could get my hands on at the library or at school. I always wanted to go on one of those expeditions. Dreamed of being an archaeologist myself you know, as a boy. My mother supported me. I was all set to study for it. I had a place at university waiting.'

'But then you never went,' said Lucy. 'Why not? You clearly have the brains for it.'

'The war,' said Mr Eastley, around a mouthful of bun.

'You were injured?'

'I wasn't able to fight myself,' he said. 'Poor eyes, you know. But my father and brother were both killed at Verdun. The money I had put away for study went to support my mother. That put paid to any ideas of university. I did odd jobs, then I started cleaning.'

'I'm sorry.'

'I was better off than many. A lot of dreams went up in smoke thanks to that war.'

There was a pause. 'So, you took cleaning shifts in museums to be in a place of history,' said Lucy. 'The mummy is in the museum now. That must have been a thrill.'

To her surprise, Mr Eastley shook his head. 'A museum is the last place he belongs, in my opinion! It's all wrong it is, great treasures like this being dug up by gentlemen like Mr Lyle who don't care much about it beyond the headlines. And the rest of that Society – rotten as they come. How would you like it if *your* ancestors' graves were dug up and shifted to a different country altogether for a load of folk to peer at?'

'Not much,' admitted Lucy. 'It's an argument I've heard before and I don't disagree. But I suppose I'm as hungry for knowledge as the Society. Shouldn't we bring great finds to light, rather than see them buried?'

'It's not right,' the man repeated stubbornly.

'Is there anything else you noticed that night?' Lucy asked him, changing back to the real reason she wanted to talk to the man. 'Aside from the drama with Dr Curry and Lyle, I mean.'

Mr Eastley licked his finger and dabbed the last few crumbs of bun into his mouth. 'I saw the lady, Mrs van Buren I think her name is, having an argument with Dr Lyle,' he said importantly.

'When?' asked Lucy keenly.

'It was after the lecture, when everyone went out into the foyer for drinks,' said Mr Eastley. 'Dr Lyle stepped off the podium, smiling, and Mrs van Buren got hold of his arm and dragged him to one side. I was sweeping up and they didn't notice me at first. I couldn't hear much, but she was whispering, *we have to end this now* and he said *nonsense, there's nothing to worry about*. And then he saw me and hustled her out.'

'The rumours are they were having an affair,' said Lucy. 'Which would fit. But I wonder if they were talking about something else. If he stole Dr Curry's research and she was helping him cover it up . . . well, maybe she'd got cold feet. Maybe his appearance at the lecture had rattled her and she was sick of the pretence.' She caught his puzzled expression and said, 'You must be thinking that I'm the most infernal busybody.'

'No, miss,' said Mr Eastley slowly. 'But I think you're treating this as a sort of game and it isn't one. Those people did something wrong, you see. Everyone on the expedition did a bad thing.'

'And so, you think it's true – that someone is punishing them?' Lucy asked.

But Mr Eastley had noticed the tearoom clock and was already standing, brushing crumbs off the front of his trousers. 'Goodness, is that the time? I must go, miss. Sorry I couldn't have been more help.'

'It's good to talk to someone about it all, someone who is as curious as I am. I hope to see you again sometime.'

'I hope not in the wake of another death,' he said seriously. 'It's not a game miss – I'd stay out of it if I were you.'

The bell tinkled as Mr Eastley walked out. Lucy sat back in her seat, watching him go, turning his collar up against the March wind.

Chapter 18

hat weekend, Lucy took her friend Freddie Carlton up on his offer of some time away in the country with some mutual friends, thinking a change of scene would be good for her. However, she had reckoned without the entire house party begging her for more details of the note and the discovery of the body, hanging off her every word. She was forced to relive the terrible scene several times before they were happy.

'And I heard that the famous Dr Lyle is one of the main suspects,' said Freddie. 'The man's a fraud, apparently. The whole Society will be investigated.'

'He'll lose his job at least,' said Lady Carlton. 'Always were rumours about him. A murky past, you know. Although I suppose he has been terribly brave, going off to these strange countries. And now he's lost it all!'

'Maybe,' said Lucy. She refused to feel much pity for Dr Lyle.

'And that Mrs van Buren,' continued Lady Carlton. 'Her husband was meant to be a gangster. Who knows what he got up to in the war – and there was talk, you know, after he died.'

'What do you mean, talk?' said Lucy keenly.

'His wife made no secret of her dislike for him. She got all the money and that big house. He died suddenly one night, alone in the house with her. The doctor attending was an old friend of hers. Yes, there were definitely *whispers*. It was convenient for her, how it worked out.'

Interesting, Lucy thought. Perhaps Mrs van Buren had a murky past too. She thought again of Dr Curry and the secrets he believed he had discovered about the members of the Society. Could the immaculate Mrs van Buren have stooped to murder, all those years ago?

'Well!' exclaimed Freddie. 'Murder on your doorstep. Anonymous notes. We all thought you throwing over Edward to go to Oxford was a terrible mistake and that your shop sounded deathly dull. Turns out, it's most exciting.'

I suppose I should feel the same, if it hadn't happened to me, Lucy thought, as she drove back to London on Sunday evening, feeling not at all rested, but, rather, more anxious than ever.

* * *

She returned to Cecil Court on Monday, having arranged to meet Felix early, before anyone would be about. The papers now talked not only of death but of the disgraced leader of the expedition.

ESTEEMED EGYPTOLOGIST INVOLVED IN DEATH

DID THE CURSE CORRUPT?

WILL THERE BE A THIRD VICTIM?

As she turned into the cobbled mews that Monday morning, Lucy felt a cold and unfamiliar sensation – dread. Walking into her cosy shop had always felt like coming home; now a shadow of apprehension had settled over it. At any moment, a printed note might arrive, heralding another terrible death.

Felix was waiting for her outside, in front of a stack of large cardboard boxes. 'Lucy, is this your doing? You've ordered another two hundred copies at least! And you told me to lay off the smut.'

'We may as well take a chance on it,' Lucy said. 'We've got nothing to lose.'

'What on earth has made you so reckless all of a sudden?' laughed Felix, lugging the boxes inside.

'Oh, nothing,' said Lucy evasively. 'I just thought we should try and up our profit margins a bit.' *But secretly,* she thought to herself, *if we're going to get taken over by Campbell's, we might as well go out with a bang.* 'Talking of profits,' she started, deciding while she had Felix alone was as good an opportunity as any other moment, 'Felix, are you all right for money? Only you mentioned your landlord was raising the rent.'

'London rents are ridiculous,' he said crossly. 'I'm all right, but I would like to discuss that raise.'

'After the next quarter, I promise,' Lucy told him. She looked at Felix, carefully hanging up his neatly brushed coat, but he didn't say anything in response. He liked finer things – but surely, he wouldn't pilfer a few shillings at a time from the till. Mr Tollesbury came down, buttoning up his coat. 'You look glum, Professor,' Lucy said, turning to him instead, to take her mind off Felix.

'Dentist,' he muttered. 'My one fear. Fancy driving me there, Felix? They might have to give me a shot.'

'You know I don't bring the car in during the week,' said Felix. 'But I'll collect you in a taxi.'

'I'll be all right.' He shuddered. 'I *hate* the dentist. Sometimes I think he's enjoying himself, doing all this work.'

As the morning wore on, and her staff and then customers began to trickle in, searching out the latest novel, familiar faces asking her for advice and recommendations, Lucy began to cheer up. Things felt almost normal. Some customers were here to snoop, she was sure; but most had no interest in lurid newspaper articles and mystical curses. She doubted that some of her customers had read a newspaper in the last five years. Mr Tollesbury came back at some point in the late afternoon with his cheek packed with cotton wool and went to lie down.

'We're doing beautiful business on the you-know-what,' said

Felix happily, as a society lady walked out with her brown paper package, flushed with the thrill of buying a forbidden book. 'I've told customers to only come to the shop between eleven and one-fifteen. I thought that would make it more mysterious.'

'Well done,' Lucy told him.

Susan, who was walking past, murmured, 'We're down another seven shillings though. I hope you haven't decided to ignore *that* little problem.'

'Not at all,' Lucy whispered back. She began to open the bills and put them neatly to one side. Her days of not opening post were over, she had sworn that much. 'In fact, I'll talk to Toby about it later—'

She paused, for Felix was looking down at an envelope in his hand, with an odd expression on his face.

'Lucy!' said Felix. 'Look.'

He held up a white envelope, their address neatly typed.

Felix swallowed. 'Is it . . . another one?'

'Looks like it,' Lucy said, trying to sound calm even as her stomach churned. 'I'll take it to the police station now.'

'Open it first,' said Felix, hovering anxiously beside her. 'It might be nothing and then you'll look silly. I'll get the others, it would be mean to leave them out.'

'It's not an afternoon at the pictures,' hissed Lucy, but Felix had gone to summon Mr Tollesbury and Toby from the book-binding room. Then, carefully, Lucy slit the envelope.

It was the same neat type face as before.

> *Two have been punished. The false face will be the third.*
> *You cannot save him, Miss Darkwether.*

And then a row of hieroglyphs, a small set of scales and a series of numbers.

'If we're right on the code,' said Susan, grabbing a pencil, 'then the time and date should at least be easy.' She began to scribble.

'Look. Two tens, a five, a two – twenty-seven. The twenty-seventh of the month. Damnit, that's today!'

'Which means our victim might already be dead.' Lucy shot to her feet, the note still in her hand. 'Come on. Susan, you ring up Inspector Hayes, don't let the desk sergeant fob you off. And then ring Max Bird and tell him this is his tip off. A deal is a deal, even though I don't like it.'

'Where are you going?' asked Susan, hurrying to the phone.

'The British Museum,' said Lucy, already running out of the door. '*The false face*. Someone who lied and deceived everybody. Who else could that be except Gordon Lyle? No one seems to believe that this note sender is worth listening, but I *do*. Someone's got to help save him.'

*　*　*

Lucy's taxi screeched to a halt outside the British Museum, standing tall and handsome in the winter sunshine. She flung some coins at the driver, pounded up the steps, too panicked to take in their beauty this time, past the reception desk, and up several flights towards Dr Lyle's office. She spun round the corner – and was met with Inspector Hayes, also breathing hard.

The sergeant was standing just inside the door, looking rather green.

'You came,' she gasped.

'It's my job,' said the inspector. There was a hard set to his mouth. 'But I'm afraid we were too late.'

He moved aside and Lucy saw Gordon Lyle seated in his usual chair, a figurine resting by his hand. Red ochre lined the desk and floor, and a fur was arranged almost tenderly around his shoulders. A hieroglyph was drawn on the wall in chalk – a set of scales. He was leaning back, neck exposed. His face in death, stripped of its character and bonhomie, was a rather silly face, with a weak chin. And, at his throat, a violent red gash.

Too late, Lucy thought numbly. She had been too late, a second time.

Lucy stepped inside. The inspector did not stop her.

'Red ochre again,' she murmured, trying to avoid looking directly at the body. 'And the figurine. The same hand, Inspector, you cannot doubt it.'

'I don't,' he said. 'Not this time. Have you got the note?'

Lucy drew it out of her bag and handed it to him. He scanned it quickly. '*The false face. The third* – but not the last?'

'It doesn't seem like it,' said Lucy. 'I can't pretend I liked Dr Lyle, but any death is a tragedy.' She crouched down next to the body. The figurine, she noticed, had a slash for a mouth, like a smile.

'He was hit on the head from behind first,' the inspector said. 'Something heavy, by the looks of things. Perhaps the poker in the fireplace, although we'll definitely need to check for fingerprints. Stunned him, but didn't kill him, I would imagine. The killer was facing him when he slit his throat.' The inspector stepped aside to let in the sergeant, followed by a surgeon and a camera man and fingerprint expert. 'If you don't mind waiting a moment, perhaps you and I might have a word next door, Miss Darkwether, while my men work.'

* * *

Lucy and the inspector sat across a round table in the office next door. Dust motes hung in the stale air. Once, Lucy would have found the presence of old books and dark wood comforting, recalling her degree and the peaceful libraries in Oxford. Now, death had penetrated even this quiet and respectable place.

The body had been examined, photographed and removed. The fingerprint expert had dusted the room.

'And found a million or so prints, including Gordon Lyle's,' the inspector said bitterly. 'He used the room to teach in – different

162

students and staff came in and out daily. It would be impossible to discern which belonged to the intruder. His colleagues say he got here as usual about eight thirty and no one saw anything of him until now.'

'Did no one hear anything?'

'The room opposite is occupied by a Professor Langley who rather defines the term "absent-minded" – no, nobody reported a sound. In spite of the lurid trappings, this was a most efficiently committed crime.'

'He *had* planned it carefully,' Lucy reminded him. 'Sent me a little note like last time.'

'I owe you an apology, Miss Darkwether,' Inspector Hayes said stiffly. 'I did not take the first note as seriously as I should have done. I confess I believed there must be a more pragmatic reason for these killings. My eyes were on those in the Society.'

Sergeant West's head appeared around the door. 'The figurine has been dusted for prints, sir – nothing doing. Want to take a look?' He set down the crude wooden figure on the desk. The inspector nodded for Lucy to go ahead and with gloved hands, she took it up.

'What do the scales mean?' asked the inspector, examining the note.

'I think they imply justice,' said Lucy thoughtfully. 'So, justice has been served here, in this room.'

'Again, the second note is addressed to you. And you were the one to find the evidence that Mr Lyle had indeed stolen from Dr Curry.'

'Outside Dakin's shop,' she reminded him.

'Hmm. Yet *you* found it. Maybe you were meant to. Our killer has made this rather . . . personal to you, Miss Darkwether. Seems to be almost directing this all through you. Can you think of any reason why?'

The inspector's words had sent a prickle down her back. 'You've got me there,' said Lucy. 'I'm as stumped as you are. I can only

163

imagine that proximity played a part – my shop is next door to Mr Dakin's. And that the killer needs someone who can decode these messages. Although why not send them to the police I can't imagine . . .'

'He knows that the police would have shelved the notes in a little pile marked crackpot,' said the sergeant, still standing in the doorway. 'You're the only way he gets attention paid.'

The inspector gave a wry smile. 'There's something in that. He must know a great deal about you, to know how you would react to receiving these notes.' His smile faded. 'Which implies he has some knowledge of you personally, Miss Darkwether. Or has been watching you for some time.'

Lucy could not repress a shiver. 'Thanks, Inspector. That makes me feel all cosy inside.'

'We are happy to offer you police protection, miss,' said the sergeant. 'Or you could leave London for a while, stay with friends.'

Lucy shook her head. 'I shall stay right here in London. If I scram, our killer might stop writing and then you won't have any clues at all.'

The inspector shifted uncomfortably. 'I must warn you—'

'Consider me warned. I'm not going anywhere. I have a business to run, Inspector, besides anything else.'

The sergeant smiled at her. 'You're a sport, miss. Didn't I say she wouldn't run, sir?'

The inspector nodded. 'You did, West. I can't say it isn't foolish behaviour though.'

'Thanks for the vote of confidence,' said Lucy. 'Now, do I get some inside information, given that I'm your line of communication to the killer?'

'I can tell you what our doctor thinks. The surgeon will examine the body, but he guesses Dr Lyle was killed around nine o'clock this morning – although the gas fire was on, which can delay rigor mortis.'

Lucy nodded. 'And no one was seen going in or out?'

'The professor across the hall says the usual cleaning staff left well before Dr Lyle arrived – they always clean on Mondays, but they're gone before eight. He seems absent-minded enough that we checked with their supervisor, who confirms it. They were both interviewed – a Mr Bennett and a Mr Eastley.' He frowned as Lucy gave a start. 'What?'

'Mr Eastley,' Lucy said thoughtfully. 'He was cleaning the night of the lecture too – *and* he was at the inquest. Seems very interested in the expedition.'

'He certainly had a lot to say,' said the inspector dryly. 'We checked him out thoroughly, but he and Mr Bennett were on shift together all morning and even had their cigarette break together. Although that hasn't stopped him having an opinion about the murder. Said he saw one particularly suspicious character, watching the museum this morning.'

'Really?' asked Lucy. 'What sort of suspicious character?'

'He and Mr Bennett went out for a cigarette just after they'd finished cleaning, about eight-thirty or so. Eastley said he noticed a man watching the museum and then, when Lyle pulled up and got out of a taxi, he waited a minute or two, hurried across the road and followed him inside. Blond man, hat pulled down over his eyes, a scar. Menacing stare, the works.' The inspector sighed and then continued. 'Unfortunately, the *only* person to see this sinister figure is Eastley. We asked the other cleaner and security guards, and no one saw him enter the museum.'

'Hard to tell with witnesses,' said the sergeant. 'This Eastley fellow might just want to be involved. The so-called "suspicious" man might have been some ordinary passer-by.'

Lucy nodded. 'He does seem *very* interested in the case,' she said. 'Mr Eastley, I mean.'

'Anyway, this menacing figure seems to have vanished into thin air. We'll keep looking, of course. I'm sure there will be plenty of other witnesses coming forward when this gets out. Only it won't be a man with a scar they saw – it'll be one of those gods with ears like a dog.'

'Anubis?' said Lucy. 'It's a jackal.'

'Whatever it is, it's wasting police time.' The inspector was silent for a moment, twirling his pencil between his fingers.

Lucy took a breath and said, 'You sound busy, both of you. Don't you think, Inspector, that we might now become allies?'

He glanced up at her. As his intelligent eyes met hers, Lucy was conscious of something – another prickle down her neck that had nothing to do with fear. She could feel her cheeks getting warm and her heart gave an odd flutter. How strange, she thought.

'Allies?'

'Yes,' Lucy said, gathering herself. 'Pool resources, so to speak. I have my knowledge of the ancient world – and the dubious honour of being the point of contact for the killer. You,' she waved a hand, 'have all the rest.'

'The rest?' said the inspector, looking amused.

'You know. Fingerprint people and witness statements and manpower and all that. Can't you let me in on this?' she said coaxingly.

His reluctant smile deepened. 'What you are suggesting is most irregular.'

'I've got something else to offer,' continued Lucy.

'What's that?'

'I'm a part of this world,' said Lucy. 'These society academics – I fit right in. For instance, Mrs Lyle. I can talk to her. Did she know that Mrs van Buren and Dr Lyle were having an affair, in Egypt? There's no smoke without fire. His wife might not have liked that. I'll talk to her – woman to woman.'

'You'll be, ah, subtle about this, will you?' asked the inspector, and Lucy thought she saw another smile.

'You mean you think I'm subtle as a brick,' said Lucy. 'You'd be surprised, Inspector. I can use a light touch when I need to.'

'Let her do it, sir,' said the sergeant. 'We could use someone familiar with these society circles. Besides, she's a sport.'

'So you keep saying,' said the inspector. He gave Lucy a look that was loaded with a heavy warning. 'I cannot include you in this investigation, Miss Darkwether, because, as I keep reminding you, you are not on the police force—'

'But—'

'However! I *can* look the other way while you pursue certain lines of inquiry. You get *one chance* to prove you can aid my investigation rather than hinder it. You can meet – unofficially – with Mrs Lyle.' He sighed. 'I've no way of stopping you so I might as well hear what comes out of it.'

Lucy beamed at him and gathered up her things. 'You will not regret this decision,' she said cheerfully.

The inspector sighed. 'I hope not. And you will let us know the *instant* you get another note?'

'As soon as it lands on the mat,' promised Lucy. 'But we'll be ready. The killer won't get lucky another time – I'm sure of it.'

Chapter 19

T he following morning was yet another busy one – but rather busier, Lucy thought with irritation, across Cecil Court at Dakin's Rare Books, which had now reopened. Clearly, the public were keen to see the site of the murder.

'Hello,' said Felix, gliding over to the woman standing in the doorway. 'Can I interest you in a—'

'Oh no,' said the woman, backing out. 'This isn't the shop I wanted. I want the one with the dead body.'

'Damn,' says Lucy, visiting Mr Tollesbury in the back room, where he was carefully disassembling a first edition of *The Wooden Pegasus*. 'Dakin really is hogging all our business. They could have asked *me* a few questions about Lyle's murder. I saw the scene too,' she harumphed. 'Which reminds me, Professor – do you remember the man we were standing with at the lecture?'

Mr Tollesbury sliced carefully through the brittle stitching of the old spine. He shook his head. 'One of the guests?'

'No, he was there cleaning. He was at the inquest too *and* he was cleaning at the museum on the morning of Dr Lyle's death too. Is that a coincidence?'

'He seems to be getting around,' said Mr Tollesbury slowly. 'Just a moment, my dear.' He unscrewed a bottle of oil of clove and poured a little onto a cloth, clasping it to his tooth. 'Although,' he said in a muffled voice, 'if he works at the museum, that wouldn't be so odd.'

'I know, but all the same, I thought about talking to him. He's clever and rather bitter, I think, about being around all these explorers when he never got to do any exploring himself. And he is very interested in these crimes. Claims he saw someone watching the museum before Dr Lyle was killed. I wonder if he knows something.'

'Or,' said Mr Tollesbury, still through the cloth, 'he just likes the attention.'

'Excuse me,' said a man, sticking his head round the shop door. 'Is this where that man was—'

'You want next door,' Lucy said crossly, and the door slammed shut.

'I'm going to get some milk,' said Lucy, standing to go out. As she left the shop, she passed Mr Dakin closing the door behind a group of customers, beaming after them. He was clearly in such a good mood he even forgot to scowl at Lucy.

'Miss Darkwether,' he said, almost civilly. 'How are you?'

'Isn't this a sad day?' Lucy began. 'First Sir Drake – then Dr Curry – and now your old friend Dr Lyle. Everyone who was in Egypt must surely be afraid. This expedition truly does seem to be cursed.'

'It is horrible,' Mr Dakin said, thrusting a handful of notes into his pocket. 'Dr Lyle was a great man, the finest Egyptologist of our age.' His pale eyes regarded her. 'We will have to hope you don't receive another note, Miss Darkwether! Out of curiosity, I understand the first note arrived the night before the murder. Yet you didn't open it till after Dr Curry's death. Why not?'

'I don't always open my post immediately,' said Lucy coldly. 'Plenty of people don't. I do *now*, of course.'

'I see.' He shook his head sadly. 'And yet a life might have been saved. You were too late to save Dr Lyle as well, weren't you?'

'I tried my best,' said Lucy through gritted teeth, indignant at the accusation. 'Dr Lyle's note I really was looking out for, but it arrived late on the day he was killed. There were all those postal strikes—' She broke off, startled at the expression on Mr Dakin's face – alert and keen. 'Are you all right, Mr Dakin?'

'The postal strikes,' said Mr Dakin slowly. 'Of *course*. We didn't have any post at all for days at a time, did we? It was lucky the killer's notes were seen at all.' He chuckled suddenly. 'Well, well! I have just had the most interesting idea.'

'What is it?' asked Lucy, but he put his finger to his lips.

'In good time, my dear, in good time. I want to think it out first, that's all.'

'The thing is,' Lucy said, 'I read a lot of detective stories and if someone has an *interesting idea* – and they don't tell anyone about it – well, they usually end up dead.'

He laughed. 'What a vivid imagination you have, my dear. Don't you worry about me. '

As she walked away, Lucy looked back over her shoulder and saw him staring into space once more, that nasty smile playing on his lips.

She went to buy milk and bread. Back at the shop, she found Toby sitting in a chair while Susan sketched.

'Keep still,' she warned him. 'It's an exercise for our class. Our teacher says it's all about tuning into the subject and I can't do that if you're fidgeting every five minutes.'

'Sorry,' said Toby. 'How much longer is it going to take, miss?'

'You can't rush these things,' said Susan, bending over her pad. 'Although apparently the Impressionists *did* dash off their paintings and put sand on their canvases and everything. I expect there's a knack to it.'

'Darling, I'm not sure Toby likes being your muse,' said Lucy.

'Toby, turn a shade to the right, will you?' Susan continued, unperturbed. 'I want to catch that shadow. You have such a striking face.'

'Thanks, miss,' said Toby, uncertainly. His hand stole up to unconsciously touch his scar, which ran behind his right eye. Lucy thought suddenly of the man who Mr Eastley had seen outside the museum. A blond man with a scar . . .

'Toby does need to work, you know,' called Mr Tollesbury, distracting Lucy from her train of thought entirely. 'We're on a deadline back here.'

'He's grumpy because of his tooth,' Lucy said.

'Coming, sir,' said Toby obediently. 'I'd better leave this for now, miss.'

The phone rang and Lucy went to answer it. 'Hello?'

There was a brief crackle and then Edward's familiar voice came down the line. 'Lucy, how are you?'

'I'm all right,' she said, feeling self-conscious with Susan listening.

'I keep leaving messages for you and you're always out,' he said.

'I've been busy,' she said. She wasn't sure why she was being so cold to Edward; he hadn't done anything wrong, other than fall in love with someone else, which was precisely what she had been telling him to do for the last two years.

'I've been thinking about you,' he said. 'I was wondering if we could have dinner in a few days. For old time's sake.'

Lucy's breath hitched but she sounded steady as she said, 'Of course. That would be lovely. Just let me know where and I'll be there.'

'Maybe I'm not cut out for this,' said Susan, tossing the sketch-book down as Lucy hung up. 'I should stick to psychiatry.'

'Or you can turn to crime,' said Lucy, looking at the portrait of Toby and pushing the thought of Mr Eastley and the man he saw out of her mind. Plenty of men in London were blond and had scars above their eye. 'Solving it, that is, with me. The inspector has given me leave to investigate – discreetly. I'm going to try and talk to Mrs Lyle.'

'Well luckily for you, I know just how to go about doing it,' said

Felix, holding out the newspaper. 'A date for Gordon Lyle's funeral in today's paper.' He looked up at Lucy over his glasses. 'The thirtieth. The wake is at his house in Chiswick.'

Lucy raised an eyebrow. 'We should go and pay our respects.'

'You mean snoop,' said Felix cheerfully. 'Just try and wait till the service is over first, will you?'

Chapter 20

On leaving Dr Lyle's office, the sergeant and inspector went straight to Somerset House. 'What are we doing here, Inspector?' said the sergeant. 'And why all the secrecy?'

'I'd like to look into something without the chief knowing,' the inspector explained. 'Has it occurred to you that there's a lot of smoke and mirrors in this case?'

'There certainly is,' said the sergeant, with a heartfelt groan. 'Every day we get at least another twenty letters, all swearing they've seen an Egyptian god stalking the streets of London.'

'Right, well let's put that aside for a minute, because I won't give up on the idea that, without any curse in the mix, it's the Society who stand to gain by Lyle and Curry's deaths. And one of them in particular.' He nodded up at the building. 'I want to check the will of the late Sir Reginald Derwent – father of Sir Hector and Sir Marcus.'

An hour later, he and the sergeant were studying the document. 'Well, well, well,' the sergeant said. 'It would seem the fortune is held in trust by Sir Marcus himself, with a yearly sum to be paid to Sir Hector on the condition that he use it *in the pursuit of ancient knowledge*. Odd sort of stipulation isn't it, sir?'

'I think Sir Reginald was an odd sort of man. Passionate about the ancient world. I assume the money was to be used to found the

Society itself, which perhaps was Sir Reginald's dream, rather than his son's, originally.'

'So, Sir Hector picked up the mantle. He founded his entire career on the study of Ancient Egypt and the Society, and he had finally seemed to triumph with the discovery of the tomb. The Society was assured funding: success and fame awaited. They brought in Dr Lyle to add some credibility . . . But then, two weeks ago, Dr Curry threatened everything, messed up Sir Hector's plans and made Lyle look like a laughing stock: Lyle was proving altogether too embarrassing for the Society. Kill Curry and Lyle, and you kill the gossip and speculation around the expedition. Sir Hector and his future career is safe.' He drew out another slip of paper. 'It seems Sir Hector isn't quite the epitome of wealthy respectability he seems. In rather deep with gambling debts. If the Society was dismantled tomorrow, his funds would end too. He would be dependent on his brother. And I doubt the chief of police would look kindly on clearing such extensive debts.'

There was silence between the two men for a few moments while they thought everything over.

'His brother is the head of Scotland Yard,' said the sergeant slowly. 'If anyone was going to orchestrate a cover-up . . .'

'The boss was very keen to write this off as suicide. He might want his brother kept out of it, without realising what part he played. Let's say Sir Hector contacted Dr Curry the night of the lecture, telling him he wanted to hear more about what happened with Dr Lyle – assured him he believed his work was stolen. We know Dr Curry got a message that night that cheered him up. What if it came from Sir Hector?'

The sergeant nodded eagerly. 'And he was regularly at the museum – he came and went as he pleased. Dr Lyle would have been completely unsuspecting when he knocked on his door yesterday morning. Dr Curry insisted he knew secrets about the Society. What if he knew about Sir Hector's gambling debts? What if Sir Hector had more than one reason to silence him?'

The two men looked at each other. 'I would rather not pursue our boss's brother as a suspect,' the inspector said. 'All the same, let's look into Sir Hector's alibi a little more, shall we?'

Chapter 21

The funeral of Dr Gordon Lyle, esteemed Egyptologist and fellow of the British Museum, was an expensive yet muted affair, with far fewer in attendance than Lucy had expected. The rumours swirling around Dr Lyle had clearly not gone away.

The vicar had spoken of Gordon Lyle's life – a young Egyptologist who had cut his teeth on digs in the north of England, before progressing to the British Museum – and then, the holy grail of every passionate Egyptologist, the discovery of an ancient tomb. An extraordinary discovery, one that would be his legacy. One that would go down in the history books.

If only Gordon Lyle had been the one who had discovered it, Lucy had thought. As it was, he was merely a common thief.

'And of course,' continued the vicar, 'Gordon Lyle was beloved of friends, family and colleagues. A devoted husband . . .'

Gordon Lyle's widow sat near the front, composed in an expensive black gown. She showed no signs of weeping. Max Bird, the journalist, had perched near the back wall of the church, writing furiously in a notebook. Mr Ahmed had concealed more than one yawn, clearly attending out of duty rather than sentiment. Mr Dakin sat near the front – still, Lucy thought, radiating self-importance. Sir Hector Derwent looked irritable. A few rows ahead she had seen the back of Mrs van Buren's head. Occasionally, the woman would turn to glance around her. She looked pale and tired.

None of them, Lucy had thought, *looked guilty*.

At last, the final hymn had finished, and people began to file out. Some stepped into waiting cars, which would carry them to the wake.

'We might as well join them,' said Lucy, ushering Susan to follow. 'After all, how often are all the suspects in a murder investigation under one roof?'

* * *

Dr Lyle's house was lavishly, if not very tastefully, furnished. It felt more like a cocktail party than a wake. Lucy wondered, as she took a cocktail from a silver tray, how much genuine grief there was in the room. Certainly, Mrs Lyle did not seem unduly bereft – she was chatting calmly enough with the vicar who had conducted the ceremony. In the corner, Max Bird was holding a glass of champagne and scrutinising the crowd.

'Who let *him* in?' said Susan.

'Who let *us* in, to be fair. Let's go talk to him,' said Lucy. 'He owes me a favour.'

'Well, Miss Darkwether,' said Max, as they approached. 'You must be almost as curious as I am. I can't imagine you were invited today, were you? Still, looks like they need to pad out the numbers. Not many here, are there? No one wants to be associated with Lyle, even now he's dead. Thanks for the tip the other day, by the way. Quite a scoop.'

'You've got some nerve,' said Susan. 'Showing up here after making up all this curse nonsense. No wonder the public are terrified.'

'I didn't make anything up,' said Max. 'I just interviewed Dr Lyle.'

'He fed you the information at first, didn't he?' said Lucy, thinking of Dr Lyle's angry phone call the week before his death. 'But then he wanted to call you off.'

Max Bird snorted. 'Said it was harming the Society's reputation, now that someone was dead. That I should put a stop to it. Well! Killing a story when it's caught the public's imagination is like trying to stop a runaway train – you can't do it. Not that I wanted to,' he added honestly. 'Sales have been through the roof. Every last inch of the front page is about the curse.' He gave a broad, satisfied smile. 'And it's going to stay that way, until they catch whoever this killer is.'

'You don't think the coverage might be hindering the police investigation? Half of London is claiming to have seen the ghost of an Egyptian king.'

Max Bird gave her a shrewd look. 'We're newspapers; we sell stories. And there's plenty here to write about. Dr Lyle was about to be sacked, did you know that?'

'No,' breathed Lucy. 'Was he really? I thought that was just gossip.'

'Nope,' said Max, looking gleeful to have been the one to share the news. 'Sir Hector was going to give him till the end of the month, to save face and attract less publicity. But Lyle was done for – academically speaking. He's being posthumously struck off the Society. The tomb won't be known as Lyle's discovery anymore.' He shook his head. 'He'll go down in history for all the wrong reasons.'

And he wasn't the only one in the Society with secrets, Lucy thought. There were questions about where Mrs van Buren had been on the morning of Dr Curry's murder – she had been seen outside Cecil Court. Sir Hector lived for the Society and Dr Curry and Dr Lyle had been about to ruin everything for him. 'Stay for one more drink,' said Lucy, pushing her glass of champagne into Max's hand, hoping she could squeeze more information out of him. 'You'll want to pay your condolences to Mrs Lyle.'

'Not exactly the picture of grief, is she?' said Susan.

Max Bird took a swig. 'Lyle burned through her money running these expeditions, then she gets wind he's having an affair with the heiress van Buren. Not surprised she cut him off, just when he was on the cusp of actually discovering something. *Then* it turns out he's been stealing someone else's research. A huge scandal.' He drained the glass. 'She's probably just sorry someone murdered him before she could. I'll wish you a good afternoon – and let me know if you get any more notes, won't you?'

'That particular deal is off, I'm afraid,' Lucy said. 'One last question. You're a journalist – well, who is *your* money on? Who's bumping them all off?'

'Ah!' said Max Bird, looking pleased. 'Now let me think. Well, I'll tell you who it *isn't* – the ghost of an Egyptian king or anyone out to avenge them. This isn't one of your mysteries you sell in your shop. No. I've covered all sorts of murders, Miss Darkwether, sordid behaviour you wouldn't believe – and the motive is always the same.'

'Which is?' asked Lucy keenly.

'Money,' he said succinctly. 'Filthy lucre. The oldest motive in the world.'

'Isn't the oldest motive revenge?' asked Susan.

Max Bird shrugged and set his glass down on an antique side table. 'If you say so. But you mark my words, follow the money, and you'll catch your man.' He strode off through the crowd.

'We should pay our respects and leave,' Susan said and they began to make their way through the room to Mrs Lyle.

'I look like a hag,' said Lucy, surveying herself in one of the gilt mirrors as they passed. 'Black is not my colour. A nice grey silk, *that* I could have pulled off. *And* I'm meeting Edward for dinner after, and I won't have time to change. Damnit.'

'Why do you care what Edward thinks?' said Susan. 'Unless you—'

'Hello, Miss Darkwether,' came a low, pleasant voice from behind them. 'You do keep popping up, don't you?'

'Mrs van Buren,' said Lucy, turning. 'I am sorry for the loss of your friend and colleague . . .'

Mrs van Buren gave the ghost of a smile. 'Oh, please Miss Darkwether. Everyone knows Dr Lyle has been thoroughly disgraced. I can't pretend to feel great grief,' she said. She glanced over Lucy's shoulder. 'Even Mrs Lyle can't pretend to that.'

Lucy followed her gaze. It was true that Mrs Lyle still looked remarkably composed, eating canapes in the corner.

'I gather you received another note on the morning of his death,' said Mrs van Buren. 'Threatening more deaths to come. How outlandish.' But Lucy caught the flash of fear in her eyes. She turned to go. 'I should make that your last drink if I were you, Miss Darkwether – I don't want Mrs Lyle's guests harassed.'

'Is she foolhardy or brave?' asked Susan, as Mrs van Buren walked away.

'Neither,' said Lucy. 'I think she's terrified, but she won't show it. Shall we have a gin and a debrief before I meet Edward?'

'Lead on, Sherlock,' Susan said. 'I'll just use the bathroom and meet you outside.'

On her way out, however, Lucy ran smack into an insignificant figure hovering in the front doorway.

'I'm sorry,' said Lucy. 'It's all that reading, I'm becoming so short-sighted, I think I might need—' She looked more closely. 'Mr Eastley, is that you?'

He had changed out of his work overalls into a shabby blue suit. 'That's right, miss. Didn't think you'd recognise me. I thought I might see you here, both of us being curious like you said. I was hoping to find you.' He took a step closer. 'I was in Dr Lyle's office the morning he was killed, did you know that?'

Lucy nodded slowly. 'The inspector mentioned your name.'

'And he was the third to die.' He looked around excitedly. 'I thought I might slip in, see if I couldn't . . . well . . .'

'Spot a murderer?' said Lucy.

He nodded, cheeks bright pink now. 'I know it's silly, miss,' he said. 'Yet I bet you're here for the same reason. Is it true you got another note, before Dr Lyle's murder? That's what the papers are saying.'

'It's true,' said Lucy. 'I got there too late, though. I was there just as the police discovered his body.'

'Gosh,' breathed Mr Eastley. 'So, you saw the crime scene.' His eyes shone longingly. 'I bet you saw all sorts of clues?'

'Did *you* see anything odd or unusual in his office that morning?' Lucy asked, dodging his comment that was more of a question.

'Nothing,' said Mr Eastley, regretfully. 'He was a tidy chap, Dr Lyle – not like that other professor over the hall, Dr Langley, his place is a right mess. Piles of papers he never wants us to touch and all sorts of things jumbled up. No, Dr Lyle keeps things shipshape. There isn't much to do in there except dust. As a matter of fact,' he went on, 'I wasn't meant to be working that day, but my manager wanted me to switch days. I was excited to see the mummy up close. I don't hold with it being there, you know. It's all wrong. What did this note say, then?'

'That more would die,' said Lucy, vaguely, not wanting to give too much away. 'Listen, Mr Eastley, I wanted to ask you about the man you saw watching the museum.'

Mr Eastley took a deep breath and launched into his narrative. 'Yes, I saw someone standing in the awning of the shop over the road, the cobbler's. He had a distinctive sort of face, miss, one I wouldn't forget. He was watching the museum. It was about eight-thirty, I remember because me and Mr Bennett had just finished up Dr Langley's office and that's when we always take our cigarette break. Mr Lyle's taxi pulled up and he got out and ran up the steps – he was always in a hurry – and that's when I saw this fellow run across the road and go up the steps too. I had to leave then and get back to work and I don't know what happened to him. Of course I didn't think much of it until afterwards.'

'Can you describe him?' said Lucy.

'Around six feet, I'd say,' said Mr Eastley. 'Fair hair, dark eyes, scar on the right cheek behind the eye, wearing a tweed cap. Some sort of overalls, a pea coat.'

Lucy swallowed. That description was excellent – and it matched Toby exactly. 'A – a scar did you say?'

'A scar right here, on the cheek,' he said firmly. 'I have a good eye for faces, like I said.' He looked at her with wistful brown eyes. 'I told the inspector about him and he said he'd asked everyone and checked it all out and no one else saw the man. I didn't like his tone. Almost like he didn't believe me. Oh well, I suppose it's only to the good. I don't want to get mixed up in anything like this.'

But the note of regret in Mr Eastley's voice made Lucy think he absolutely *did* want to be mixed up in 'all this'. Lucy considered him. The sergeant had warned her about people like Mr Eastley, who haunted crime scenes, who contacted the police thinking they had seen the killer, who bothered his sergeants with lurid descriptions of striking men with memorable features. Time wasters.

And yet.

Dark eyes, fair hair, a scar on the cheek. Overalls and a tweed cap.

Certainly, that description matched her very own bookbinding assistant. The question was, what was she going to do about it?

* * *

After she found Susan again for a drink, Lucy went directly from Chiswick to meet Edward at the Palm Tree in Soho, which was known for being one of the hottest new nightspots and for hosting a rowdy and mixed crowd. Lucy had been the one to suggest it to Edward, partly out of mischief – he had always been so staid. They lingered over bad cocktails, then danced.

'I'd forgotten what a good dancer you are, Edward,' Lucy said. It was true; they moved comfortably together.

'And you. All those lessons with Madam paid off. Remember those? Your mother would organise them every summer.'

Lucy groaned. 'What a blight on the holiday they were.' She tilted her head back so she could look him in the eye. 'Let's not ignore the elephant in the room. When is this wedding of yours?'

'Helen says we need to be sensible and wait – she has a five-year business plan for the ranch.'

'A five-year business plan! How romantic,' said Lucy, resting her head against his chest again.

She felt his rumble of laughter against her ear. 'Come on,' he said. 'Let's eat, shall we? I've reserved a table at Wiltons – it's a bit dull, but I thought we could chat properly there. It would be quiet at least.' A woman sitting at a table near them, whose argument with her companion had become increasingly heated, rose and tossed her drink in his face. Edward flinched. 'This place is a bit too exciting for me.'

'Same old Edward,' said Lucy fondly. 'Let's go – I want to talk to you properly too.'

They did not, though, find themselves chatting much over the meal. The hushed surroundings constrained them almost as much as the chaos of the Palm Tree had. Lucy was distracted, her mind running along other channels – of dusty archaeological digs, hot sun and ancient curses – and Edward, never the most animated, followed her lead. They gossiped about old friends and London haunts and then they fell silent. Had she and Edward, who had known each other their whole lives, Lucy thought uneasily, run out of things to talk about?

Not at all, she told herself. We're simply comfortable enough to sit in silence.

They were finishing their coffee when Lucy looked up and saw a familiar, although unexpected, figure crossing the room. 'Well, well,' she said. 'It's Inspector Hayes – I didn't think he dined in restaurants like this.'

'And you call *me* a snob,' said Edward. 'Where do you expect him to be – the officer's caff?'

'He doesn't seem like a restaurant type,' said Lucy. 'I thought he'd be above eating somehow. Although I did once see him eat a sandwich.'

Lucy watched as the inspector took his seat opposite a middle-aged man with a fine white moustache. 'I recognise the other man too,' she said. 'That's Sir Marcus Derwent, head of Scotland Yard – my father knows him. His brother is Sir Hector, from the Egyptian Society. Perhaps our inspector is debriefing Sir Marcus about the case.' She put down her napkin. 'Let's go and say hello.'

'I'll wait here,' said Edward, looking uncomfortable. 'This isn't a game, Lucy.'

'So people keep telling me,' said Lucy. 'And yet our killer thinks it's a game, doesn't he? Writing his notes, dropping his clues. Maybe someone needs to play his game to stop him.'

She walked across the plush carpet towards where the inspector sat, with Sir Marcus. His eyes widened only slightly when he saw her. She ignored him and smiled winningly at Sir Marcus.

'Do excuse me for interrupting. You won't remember me at all, sir,' she said, 'but you used to visit my parents a lot when I was growing up.'

'Lucy Darkwether,' said Sir Marcus, standing and giving Lucy a hearty embrace. He was a bluff, military type who had served only briefly but incorporated it so entirely into his personality that Lucy recalled she and John used to call him The General. 'Why, you must have been nine years old when I saw you last.' He pinched her cheek and Lucy flinched. He had always done that and she had always hated it. 'You look wonderful, my dear. The spit of your dear mother. How's your father?'

'Exhausted by Mother's parties – and by Mother in general.'

'Ha! Poor man, poor man. There's a reason I never married. Sit down for a moment, won't you? This is Inspector Hayes.'

'The inspector and I know each other,' said Lucy, slipping into a seat a waiter had set out. 'He's investigating the murder on my doorstep.'

'Miss Darkwether believes she's an amateur detective,' said the inspector. 'Thinks she can put us dolts on the force straight on this mummy business.'

Sir Marcus laughed. 'Of course, you always did love a good story, Lucy, I remember that. Always with your head in a book, she was, Hayes. The inspector and I were just discussing the case in fact. These notes, you know – the work of a maniac, who has got lucky twice. But we need to start rounding up some suspects or the public will get frightened – and then we'll have a mass panic on our hands.'

'Or,' the inspector said stubbornly, 'we should be looking closer to home. At the members of the Society.'

Sir Marcus tutted and shook his head. 'We need to stop bothering them,' he said. 'These notes, that's where the case is.'

'I'm afraid I've been pestering the inspector dreadfully for information,' Lucy said. 'He's been getting annoyed with me.'

'Oh, pshaw,' said Sir Marcus. He smiled fondly at Lucy. 'I can't imagine anyone getting annoyed with *you*, my dear.'

Lucy was sure she could hear the inspector's jaw clenching.

'He even thought *I* might be a person of interest at one point,' Lucy said, unable to resist. 'Thought I might have staged a nasty prank on poor Mr Dakin that turned deadly.'

Sir Marcus burst out laughing; the inspector looked unamused. 'Person of interest! You're barking up the wrong tree there, my boy. Why, I was at school with Miss Darkwether's father, and we used to have quite the time. Excuse me while I make a phone call – Hayes, you can tell Miss Darkwether anything she wants.' He winked at the inspector. 'Within reason, of course.'

Sir Marcus bustled off and Lucy ordered a drink. Inspector Hayes looked at her stonily.

'Friends in high places, I see,' he said. 'No wonder you thought you could argue your way into the investigation. I suppose the normal rules don't apply if your father was at school with the head of Scotland Yard.'

'I do feel a bit ashamed,' admitted Lucy. 'But I wanted to tell *you* something. I went to the wake and saw Mrs van Buren. I think she's absolutely terrified she's next, which speaks to a guilty conscience doesn't it? I heard there are stories about her – that she was all alone with her wealthy, criminal husband when he died. Did you know that?'

The inspector gave a nod. 'She was alone with him in the house when he died. He was a heavy drinker and drug user. A small quantity of cocaine was found beside his body. The doctor said he died of heart failure. An unpleasant scandal, but nothing that directly implicated her.'

'She inherited all his ill-gotten money,' said Lucy. 'Inspector, what if she believes she *deserves* to be punished? That would explain her strange behaviour. She believes the curse will get her, whatever she does. The question is, why is she so guilty? Is it because of her husband's death – or a more recent murder?'

'Regardless, it won't be a curse that gets her,' the inspector said. 'Sir Marcus isn't taking any chances with her – or any of them. We've got men posted outside her flat round the clock. The sergeant is trying to persuade her to leave the city. Anything else?'

'Mr Bird said Mrs van Buren may have taken a detour to Cecil Court on the morning of the murder, is that true too?'

'It's looking likely, but she's refusing to elaborate. A taxi driver claims he dropped her off just after eleven-fifteen. And she was at the lecture at the museum by quarter to twelve. One of my men timed the journey in a taxi. It's cutting it very fine if she also had to break into Dakin's, kill Curry, then make it to the museum.'

'Mr Eastley was at the wake too. Cropping up again, which is interesting isn't it? He told me all about the mysterious man who was watching the museum.'

'A man who no one else saw. Who seems to have vanished into thin air the moment he went up the museum steps. We asked the security guards and staff. No one went into Dr Lyle's office and certainly not a six-foot blond with a tweed cap. I'm starting to think Mr Eastley just likes to involve himself.'

There was, Lucy decided, no need to tell the inspector the description might have easily described Toby. Her shy bookbinding clerk could surely have nothing to do with the killings and, as the inspector said, Mr Eastley was a busybody.

'Why are you having dinner with Sir Marcus?' she asked abruptly.

For a moment, she thought the inspector was going to tell her it was none of her business. Then, reluctantly, he said, 'Sir Hector is refusing any further interviews. Which is making things difficult. The sergeant and I did some digging, and his fortune is conditional on the perpetuation of the Society. He gained something out of both deaths – the scandal associated with Curry and Lyle went away. But the chief wants this sewn up and his brother kept out of it. Wants us to focus exclusively on the notes.'

'In short, he wants an arrest, and he wants one now?'

'At any cost.' The inspector sighed and pushed away his drink. 'He thinks we're dealing with a madman who should be easy enough to catch. As though he's walking around with a sign on his back that says *killer*. It doesn't help that half of London is showing up at Scotland Yard to tell me they've seen Isis or Osiris or whoever it is lurking in their woodshed.' He gave her a rather disarming smile. 'Forgive me, Miss Darkwether. This case is proving more frustrating than I had at first imagined. I too underestimated our killer.'

'The question is, Inspector, are you going to be able to investigate the members of the Society as you would like, if your boss wants you to look in another direction entirely?'

'What would you suggest?' he asked. The hard lines of his face were softer in the candlelight.

Lucy thought for a moment. 'It's so frustrating!' she cried at last. 'There *are* human motives here – Sir Archibald's death benefitted the museum. Dr Curry's benefitted Dr Lyle. Dr Lyle's benefitted his wife, who knew about his affair, as well as Sir Hector and Mrs van Buren, who got to protect the Society.' She thought for a moment. 'If only you had someone who moved in those circles,' she said slowly. 'Who could do some digging without Sir Marcus knowing.'

The inspector smiled at her. 'If only I did.'

Chapter 22

allo people,' said Lucy, breezing into her drawing room. 'What a shocking night. Cocktails?'

It was Friday. The rain lashed and branches scraped against Lucy's windows. She had gathered her staff at her flat after work. Mr Tollesbury and Susan had joined her for dinner many times and knew the flat well, but Felix had always politely yet firmly declined any invitations, and Toby had never been before. He sat perched awkwardly on her sofa and looking around at the cluttered room. The mantlepiece was stuffed with invitations and candles and paper flowers, the sofas strewn with silk cushions and there was an abundance of plants, spilling out of bowls and pots, giving the impression of a greenhouse. A gramophone played a record and Mrs Thorpe had brought in the drinks trolley. Lucy began to mix the drinks herself.

'I'll take one,' said Felix, running a hand distractedly through his hair. 'It's been a trying day. Although your illicit orders are selling like hot cakes. Shall I make another order, Lucy?'

'Please,' Lucy told him. She could see the money pouring in – but whether it would be enough to win her bet, she had no idea.

'It's a bit stressful, Lucy. I know it was my idea, but the strain is getting to me. Lady Lucas has requested several copies, and she can't collect until Tuesday. It's like I'm sitting on stolen goods.'

'You're doing a marvellous job coping under pressure,' Lucy reassured him. 'Have you dipped into the novel yourself, out of interest?'

'Of course I have darling,' said Felix, winking at her. 'Very earthy.'

'Save me a copy, if there are any to spare,' said Lucy, handing him a glass. 'Here, Toby, you must have a drink too. I make a mean martini.'

'Thanks,' said Toby, accepting a glass. He sniffed it cautiously, took a sip and coughed. 'It's strong,' he gasped, wiping his watering eyes.

'That's the point,' said Lucy, taking a seat.

Susan took a drink but Mr Tollesbury declined. 'I'd rather keep my wits about me until I find out what you're up to, my dear,' he said. 'I can tell by the look in your eye that there's *something*. It's the look you'd give me when you just *had* to have an essay extension for very urgent reasons.'

She grinned at him. 'Fair cop. I've asked you all to come here because I get the strong impression that Sir Marcus is scuppering the police investigation. He doesn't want his Society pals interrogated, despite them all having a juicy motive for the murders of Dr Curry and Dr Lyle. I was thinking I would have to interview everyone myself, when I realised I was ignoring the talent under my own roof,' said Lucy. 'I need your help – division of labour and all that.'

She looked round at them. Felix shifted uneasily. Mr Tollesbury wore a worried frown, Toby looked still more hunted, and Susan gnawed at her lip.

'I'm not sure,' said Mr Tollesbury at last, 'why we're getting involved in this at all.'

'You're thinking that Dr Lyle wasn't a nice man so why should we bother ourselves,' said Lucy. 'But murder is murder. The notes are coming to me, and I want to know why.'

There was a pause and then Susan sighed. 'Oh, of course I'll help,' she said. 'How can I resist those eyes?'

'Speak for yourself,' said Felix coldly. 'I can resist them fine. I don't want a knife in the back, thank you. Shouldn't we leave this to the handsome inspector?'

Lucy shook her head. 'The higher ups are taking over. Which is in itself suspicious. Why is Sir Marcus so keen to shut down any investigation into the Society and his own brother? Sir Hector certainly needs investigating – either as a suspect or as our next potential victim. Unfortunately, he wasn't forthcoming with me, a mere woman. Mr Tollesbury, I thought perhaps you might try instead?'

Mr Tollesbury sighed dramatically, but Lucy knew he wouldn't take much persuasion. 'If you wish,' he said. 'Hard to imagine him as a killer, though.'

'I know,' said Lucy. 'But then someone has to be. There's also Mrs van Buren. She had a motive to kill both Lyle and Curry. She was seen outside Cecil Court on the morning of the murder but denies it.'

'A knife that sharp – it could have been a woman,' said Susan thoughtfully.

'Either way, I think she is frightened, but she won't leave the city. Could you speak to her as well, try and find out more – *and* persuade her of the potential danger?'

Mr Tollesbury bowed his head. 'I shall try.'

'Susan, I would like you to approach this from the psychological angle once more. A more detailed profile on our killer, if you please.'

Susan sighed. 'I've told you already Lucy, it's an inexact science.'

'Look.' Lucy held out a book, showing a suited man frowning down at a piece of paper. 'This is by a man called Durand – he used psychological profiling to track down Le Taureau.'

'Who's that?' asked Mr Tollesbury blankly.

'The century's most prolific serial killer,' said Toby, looking interested at last. 'They called him Le Taureau in the press.'

'Right, Toby knows his true crime. Le Taureau cut a swathe of terror throughout the poorer districts of Paris. Nine victims, I think. Eventually, this man Durand had tripped up an innocuous-seeming suspect – seemingly no more than a bystander – in a series of lies that resulted in their dramatic confession. Anyway, can't you have a shot? Look at our pool of suspects and see if there are any inconsistencies that might point to a bigger lie. Any psychological traits that might indicate a killer . . .'

'All right,' said Susan, scribbling. 'I'll do my best. You want to know if any of our Society fits a profile?'

'Yes please. And talk to Sergeant West – he's much chattier than the inspector. Felix, I'd like you to go and talk to the museum cleaners. And this Professor Langley across the hall – did he really hear nothing at all? People always tell *you* things – you have a disarming kind of face.'

'I too will do my best,' said Felix. 'But I'm not happy about any of this.'

'Toby, you go with him,' said Lucy. She added, thinking of Mr Eastley's mysterious figure, 'You – you haven't been to the museum before, have you?'

She thought a faint flush came to Toby's cheeks, but she couldn't be sure. 'Never, miss.'

Lucy chewed her lip. It was ridiculous to think of Toby spying on the museum. Why on earth should he?

'What will *you* be doing, while we're all running around doing our errands?' Mr Tollesbury asked.

'I'm going to visit the newest grieving widow,' said Lucy. 'Mrs Lyle. She has a terrific motive for killing Lyle – he'd spent all her money, *and* he was reportedly having an affair with Mrs van Buren.' She frowned. 'Unfortunately, I don't see why she'd murder Dr Curry.'

'She looks so calm,' said Susan. Her eyes lit up. 'Although she might be the sort who bottles it all up and then snaps. Very interesting psychologically.'

'And I'm going to speak to Dakin again. He was very strange the other day, dropping hints.'

'What sort of hints?' asked Mr Tollesbury, leaning forward.

'Implying he knows something. I doubt he does, really – but all the same, this could put him in danger. In books, it's always the one who goes around hinting who winds up dead.'

'I can think of worse things,' said Felix. 'In fact, I'll give the killer a hand if Dakin's next.'

PART TWO

Chapter 23

Mr Tollesbury had arranged to meet Sir Hector Derwent at his club. He had made the appointment by mentioning his erstwhile position as professor at Oxford and alluding to various pieces in his personal collection that he wanted to run past Sir Hector as an amateur expert in the antiquities. An appeal to his ego, his life's passion, and the old school tie. It was duplicitous, but, Mr Tollesbury thought, needs must.

'Hello, old chap,' said Sir Hector, standing and shaking hands across the table. 'Nice to see you again. I thought I recognised your name. Eton, wasn't it?'

Mr Tollesbury, who had attended his local grammar school till he was fourteen, smiled, cursing Lucy for forcing him to tell such lies. 'Of course,' he said, in his most cultivated tones. 'I thought *you* seemed familiar – I'd have been a good few years ahead of you though. Did you have that awful Latin teacher, what was his name . . .'

Sir Hector needed no more encouragement and, to Mr Tollesbury's relief, launched into a detailed account of his time at Eton, which seemed to have mostly involved bullying younger boys. The two men ordered steak pie and dumplings. Then Sir Hector sat back in his chair and said, 'So you want some advice, do you? What have you got for me then?'

Mr Tollesbury described his fictional antique pieces in detail. When he had finished, Sir Hector held forth in turn for the next forty minutes, uninterrupted, with his views.

As he talked, Mr Tollesbury studied him. A man who looked intimidating – dark brows, a forceful, carrying voice, broad shoulders, all the trappings of wealth and power. Passionate about the Society. But perhaps, underneath all that, not very bright.

'Quite shocking, this business with poor Lyle,' Mr Tollesbury said, when Sir Hector had paused. He took a sip of the wine, which was too rich for him. 'Although I'd been hearing all sorts of rumours about him.'

Sir Hector's heavy brows descended. 'Lyle's death may have been a blessing in disguise,' he said shortly. 'What sort of rumours?'

'I try not to listen to gossip,' said Mr Tollesbury loftily. 'But there were all those stories that he stole research and then fired the chap. And there's talk of an affair . . .'

Sir Hector let out a noise of disgust. 'Everyone thought the sun shone from Lyle's backside. *I* never trusted the chap! Oily sort of fellow, always talking on and on. *Not* out of the top drawer, you know. But the board loved him, so did the public – it's how we got hold of funding. And his wife would always support the expeditions. He got too damned cocky though. Started to think the Society was nothing without him! When his wife cut the purse strings – well, we were stuck.' He forked a piece of kidney into his mouth. 'Luckily that American lady came through, Mrs van Buren. *Her* background though . . . her husband was nothing short of a criminal. I tell you, the Society needs some fresh blood.'

Mr Tollesbury nodded sympathetically. 'You must have worked so hard to build the Society,' he said. 'To fund the expedition. You unearthed what will surely be one of the greatest discoveries of the twentieth century.'

'And those fools were about to ruin it all! Rumours and scandal and gossip. First this Dr Curry, then Lyle.' He swirled his wine glass with a sour expression. 'Better off without the lot of them.' He leaned forward. 'My brother is heading up the investigation, you know. Says he doesn't care who swings for this, so long as they catch someone soon. *I* certainly don't. This letter-writer, stalking about with a blade – whoever it is, they did me a favour.' He frowned. '*I've* got to be careful, of course, if there really is a maniac on the loose. But the Yard has assured me of complete protection.'

'I suppose the killer believes he's doing the right thing,' said Mr Tollesbury lightly. 'Avenging the king's disturbance. Many believe that he should have remained in Egypt, you know.'

'Only a fool would think that,' said Sir Hector. His face was the colour of his wine now and his voice was slurred. He lit a cigar with difficulty. 'The pursuit of knowledge, you know – that's all there is, the most important thing.' He gave a bark of a laugh. 'Although given the nightmare we've had since we found the tomb, maybe I *do* believe in the curse.'

'Really?' asked Mr Tollesbury, wiping his eyes behind his glasses. The smoke from the cigar was making them water.

'First that old fool died, Sir Archibald,' said Sir Hector viciously. 'Then it turned out Lyle was feeding stories to the press. And then Dr Curry accused the Society of fraud.'

'That must have been embarrassing,' said Mr Tollesbury sympathetically.

'Embarrassing! My god! I was furious. If that had got out – if the board had taken it seriously – we would have had our funding cut. The Society might never have been able to return to Egypt!' His fist clenched around his glass and Mr Tollesbury became aware once more of the force and physicality of the man. 'Curry *had* to be stopped.'

'And someone did stop him,' said Mr Tollesbury quietly. 'The very next night.'

'Yes – yes.' Sir Hector fell silent, suddenly sombre. 'Yes, they did.'

'Lyle too,' went on Mr Tollesbury. 'Two people who had brought disgrace on the expedition were silenced, forever. No one need ever find out. As you say, whoever killed them did you a favour.'

Sir Hector had gone from rich puce to pale. He set down his cigar. 'Now, look here,' he said uncertainly, the bluster fading from his voice. 'Whoever killed them is clearly unstable. If you think – if you're suggesting . . .'

'I'm not suggesting anything,' said Mr Tollesbury, cleaning his glasses on his napkin. 'I'm merely . . . noticing how convenient their deaths were, to you and the Society. And your brother is the head of Scotland Yard. If anyone could successfully cover up a crime, it would be the two of you. As you say, you don't care who swings for it so long as it goes away.' He stood. 'Thank you for lunch, Sir Hector, and for your help. It has been most enlightening.'

When he left, Sir Hector no longer looked like a forceful and overpowering man. Instead, he had the scared look of a bully receiving a taste of his own medicine.

Outside, taking in deep, cleansing breaths of chill air, Mr Tollesbury glanced at this watch and saw that he would still have time to see Mrs van Buren that afternoon. He shook his head. Yes, a foolish man, Sir Hector Derwent , he thought – and perhaps also a dangerous one.

* * *

When he reached Ashbourne Square, Mr Tollesbury cast an eye around the square. Elegant, quiet, moneyed. His sharp eyes took in two plainclothes officers watching the house, one smoking a cigarette and the other pretending to read a newspaper. He was certain they had noticed him. Well, he had nothing to hide.

He was received by a dignified butler to whom he gave his card. He would not bother with a fake background this time; he did not get the impression it was worth lying to Mrs van Buren. He dusted a marble statue of Psyche while he waited, before being led upstairs into the drawing room.

He shared Lucy's first impressions – that it was a beautiful room and a pleasure for anyone with an interest in the antiquities. Mrs van Buren clearly had the soul of a true collector. It made him even more curious about the woman herself.

'Mr Tollesbury?' she asked, turning. She was frowning down at his card. 'Of Cecil Court Books. Your name is familiar to me, but I can't place it.'

'I work in antiquities,' he explained. 'I have consulted with the museum once or twice.'

Her brow cleared. 'Of course. You wrote that monograph on the Hans Sloane collection.'

'That was me,' said Mr Tollesbury, pleased that his modest work had been recognised. He nodded to the cabinet beside the fireplace, where there sat a small ushabti. 'This is exquisite.'

Moving deliberately, she took a pair of white gloves and unlocked the pretty glass cabinet. She drew out the piece and handed it to him. He sat with it at a low table and turned it to the light.

'It is in immaculate condition,' he said, admiring the object.

'It certainly is,' she said. 'I have another in my bedroom that is really extraordinary, I shall show you.' She gave him a half-smile. 'Cecil Court Books? That girl sent you didn't she – Lucy Darkwether. She has a bee in her bonnet about this curse business and won't leave it alone – or *me* alone, for that matter.'

'She is afraid for good reason,' said Mr Tollesbury, gently setting down the piece. 'Three people have died. She wants to convince you of the very real danger.'

'Three people?' Her voice was calm, but Mr Tollesbury noticed her convulsive swallow. 'You – you also believe that Sir Archibald Drake died an unnatural death?'

'It's hard not to wonder,' he said.

The words burst out of her as though she had been brooding on them for some time. 'None of this makes sense! For a start, the idea that Ancient Egyptians believed in exerting revenge against those who disturbed their tombs is exaggerated. That's largely a myth of our own making, here in the West. It seems an odd way to protect the interests of a dead king. And all those silly trappings, jumbled together – the red ochre and furs and the figurine. It's not ritual – it's a spectacle!'

Mr Tollesbury bowed his head. 'That is all true – you are a scholar, Mrs van Buren, and a sensible woman. And yet . . .'

'And yet,' she said, broodingly. 'And yet – the tomb has power, Mr Tollesbury. I don't believe that we should have moved the king after all. Maybe this is our punishment.'

'Do you believe the Society needed punishing?' asked Mr Tollesbury gently.

She gave a harsh laugh. 'Oh yes. Sir Archibald was a pig-headed old fool, with more money than sense. Dr Curry was obsessed with finding the tomb for no other reason than his own glory. Lyle might have fooled me for a time, but he was a liar who used people. Me, Dr Curry, countless others. Sir Hector is a bully. The whole expedition was full of fools who deserved retribution.'

'And you?' asked Mr Tollesbury in a low voice. 'What had *you* done, that you would deserve to be punished?'

A shadow crossed her face, then she gave another brittle laugh. 'Thousands of things, I expect,' she said. 'Can I tell you something, Mr Tollesbury? And you'll promise not to tell the police?'

'Of course,' he said gently.

'I did try to stop it though, you know.' Her voice was small and vulnerable now, in contrast to her previous poise. 'I admit that I was frightened by the story, of a curse. Sir Archibald's death had shaken me. And I knew that what we had done in Egypt was wrong – both in removing the mummy and in our treatment of Dr Curry. I came to Cecil Court the morning of the exhibition. I thought I might be able to speak to Dakin, to convince him to call it off. That to flaunt the mummy in an exhibition was too dangerous. But he had already left.' Her brow creased. 'At least . . .'

'At least?' said Mr Tollesbury sharply, leaning forwards.

'At least, I thought, at first, I could hear someone moving about inside. When I knocked, though, there was silence. I waited for a while, then I left.'

'Did you hear anything else?' asked Mr Tollesbury urgently. 'Anything that could be a clue as to who was inside?' For surely, he thought, what Mrs van Buren had overheard that morning was the murder of Dr Curry.

She thought a moment. 'I thought I heard . . . *laughing*,' she said. 'Only I can't have done. Dr Curry was hardly laughing as he was being murdered, was he?'

Mr Tollesbury sat back. 'No,' he said thoughtfully. 'I suppose not. My dear lady – are you sure you shouldn't go to the police with this?'

'I shan't tell them anything,' she said decisively. 'I know better than to get more mixed up with the police. That inspector suspects me already – I was seen. But they haven't much proof to go on. I made a call to Sir Hector, and he's told his brother to call off the police. Money talks, Mr Tollesbury.'

They sat in silence for a minute, while Mr Tollesbury wondered what to do. Would Mrs van Buren really insist on keeping quiet about what she had heard? Or might she be persuaded to speak? 'You've a beautiful house,' he said, changing the subject, hoping it might relax her while he came to a decision.

'It was my late husband's,' said Mrs van Buren.

'I lost my wife – and my daughter,' he said. 'It was many years ago, but that pain of grief, it doesn't really go away. I do sympathise.'

'Don't waste sympathy on me,' said Mrs van Buren, a slight curl to her lip. 'My husband wasn't a good man, Mr Tollesbury, although he made a great deal of money. He died because of his own sins and appetites. Your loss is far greater than mine.' She rose abruptly and went to the window. 'I have also done wicked things, I'm afraid, in the pursuit of money. If this ridiculous curse should punish anyone, perhaps it should be me. But I have tried to spend my fortune wisely and create something beautiful.'

Punished. So, Lucy's theory was correct. 'You have succeeded,' he said gently. 'I confess I could spend days here, looking through your collection. Do you live here alone?'

'My sister Amelia has the downstairs apartment,' said Mrs van Buren. 'She doesn't come up here much – she dislikes the *clutter*, as she calls it.' She smiled wryly. 'She has decorated her own apartment in quite a different style.' She stood. 'Thank you for listening to me, Mr Tollesbury. And – can I ask you to pass Miss Darkwether a message?'

'Of course,' he said, realising that the interview was at an end.

'If the curse reached Sir Archibald Drake in Egypt and Dr Curry and Dr Lyle in Bloomsbury, what could I possibly do to stop it? Please tell Miss Darkwether to stop worrying. I accept my fate.'

The professor sighed. 'I suppose if that's what you believe, then there's nothing more to say. But I do not believe you need punishing, Mrs van Buren. I prefer to believe that everyone can be redeemed.'

'That,' she said with a smile, 'is because you don't know how wicked I have been. Now, shall I fetch the shabti? It really is quite extraordinary.'

Chapter 24

hile Mr Tollesbury was dining with Sir Hector, Felix and Toby strode up the steps of the British Museum, past the front desk and a guard reading a magazine, towards the back stairs which led to the staff and professors' offices.

'No one has even asked what we're doing here. A child could break in,' said Felix indignantly, stopping and looking about. 'Where's all the security? Lyle was only murdered last week!'

'There's two coppers by the back stairs,' said Toby, assessing the figures shrewdly. 'And that fellow there, with the handbook? That's another. They'll have clocked us all right. Come on, it's up here.'

They hurried on up the stairs towards the staff section and stopped before a wooden door that was ajar. Felix peered at the worn brass nameplate. 'Professor Langley – this is it. And Dr Lyle's office was opposite.'

They turned to look at Dr Lyle's office door, which was shut and, they realised after trying the handle, locked. There were holes where a nameplate had been removed.

'I could pick the lock,' said Toby. Felix looked sternly at him and his ears went pink. 'If you want.'

Felix shook his head. 'I must hear more about your idyllic rural upbringing some time. You can spot a plain-clothes copper at twenty paces *and* pick locks?'

Toby shrugged evasively. 'I picked things up here and there.'

'Well, I don't think Lucy would want us to break in. Besides, she saw all there was to see. We'll talk to Dr Langley instead.' He raised his hand and knocked on the door.

Professor Langley appeared to be a befuddled professor out of central casting – dishevelled, with a straggling beard, smeared horn-rimmed glasses, wearing a tweed suit with missing buttons and a tie stained with what might have been soup. A handkerchief protruded from one worn sleeve. *These academics*, Felix thought, *could do with smartening up a bit*.

Professor Langley accepted their appearance at his door with delight and forced cups of weak tea in filthy, chipped cups on them both. He didn't question why they were there; he seemed merely happy to have humans to speak to. Two tortoiseshell cats wound around Felix's ankles.

'I have some biscuits in here somewhere,' the professor said, rummaging in a cluttered drawer. 'Or some fruit cake. I'm sure there's something.' He peered at a label. 'No, that's fish.'

'We don't need anything, really,' said Felix, picking cat hair from his trousers. He took out Susan's sketchpad, which he had taken along to make notes in. 'We wanted to speak to you about the tragic death across the—'

'Ah, tragic, is it?' cried Dr Langley, chuckling. 'You young people have the modern idea of death. Why, the Ancient Egyptians believed that death was merely a continuation of life. The afterlife was not much different from the world they inhabited, so death was no tragedy but rather a transition . . .'

At length, he spoke about Egyptian burial practices and ideas on life after death and how they differed from the Christian tradition. He segued without pausing to the parlous state of research funding. He unearthed a packet of rich tea biscuits and began to eat them while still talking. Felix struggled in vain to stem the flow while Toby quietly drank his tea and allowed one of the cats to perch on his knee.

'We came,' Felix broke in desperately at last when Professor Langley momentarily drew breath, 'because we wanted to ask you a few questions about Dr Lyle's murder.'

'Oh, you knew Lyle, did you?' Professor Langley asked, looking at him with watery blue eyes. He took a mouthful of stale biscuit, dropping crumbs down his front. 'In the field yourself?'

'In a way,' said Felix, unblushingly. 'I'm *full* of admiration for what you do in the pursuit of knowledge. What was Dr Lyle like as a colleague?'

'Man was a fool,' said Langley, with a surprising cackle. 'He was good at talking the talk. Not above casting an eye at other people's notes, if you know what I mean.'

'So, the rumours about his stealing Dr Curry's research . . .' Felix let his sentence trail off meaningfully.

'I heard them arguing one day,' Professor Langley said. 'Dr Curry seemed upset, and Dr Lyle was talking him down. Saying he would *tell everyone the truth in good time*, he wanted to be certain the research was correct first, secure funding and all that. Wouldn't be surprised if he convinced Dr Curry to lead them to the tomb, promising him he would get credit for it in the end – and then reneged on his promise the minute he had a glimpse of Egyptian gold.' He laughed again. 'Nasty piece of work. Day to day I didn't speak to him much. His classes were very popular, of course. *I* have to work to drum up much interest in my class on the Predynastic period. They have me teaching *undergraduates*. If I had found a mummy's tomb, now!' He sighed again. 'Yes, Lyle was bound for big things – till it all came tumbling down. It all came out at the inquest, didn't it? The Society will collapse next, mark my words. Can't survive a scandal like that – the funders will be off like rats deserting a sinking ship.'

'Did you see anyone go into Dr Lyle's office on the morning of the murder?' asked Felix.

'I already told the police, my boy – not a soul. Now, if it was *last* week! Last Thursday morning I think it was, because I remember it was before the department meeting, there was a very suspicious chap here, roughly dressed, not the sort you see in the museum. Standing right outside Dr Lyle's door with his back to me. I said hello to him, and he just grunted, very rudely, then turned on his heel and left.' His eyes widened. 'Do you think he was . . . casing the joint, as they say?'

'Could well be,' said Felix. 'But on the morning of his death, nothing?'

'Nothing. Two or three cleaners, but that's it. Are you sure you won't have a biscuit?'

Felix took a biscuit with every appearance of pleasure. 'So, you saw the cleaners enter . . .'

'Oh yes, saw the lot of 'em go in, two or three – but they'd left his office by just gone eight, well before Dr Lyle even arrived. I know because they came over the hall and did mine. I always watch them like a hawk, you know, in case they disturb my papers. I have a system.' The professor extended a hand and Felix and Toby looked respectfully at the drifts of paper and cups of cold coffee covering the desk in what seemed like complete chaos. 'Dr Lyle starts later than me, got here about eight-thirty. They'd gone downstairs by then.'

'And after that, no one? No one brought him tea or anything like that?'

Professor Langley indicated a gas ring in the corner. 'We make our own tea and coffee. If we want anything else, we go to the canteen. They do a soup with a roll, for a shilling. It's going up next month though, they said, which seems most unfair when—'

'It does indeed!' broke in Felix warmly. 'Did you exchange words with Dr Lyle that morning?'

'I stuck my head out when I heard him coming down the corridor,' said the professor, recalling. 'I said good morning and told him I'd read a piece about the mummy and how it was cursing everyone! I thought Dr Lyle might find it amusing, but he didn't seem to, he cut me off and said he had work to do. He looked to be in a filthy mood. He shut his door.' Dr Langley added, mournfully, 'but then he always shuts his door.'

I can understand why, thought Felix. He felt a flicker of sympathy for the late Dr Lyle.

'So once the cleaners had left his office just after eight, no one came in or out,' said Felix. *Which was impossible*, he thought. Someone *had* gone in and hit Dr Lyle over the head, cut his throat, and come back out again. The professor must have simply missed them.

'Not till the police arrived,' said Dr Langley. 'It was quite a shock, when they came running in. Nothing like this has ever happened here.' He crumpled up the empty packet of biscuits. 'If you ask me, it's not a bad thing.'

'Not a bad thing Dr Lyle *died*?' asked Felix, startled.

'Well, that's perhaps a little far. But that expedition was bad news from the start.' The professor shook his head. 'Hubris, you know, it gets you in the end. I don't fancy it myself. If it had been Anatolia – Turkey, as they're calling it now – I might have been tempted . . .'

At last, Felix and Toby managed to escape from the stale little room, with Felix offering profuse thanks, and left Dr Langley to his work. They stood in the corridor taking in deep breaths of air.

'Phew!' whispered Toby. 'He's a talker, isn't he?'

'He certainly is. I could imagine Dr Lyle murdering *him*, just for some quiet. But it hasn't got us any further forward. The cleaners left Dr Lyle's office at eight to clean Dr Langley's, and both men were downstairs smoking before the time Dr Lyle even arrived. And no one else went in or out.'

Toby scratched his head. 'That's not possible,' he said. 'Is it?'

'Of course it's not,' said Felix briskly. 'The old boy was busy with his bits of paper and didn't notice the killer. He was shortsighted too, did you notice those thick glasses? Unfortunate that he was the only possible witness, but there you go. Let's go talk to the security staff.'

The head of museum security was a burly man with a defensive air. 'I told the police already, I was having my tea when Dr Lyle was killed,' Mr Herbert snapped. 'We can't be expected to search everyone on the off chance they're going to murder someone, can we?'

'Of course you can't,' said Felix soothingly. 'How on earth could you have known that such an outrageous thing would happen on such an ordinary morning?'

'Well, quite,' said Mr Herbert, somewhat mollified.

'So, no one looked suspicious?'

'Between us, half of this lot are off their rocker,' Mr Herbert said confidingly. 'Muttering to themselves about some bit of old pottery or dust. Nothing was any stranger than *normal*. Lyle was in a terrible mood. Plenty of rumours he was for the chop – from his job, I mean.'

'And the cleaners on shift that morning – they didn't see anything?'

'The sergeant spoke to them both. It was Eastley and Bennett upstairs that morning – I think Eastley is still here now, you could catch him. He's already told the police everything though. He'll be in the staff room.' Mr Herbert smirked. 'Fancies himself as smart as one of the professors, he does.'

'Mr Eastley is that chap who keeps cropping up,' said Felix to Toby in an undertone, as they headed out. 'Shall we speak to him anyway?'

'You go,' said Toby. 'I need a smoke.' He looked around, looking, Felix thought, rather tense. 'This place gives me the creeps,' he added.

'Are you all right?' asked Felix. 'You've gone a bit pale.'

'Dr Lyle died here, didn't he?' said Toby. He swallowed. 'Gives me the creeps,' he said again. He patted his pocket and took out a cigarette. 'I'll be all right after some fresh air. See you outside.'

Felix found Mr Eastley folding away his overalls in the dimly lit staff room, which smelled of stale coffee and socks. His eyes lit up when Felix explained they wanted to go back over the morning of Dr Lyle's death.

'Happy to help, sir,' said Mr Eastley, buttoning up his cardigan and assuming a self-important air. 'I was one of the last people in that room before the killer arrived. *I* think the police must have missed something, myself. These sorts of cases, everything might be a clue.'

'You like reading mysteries?' asked Felix, eyeing the shelves. 'I like 'em too. I see you've got all the greats. The ones from America are my favourite, with the gangsters.'

'I prefer the Brits myself,' Mr Eastley said. 'Less grimy, you know?'

'So much more civilised,' Felix agreed. 'I know everyone will have asked you this – but did you see anything suspicious on the morning of Dr Lyle's death? In his study, for instance?'

'I already told the police and Miss Darkwether I didn't,' said Mr Eastley regretfully. 'It's a shame really, but it was a completely normal day. At least, that's how it seemed. We're only meant to do a quick clean in the mornings. I dusted and did windows as usual while Mr Bennett did the floors, then we shut the door and locked it and went over the hall to Professor Langley's. He's a difficult sort, always hounding you about moving some scrap of paper or accusing you of losing things. Hard to get much done. Then we finished up and went downstairs for a smoke. It's just those two offices used up here – the others are all empty along that corridor.'

'You're right, it sounds like an ordinary day,' said Felix and Mr Eastley sighed.

'It was,' he said, in disappointed tones. His expression brightened. 'There was the man opposite, of course, I saw him when I was smoking. Medium height, scar on his right cheek, right up by his eye, tweed cap pulled low, menacing air. He was watching the museum, I'm sure of it.' Mr Eastley lowered his voice. 'And then Dr Lyle arrived, and the man *followed him inside*.'

'I think Lucy mentioned it.' Slowly, an unpleasant thought occurring to him, Felix said, 'A scar on his *right* cheek, did you say – by his eye?'

'Yes.' He shook his head. 'Strange he seems to have vanished into thin air.'

Felix hesitated, then pulled out Susan's sketchpad. 'Can I show you something, Mr Eastley?' he said.

* * *

Felix joined Toby on the low wall beside the museum. Toby was smoking and staring out at the street.

'Well, that's us,' said Felix lightly. Toby started when he spoke. 'I had a good chat to Mr Eastley.'

'Anything useful?'

'Not really,' said Felix, his fingers grazing the folded sketch in his pocket. 'Eastley just confirmed what Langley said – no one was seen going in or out of that room once the cleaners left. Claims he saw a chap following Lyle outside, but the police have already checked that out and nothing doing.' He studied Toby closely as he added, 'So he must have been wrong.'

'Must have been,' said Toby absently. 'What's next? Back to the shop to report back to the boss?'

They walked over to the tube in silence. Felix was thinking that it was odd that Toby, who had never been to the British Museum before, had been able to lead the way so confidently upstairs to Dr Lyle's office. How rattled and shaken Toby had been by being inside the museum itself. About the man who Mr Eastley had seen outside, watching the museum, a man he had been so certain to have seen on the day of the murder, who so exactly matched Toby's description.

His fingers closed around the sketch in his pocket.

* * *

Meanwhile, Lucy set off to see Mrs Lyle. First, she paused at Mr Dakin's shop, on the pretext of giving him some misdelivered mail, but really . . .

'It's quieter than I expected,' Lucy said, looking around at the empty shop and setting the handful of circulars down on the counter. 'I thought you'd still be packed full of people desperate to see the scene of the crime.'

'It was,' said Mr Dakin glumly, coming out from behind his desk. 'They've moved on now.' He scowled. 'I put a lot of money into that exhibition, you know, and I won't see a penny of it. That's what the others don't understand – Sir Hector and Mrs van Buren. *They* won't suffer. Whereas my business has been dealt a great blow. I thought I could recoup my losses – now I'm not so sure.'

'The murder was a blow for us both there,' Lucy admitted.

'Although I might still be able to get something out of it,' said Mr Dakin thoughtfully. 'If I play my cards right.'

Lucy tensed. 'Enough with the hints. You're an observant man, Mr Dakin. Is there anything the police are missing?'

'Well, those notes did come to *you*, Miss Darkwether. Interesting that, isn't it? Why not me – or the police? Why you?'

'I don't know – there doesn't seem to be any logical reason. Do you think there will be another letter?' Lucy asked curiously.

Mr Dakin startled her by giving a sudden laugh. 'I imagine so,' he said. 'Yes, I imagine you will receive at least *one* more, Miss Darkwether.'

*　*　*

Lucy had been inside Dr Lyle's house at the wake, but now she examined it properly. It was a vast, Victorian house which evoked old-world grandeur – and yet, thought Lucy, much like Dr Lyle himself, it had a faintly manufactured sheen. The brocade was new and the furniture expensive, heavy and solid but ill-matched. The blowsy bowl of roses on the hall table was shedding petals onto the marble. Even the ancient butler, who peered at Lucy down his nose, seemed to be playing a part.

Lucy took a seat on a striped couch in the drawing room. She stood when the widow came in.

Mrs Lyle was a handsome woman with florid colouring. She looked well rested, as though, Lucy thought, she had not spent even one sleepless night grieving her husband and was wearing a set of expensive pearls. Mrs Lyle had been Lady Dartington before her marriage to the ambitious young archaeologist Gordon Lyle. He had squandered the majority of her fortune on expeditions and then, when he was finally on the brink of success, had betrayed her by having an affair. If anyone had a motive, Lucy thought, it was her.

'Mrs Lyle,' said Lucy, holding out her hand. 'You might remember me, Lucy Darkwether? We met at your husband's lecture at the British Museum.'

'No,' Mrs Lyle said, her pleasant, uninquiring expression unchanging. 'I don't think that I do recall you, Miss Darkwether.'

This was not encouraging, but Lucy sat down again anyway.

'I own a bookshop in Cecil Court,' she said. 'And my own interest is in Egyptology. Your husband made an extraordinary contribution to the field with the discovery of the tomb. You must have been proud of him.'

'I suppose,' said Mrs Lyle, taking her seat and pressing the bell for the maid. 'Gordon was certainly most pleased with the results of the expedition – his name in the history books at last, or so he thought. Didn't work out that way though, did it? Tea?'

The ladies sat in silence while a maid brought and poured tea. Mrs Lyle handed Lucy a cup and said, 'I have a lot to be doing today, Miss Darkwether. A sudden death brings with it an awful lot of responsibility, as I'm sure you can imagine. How can I help you? I have a feeling this isn't a social call.'

'I should cut to the chase,' said Lucy, setting down her cup. The widow did not seem bereft, so she thought she may as well speak plainly. 'I have a personal interest in your husband's death. I got there too late to save him, but you may have heard that there was a note that foretold his death. Well, it was sent to me.'

'Whoever is doing this – writing these notes and killing – they must be some sort of lunatic,' said Mrs Lyle. 'That's what Sir Marcus thinks. He feels a man like that should be easy to catch. He says they should be making an arrest very soon, any day now.'

'I know that's what he *wants*. But your husband had other enemies, didn't he?'

Mrs Lyle laughed. 'Enemies? How long have you got, Miss Darkwether? The list would be long.'

'Can I ask you a delicate question?' Lucy asked. 'Why did you withdraw funding for his most recent expedition?'

Mrs Lyle took a deep breath and then exhaled, clearly deciding whether or not she wanted to share her story with this stranger who had landed at her front door. 'I heard stories about Gordon before we married, not that I paid attention. About various unpleasant affairs. Once we got married, he was careful about that sort of thing. Knew which side his bread was buttered and didn't want to give me grounds for a divorce. But he slipped up in the end with Mrs van Buren. I knew that months ago. But I drew the line at being made a fool of. Let him get the money from *her*, I thought.'

Lucy nodded. 'I'm sorry for such an insensitive question – but the police must have asked you about an alibi?'

Mrs Lyle smiled. 'Not exactly subtle are you, Miss Darkwether? I already told the police. I was here all morning – my maid can testify to that.'

'That *is* lucky,' said Lucy, thinking that a maid might be paid to lie. 'Is there anything else you can tell me about your husband's last hours? How was his state of mind in the run up to his death?'

The widow looked thoughtful. 'In the week before, I thought he seemed a little . . . rattled.' She shrugged a grey-clad shoulder. 'I caught him looking out of the window a few times. Perhaps the curse of the mummy stories *was* getting to him – although he wasn't usually superstitious. Too hard-nosed for that. Maybe it was his conscience.'

'That's interesting,' said Lucy. 'Perhaps you're right – perhaps his conscience had awoken.' She stood. 'I'll leave you to the rest of your morning, Mrs Lyle. Thank you for your time.'

'It was an unexpected pleasure.' Mrs Lyle smiled broadly. 'Does the inspector know you're playing amateur detective, Miss Darkwether?'

'Yes,' said Lucy, 'and I think he's coming around to the idea.'

Chapter 25

'All right, team,' said Lucy the following day. 'Let's have it.'

It was a fine day, with a hint of spring – April had just begun– and Lucy had gathered her staff in Soho Square, to debrief her on their progress so far. While her demeanour was calm, her thoughts ran anxiously around her head. Toby, who matched Mr Eastley's description of the sinister man watching the museum. The bet with Bryan Campbell that she saw no chance of winning. The killer who might at any moment strike again . . .

'I'll go first, shall I?' said Felix. 'Toby and I went to the British Museum and showed our friendly faces. We spoke to Dr Langley, who saw nothing except two or three cleaners, as the inspector already told you. I spoke to your Mr Eastley who seems *devastated* not to have seen a vital clue – of course there is the mystery man, who only Eastley saw.'

'Oh yes, him,' said Lucy. 'Did he, er, describe him to you?'

'He did,' said Felix, meeting her eye. A look passed between them.

'He's sailing close to the wind, this killer,' mused Susan. 'These are daring, audacious crimes. He could have committed them without writing the notes, but he didn't. Why? What is it about sending the notes that's so important for him?'

'I wish I knew. You keep saying *he*,' said Lucy. 'A woman could have committed the crimes, couldn't they, with a deadly blade?'

'Yes, I suppose they could,' said Susan doubtfully. 'You're right, Lucy – I do assume it's a man.'

Lucy thought of Mrs Lyle and large, capable, neat hands.

'They're quite mad, I suppose?' Felix said.

Susan hesitated. 'Everything would point to an unbalanced mind, an obsessive interest in the expedition,' she said slowly. 'All this talk of vengeance, using codes and numbers. Whereas the murders themselves are very efficient.'

'So, you're arguing that our vengeful letter-writer and the killer are different people?' mused Felix.

'I think that's a distinct possibility,' Susan asked.

'In which case, let's return to the Society, who all have a very sane and practical motive for murder. Did you find anything out from Sir Hector and Mrs van Buren, Professor?'

'Mr Ahmed's assessment of Sir Hector is fairly accurate, I should think,' said Mr Tollesbury. 'A bully who was happy to throw Dr Curry under a bus for the sake of the expedition and to keep Lyle's reputation squeaky clean. I shouldn't put murder past him at all.'

'Unfortunately, Sir Hector has iron-clad alibis for both crimes,' said Lucy.

'Mrs van Buren seems to believe them all deserving of this curse, including herself. She referred to deserving punishment.'

'There are rumours that her husband died in suspicious circumstances,' said Lucy thoughtfully. 'She hated him and wanted his fortune. Could he have died by her hand?'

'There must be some reason for her guilt,' said Mr Tollesbury. 'Oh, and the sergeant is right. She *was* at Cecil Court on the morning of the murder, although she'll deny it in court.'

'What was she doing there?' asked Lucy. 'If she wasn't murdering Dr Curry, that is.'

'She says she wanted to call off the exhibition,' said Mr Tollesbury. 'Her conscience was getting to her – out of all of them, I think she is the most superstitious. She truly believes in a curse.

She also thinks she heard people talking inside Mr Dakin's shop around eleven-fifteen or so.'

'What!' cried Lucy. 'Why, she could have heard the killer.'

'Perhaps, but she isn't too sure she heard anything at all. She's adamant that she will deny it to the police at any rate.' He shook his head, his expression troubled. 'I do wish she would reconsider.'

'Mr Ahmed, Mrs van Buren and Sir Hector,' said Lucy. 'All of them connected to the expedition; any one of them could be the next to die.'

In silence, they walked back to the shop. Felix and Lucy fell back to walk side by side, out of earshot of their colleagues. 'Are we just going to ignore the fact that Eastley's description of a mysterious scarred man watching the museum matches someone we know very well?' Felix murmured.

'I think so – for now,' Lucy said. 'I'm with the inspector. I think the killer is one of the Society and this man is just a figment of Mr Eastley's imagination. It's a coincidence that he described Toby.'

'In that case,' said Felix, pushing a piece of paper into her hand, 'you should hang onto Susan's sketch of Toby. Because Mr Eastley identified it as the same man – and he seems utterly certain.'

Chapter 26

The third day of April dawned, but without a glimmer of spring. Instead, it was grey and foggy. They were all tense in the shop, as though each expected something terrible to happen. Which, Lucy thought worriedly, was horribly likely.

Whether it was the weather or the worries building up, Lucy's nerves felt at breaking point. She made tea and toast and then left it untasted on her plate, her eyes on the heavy curtain which kept out the draught from the front door and hid the letterbox from view. For some reason, she had a strong sense that today another note would arrive.

The ticking of the old clock felt ominous, each strike a death knell. The air, heavy with the smell of old books, Toby's bookbinding glue and the professor's pipe smoke drifting through from the next room. It felt oppressive, thick. Any moment now she expected to hear the creak of the letterbox, followed by the sound of letters falling on the mat.

She was not the only one to be nervous, she could tell. Felix was checking figures and humming the same line from a popular musical comedy, but his knuckles were white on his pencil. Susan was frowning over the accounts.

Lucy pushed away her plate. 'The post is late today, isn't it?' she said in a voice that didn't quite sound like her own.

'Fall out from all these strikes,' murmured Felix. 'Maybe our letter-writer should find a more reliable means of communication.'

Lucy's stomach twisted. So, Felix *was* thinking about it too. 'Perhaps there won't be a letter,' she said hopefully. 'Perhaps that's the end of it. He's had his fun, had a lot of attention in the press and he's given up.'

'Perhaps,' said Mr Tollesbury, coming in with a tea tray and a copy of the *Mirror*.

At that very moment, Lucy heard the brisk tread of their postman on the cobbles and, seconds later, there was the slap of their post landing on the mat. They all looked at each other.

Slowly, Mr Tollesbury went to the front door, pulling back the curtain and stooping to gather the little pile of post. He returned with a handful of bills and circulars – and there it was. A stiff, white envelope.

Lucy took it with a hand that shook. That neat, precise typeface. She had come to hate the sight of it.

'Speak of the devil,' she said, striving to sound calm.

'I'll open it,' volunteered Felix.

Lucy swallowed. 'No,' she said. 'I will. It's addressed to me, isn't it?'

She slit the envelope with a paperknife. She drew out another slim sheet of card and considered it for a moment.

> *The fourth will sleep amongst their ill-gotten gains,*
> *for all eternity.*

Lucy thought for a moment. 'So – Dr Curry was the architect of the expedition. Dr Lyle the *false face*. Ill-gotten gains can only refer to . . .'

'Mrs van Buren,' said Susan grimly. 'I'll call up the Yard, shall I?'

* * *

When Lucy arrived at the police station, she could hear the furious tones of Sir Marcus Derwent from the corridor. Short, explosive phrases drifted down the corridor. 'Utterly ridiculous . . . gone on long enough . . . insulting . . . tonight, we will make our arrest.'

Sergeant West, who was collecting paperwork from the front desk. grinned at her.

'Sir Marcus is rather upset,' he said. 'Nice to see you again, miss. Shall I take you in?'

'Thanks. The inspector wanted me to bring the note,' said Lucy, as they walked along the corridor towards the office. 'He thought it might help convince Mrs van Buren of the very real danger she's in.'

The sergeant sighed. '*She's* here too. We brought her in as soon as you called. Being awful stubborn, miss, refusing to leave London although I'm sure a rich lady like her has plenty of places to go. I can't figure out why. Some folk get like that when they're scared. Sir Marcus thinks it's an embarrassment—'

'This is an embarrassment!' cried Sir Marcus's voice, as if on cue. 'Lunatic like this should be easy to find!'

The sergeant shook his head. 'How you can be head of the Yard all these years and still think killers *look* like killers I don't know.'

Outside the inspector's office, the sergeant rapped on the door and three separate voices called impatiently for her to come in.

She went inside the office, where Sir Marcus, Mrs van Buren and the inspector sat. Without a word, she handed Mrs van Buren the note. The woman read it and then put it on the table before her. Lucy thought she looked pale and tired, with dark circles under her eyes. '*Ill-gotten gains*. I'm assuming the killer is referring to the fortune my husband left to me, which I used to fund the expedition.'

'Whether or not you believe this letter-writer means to kill, I would strongly advise you leave London, Mrs van Buren,' the inspector said. 'Name your location and my officers will drive you there now, under another name. You can take your sister with you, if that suits. Remain there for at least a week, or until an arrest is made.'

Mrs van Buren shook her head. 'A week in a remote location with my sister? I will take my chances with a killer, thank you, Inspector.'

Sir Marcus nodded. 'Quite right. It won't be necessary. We'll have the streets of Bloomsbury crawling with officers. If he's in the vicinity of Ashbourne Square, we'll have him.'

'I would prefer her to leave London, tonight,' persisted the inspector.

'I will not be leaving,' Mrs van Buren said firmly. 'I have a head-ache and wish to lie down. My sister will be in the apartment downstairs, and you will have your men stationed around the house.'

'And inside,' the inspector said quickly. 'I should like a man by your front door all night.'

'If you believe it will do any good, then please do.' She stood, her expression resolute. 'If I am to be punished, however, then I will surrender to my fate. Unless you mean to keep me here, Inspector?'

'Of course you are free to leave, my dear Lady,' said Sir Marcus hastily. 'You have nothing to fear.'

The inspector let out a breath. 'Sergeant West will drive you home,' he said.

In the doorway, Mrs van Buren stopped and met Lucy's eye. 'We must all pay some time, Miss Darkwether,' she said, with a faint smile. There was a low, vibrating intensity in her voice. She turned and walked out.

'We mustn't annoy people like Mrs van Buren,' fretted Sir Marcus from inside the room. 'She is *crucial* to the Society's success; my brother is quite certain about that. Without her, the funding will dry up. All the same, I have a job to do as well. Have her house surrounded. Men on every corner. Officers inside her apartment, by the front door. No one so much as walks down the pavement without being brought in . . .'

Lucy watched as Mrs van Buren walked down the corridor, her head held high, as though resigned to her fate. Somehow, in spite of her scepticism about the curse, she had a feeling that all of Sir Marcus's precautions wouldn't save the next victim.

Chapter 27

When the phone rang just before six the next morning, Lucy sprang for it. She had been awake since the early hours. She had gone into her kitchen, careful not to make a sound to wake Mrs Thorpe, and made herself a pot of strong, black coffee. The pale grey of dawn had only just begun to creep across the sky when the phone rang. She knew who it must be.

'Yes?' she said into the receiver.

'It happened,' said Inspector Hayes, in dispassionate terms. 'Mrs van Buren died in her sleep last night.'

'No,' cried Lucy. 'In her *sleep*? I don't believe for a minute this was a natural death.'

'I never said it was,' the inspector said. 'The doctor believes it to be CO intoxication – poisoning from a faulty gas fire. My men kept watch all night and not a soul went in or out, except officers changing shifts. The officer on the night shift was meant to change over at four and never came out. One of my men knocked on the door just after and, when there was no answer, they broke it down. The officer inside the apartment was unconscious and so was Mrs van Buren's sister, who slept in the lower apartment. Both were thankfully revived in the fresh air. Mrs van Buren, who slept upstairs, was dead.'

Lucy sank down onto the chair. 'Well, that's not very sporting,' she said, in a voice that was not quite steady. 'What happened to slitting throats?'

'He's getting inventive,' said the inspector. 'All the windows were tightly shut according to our own instructions. Our men are checking the fireplace now – a vent might have been tampered with, causing a slow release of the toxic gas. I should have been firmer with Sir Marcus and Mrs van Buren and had her sent away. I admit I had a lingering doubt – surely, the killer could not get past my men – but, tragically, I have been proved wrong.'

'You couldn't have done anything,' said Lucy sadly. 'Mrs van Buren was determined not to listen to us. She was resigned.'

'She seemed ready to die,' said the inspector. 'I was so sure that the killer was someone in the Society, but it appears I was terribly wrong. Sir Marcus is bringing in expert help.'

'Expert help?'

'Yes,' said the inspector, in drier tones than usual. 'In fact, he's a celebrity – and he's arriving at the station this morning, if you would care to join us. He's very keen to meet you.'

*　*　*

'Ah, Miss Darkwether,' said the inspector, when Lucy arrived a few hours later. He looked worn and tired. He was sitting across the desk from Sir Marcus Derwent and a tall, elegant man in his fifties with crisp, wavy hair. 'May I introduce you to Luke Durand, a criminal profiler, offering his expertise in the case.'

'Pleased to meet you, Mr Durand,' Lucy said, shaking the man's hand admiringly. 'I know of your work, of course. You tracked down the Le Taureau killer in Paris two years ago, using psychological profiling. I bought your book on the subject.'

Mr Durand said, 'Thank you for coming in, Miss Darkwether. Sir Marcus called me in last night to see if I could offer any insights. I did not imagine I would arrive to tragedy.'

'We had half the force in the surrounding area. Can't have our great and good being picked off like this,' said Sir Marcus angrily. Beneath his bluff manner, Lucy thought he seemed frightened.

'Damnit, my own brother is at risk! This killer has a madman's cunning. If manpower can't help, I thought the force could use some psychological insight.'

'I must tune in to the mind of the killer,' said Mr Durand. 'That is why I wished to meet with Miss Darkwether, as the recipient of his letters.'

'A dubious honour,' said Lucy.

'And yet,' said Mr Durand, regarding her with his piercing eyes. 'He has chosen you for a reason. We simply must discover what it is. It will make sense to *him*.'

'The psychology, that's right,' muttered Sir Marcus. 'Not that I'm sure about that sort of thing, under normal circumstances. But this situation is unprecedented. Time to admit we need help from some experts. God knows, we've tried everything else! Where are we at, Inspector?'

The inspector responded, 'We know that no one went in or out of Mrs van Buren's house in Ashbourne Square on the day of the murder, but we are now reviewing the previous week to see if any workmen were seen. No reports so far. It seems the fireplace vents were tampered with. Our expert believes it was a slow leak – odourless.'

'Mrs van Buren was complaining of a headache, wasn't she?' said Lucy. 'When she was at the station yesterday.'

'That's one of the symptoms,' said the inspector. 'Of course, it would have been hard to know exactly *when* she would die.'

'So, it was only coincidence that she died when she did?' asked Mr Durand thoughtfully. 'A little haphazard.'

'Someone with expert knowledge might have had a rough sense of when the gas would reach deadly levels,' said the inspector. 'But they could not have known precisely. Officers retrieved this from the scene – it was amongst her post, addressed to her.'

The inspector held a small paper package, loosely wrapped. Mr Durand took it. Inside, a piece of rough cloth swaddled a small figure. It had small lines for eyes, as though they were closed in sleep, and its hands rested by its side.

'The victim is sleeping the eternal sleep,' Durand said breathlessly. 'Entombed in her own collection. Her spoils . . .' He consulted a page of notes. 'I have compiled a preliminary profile of the killer. An expert in the ancient world, of course, given the tomb attribute—'

Lucy could not resist breaking in. 'I'd argue that actually anyone with a *rudimentary* knowledge could have staged Dr Curry's murder. They don't seem to have adhered particularly closely to a period or . . .'

'Nonsense,' barked Sir Marcus. 'Not like the average man on the street knows anything about red ochre, do they? Well, then. It's an expert.'

'This is someone who craves attention,' persisted Mr Durand. 'That's his aim – to get noticed, to get written about in the press.'

'Damnit, we've given him exactly that,' snapped Sir Marcus. 'Bloody Max Bird won't leave the story alone.'

'So, you think our killer cares less about avenging the king than he does the attention?' asked Lucy. 'That's interesting.'

Mr Durand nodded. 'The cause is secondary – the *attention* is what he wants. He's feeding off each crime, each news story, growing more confident by the day. But it will make him careless. That's how Le Taureau was finally caught, in Paris. He got sloppy, carried away. Once he was brought in, that was it. A careless slip of the tongue, a few inconsistencies – and we had him.'

'How many people did he kill before that happened?' asked Lucy uneasily. 'Wasn't it . . . nine?'

'No!' roared Sir Marcus. 'Nine! No, damnit. This ends here, if I have to put the entire police force on it.'

'If we can only make an arrest,' continued Mr Durand, calmly, 'then I'll break him, whatever his story is, however clever. Once these cocky attention seekers are arrested, they fall apart, they've got nothing left. They like to boast, these killers, and sooner or later that will give them away. Sometimes I think they almost *want* to get caught. We are dealing with a sick man.'

'Well, you don't murder three people if you're not,' snapped Sir Marcus. He composed himself and drew out a pipe. 'What would you suggest? Crack down on the press?'

'On the contrary, I should let the press run wild,' said Durand thoughtfully. 'The more attention the better. He'll slip up then, I'm sure of it.'

'You don't think that will bring more attention seekers out of the woodwork?' Lucy asked.

Sir Marcus seemed to notice Lucy properly for the first time. 'You must go now, my dear,' he said reproachfully. 'Your father would be cross with me if he knew you were here. He's probably worried enough, what with these unpleasant notes being sent to your door. I hope he doesn't blame me for all this. Please assure him we are doing all we can. An arrest will be imminent.'

The number of people Sir Marcus was promising an arrest to was growing. Lucy gathered up her coat and hat. 'Goodbye, Mr Durand. And have you any idea why he's picked on me?'

Mr Durand touched a finger thoughtfully to his temple. 'Have you come across anyone related to this case, beyond the members of the Society? Anyone on the outskirts? That will be the connection, I should think. Someone unexpected. They see you as their link to the expedition.'

'I don't know who that could be,' Lucy said. 'I'll think about it. Good luck, anyway. Inspector, do you think you could show me out?'

They walked out of the building in silence. Lucy shot the inspector a sidelong look. 'Have you been . . . replaced by Mr Durand?' she inquired.

'Not exactly,' he said stiffly. 'As you can tell, Scotland Yard are concerned that the case is dragging on. That it's going to cause more public panic.'

'And so, the official line is you're looking for a deranged letter-writer. What about you? Who do you suspect?'

He lowered his voice, drawing her closer. 'I believe the most likely suspect is someone the chief won't consider.'

'Sir Hector,' said Lucy.

'He has a motive to kill everyone on the board,' said the inspector. 'He's poured everything he has into that expedition, only for Lyle and Curry to discredit it, possibly beyond repair. There's talk of the Society being shut down. As for Mrs van Buren, she could have overheard something suspicious that day in Cecil Court. Identified him as the killer. He could be tying up loose ends.'

'So, you just have to let him go?' whispered Lucy. 'He could be plotting to kill someone else as we speak.'

The inspector's jaw hardened. 'There's men posted inside Sir Hector's house right now under the guise of protection. But I've told them to call me if he so much as makes a phone call.' He sighed. 'Although I have a feeling that's my promotion down the drain.'

Chapter 28

ucy walked back to the shop, trying to clear her head. She was starting to feel more human when, at the turning to Cecil Court, she saw with a sinking heart that Mr Dakin was pacing, clearly waiting for someone. When he saw her, he leapt forward.

'Miss Darkwether, tell me – is it true?' he cried. 'Another murder – another member of the Society, dead? Poor Mrs van Buren. It is too terrible.' He didn't look upset though, Lucy thought. He looked almost excited.

'It's true,' said Lucy, trying to edge past him. 'She refused to leave her flat for protection.'

'Foolish, most foolish,' said Mr Dakin. 'This killer is in deadly earnest. And you received a note, Miss Darkwether, as usual? Just like all the others?'

'I did yes – by that morning's post.'

'Ah by the post?' said Mr Dakin. His eyes were fixed on hers. 'They *all* came in the post didn't they – including the first, the one for Dr Curry?'

'Yes,' said Lucy, rather taken aback. 'How else would they have arrived?'

Mr Dakin nodded rapidly. 'Quite,' he murmured, bouncing on his heels. 'How else would they, as you say? I'll let you get on, my dear. I only wanted to confirm the – the very sad truth.'

He gave her a cheerful wave and bustled off, leaving Lucy staring after him, torn between irritation and worry.

She quite often longed to murder Mr Dakin herself – but she certainly didn't want anyone else to.

*   *   *

It was the next morning that Lucy received a note requesting an interview with the deceased Mrs van Buren's sister, Amelia Bright, the woman who would inherit Mrs van Buren's immense fortune.

She suggested meeting at the Palm Court tearoom. When Lucy arrived, she was led over to a table where Amelia Bright sat. She was a woman in her late forties, with thin lips enhanced by a lot of lipstick. She beamed at Lucy and shook hands. Despite her obvious friendliness, Lucy felt an instant aversion.

'I am sorry for your terrible loss,' said Lucy. 'It seems inadequate, but I truly am. I only met Mrs van Buren a few times, but she seemed like a remarkable woman. She did what I have longed to do since I was a young girl – attended expeditions in Egypt.'

'Oh yes, Moira was intrepid,' said Miss Bright, with a sad trill of a laugh. 'She never worried about personal danger. I can't count the times she has travelled to wild places, without thought of her own safety.' She gave a sorrowful sniff. 'If only she had, perhaps she might still be here today. She might have taken these dreadful warnings more seriously. Why, I haven't been back to the house since – I simply couldn't. The workmen have made it quite safe, apparently, but all the same . . .'

'How much of this strange business did Mrs van Buren discuss with you?' inquired Lucy.

'Only what I could prise out of her. Most of it I read about in the papers. She pooh-poohed the whole affair,' said the woman. 'But all the same, I could tell she was scared. I will admit I was frightened, myself – for her of course – but I lived there too, directly underneath her apartment. I was as much a target, indirectly. I suggested we move to the countryside for a time, use fake names, throw the killer off the scent. She told me to stop being

238

such a goose and to get on the next train if I was worried. Then I heard that the note had come . . .' She shuddered.

'Did you try to persuade her to leave?' asked Lucy.

'Of course! She wasn't having it. Told me there would be men outside, and inside too, by the front door – that no one could get in. I agreed to stay – it's hard to argue with my sister. When I think it could have had tragic consequences.'

'I rather think it did,' said Lucy, bewildered.

Miss Bright said, 'I meant, for *me*.'

'I see,' said Lucy, and she did. In Miss Bright's world, it seemed, there was only one person of importance. 'Are you her only relative?'

'Yes – our poor parents died years ago. And then Moira's husband died, as you know, about six years ago. He was a very wealthy man and left her most comfortably off. Of course,' she lowered her voice, '*I* should not have been comfortable taking his money. The stories I heard about what he did in the war . . .' She shook her head piously. 'I'm surprised my sister could tolerate it. Of course, she has since spent a great deal of it on her *collecting*.'

The pursed lips of Amelia Bright told Lucy exactly what she thought of such delicious money being wasted on old and dusty artefacts. Amelia Bright, Lucy thought, would spend the late Mr van Buren's fortune quite differently – and she would, in the end, have no scruples about accepting the tainted money.

An old motive, money: one of the oldest in the world as Max Bird had said. Another suspect with a compelling motive for murder. And yet, Lucy was sure the killer was outside of this room.

'Will you stay on at the house, do you think – or are the memories too painful?'

'The memories *will* be painful,' said Miss Bright, her eyes darting around. 'But my sister would want her home lived in. Once upstairs is cleaned up and modernised a bit, you know, it will be a lovely place to live. Some of these dusty antiques could go, clear a bit of space.'

Miss Bright was wasting no time taking possession of what was now hers.

'There is something I wanted to ask you, Miss Darkwether,' said Miss Bright, in a deceptively casual tone. 'The solicitor says that, the week before my sister died, she wrote a new will. It is most surprising. And she says that *you* are named.'

'Me?' Lucy stared at the woman in absolute astonishment. 'But I barely even knew her!'

'That's what I said,' said Miss Bright, stirring her cup of tea. 'And yet the solicitor is *insistent* that you are there when the will is read out. It is . . . most odd.'

An uneasy silence fell. Miss Bright regarded Lucy with outright suspicion now.

'All I can think,' said Lucy eventually, 'is that she means to leave me some – some token. She knew that I was interested in Egyptology. A fellow woman in the field.'

Miss Bright dabbed her lips with her napkin. 'I hope you're right, Miss Darkwether,' she said coolly. 'I shouldn't like to contest the will or anything unpleasant like that.'

'I'm sure it won't come to that,' said Lucy. Her mind was racing. Why on earth had Mrs van Buren named her in the will – and was it connected to the case?

* * *

Lucy walked to the British Museum and stood outside for a long time, looking up. The seat of so much knowledge and culture – and yet she was starting to wonder. So much within its walls had been gathered at a terrible cost. As she turned to leave, she noticed a familiar figure, hunched and shabby, sitting across the street, seemingly lost in thought and chewing his nails.

'Mr Eastley,' she said, approaching. 'Of course. We have got to stop meeting like this.'

'Eh?' He blinked at her. 'Oh, hello, Miss Darkwether. I was miles away.' He held up an unopened greaseproof packet. 'I came out here to have my lunch. What are you doing here?'

'I keep thinking about the museum and the mummy,' she admitted. 'So much blood shed in the name of discovery. So, I came to see it for myself.'

'I saw the papers – Mrs van Buren is the latest victim. Miss Darkwether, I'm glad you're here. There's something I must ask you, something that is worrying me terribly. I trust you. If I knew something – but it might cause suspicion to fall on *me* . . .' He twisted his hands anxiously. 'Well, in my shoes – would you tell the police?'

Lucy sat down beside him. 'What is it that you know?' she asked gently. '*I* won't tell the police unless you want me to, I promise.'

He wet his lips, then nodded. 'I was *there*,' he whispered. 'I was there the night she died. Mrs van Buren.'

'What?' gasped Lucy. 'You went to Ashbourne Square?'

'Not in the square itself. There were too many police to get close. I was a few streets over.'

'But why?' asked Lucy.

'Oh, I know how it sounds! But there was so much talk about who the next victim would be and I was certain it must be Mrs van Buren. I had the strongest feeling. I couldn't resist walking near where I knew she lived. *And I saw him.*'

'Saw who?' asked Lucy, her heart starting to thump in her chest.

'The same man I saw watching the museum the morning Dr Lyle was killed. Unmistakeable. Standing under a streetlight, looking in the direction of Ashbourne Square – it was foggy, but it was the same man, I'm sure of it. I saw his scar.' He looked up at Lucy, his brown eyes wide and frightened. 'But if I tell the police about it, they'll know that I was there!'

Lucy swallowed. Again, the mysterious man who appeared only to Mr Eastley. It was too wild to be true. And yet . . . She thought back to the Friday night. Where had Toby been? At the pictures as usual, she thought. Although, was that *really* where he went so often? She had discounted him being the man who Mr Eastley had seen – she had half-thought that Mr Eastley hadn't seen anyone at all. But perhaps that had been a mistake.

And now, Mrs van Buren was dead.

'He could be here right now, watching,' said Mr Eastley, looking around with hunted eyes. 'He could have seen me. He could know that I saw *him*.'

'I doubt it,' Lucy said, repressing a shiver. 'Mr Eastley, I think you should talk to the inspector. Go along to the Yard right now, by bus. I think you should tell him exactly what you saw. Anything that can prevent more deaths is worth doing.'

Mr Eastley's anxious expression relaxed. 'If you think that's best,' he said. 'I suppose it is the right thing to do, only I'm afraid. But if I don't speak out, more innocent people die.' He rose. 'If I go to the station now, I'll be back for my afternoon shift. Perhaps whoever this killer is, they have been somehow influenced by an ancient power in a way they themselves cannot fathom.'

His voice was serious. Lucy could no longer laugh at the idea of an ancient power. 'The tomb opening was a great opportunity for discovery and knowledge,' she said. 'But I confess that, more and more, I agree with you Mr Eastley. Maybe the king's body should have always remained in Egypt.'

'A terrible lesson will have been learned,' he said importantly. 'I must go. Goodbye, Miss Darkwether. I hope the next time we meet, this is all far behind us.'

Lucy watched him hurry across the road to the bus stop, then stood.

Blindly, she walked through the museum, until she reached the Ancient Egyptian section. Dust hung in the air, which seemed thick with the past. Countless tombs, unopened for centuries – now on display, so far from where they had been laid to rest. She paused by the facsimile of the death mask and considered its bland expression. So much pain and suffering brought along with it. And yet

– she was certain that behind all this talk of a curse, all the red ochre and thick furs, there was another motive at play entirely.

On the way back through the streets of London, she wrestled with her conscience on another matter entirely. The man whom Mr Eastley had seen at the museum and near Ashbourne Square, matched the description of Toby Calvert, who right now was under her roof. Of that there was no doubt. And, while Toby had an alibi for the morning of Dr Curry's murder, he had – as far as Lucy knew – no such alibi for the crimes that followed. *Could* Toby be a killer? Or was that only a coincidence, and there was another hand behind this entirely?

Lucy suddenly became aware that a fog had descended with a frightening suddenness. The sound around her was muffled and she could barely see her hand in front of her, as though a veil had descended. Even her own footsteps sounded muted. Lucy had the feeling that, were she to scream, even that would be swallowed up and choked by the thick white shroud.

She stopped, her heart pounding. She thought of Mr Dakin, his eyes fixed on hers. '*Well, those notes did come to you, Miss Darkwether. Interesting that, isn't it? Why not me – or the police? Why you?*'

It was a question she could not answer. Why *her*? All this time, someone had been watching her, deciding that she would be the recipient of their twisted games. Writing her letters. The killer. He could be right behind her. In the thick silence, she was sure she could hear footsteps, moving stealthily in the fog, inexorable as the curse which had followed its victims from Egypt to the heart of London.

It's just my mind playing tricks, she told herself. Just her mind. There was no one following her and there was certainly no curse. She forced herself to draw long, slow breaths, counting in her head. Slowly, her heart began to stop racing. She was safe. She was alone.

Lucy walked on.

Her suspicions could not be ignored, not without risking more deaths. And yet it was all so ridiculous! Toby Calvert, so shy as to barely string a sentence together, clever with his hands, but, before these killings, without much idea of what a hieroglyph was. The idea that it was *he* writing those taunting notes was absurd. No one was such a good actor – and she had known Toby for months.

Unless . . .

She stopped again, struck by an unpleasant thought.

Unless Toby could be *working* for someone.

He needed money; Susan had overheard him borrowing from Mr Tollesbury. Sums had been going missing from the till for weeks. What if he had been desperate? What if those small sums weren't enough? What if someone had offered Toby a far larger sum of money – to kill in this extraordinary and elaborate way. A solution to all his problems. But who would do such a thing?

Someone powerful, unscrupulous, of great social standing, someone with the will to destroy – but who was unwilling to do the deed themselves. Someone who could hide behind a mask of respectability while paying a young man to do his dirty work. Someone with a grudge against those who had brought scandal on the Society. Someone who wanted them dead, but to be as far removed from the crime as possible.

Someone like Sir Hector Derwent.

Chapter 29

T he inspector has a secret theory as to the killer,' Lucy told her staff the following morning, as they set up the shop for the day. She watched Toby closely as she said, 'Sir Hector.'

Toby, however, didn't flinch, and she went on. 'It adds up. Dr Curry was about to expose his precious Society as a fraud, so he had to die. Dr Lyle was a liability – he had stolen research and lied about it. Mrs van Buren had conspired to betray Dr Curry and had been having an affair with Dr Lyle. Besides, she might have recognised Sir Hector's voice inside Mr Dakin's shop on the morning of the murder.'

'He didn't have the opportunity though,' said Susan. 'On the morning of Dr Lyle's murder, he was in Oxford.'

'Unless he had someone working for him,' said Lucy, watching Toby over the rim of her coffee cup. 'Unless—'

The bell rang and a tall man stepped through the door. 'Edward!' Lucy cried. Her surprise was mixed with displeasure although she couldn't entirely tell why. It was Edward – of course she should be happy to see him. 'What on earth are you doing here?'

He looked around him. 'You kept avoiding my calls. I thought I should see the famous shop,' he said. 'So, this is it!'

'Well, come in,' said Lucy heartily. She was conscious of embarrassment and of Felix and Susan shooting Edward keen glances. 'Let me introduce you to everyone. Everyone, this is Edward.'

In the first few months after she had opened Cecil Court Books, well-meaning society friends had come to the shop and tried to look interested as Lucy had shown them around. Pityingly, they had bought a few copies of the latest fiction titles and told her how marvellous and independent she was. One by one, the visits had fallen away. Lucy didn't mind; she had liked it that way. And now, here was Edward, where he had no business to be.

'Delighted,' said Felix, taking Edward's hand and shaking it vigorously. 'I've heard so much about you.'

'This is Professor Tollesbury,' Lucy said. 'My professor from college. And this is Toby.' Toby, who, she thought, might be a killer, was looking particularly angelic that morning with the spring sunlight catching his blond hair.

Edward decorously shook hands with them both. 'So, you taught Lucy?' he said to the professor.

Mr Tollesbury said fondly, 'Lucy was my finest student. So clever. Although she was terrible at meeting deadlines.'

Edward said, 'We were all so proud of Lucy, going to Oxford. We expected great things, afterwards.'

There was a pause, in which Edward regarded the shop. Running a dingy bookshop, his silence implied, was not one of those great things. If Lucy was going to walk away from their engagement and a life of respectability, surely, she could have done better than this?

'It's . . . smaller than I expected,' he said at last. 'Very cosy.'

'Were you expecting Campbell's?' asked Lucy tartly. 'Two floors and literary luncheons?'

'Campbell's – now that's quite an emporium,' he said admiringly. 'I stopped by there the other week to do some shopping for Mother.'

'We had Eleanor Valentine in here over the summer, reading her memoirs,' said Lucy weakly.

'How fascinating,' said Edward. 'Who is Eleanor Valentine?'

'She's a famous actress who – oh, never mind Edward. You've been in the Argentine too long to understand.'

'I see.' He glanced around the shelves. 'Are there any books you'd recommend? I'd like to buy something.'

I don't want your pity, Lucy thought, but Felix, ever with an eye to a sale, swept in. 'We have something new in, very racy, only available on the continent, if you would be interested.' He dropped an eyelid in a faint wink. 'I'd have to give it to you in the backroom, of course. It's not precisely legal—'

'Not precisely legal?' said Edward, looking startled.

'Felix! That's not for Edward,' snapped Lucy, shooting Felix a cross look. 'Edward would like something – something about cattle, perhaps, or farming.'

Felix took Edward round the corner and Lucy let out a groan. Susan, who was unwrapping parcels that had arrived in the morning's post, said sympathetically, 'All *my* friends have stopped visiting. I think I prefer it that way.'

'He's going to tell everyone what a disaster it is,' sighed Lucy. 'Why do I still care so much for what Edward thinks?'

'Only you can answer that,' said Susan enigmatically, stacking post.

Edward emerged from Felix's clutches, holding a stack of books. 'I've got a book about hardy perennials and a stack of new novels for Mother,' he said, smiling down at her. 'Now, can I take you out for lunch?'

'I'm not sure I can go,' said Lucy. 'We're dreadfully busy.'

Edward looked pointedly around the shop, which was empty except for an elderly gentleman in the corner, examining a collection of Oscar Wilde poems.

'I'll wait for you,' he said gently. 'We could go around the corner, to Daphne's.'

Lucy paused but couldn't think of a better excuse. 'All right,' she said ungraciously. She felt as though her beloved shop had been judged and found wanting. *Just go back to Argentina and run your ranch*, she thought rudely, but did not say.

Just then, the bell above the door jangled and Bryan Campbell stepped inside.

'Hello,' he said, looking around at them all cheerfully. 'I thought I would pay you a little visit, Miss Darkwether – take you out to lunch, if you're free. Quiet in here, isn't it? You haven't forgotten our little bet, have you?'

'What bet?' asked Felix with interest. 'You haven't been gambling have you, Lucy?'

'Have you been up to something?' asked Susan.

'No,' said Lucy, 'I—'

'Actually,' said Edward, eyeing Bryan with dislike, 'Miss Darkwether is coming out for dinner with *me*.'

'Excuse me,' said Lucy firmly. 'But I really am not sure—'

'Lucy!' cried Susan. 'Look!' She had paused in her sorting and was holding out a white envelope. 'This was in this morning's post.'

'Another?' cried Mr Tollesbury.

'Is that one of the famous letters?' drawled Bryan. 'How thrilling to be on the spot.'

'Oh, not again,' said Felix, looking green.

'We must call the police immediately, Lucy,' Edward said.

'Will everyone be quiet!' Lucy shouted above the hubbub. This is *my* shop and this is addressed to *me*.' She took a deep breath to compose herself. 'I'm going to open it first.' She slit the envelope and read aloud, her voice clear and calm in the quiet room.

> *The host saw what you tried to conceal. He shall be found at midnight at the needle, to make good your secret.*

Lucy lowered the paper, thoroughly confused. 'Has he given up on hieroglyphs?' she asked, bewildered, to the room at large. 'The needle – why that's too obvious, isn't it? Cleopatra's Needle on the Victoria Embankment.'

'Obvious to who, exactly?' muttered Felix.

'Call the police, Lucy,' Mr Tollesbury said, looking at the clock. 'It's only noon now. This is their chance to be ready. Finally, they have enough warning.'

She nodded and stretched out a hand to the telephone. 'I'll call the inspector – and he'll want to see the note. A taxi to the police station, I think – right away.'

'I'll go with you, Lucy,' said Edward possessively.

'I've got my car outside,' said Bryan. 'Plenty of room.'

Edward glared at him. 'With the traffic at this time, we're better off getting the tube.'

'Oh, I know all sorts of short cuts,' said Bryan, smiling at him. 'It's a Rolls. Fast and comfortable.'

'Let's just go, for goodness' sake,' snapped Lucy, pulling on her coat. 'Bryan, we'll take your car. Edward, you can come for all I care.'

Inside Bryan's car, Lucy found herself sitting next to Bryan, with Edward and Susan in the back. Bryan did indeed know short cuts and drove fast and well. Maybe he *could* be of use, Lucy found herself thinking.

At Scotland Yard, they waited in the foyer until Mr Durand, the inspector and the sergeant all hurried in. When they entered, Lucy came forward, holding out the note. 'Did you call Sir Hector?' she asked, slightly out of breath, and without preamble. 'He need to be warned.'

The inspector was looking past her at Edward, Bryan and Susan. 'And who are all these people?' he asked bluntly. 'I can't believe Miss Darkwether needs *three* escorts.'

Edward opened his mouth indignantly, but Bryan guided him out with an amused smile. 'We'll get out of your hair, Inspector. Lucy, we'll be just outside.'

'Well?' Lucy demanded, ignoring what was going on behind her. 'Have you warned him?'

The inspector nodded. 'I've spoken to Sir Hector to try and persuade him and his family to leave London. He will consider a visit to his country estate, accompanied by a police escort. He was most concerned as to whether the note named him. Can I see it?'

Lucy handed him the note and the inspector studied it in silence.

'He seems to have abandoned the hieroglyphs,' the inspector said thoughtfully. 'Cleopatra's Needle, is that what you're thinking?'

'Yes, and at midnight – that's plenty of time to get ready,' said Lucy. 'This could be your chance.'

'It reads a bit oddly doesn't it, miss?' the sergeant said, staring at the note. 'Not bothering with the code or the drawings. And the paper is different – regular stationary, not that fancy card. We'll see what the team say. It might be that someone is copycatting, you know. We'll treat it seriously of course.'

'It *is* odd, for him to change his style,' said Mr Durand, looking puzzled. 'Very unusual, psychologically.'

'And neither Mr Ahmed nor Sir Hector fits the description of *host*,' said Lucy, worrying a fingernail. 'I can't help feeling we're missing something here.'

'Either way, we'll be ready for him,' the inspector said firmly. 'We've hours yet and half the force heading to the Embankment. Our letter-writer won't know what hit them.'

Chapter 30

Lucy and Susan watched as the last police car peeled off into the darkness.

'I suppose we have to wait for word now,' Lucy said reluctantly. 'By midnight they could have caught the letter-writer. We can finally get some answers.' She groaned. 'That's still two hours away. I hate waiting. I wish I could be closer to the action, somehow.' Her eyes lit on Bryan's car. 'Unless . . .'

'Lucy, no,' insisted Edward. 'I'm taking you home – now.'

'I just want to be nearby,' Lucy said, looking up at Bryan persuasively.

'Come on, Vyse, don't be such a stick in the mud,' Bryan said easily. 'We won't go anywhere near Embankment. Where's your sense of adventure?' He patted his breast-pocket. 'I've got my old war revolver with me. I don't think you need to worry.'

'It's not me I'm worried for,' snapped Edward.

'Please, Edward,' said Lucy. 'I can't just sit at home and wait for a phone call, not this time. And there's something awfully odd about that note. It doesn't fit the style – it wasn't even a proper code really. And nothing to do with Ancient Egypt. I can't help thinking it's important that we go.' She nudged him. 'What about your adventurous spirit that took you to the Argentine?'

'The Argentine, really?' said Bryan Campbell, looking amused. 'That *is* more adventurous than I expected. I've been all over, of course, with the war.'

'Please, Edward,' begged Lucy. 'The first sign of danger and we'll turn back.'

Edward met her beseeching gaze and sighed. 'All right,' he said, 'but we stay in the car.'

* * *

'I think this is as far as we can get,' whispered Bryan, parking up. They were a few streets over from Embankment, near the Thames wall; the streets were empty. Lucy looked out into the inky darkness, punctuated by a few greasy streetlights, knowing that the letter-writer was out there – and the police were waiting.

'Why are you whispering?' said Lucy. 'The killer can't hear us.'

Bryan laughed and his teeth shone in the darkness. 'I don't know exactly.'

'I don't understand what we're doing here at all,' muttered Edward sullenly. 'The police will have the area covered.'

'I know,' Lucy said. 'Don't look so worried, Edward – we're a good way off any danger. I just wanted to be nearby, for some reason.'

'It's nice to get out for a jaunt,' said Bryan blandly. 'You can see the stars for a change. And besides . . .'

'You have your war revolver,' said Edward coldly. '*Were* you in the war? You did mention it, once or twice.'

'What did *you* do in the war?' Bryan asked interestedly.

'I was too young for it,' said Edward coldly.

They sat in silence for a while. Suddenly Susan tugged at Lucy's sleeve.

'Look,' she whispered. 'A man, over there – by the wall, by the streetlight.'

They could just make out a dark shape lurking in the larger shadow of the wall. As though they had waited long enough, the figure began to walk, hands in pockets, head bent against the wind.

'People,' Lucy said in a low voice. 'My gut says we should follow him.'

'Absolutely not,' snapped Edward. 'That's what the police are for. And you said yourself, we're nowhere near the shoreline. He's probably just some chap out for an evening walk.'

'I'm sure you're right, but I have a feeling,' said Lucy slowly. 'Come on, he's getting away from us.'

Before anyone could stop her, she slipped out of the car. She could hear the others following as fast as they dared. Their target's progress was somewhat erratic. Sometimes he moved forward at a brisk trot; sometimes he slowed down till he almost came to a stop. Once a streetlight caught the gleam of a bald head. Once he circled the block. They tailed him closely until, suddenly, they rounded a corner and saw – nothing. They were at the beach itself.

'Damn,' cried Edward. 'He lost us.' His jaw was set and tense, and his nerves seemed to have fallen away; it was much more dashing, Lucy thought.

'That shows he was up to no good,' said Bryan. 'Everyone listen a minute.'

In the near distance, they heard the sound of footsteps running along the street parallel to the river.

'He's gone that way,' hissed Bryan, pointing. His eyes were shining in the streetlight and a lock of hair fell over his forehead. He drew his revolver. 'Let's go.'

He set off at a run and Edward, who seemed to have caught his excitement, followed. Lucy and Susan started after, but after a few paces Lucy skidded to a halt.

'Susan,' she whispered. 'Do you hear that?'

Bryan and Edward's footsteps had faded into the distance. In the silence, broken only by the lapping water, they heard something. The stealthy tread of a person who did not want to be heard – on stone.

'He doubled back,' said Lucy. 'He's walking along the shoreline.'

She and Susan clung to the wall, making themselves invisible in the darkness, until they could see again the darker shadow of a figure ahead, feet crunching over the pebbles. Then silence.

'The beach,' Lucy said in an agonised whisper, looking over the barrier. 'Do we go down?'

Susan eyed the inky water uneasily. 'I think we should wait for—'

A sudden scream rent the air, followed by running footsteps. Lucy and Susan looked at each other, faces bleached and frightened in the lamplight. Then they ran in the direction of the cry, down the steps onto the beach, slippery with seaweed, landing on the beach itself, feet sinking in stones.

Susan caught her breath. 'Look! I see something, just up ahead.'

Some ten feet ahead was a dark heap that might have been a bundle of old clothes. Susan put on a burst of speed and dropped to her knees beside the ominous huddle, feeling for a pulse.

Rain blew Lucy's hair into her face, but as the moon passed behind a cloud, she saw the victim clearly. A man of fifty or so, with a domed head and shattered horn-rimmed glasses that were spattered with rain. He lay, his eyes shut, a gory stain spreading across his shirt.

'Mr Dakin,' breathed Lucy. 'Oh no. *The host*. Of course. He hosted the exhibition. We thought we were following the killer, but it was the victim, all along. Although we're a good way off the Needle . . .'

'Our killer got in there early.' Susan bundled her scarf up and held it there. Then she looked up at Lucy, who was feeling quite ill. 'He's alive. Just. Bryan and Edward won't be too far off. We need to get help, now—'

Dakin's lashes fluttered and he groaned. His mouth worked and he let out a faint breath of a laugh. 'It was him. I knew it. I was right. It was *him*.'

'Who?' cried Lucy. 'Who did this?' But his eyelids fluttered shut.

'Go for help, Lucy,' said Susan impatiently, her wet glasses glinting in the moonlight. 'I'll stay with him. We passed a few houses back there by the wall. Hammer on some doors, send down anyone with medical knowledge and ask to phone for an ambulance, tell them it's a knife wound to the abdomen.'

Lucy set off at a run back to the river wall. A sharp breeze blew off the river, bringing with it the smell of sewage, rust, vegetation. The pebbles made the running difficult, her ankle turning, boots slipping. The killer would still be here, on the beach, she thought. She forced the thought away.

As she neared the steps she saw a shadow at the top, melting into the darkness. As fast as she dared, she raced up, skidding onto the pavement. Footsteps ran across the road, passing under wall sconces too fast for her to catch more than a glimpse – an overcoat, a dark hat clamped to the head. The figure darted down a corner: Lucy turned, followed, heard a dull clang, then she stumbled into an alley and – nothing. The figure was gone. Only a few scraps of paper drifted across the alley along with wisps of smoke.

'Damnit,' whispered Lucy. Sweat cooled on her forehead, and she began to shiver. 'Where did you go?'

Chapter 31

octor says it's touch and go whether he pulls through or not,' said the inspector, looking down at the still figure in the hospital bed. Mr Dakin had been taken to the nearest hospital, the newly opened St George's. 'The doctors have done all they can, but he won't regain consciousness any time soon they think. Miss Darkwether, what you did tonight was dangerous.'

'If I hadn't, he'd be dead!' cried Lucy. 'Where were you and your men?'

'We were waiting where you insisted the killer would be!'

They stared at each other angrily for a minute, and then Lucy shook her head. 'The killer didn't play fair. He got Mr Dakin while he was walking to the meeting place. But what made Mr Dakin come all the way out here? Did he have a note on him, anything like that?'

'Nothing,' said the inspector. He let out a long breath. 'I apologise for losing my temper, Miss Darkwether. I don't like having my witnesses attacked.'

'At least now there's a chance we can identify them,' Lucy said. 'Mr Dakin saw his attacker, he recognised him. He could tell us who it was.'

'If he regains consciousness,' said the inspector. 'Tell me exactly what he said again, when you found him.'

'It was only a few words,' said Lucy, trying to recall Mr Dakin's rain-soaked face, his lips moving. 'He said something like – *it was him, it was him.* Something about how he'd been right. And then he laughed.'

'Hard to know what was funny,' said the inspector. 'But you're right; it indicates he saw his assailant. It also tells us that our killer is a man.'

'Mr Dakin was never even on my list of possible victims,' said Lucy remorsefully. 'I was so sure the next victim would be either Sir Hector Derwent or at a pinch, Mr Ahmed. Those who were in Egypt.' She swayed suddenly, feeling dizzy and ill. The inspector took her by the arm and sat her down in a chair.

'I'm going to fetch a cup of tea,' he said, more gently. 'My sergeant is always telling me it's wonderful for shock.'

When he returned, with a cup of strong, steaming brown liquid, Lucy was sitting up with more purpose.

'That'll teach me to chase a killer after eating only a slice of fruit cake all day,' she said, sipping the hot tea. 'I feel such a fool.'

The inspector said, 'You and me both, Miss Darkwether. The killer outsmarted us. It might interest you to know that Sir Hector was in his house in Oxford tonight; he had friends staying that evening. So that rules him out.'

'Unless someone is acting on his behalf,' Lucy said, her mind jumping back to Toby. 'How did the killer lure Mr Dakin all the way out there?'

'Until he regains consciousness, that part will be a mystery. Yet again, the weapon is missing.'

The weapon. Dimly, something stirred in Lucy's mind, but then it was gone.

'This figure you think you saw,' the inspector went on, 'nothing more has come back to you there, has it?'

'No,' said Lucy regretfully. 'I think I saw an overcoat flapping as he ran, a hat maybe, but that was all. I think he was tall – not as tall as you, maybe. I don't know if he saw me or not.'

'Let's hope not. Mr Durand already thinks the killer has a special interest in you – let's not give him any more reason to pay you attention. Let tonight be a wake-up call, Miss Darkwether. Do you want to wind up dead like Mrs van Buren or in a coma like Mr Dakin?'

'Not particularly,' said Lucy, with spirit. 'But I'm in this, as much as you are. Something has to be done.' She thought of Toby, back at Cecil Court Books, and her jaw hardened. She had ignored her suspicions long enough; it was time to face them.

* * *

Susan was waiting for her outside the hospital. The darkness was fading slightly to grey – dawn was coming. 'Let's get a taxi,' she said.

'Do you mind if we walk for a while?' Lucy said. 'I doubt the killer is still hanging around. I just want to check something.'

They headed back the way they had walked last night. The beach where Mr Dakin had been stabbed had been cordoned off, but the pavements were clear.

'This is where I think I saw a figure,' said Lucy, pointing to the wall. 'If there even was anyone. I might have imagined it.' She heard in her mind that dull clang of metal on stone. 'We'd turned this corner . . . and I think I heard the sound of metal . . .' She stopped and turned in a circle. Then she walked along, tracing her footsteps until she reached the alley. 'This weapon the police can never lay hands on. Well, what if he dropped it tonight?'

'He might have slammed into a dustbin or kicked a can or something.' Susan shivered. 'Lucy, I think we should come back later, preferably with a burly officer.'

'Perhaps.' Lucy scanned the alleyway. Piles of refuse, rags, amidst the mist pooling at their feet. 'Let's just see.'

Up and down the alley they went, combing every inch in the dim early morning light. 'The smell is terrible,' said Susan, crouching down to peer under a sheet of cardboard. 'Like a dead rat.'

'There are probably tons of them here,' said Lucy, digging through the rubbish with her foot. 'You're right, I must have – oh.'

There it was, covered in a silt of food wrappers. A slim knife, with a wooden handle, stained with blood.

Susan sat back on her heels. 'Lucy,' she breathed. 'I believe you have found the murder weapon. Let's take it back to the station and make the inspector's day.'

But Lucy was still staring at the knife with disbelieving eyes. She had seen that knife before. Nausea rose up in her throat. She had tried to deny the truth – but she could do so no longer.

'Not yet,' she said, with difficulty. 'Let's take it back to the shop first. I have a feeling I know whose knife this is. And I want so much to be wrong.'

* * *

'Lucy, Susan!' said Mr Tollesbury sharply when they came in. He was sitting with Felix beside the fire. 'Thank goodness. We rang the station, and the sergeant said you'd left the hospital an hour ago. Mrs Thorpe said you'd never made it home. We were starting to get worried.'

'What are you doing here, Felix?' said Lucy. She still felt dazed – exhaustion, she supposed.

'Mr Tollesbury called me up a few hours ago and explained. I came straight back. They got *Dakin*? We never even had him on our list.'

'The killer is a tricky customer,' said Lucy. She looked around. The knife was wrapped in old newspaper and tucked into her coat; she could feel it pressing against her chest. 'Where's Toby?'

'In bed asleep, I assume,' said Mr Tollesbury. He wore his usual plaid dressing gown with frayed sleeves. Morning light had begun to filter into the shop, casting everyone in a dramatic, blueish hue.

'Has he been here all night?'

'Of course,' said Mr Tollesbury, frowning at her. 'He went up to bed early. You look quite ill, Lucy, sit down—'

'We found something,' said Lucy. She took the slender bundle from her coat. 'Fellow detectives, I give you – the murder weapon.' Her voice sounded unsteady to her own ears.

With a rather pathetic flourish, she laid the bundle on the table. The paper fell open, revealing the knife. She heard Mr Tollesbury take in a deep breath.

'The man who stabbed Mr Dakin dropped it. I wondered,' Lucy said slowly, 'whether any of you recognised it.'

Felix frowned. 'Why on earth would we?'

But Lucy's eyes were on Mr Tollesbury, who was looking down at the knife with a sad expression in his eyes.

'Do *you* recognise this knife, Professor?' she asked softly. She moved the paper aside, revealing initials carved into the handle, filled with dried blood. TC.

Mr Tollesbury's eyes met hers and a look passed between them. 'I'm not sure,' he said quietly.

'That's a lie,' said Lucy. Her voice cracked. 'I think you recognise that knife because you gave it to—'

The door opened then, and Toby came in. His hair was rumpled and Lucy noticed with a pang that his pyjama trousers were slightly too short, stopping above his ankle and giving him the look of an overgrown child.

'Thought I heard something down here.' His eyes fell on the knife and widened, and he stopped short. 'That's mine.'

'Your best bookbinding knife, which went missing a few weeks ago – the day before Dr Curry was murdered, if I remember right,' said Lucy. Slowly, Toby came forward and held out his hand. His fingers did not quite touch the knife.

'I'm assuming it wasn't covered in blood when you lost it,' said Lucy, trying to keep her voice calm. He shook his head, still staring at it in bewilderment. 'Toby, where were you when Dr Curry was killed?'

Toby swallowed. 'I was here,' he said unconvincingly. 'I was with Mr Tollesbury all morning, working.'

She swung round to look at the professor. Again, avoiding Lucy's eye, Mr Tollesbury said, 'That's right.'

'You've always been a rotten liar, Professor,' said Lucy. 'The question is, why have you been covering for Toby?'

There was a long and horrible pause. Then Toby said at last, 'I asked him to, miss. I got scared.'

'Well, I realised too,' said Felix. 'I showed Susan's sketch to Mr Eastley – he insisted it was the man he saw outside the museum. You, Toby. I didn't want to believe it. Lucy and I didn't want to give you up until we were sure.'

Which, Lucy thought miserably, it seemed they were.

Toby looked around at them all and his expression hardened. 'Will you call the police now, miss?'

A knock on the door made them all jump. The atmosphere in the shop had been so intense that no one had heard the sound of an engine or footsteps on cobbles.

'Maybe I don't have to call anyone,' said Lucy, taking Susan's portrait of Toby out from her pocket and smoothing it with her hand. 'It seems Inspector Hayes has figured this out on his own.'

Chapter 32

What made you decide to arrest Toby?' said Lucy. She sat across from the inspector and his sergeant at a small table in the station. The room was stuffy and overheated.

'What made *you* decide to harbour a potential killer rather than turning him in?' said the sergeant. 'You knew he matched Mr Eastley's description of a man he saw at two separate crime scenes.'

The inspector said nothing. He looked lost in thought.

'I couldn't believe it was him,' said Lucy. 'I still don't.'

'Firstly,' said the inspector, rousing himself, 'Mr Calvert *isn't* under arrest – he's detained under suspicion. Secondly, we realised early on that the description of Mr Eastley's, describing the man he saw hanging around two separate crime scenes, matched that of your apprentice. Even if he did always make sure to lurk in the shadows when we were in the shop. I think you realised that too, Miss Darkwether.'

Lucy flushed. 'Blond, average height, a scar above his right eye. There must be thousands of young men in London matching that description. Besides, you thought Mr Eastley was a busybody.'

'Even busybodies can be useful sometimes. You're right – at first, we dismissed it as an unlikely coincidence. Still, it interested us enough that we did some digging.'

'We found quite a lot actually,' said the sergeant. He flipped open a file. 'We interviewed all your staff as procedure. Everyone's alibis checked out, with the exception of one. Toby Calvert lied about his whereabouts on the morning of Dr Curry's murder – he said he never left your shop, and your professor corroborated that, said they were in the room together all day. But he was seen by a few locals in front of Cecil Court just after eleven. Could be nothing, we thought – people forget they've popped out or they get nervous around the police and lie for some other reason.

'But Mr Eastley also saw a man matching Mr Calvert's description at the British Museum on the morning of Dr Lyle's murder, watching the museum. Described him right down to the scar on his cheek. Mr Eastley, who visited us yesterday at your suggestion, is also willing to testify that he saw a man fitting Mr Calvert's description near Ashbourne Square on the night before Mrs van Buren's murder. Mr Calvert has no alibi for that night – he claims he went to the pictures but wasn't seen by anyone. *You* saw a figure running from the scene along the Thames – would you say he fit Mr Calvert's description?'

Lucy shrugged. 'It would fit *many* people's description. Fairly tall, some sort of cap, an overcoat. It was dark, impossible to tell. This all seems extremely circumstantial.'

The inspector nodded. 'We have only his word that he was at Cecil Court in bed last night. Then there's his previous.'

'His previous?' said Lucy. She looked between sergeant and inspector.

The inspector reached for the folder. 'What do you really know about the man who calls himself Toby Calvert?' he asked.

'Who *calls himself*?' said Lucy, a cold feeling settling in her chest.

'What do you know of him?' persisted the inspector.

Lucy gathered herself. 'Not much. Mr Tollesbury hired him. He grew up in a small Yorkshire village, parents are factory workers. Seemed a nice boy.'

The inspector shook his head. 'Not a small village in Yorkshire, and no parents to speak of. Not such a nice boy either. Toby Calvert – or Tobias Turner, as he was born – grew up in a foster

264

home near Bradford. He got in trouble there, petty theft, fighting. He was sixteen when he committed one instance of armed robbery, robbed a tobacconist and did time – only got eight months, he got a scar in a fight just above his right eye. Inside, Turner met a well-known forger who spotted promise and took the boy under his wing. Upon release, Turner joined his ring and did nicely for himself before the Yard broke up their organisation. Most of the ring were arrested – Turner eluded the police and went to ground. I thought he seemed familiar when I first saw him in your shop. His photo was in the papers at the time. The press wrote about it – the baby-faced criminal.'

Lucy shook her head. 'A *forgery ring*?' She thought of Toby deftly reproducing the hieroglyphs from memory, his sure strokes replicating them so accurately.

'The knife that you found is his,' the inspector went on. 'He admits that much, although he can hardly do otherwise when his initials are on the handle. It's covered in both Dakin's blood and Mr Turner's fingerprints. Claims he lost it two weeks ago or thereabouts. Forensics say the same knife is a likely fit for the murders of Dr Curry and Dr Lyle. All Mr Turner will say is that he didn't kill anyone. Other than that, he won't say a word to help himself, not even to our duty solicitor.'

Lucy thought for a moment, brow furrowed, then shook her head. 'Toby – Tobias Turner – whoever he is – might have been a crook and a forger. But one thing he isn't – and that's interested in the ancient world. He *can't* be behind these crimes.'

'A clever act?' said the inspector. 'He worked in your shop, had access to books on Egyptology, heard you talking about the exhibition. You said yourself whoever arranged this didn't need to be an expert. I think he could have cobbled together enough to set the scene.' He pushed a pile of papers towards Lucy. 'These were found in his room.'

Lucy examined them. Newspaper clippings about Gordon Lyle and his discoveries, going back years. A brochure for the museum with its opening times. Photos of Lyle cut from magazines, attending society parties, beaming out at the camera. An item about his appointment to the Society. Lucy caught her breath.

'It seems that Toby Calvert had a special interest in Dr Lyle,' the inspector said neutrally.

'But what motive did he have to kill Dr Curry? To hide his research papers in Cecil Court?' The inspector shook his head and Lucy stood, her face pale. 'Can I see him? I'm perhaps the nearest thing he has to a family member, it sounds like. Maybe I can persuade him to talk.'

After a moment, the inspector inclined his head. 'Five minutes. And I would urge him to share what he knows. It won't look good in court, this silence. Sir Marcus will throw everything at this to get a conviction – he wants this case closed before any more gossip emerges about his brother. Mr Durand has already insisted he can break a suspect, given enough time.'

'Toby isn't your killer,' Lucy said firmly, pulling on her gloves, ignoring the voice of doubt in her own mind. 'That's not what I'm worried about, Inspector.'

'No?'

'No. I'm worried because we're wasting time. Because while Sir Marcus and Mr Durand are building a case against Toby, the real killer is still out there.'

Chapter 33

oby Calvert – or Tobias Turner – no longer looked like Mr Tollesbury's shy, boyish apprentice. With dirty hair, his eyes darting nervously, a belligerent expression and his hands cuffed before him, he looked like a cornered criminal.

Which, Lucy thought, by all accounts he was.

'Toby,' said Lucy, taking a seat, 'we have to be quick, we've only got five minutes. What were you doing in Cecil Court on the morning of Dr Curry's murder?'

He gave a shrug, avoiding her eye. 'Not a crime is it? I live there.'

'But you told the police you didn't go outside the shop all morning. Why did you?'

'Fresh air, a smoke.' He shot her a sly look. 'Is that a crime too?'

'No,' said Lucy, keeping rein on her temper. 'So, you asked the professor to lie for you.'

Toby nodded reluctantly, then sighed, before eventually starting to talk properly. 'I've got a dodgy past, miss. When you came back that evening saying there had been a body and I knew the police were coming, I got scared. The police might have recognised me. While the sergeant was talking to Susan, I asked the professor to say I'd not gone out all morning, just in case.'

'You were also seen outside the British Museum on the morning Dr Lyle was killed. Watching the place, waiting for Dr Lyle to arrive and then you followed him inside. You told me you'd never been inside the museum before.'

'I hadn't!' said Toby sullenly. 'I never went there. You know I'm not interested in museums.'

'Felix said you certainly knew your way around when you went there the other day,' Lucy said. 'The inspector found the brochure in your room. Along with a lot of clippings about Dr Lyle. Can you explain that?'

He winced and glanced away.

'And what were you doing all the way over near Ashbourne Square?'

'I wasn't! Why would I go there?'

'For heaven's sake, Toby!' Lucy exploded. 'It was *your* knife used to attack three people! You changed your name! You lied about your past! You have a criminal record and you have no alibi for the killings. And for some reason you've been compiling a little dossier on Dr Lyle in your bedroom. Do you want to go to jail again? Because at this rate you could and not as an accomplice for robbery. You're an adult now and this is murder. You could hang.'

Toby said nothing, but Lucy thought he looked afraid.

'Toby, I'm on your side. I know you had no reason to commit these crimes. But did someone put you up to this? Did someone tell you to kill Dr Curry? His research papers were found stashed in Cecil Court. Did you put them there?'

'I didn't put any papers anywhere,' Toby said.

'There's no reason you should pay for someone else's crime. Even if they're rich and powerful, you mustn't be scared to tell me—'

'I'm not working for anyone,' he said. 'I told you. I didn't *do* anything. They're fixing this on me because I've got a record.'

The sergeant rapped on the door. 'Time's up, miss.'

Lucy stood. 'A lawyer will visit – Mr Walker, he's a dear, he's got my brother John out of all sorts of scrapes in the past, although I imagine *this* will be something of a challenge. I'll call him up now. He'll tell you not to say another word until you've put your story together.' She took a deep breath. 'It's small fry compared to all this, but I can't help wondering. Did you take money from the till at Cecil Court?'

Toby hung his head. 'I might have taken a shilling or two, to place bets.'

Well, that was one mystery solved. 'And to think I felt sorry for you,' said Lucy.

Chapter 34

ARREST MADE IN EGYPTIAN CURSE CASE!
London freed from reign of terror.

ohn dropped the newspaper onto the white table-cloth at the Ritz. He, Edward, Lucy and Maggie were dining before an evening at the theatre. 'Success for the sleuths at Scotland Yard at last!' he cried. '*The law triumphs and the dark forces of the supernatural were shown to be nothing more than a petty crook with a bloodlust.* Well, well. What on earth made him do it, Lucy?'

'That's the question,' said Lucy. 'One I imagine Sir Marcus is trying hard to answer at this moment.'

Despite the tinkle of crystal, the soothing jazz and the chatter in the room, Lucy felt tired, cold and a little sick. The oysters on their bed of ice looked repulsively grey and pallid.

'Might be one of those psychopaths, I suppose, who don't have a reason except to themselves,' mused John.

'*Tobias Turner, known to his employer as Toby Calvert, was formally arrested last night after being detained on suspicion. He worked as a bookbinder at Cecil Court Books,*' said Maggie, continuing to read. She wore a white silk gown, her auburn hair a rich red cloud against her pale shoulders. 'Under your roof all that time. Did you really have no idea?'

'Not for the longest time,' said Lucy, stirring the remains of her martini with a cocktail stick. Edward shot her a sympathetic look across the table. 'I suppose I—'

There was a crash and Lucy jumped, spilling what remained of her drink. Edward squeezed her hand. 'Just a waiter dropping something,' he whispered. 'You're frightfully nervy, and no wonder.'

'Just – just a waiter,' she repeated. It was true – she *was* nervy. The dim lights of the restaurant only seemed to bring out the shadows in people's faces, as though they wore masks, wreathed in cigarette smoke. And Lucy was troubled by an uneasy sense that, in spite of Toby's arrest, she had missed something that had been under her nose all this time.

'*The police are reserving the evidence for the trial, but Sir Marcus can reveal that the weapon found at the scene of Mr Dakin's attack was known to belong to Mr Turner!*' Maggie laid down the paper. 'Phew.'

'But the thing is, I don't think Toby did it. Not on his own, at any rate.' And yet Lucy could feel the cold chill of doubt in her chest. Toby, who had stolen from her and used a false name. Could she really trust him?

'Of course you don't,' said Edward gently. 'You always were tender-hearted, Lucy.'

'I might be tender-hearted, but that's not why,' said Lucy, with spirit. She gestured to the waiter for another drink. 'Toby Calvert – or Tobias Turner – might have been a crook, but unless he's been playing an extremely long game, he knew next to nothing about Egyptology. Whoever wrote those notes had at least *some* knowledge of the Egyptian world, enough to arrange the bodies in the correct way, to line the room with red ochre, to supply furs to keep them warm on their journey to the afterlife—'

'It all seems silly to me,' said Maggie. 'All that set design. Like a bad play, out in the sticks.'

'Maggie used to be an actress,' explained John. 'In her youth.'

His fiancée socked him on the shoulder, not too lightly. 'In my youth!'

'You gave up the boards for love,' said John.

Maggie laughed. 'Silly boy,' she said. 'What I mean is, that's just set dressing – it's the sort of thing you'd use as misdirection. Have the audience looking at the Egyptian nonsense, vengeance for a king, when all along it's something else.' She glanced at her watch. 'We should go, or we'll miss the start. You'll enjoy it, Lucy, it's a mystery play.'

'Oh, good,' said Lucy sourly. As if she hadn't had enough of murder. She thought of her bet with Bryan Campbell, hanging over her, the illicit books in her back room which could bring disgrace on them all. The fact she had been harbouring a criminal all these months; the thefts which had made her so suspicious of everyone. The oppressive cloud of superstition and death that hung over Cecil Court along with the police and reporters.

Lucy wasn't superstitious; but it was hard not to feel as though they were, in their own way, haunted by a curse of sorts. That everything she had fought so hard to build was slipping through her fingers, like sand in the desert.

'Come on,' said Maggie, standing and arranging her furs. 'We can take bets on who the killer is at the interval. It's always the one you least suspect.'

* * *

The lights came up on Drury Lane. The audience were easily thrilled and the applause had gone on for some time. Now, they began to collect their belongings, their furs and evening bags, chattering happily. There were low chuckles and occasional bursts of satisfied laughter. The audience had paid for a good mystery and got one.

'I liked it when real water came out of the tap,' said John, stretching. 'How on earth did they manage that?'

Lucy had not enjoyed the play much. She had found it all too unreal to be enjoyable. The corpse, a platinum blonde discovered in a pool of bright red blood, lying very still, had been unable to repress a faint sneeze. She kept thinking she saw something in the shadows at the edge of the stage – a figure moving, just out of sight. Truly, she needed to put death and murder out of her mind.

In the foyer, the others were talking about going on to a night-club. 'I think, if you don't mind, I'm going home to bed,' she broke in. 'It's been a long day. Long few weeks.'

'Of course, old thing,' said John guiltily. 'Sorry for poking fun earlier. Let me get you a taxi.'

'I'll get my own, thanks,' said Lucy. She squeezed his hand and smiled at Edward and Maggie. 'Enjoy yourselves.'

* * *

In a taxi bearing her homeward, her head fell back against the seat. London rushed past her, a smudge of lights in the dark. Lucy was tired, so tired. She could fall asleep right here, she thought, in the taxi. She began to drift, letting the streets and houses outside her window blur. Snatches of memories flickered through her mind.

Toby watching the museum, cap tugged down over his eyes—

Something was niggling at the edges of her brain.

Toby, who had conveniently been seen outside every crime scene, with his distinctive scar, which made him so easy to describe and identify. At Cecil Court, or watching the museum from a distance, or near Ashbourne Square.

And then she thought of another figure, ever present, quietly yet obstinately inserting themselves into the investigation. Always watching, insistent that they had seen Toby through the fog . . .

Lucy's eyes snapped open. She sat bolt upright and leant forward.

'Excuse me,' she said to the driver. 'Would you mind making a different stop?'

Chapter 35

ucy gave the taxi driver a note to deliver immediately to Scotland Yard, tipped him lavishly, drew a deep breath, then knocked long and hard until the side door to the British Museum cracked open. The startled eyes of Mr Eastley looked out.

'Mr Eastley!' cried Lucy. 'I'm so glad you're here. I was hoping you worked this shift – I suddenly thought of something I wanted to ask you. Would it be all right if I came in? I won't disturb you long.'

'All right,' Mr Eastley said uncertainly. He stood away from the door and let her in. 'I've never had anyone come here when I was working before,' he said, glancing around worriedly. 'It's not the sort of thing the museum would like. Come into the staff room, will you?'

Inside the dingy room, lit by one naked bulb, Mr Eastley shut the door and opened a tin of biscuits which he regarded dubiously. He held them out. 'Biscuit? They've been here a while I should think, but it's all there is.'

'No thank you, I had dinner only a few hours ago,' said Lucy. She sat down on an uncomfortable chair. 'I was at the theatre – it was a lot of tripe. But something occurred to me in the taxi, and I wanted to ask you about it.'

'All right, miss.' Mr Eastley took a bite of biscuit and shook his head. 'Stale,' he said sadly. 'Go on miss, what is it?'

'Mr Eastley,' Lucy said. She dug into her evening bag. 'I wanted to show you something – a portrait my friend Susan drew. Don't judge too harshly, she's only learning, but you'll get the gist. Is this the man you saw on the day of Dr Lyle's murder, outside the British Museum? The man who the police arrested?'

She held out the portrait of Toby that Susan had drawn. Mr Eastley's brow cleared.

'That's right, that's the man I saw – Mr Fletcher showed me this same drawing. The police called me in today and explained he'd been apprehended. And then it was in all the papers. It's a relief – I was starting to think I might have imagined the whole thing. You were right to make me go. A Mr Turner wasn't it? I was surprised to see he worked at your shop.'

'I knew him as Toby Calvert,' Lucy said slowly. 'He was born Mr Turner. And yes, he works for me. Well, that seems to settle it.'

'Settle what?' said Mr Eastley, looking mystified. 'He's already been arrested, hasn't he?'

'On your evidence. And you *did* see him – I know that. Only it wasn't outside any crime scene.'

'It – it wasn't?' said Mr Eastley, looking bewildered.

'No. I think you saw him once – at the British Museum. Only it was a good week before Dr Lyle's death, while you were cleaning. Dr Langley noticed him too, hovering outside Dr Lyle's office. You got a good look at him as he passed and thought he had a striking face. You've always had a photographic memory, you said – well, this face stuck. And when you decided to go to the police to describe a man you saw on the morning of Dr Lyle's death, you picked him. You could describe him accurately down to his distinctive scar. A scar you *couldn't* have seen outside the museum, though – not at a distance, with his cap pulled down. Nor across Ashbourne Square on a foggy night. It's above his right eye – you wouldn't have noticed that at all. And you have poor eyesight, Mr Eastley. It's what kept you out of the war – you told me that.'

He stared at her. The little room was silent, the atmosphere oppressive.

'You're taller than I thought,' said Lucy. 'I'd have thought you under six foot, but you must be a good six-two or three. The man I saw by the river, the man who stabbed Dakin – he was about that height. You stoop.'

Mr Eastley smiled. 'I always have.'

Lucy stood. 'It *was* you I saw along the river, wasn't it? A man of your height and build. The police thought you were a busybody – they thought that's why you kept hanging around the crime scenes, impressing upon them the sinister figure you'd seen. But maybe you were there for another purpose entirely.'

Mr Eastley's gaze skittered away from Lucy. 'What purpose?' he asked.

'You told me straight out, but I didn't listen. You believed the tomb shouldn't have been opened. You were sick of fools like Dr Lyle trampling all over sacred ground, for squandering the opportunity you would have given anything for, to learn and study the Ancients. You had been passed over all your life, your dreams and ambitions crushed. Seeing Dr Lyle showboating on the stage, showing off when he'd desecrated a sacred tomb – was that the moment you decided you'd had enough? Was that when you realised it was time to make those idiots listen?'

Mr Eastley shook his head. When he spoke, his voice was high and frightened. 'They made a mistake. They should never have opened that tomb.'

'I thought so,' said Lucy.

But she was the one who had made a mistake. She realised it in the moment Mr Eastley's eyes narrowed. It was the look of a trapped animal with nowhere to go, cornered and dangerous. Lucy turned to run, when something exploded in the back of her head, and all she felt was pain and then nothing.

* * *

When she came to, she was sitting on the uncomfortable chair and her hands were tied before her. Mr Eastley was crouched in front of her, looking up at her anxiously. In one hand, he had a knife – small, but viciously sharp.

Lucy's head was swimming, and she felt sick.

'Are those ropes too tight?' he asked solicitously.

'Yes,' said Lucy through gritted teeth. 'They hurt. Will you untie me?'

He shook his head regretfully. 'You know I can't, miss.'

Lucy's teeth were chattering. It was freezing down here in the museum basement. Oddly enough, she wasn't yet truly afraid. It still seemed faintly ridiculous that Mr Eastley, with his earnest theories and pomposity, should be the killer they had been searching for all this time, the writer of those cocksure, teasing notes.

'When did you decide to kill them?' she asked.

'*I* didn't decide anything,' said Mr Eastley, rocking back on his heels. 'It was decided *for* me. I believe in justice.'

'We have that in common,' said Lucy, straining against the ropes. She thought she heard a creak outside and added, 'You won't get away with this.'

'No one knows you're here though, do they? Poor, simple, irritating Mr Eastley, so eager to waste police time – no one would think I would hurt anyone. It's one advantage to being so inconspicuous. If no one notices you, you can get away with a lot.'

Lucy had a nasty feeling he might be right. She wondered whether she was imagining another creak of floorboards outside.

'You were drawn to the story of the tomb opening,' she said. Keep them talking until the cavalry arrived: that's what the hero always did in detective novels. Except she wasn't so sure the cavalry *was* coming. 'You've always loved history.'

Mr Eastley sat back, his eyes bright and alert. 'Always. I was bullied as a child and books were my escape – quite literally. I would hide in the library and read about Pharaohs, pyramids, treasure. As I got older, I read more deeply. I felt a real affinity with those kings. I knew I was meant for more than my ordinary, suburban life. I think you understand that, don't you Miss Darkwether? The spell that books can cast?'

Lucy nodded. 'Absolutely,' she assured him. 'But then you were denied the chance to study.'

His face hardened. 'Instead, I sweep floors. I got this job at the museum so I could at least be in a place of history and learning. I followed the expedition to Egypt from the beginning, read everything in the papers. So much promise, so much knowledge, they were all so *lucky*. I was excited when I found out I was to clean Dr Lyle's office. A great man, I thought. I thought I might catch a glimpse of his studies.

'Then I got to know him better. He never noticed me, but I noticed *him*. He wasn't a great man at all! – he was rude, petty, a charlatan. Him, Sir Archibald, Sir Hector and Mrs van Buren, all of them driven by greed, happy to turn a sacred king into a cheap side show. Fighting like dogs over him.

'When the news came that Sir Archibald Drake had died on the very day the tomb was opened, I understood. It was divine retribution, the king making his displeasure known. He wanted all who defiled his tomb dead and would act through me. I made sure I was working at the museum the night of Dr Lyle's lecture. I'd thought *he* should be next. But then Dr Curry arrived. I realised he'd been the brains behind it all. Without him the tomb would never have been touched. I changed my mind about who should be the second. Then it would be Lyle. And then Mrs van Buren.'

Keep him talking, Lucy thought; anything to buy some time.

'Mr Dakin isn't on your list,' she said. 'Why did you stab him?'

'The powers act in mysterious ways,' said Mr Eastley.

'So, you never saw Toby outside the museum.'

Mr Eastley laughed. 'Of course not – I saw him in the corridor a week before the lecture, outside Lyle's office. He was hovering about, looking shifty. I didn't know he worked in your shop, of course! I didn't think the police would ever find him. That was a coincidence, wasn't it? And he turned out not to have an alibi.' He shook his head, as though awed by his own good fortune. 'I was truly aided by the divine king.'

'And why *me*? What made you write the notes to me?'

To her surprise, Mr Eastley looked briefly confused. Then he rallied. 'Why not? You were next door, that's all. I wanted to herald the events,' he went on loftily. 'I wanted to—' A slight noise in the corridor outside made them turn. Mr Eastley's hand tightened on the handle of his knife.

'That's the police,' said Lucy, trying to sound calm. 'I'm afraid the game is up, Mr Eastley. Untie me, won't you? They'll go easier on you, if you do. After all, pretty much everyone who needed punishing is already dead.'

'No,' he said quietly. 'There's one more person left to punish.' A cold smile crossed his face. 'You, Miss Darkwether. You wanted those tomb artefacts as much as Dakin. You supported the expedition, you agreed with those thieves. You don't deserve my mercy. The door is locked. I think I can act before anyone can save you.'

And there it was, thought Lucy, her hands flexing helplessly at the rope, as she met his eyes. The expression of a killer.

Mr Eastley advanced and raised his knife. He brought it down as Lucy flung herself to the side, hitting the ground hard – just as wood splintering sounded and the door was kicked open.

Chapter 36

hy don't we start again from the beginning?'

Inspector Hayes and Sergeant West were sitting across the wide table from Mr Eastley. They had been in the room for a little under two hours. Behind a one-way mirror was Sir Marcus Derwent, pacing impatiently, and Mr Durand, watching with rapt attention. Lucy, who had received a long graze across her ribs but was otherwise unharmed, was being examined by the police doctor in a nearby hospital.

Mr Eastley's eyes darted from side to side. He looked frightened and cornered, an unlikely killer, but Hayes knew that looks had little to do with anything. Beside him sat the duty solicitor, scanning the notes they had made so far. Confused, repetitive notes, full of glaring holes and omissions, but with one clear fact reiterated – Mr Eastley was determined to confess to the murders of four people.

Mr Eastley nodded eagerly. 'They needed to be punished. I meant to kill them—'

'I know, to kill them all. Even Sir Archibald Drake, all the way in Egypt?'

'N-o,' said Mr Eastley, hesitating slightly. 'No, that must have been the curse. It was at the lecture that I realised they all had to . . .'

'Yes, they all had to die,' said Inspector Hayes wearily. 'Can you tell me *how* you did it? For instance, how did you murder Dr Curry?'

The man rubbed his forehead. 'A knife.'

'How did you manage to get inside Dakin's shop?'

Mr Eastley hesitated. 'The – the door was open.'

'It wasn't. All of this is in the papers. Dr Lyle was killed when you were smoking outside – there were witnesses. And Mrs van Buren died from gas poisoning. The vent in her chimney was tampered with – that took expert knowledge.' The inspector waited. 'How did you manage that?'

Mr Eastley looked flustered. The inspector sighed. 'How did you arrange to meet Mr Dakin?'

'I didn't arrange anything. It was simply coincidence,' he said firmly.

'What about the notes? Why did you write them to Miss Darkwether?'

'I wanted to explain,' said Mr Eastley crossly. He rubbed his forehead again. 'Stop badgering me. I'm so tired. I've told you I did it haven't I?'

The inspector sat back. 'Yes, you've told us you did it,' he said. He glanced towards the screen, behind which Sir Marcus and Mr Durand waited. If he pushed Mr Eastley now, he thought, he might well get a written confession to anything he wanted, if only to get out of here and rest. A man who felt himself ignored and longed to insert himself into the heart of the action, even at risk to his own life.

And yet, was he truly a killer?

The inspector shut his file and pushed back his chair.

'We're *all* getting tired, Mr Eastley. I suggest we pause this for now.'

* * *

'Why on earth did you leave it there?' spluttered Sir Marcus, as they gathered in the corridor outside. He flung an indignant hand towards the glass panel in the door. They could see the duty solicitor talking to his client earnestly, but Mr Eastley only hung his head.

'A fascinating study,' said Mr Durand, watching with rapt attention. 'Craving attention, yet hiding in the shadows. Yes, this all falls into place now. He is undoubtedly the author of those letters. A few minutes alone with him and I shall make him confess.'

'I don't think getting a formal confession will be a problem,' the inspector said drily. 'In fact, he's *dying* to confess.'

'Well then, one of you get it in writing,' snapped Sir Marcus. 'This case is closed. Either him or Calvert – one of them swings, I don't care who.' He turned and stormed out of the room. Durand followed eagerly.

'You were right to send men to the museum tonight, sir,' said the sergeant.

The inspector nodded. 'I have learnt by now Miss Darkwether was worth listening to.'

'Well, that's that,' said the sergeant, stretching. 'Case closed. A full confession incoming, especially once Durand gets his hands on him. A few loose ends tied up and we're done. Tobias Turner can walk out a free man and Sir Marcus can get off our back. Simple.'

'Very simple,' murmured the inspector. The sergeant looked at him curiously. 'What's bothering you, sir?'

'*All* of it. Eastley can't explain how he broke into the locked shop to stab Dr Curry, nor how he managed to kill Dr Lyle at the same time as smoking a cigarette with Bennett. He has no knowledge of air vents or gas poisoning . . . These were efficient crimes. Clever crimes. Practical. Mr Eastley may be book clever, but he doesn't seem a practical man.'

'I know what you mean,' said the sergeant. 'Mr Eastley is the sort who talks a lot and likes hanging around crime scenes and to feel important – but those sorts don't usually *do* anything. These are the crimes of someone who acts. This is an unconvincing confession, to put it mildly. But what can we do about it?'

The inspector said nothing. He was thinking.

Chapter 37

I t was getting light when the taxi carrying Lucy reached Cecil Court Books. She climbed out gingerly, holding her side, which had been carefully cleaned and bandaged. She had rung up Mrs Thorpe and explained, then asked her to send on a message. The doctor had insisted she be driven straight home for rest, but when she had finally escaped into a cab, she had asked to be driven to her shop instead. After all, it was more truly her home than anywhere else.

In the taxi, a jumble of images rushed through her exhausted mind. She was back in Mr Dakin's shop, stepping into a dusty tomb from long ago, smelling incense. She saw Sir Archibald, lying sightless under a blue sky, Sir Archibald whose death had started this whole chain of events. Greasepaint, cardboard scenery, water running from the tap, all very convincing, yet none of it quite real. She heard Maggie's low, husky voice. *Set dressing.*

And then the inspector's voice came to her. *'All very dramatic, isn't it? A curse and a long-dead king. Most crimes are committed for far simpler reasons. Money. Lust. Revenge.'*

Mr Tollesbury was waiting up for her, as Lucy had known he would be. He wore his old, worn dressing gown and looked as welcoming and familiar as always.

'My dear,' he said, as she stumbled through the door, white faced, so tired that her eyes were swimming. 'Mrs Thorpe rang me with your message. Said you were coming straight here and would need looking after. I put the kettle on as soon as I heard the car outside.' He held out his arms. 'Come here.'

Lucy let him put his arms around her and rested her head on his chest. She breathed in pipe smoke. She clung to him until the kettle began to come to a boil and he gently detached himself. Then she sat obediently at the old wooden table he used for his bookbinding, letting out a faint yelp.

'Did he hurt you badly?'

'It's only a scratch, the doctors said. I'll be all right. I was lucky.'

There was the sound of china being set on a tray. Lucy knew precisely which cups the professor would use – the delicate rose pattern.

'It was awful, Professor,' Lucy said. 'When I came to and was tied up, I felt so helpless and silly. I was playing at finding the murderer – but it wasn't a game at all, it was real.'

Mr Tollesbury poured hot water into the teapot. 'Why on earth did you go over to the museum on your own?' he chided.

Tears came to Lucy's eyes. 'I don't know. The idea only came to me in the taxi. Mr Eastley was always hanging around, but why? He *was* close to the Society, just not in the way we thought. He understood the Ancient Egyptian burial rites. He passionately opposed the tomb opening. And, most of all, he resented the Society for getting to do everything that had been denied to him. The dogged way he described Toby, when actually he couldn't have seen his scar at that distance. He was so obvious, I didn't see it until it was nearly too late. But truly, I didn't think Eastley would be dangerous. Even now, I can't believe it.'

Mr Tollesbury poured her a cup of tea into a dainty Dresden cup and pushed it over to her. 'Drink this, my dear. You've had a terrible shock.' He poured his own cup and sat, looking at her fondly.

Lucy eyed her cup. It was fragrant and steaming, but what she would have liked was a strong cocktail. 'No one makes a cup of tea like you,' she said gratefully, lifting it to her lips.

'You were always brave, Lucy. Like to look things in the eye, squarely, see them for what they are. It's over now though. No more notes, no more police, no more murders. You don't have to worry about it anymore.'

There was a silence. 'It would be nice if that was true,' said Lucy. She set the delicate cup on its saucer. Rosebuds, partly opened. 'There's one problem though. Mr Eastley didn't kill all those people, did he Mr Tollesbury? And neither did an Ancient Egyptian curse. You did.'

* * *

'Mr Ahmed said it right at the start, but I didn't listen,' said Lucy. 'He doesn't have an ounce of superstition in him. He saw right past all the curse nonsense and said whoever was doing this had a very *human* motive. Well, what are the human motives for murder? Money, of course. Fear. Jealousy. Passion. And *revenge*.' She waited a moment, eyes on her teacup, watching it blur with tears. 'Only you weren't trying to avenge any king. You were avenging someone else.'

Mr Tollesbury laughed, his old, familiar laugh, which brought a pang to Lucy's heart. She lifted her head and looked at him, squarely, right in the eyes.

'Of course not,' he said. His gaze shifted past her, to somewhere long ago. 'I wanted vengeance for someone far dearer to me than any dead king.'

'Rose,' whispered Lucy. Her chest tightened as cold realisation set in. She had known it, she had realised, and yet she had hoped so desperately that she was wrong. 'Your daughter Rose. Did Rose really die from Spanish flu, Professor? Or was it something else?'

'*He* killed her,' snapped Mr Tollesbury. 'As surely as if he put a gun to her head.'

'Gordon Lyle,' said Lucy. 'A serial philanderer. Someone who seduced women wherever he went and then abandoned them without a second thought.'

287

'He left Rose pregnant at sixteen, her dreams in tatters,' said Mr Tollesbury. He was still looking past her. 'Abandoned her – a frightened child. She was too scared to tell us until the night she died, when she was too far gone for help. She took sleeping pills. My wife died of grief. Lyle took everything from me.'

'So, you swore vengeance,' whispered Lucy.

'Yes. When Rosie died, I swore whoever had done that to her would pay. I don't look like an avenger, do I my dear? No mask, sword or black cloak. But I have nursed vengeance in my heart for twenty-five years. I just didn't know *who* I needed to make pay.'

'She didn't tell you?'

Mr Tollesbury shook his head. 'Rose never told me his name,' he said. 'She was loyal even when he deserted her, even when she was dying. She said the man laughed in her face when she told him she was pregnant. All I knew about the man is that they were attached to the dig that came to the village, but they'd moved on by then. When the famous hoard was discovered, there was great excitement – all these archaeologists and historians coming and journalists too. Rosie was most excited of all, she loved the idea of digging up treasures from the past. She'd not always had it easy, Rosie – she was born lame – but she was as cheerful as anything. I was working as a plumber then, doing nicely for myself. We had a cottage on the edge of the village. My wife made a little extra money by selling sandwiches and beer to the people at the dig. Rosie would carry it down for her. That's how she met him, I suppose.

'The night Rosie died, all my dreams changed. I'd always been interested in history, as a hobby, but it wasn't for boys like me – well, now I applied myself. I thought it might, one day, bring me closer to the man who had killed her.

'Plenty of people reinvent themselves. I reinvented myself, over the years, as Professor Tollesbury. It's not hard to falsify credentials, Lucy, not hard to play a part. I aimed high – for Oxford, in fact – and I fooled the board who interviewed me. They never looked past my accent and tweed suit. Antiquity teachers were in short supply.' His gaze landed on her and she was struck anew by the sadness in it. 'If anyone had a right to vengeance, it was me.'

'All this time, you waited, trying to discover who the seducer might be,' said Lucy. 'Then, one night, you found out. The night of the lecture.' She thought back to Gordon Lyle, holding forth in his big, booming voice. *Why, she had a club foot and a squint eye!* 'Of course. He told you, right to your face, with all the details that made you realise that Gordon Lyle was that young archaeologist who had seduced and ruined your daughter.'

'Joking about it – one of his sordid little stories. He had hurt so many people, over the years. He deserved to pay. But this was not a crime that could be punishable by law. There was only one way.'

'Murder,' said Lucy. 'But Dr Lyle was eminent, wealthy, well connected. Famous throughout the country. If he was killed, there would be an investigation. His past connections would be examined. You needed a distraction, to send the investigation immediately in the wrong direction. You needed some set dressing. You needed a story.'

'People love stories,' said Mr Tollesbury dreamily. 'Look around you, Lucy – this whole shop is testament to that.'

'It's why you were such a good teacher – you always span a terrific yarn. You were shocked when Dr Lyle revealed he was the man behind Rose's death all those years ago, but you thought quickly. You wanted him dead – and not just dead, but *discredited*. Ruined, even after death. You wanted him stripped for ever of all his glory.'

'Men like that are untouchable,' said Mr Tollesbury. 'Someone had to hold him to account.'

'Dr Curry had made his explosive accusations during the lecture, but he was easy to dismiss. You knew it wouldn't worry Lyle for long. You had an idea, though, as Dr Lyle was talking. The sudden death of Sir Archibald Drake had already started rumours of an Ancient Egyptian curse – well, what if those rumours became reality?'

289

He nodded, looking pleased. 'The public would eat up a curse if there was another death. And, as for the police, if a madman was killing members of the expedition, no one would think to look for another motive for *one* of the deaths. They wouldn't look too deeply into Dr Lyle's unsavoury past. But it had to be sensational. Something the press and public couldn't ignore. What if Dr Curry died at the exhibition the following night? Mr Dakin was worried about it – it was easy to suggest he decorate the room like a tomb. I knew he would be delighted by such a theatrical concept and would think it was all his own idea. And, while I was talking to him, I relieved him of his keys.'

'But you needed evidence of a serial killer avenging the tomb opening,' Lucy said. 'That's why you needed me to be involved. You needed to make sure I opened the note and took it to the police.'

She drew a deep breath and looked to him for an answer, much as she had in class.

Mr Tollesbury nodded. 'Top marks, Lucy. I had Dr Curry's address, from when I put him in the taxi, and Mr Dakin's keys – those were easy to filch. I went to Dr Curry's house that night, told him I believed him. He knew me to be a respectable, eminent professor. The fool was so relieved to be listened to at last, he would have done anything I said. He was a sly little man, listened to gossip and rumours and believed he had one over on the members of the Society. Mrs van Buren, he hinted she had killed her first husband. Sir Hector had been indiscreet regarding his gambling debts. And Dr Lyle was a charlatan, of course.'

'So, Dr Curry intended to blackmail them?' asked Lucy.

'He intended to try. But I told him I had a better idea, one that would keep within the law. I told him Dr Lyle had pulled this sort of stunt before, that it was time he was brought down. But we had to be careful. The museum and public would always believe Dr Lyle over us, would do their utmost to cover up the truth. We had to put our heads together and come up with something ingenious, daring, outrageous, to expose Dr Lyle.'

'You persuaded him to come to the crime scene?'

'Desperate people are suggestible, Lucy. If Curry confronted Lyle in the tomb, there would be a captive audience – the museum board, high society, the newspapers present. Curry could publicly accuse him all over again – but properly this time, when Lyle would have no means of escape and plenty of press there to record it.' The professor snorted. 'Silly fool. I let Dr Curry into the shop with Dakin's key before dawn, told him to hide in the sarcophagus. I locked up, then dropped the keys on the mat outside. He was already in the room when Mr Dakin checked it a few hours later. Mr Dakin dressed the room, left for his breakfast. Toby told me he was going out for a bit that morning, which was a piece of luck – I had planned to say I was going to bed with toothache, but I didn't need to. I waited till he'd gone, then I knocked on the door and Dr Curry let me in. I had the ochre and furs upstairs – I have plenty of relics from my time in the field. It took no time to knock up a shabti with a gash across the throat. Curry and I decorated the room together. I told him it would scare Lyle.'

'Mrs van Buren heard you laughing together,' Lucy remembered.

'Yes, he thought it all a good joke. I heard knocking, but didn't realise whoever it was had heard us. Don't feel too bad for Dr Curry, Lucy. He didn't feel a thing. He was half asleep by the time I had him rigged up.'

'You drugged him,' murmured Lucy.

'It was cold in the shop,' said Mr Tollesbury. 'I brought a thermos of tea with me, along with the props and Toby's knife, and insisted he drank it. I didn't want him to suffer – or put up too much of a fight. I was back at the flat well before eleven-thirty. I narrowly missed Toby coming back, looking guilty as anything. When he came to me later that evening and told me he was scared of the police, I told him I would cover for him.'

'But in reality, he was providing *you* with the alibi. Pretending you were both together. And then, the next step of your plan. To discredit Dr Lyle.'

He smiled. 'Dr Curry had brought me his pathetic bundle of evidence to use against Lyle that night – well, I *did* use it. I hid it in Cecil Court, under some old wooden boards. I thought I could pretend to stumble across it myself one day – but I didn't need to, because you found it and took it to the police. I was determined that Lyle would be discredited. His name would be associated not with the expedition but with shame and disgrace. And *then* he would die. Exactly when I chose.'

'Timing was crucial, so you couldn't risk the notes getting lost in the post,' Lucy went on. 'You slipped them in with the regular post when it arrived at the shop. You'd used stamps from your collection so there would be a postmark. I wondered why you did that, when you could have easily posted them from different boroughs during a walk. But you needed to be sure *when* I got the letters.'

He bowed his head.

'The next murder was the most important. You couldn't take any chances. You went to the British Museum that morning early wearing a pair of Toby's overalls and waited in the recess beside Dr Lyle's office. The regular cleaning staff came – you slipped in when they came out and crossed over into Langley's office. I think he saw you – he mentioned two or *three* cleaners to Felix. You hid in his office . . .'

'That hideous screen,' said Mr Tollesbury. 'I waited behind that. He was surprised to see me when I came out – amused, when I explained who I was.'

'Did you ask him about Rose?'

'Of course,' said Mr Tollesbury. 'I reminded him of the whole sorry tale. I gave him the chance to apologise. He didn't even remember Rose's name. He laughed at me, called me pathetic. Told me to get out. I told him I was leaving and then, when he turned away . . . I had to stun him first, I'm only an old man. But he was conscious, just. I took my time telling him how he'd die. I wanted him to feel everything.'

'Why did you need to kill Mrs van Buren?' asked Lucy. 'You had what you wanted – Dr Lyle discredited, dead. You could have just stopped there.'

'That was your fault, Lucy,' Mr Tollesbury said reproachfully. 'You asked me to speak to her and she told me she'd been outside Dakin's shop – while me and Dr Curry were inside. She didn't seem to have heard much, but she *could* have done. For all I knew, she recognised my voice, suspected me. I was a plumber when I was a young man – I know those old buildings would have a gas flu in the fireplace and I knew that a slow leak could kill someone over time. I sent her out of the room on a pretext. I wasn't sure if it would work, but I did my best. I waited a few days, then sent the note. I posted the shabti to her flat.'

'You found an unexpected ally in Mr Eastley,' Lucy said. 'His confession must have surprised you.'

Mr Tollesbury laughed. 'Mr Eastley, now – he really *was* an unexpected gift. I could not have dreamt of a more likely suspect. But actually, Toby was always meant to be *the fall guy*, as they say in those terrible American books he reads.'

'That's why you used his knife. Only Toby's fingerprints remained because you were wearing gloves.' She eyed Mr Tollesbury. 'You're wearing them now, Professor.'

'That's right,' he said. 'Are you feeling sleepy, Lucy?'

'A little, now you mention it. You wanted to call it quits once Mrs van Buren died. But someone had put two and two together – someone who was sharper than they seemed. Mr Dakin.'

'Appearances can be deceiving,' said Mr Tollesbury. 'I admit, I always thought the man was an idiot.'

'He surprised you there,' said Lucy. 'He realised that there was no way all the notes could be arriving in the post. The postman was only coming once a week, because of the strikes. He was always peering out into Cecil Court. No errand boy came on the morning of Dr Lyle's death, delivering a letter. It began to dawn on Mr Dakin that if nobody had delivered the anonymous letters, yet the letters were on the mat, then the person sending the notes *had to be someone within the shop*.'

Mr Tollesbury let out a breath. 'That pompous, interfering—'

'Don't forget greedy. Dr Curry's murder had ruined him financially. Mr Dakin saw an opportunity for blackmail. He decided to take matters into his own hands, didn't he? I thought he seemed very pleased with himself, before that last note came.'

'Silly man,' said Mr Tollesbury irritably. 'He sent his own cryptic message, knowing that only one person would respond to the threat of blackmail – the killer. I was confused when that message arrived. The note looked different too – different paper, a different typewriter. But I knew what it meant. I thought Dakin had seen something. I urged you to go to the police – I knew that the Needle would be surrounded by the law. While you were at the police station and Toby was in bed, I waited in Cecil Court for Dakin to leave.'

Lucy nodded, imagining the moment. 'You followed him, dressed in Toby's overalls and a cap pulled down over your eyes. You took Toby's knife . . .'

'I only wanted to kill one person,' said Mr Tollesbury.

'And yet you've murdered three. So far.'

'So far, indeed,' said Mr Tollesbury amiably. 'So, Mr Dakin was taking a stab in the dark, so to speak? He knew the killer was in the shop, but that was all. Well, well. I struck well before the meeting point, on what I thought was a nice, deserted bit of shoreline. I didn't expect you to be on the scene. Still, it played into my hands – I made sure to drop the knife nice and loudly so that one of you went looking for it.'

Lucy shook her head. 'I won't forgive you for that, you know. For framing Toby.'

'Collateral damage,' said Mr Tollesbury. 'I think Sir Marcus might have got his conviction, in the end. If Mr Eastley hadn't been so obliging.'

'He was desperate to be arrested. But I wonder whether his story holds up. I imagine the inspector will see through it. How long have you been dreaming of your vengeance, Mr Tollesbury?'

'For twenty-five years,' whispered Mr Tollesbury. 'Ever since she died. My little Rosie.' He leaned forward. 'Are you feeling all right Lucy? You look rather pale.'

Lucy put a hand to her chest. Her eyes drooped. 'The tea,' she murmured. 'You put something in it . . .'

'I had no choice,' said Mr Tollesbury. His eyes were full of tears. 'It's a shame. I'm fond of you, Lucy. My best student.'

'Or at least the most curious,' said Lucy.

Mr Tollesbury stood and took a step closer. Lucy saw the glint of steel in his hand. He raised the knife – an ordinary kitchen knife, she saw – and Lucy sprang. She gripped his wrist, bending it backwards until, with a cry of pain, he dropped it. Lucy shoved him back with all her strength.

'I didn't drink the tea, Mr Tollesbury,' she told him, ducking and picking up the knife. 'I'm not stupid.'

He staggered, catching himself on the back of the chair. She watched him as she edged towards the phone, holding the knife in a firm grip.

'You're making a mistake, Lucy,' he said, his voice cracking. 'If you call the police on me – an old man—'

'Please,' said Lucy, 'spare me.'

'Then,' he said, his eyes pitiless now, 'I may need to take more drastic measures.' He drew a revolver from his breast pocket and drew back the barrel with the sound of a deadly click.

'Not so fast,' came a cold voice. 'Step away, Professor.' Susan stepped from the shadows, a pearl-handled revolver in her gloved hand. 'I'm a mean shot. And you always told us to question authority.'

Chapter 38

But why on earth were you at the museum the week before Dr Curry died?' Lucy asked Toby. 'You can tell us the truth *now*, can't you?'

They were in her sitting room – Felix with Susan's feet in his lap, Toby perched on the edge of the sofa as usual. A martini sat untouched at his elbow. *I must remember to get in some beer next time*, Lucy thought. The newcomers in the room were the inspector and the sergeant, both looking rather out of place. Both had declined a drink.

'I wanted to see Dr Lyle,' said Toby. 'I went to the museum and found his office, but I got too scared to knock – that old professor over the hall saw me and I got nervous. In the end, I left him a note instead, pushed under the door, asking him to meet me near Cecil Court the next week.'

'But why? What was Dr Lyle to you?'

Toby reached into his breast pocket and produced an envelope, worn soft as satin. He drew out a letter, unfolded it, and handed it carefully to Lucy.

Dear Tobias,
It is good to hear from you. Your mother would have been happy to know you were well cared for.

You asked me if I knew who your father was. I have thought long and hard before replying. It sits badly with me to betray my sister's confidence, but I believe you should know.

Your mother gave me a name before she died and begged me to tell no one. Your father's name was Gordon Lyle – a well-known figure, living in London. Your mother was a servant in his house-hold when he was a young man. There's no point in writing to him – she wrote when she found out and again when you were born, and he wanted nothing to do with you or her.

We did what we thought was the best thing for you and your poor mother, placing you with Christian people. We think of you often.

Very best,
John Turner.

'Gordon Lyle was your father?' Lucy said.

'That's what my uncle told me – I was sixteen then. I'd always been curious. After that, I couldn't stop thinking about Gordon Lyle. He was often in the papers, you know – he was famous in his way. Always travelling to wild lands, digging up ancient tombs. I collected everything I could find about him. When my work got, er, thrown up in the air . . .'

Lucy nodded. 'When your boss went to jail again.'

'Yeah. I started to think, what if I went to London and found my father? He hadn't wanted to know all those years ago, but he might feel different now I was older. He'd only been a young man himself when I was born. Had nothing to lose, so I came.

'I knew he worked at the British Museum, so I looked for work nearby. Didn't have much luck and Dr Lyle was in Egypt anyway. Then Mr Tollesbury gave me a chance here. Didn't ask for refer-ences or qualifications, once he saw I could do the job. Always very kind to me. I liked it, knowing something you all didn't about the famous Gordon Lyle.

'When he got back from Egypt, I finally plucked up the courage to go and find him, but I lost my nerve like I said. I left him a note, telling him who I was and asking him to meet near Cecil Court the morning of the exhibition. But he never came—'

Toby swallowed and Lucy looked away. She couldn't imagine that Gordon Lyle would have looked kindly on his offspring appearing from the past at his place of work. His reaction would have given Toby nothing more than heartbreak. But she ached for the lad nonetheless, that he missed the chance to meet his father. She recalled Mrs Lyle mentioning how nervy her husband had been in the week before his death. Having an illegitimate son appear on the eve of his triumph must have added to the strain. Of course he had never gone to meet Toby; Lucy imagined he had swiftly burnt the note and hoped it would go away. Dr Lyle, it seemed, had a history of hoping past indiscretions would go away.

'So that's why you were outside on the morning of Dr Curry's murder,' she said. 'You were waiting to meet Mr Lyle.'

'Yeah. But he never came so I went back to the shop. When I found out about the murder and that the police were coming, I was scared. I asked the professor what I should do – I told him I had a record, and they might recognise me. He told me not to worry, that we should tell the police that I'd not left the shop, that we were here all morning together. And then after that – everything seemed to go wrong. That Mr Eastley had seen me, described me to the police. And it was my knife that stabbed Mr Dakin.'

'He should pull through,' said the sergeant comfortably. 'He's conscious. It scared the life out of him. He's admitted to the blackmail attempt.'

'Did the professor drop the knife on purpose?' said Toby quietly. 'To pin it on me?'

'You were framed,' said the inspector. 'Your knife, your fingerprints. A criminal record. But then Mr Eastley appeared. We went from having no suspects, to having two. And neither of them quite convinced me.'

'I hope Mr Eastley gets the help he needs,' said Susan thoughtfully. 'Even if he did nearly kill Lucy.'

Toby said, 'He *was* kind in some ways. Mr Tollesbury, I mean. Offering me a job when no one else would have.'

'He donated to our political fund,' said Susan.

'And he was my guarantor for this shop,' added Lucy. 'But this had been his life's obsession. Revenge. It's like you said, Susan. The oldest motive in the world. Older than money even.'

'He'll hang,' said the sergeant. 'Unless the jury take pity on him, with that story.'

Lucy shivered. The professor always had been good at spinning stories. Perhaps he would be able to tell the jury a good enough one.

'What did Mrs van Buren leave you in her will, Lucy?' asked Susan suddenly. 'I'm dying to know. Is it her house? A first edition? One of those statues?'

'No,' said Lucy. 'She left me a good chunk of her fortune. I should imagine her sister will contest it with all her might. But it's on the condition that I do something *good* with it. She was trying to redeem herself from beyond the grave. I'm not sure why she picked on me.'

'I think she did kill her husband,' Susan said.

'I think you're right,' said the inspector. 'Not that anyone could prove it. But between us, I do think she killed him.'

'What worthy cause can you find?' Susan asked. 'More artistic endeavours?'

'I'm not sure,' said Lucy. 'But it won't go to another expedition or buying some artefacts. If she trusted me, I'm going to use it to help some real people.'

'Lucy,' said Felix nervously, finishing his drink. 'I know this isn't the best time, given – well, given, er, everything – but there's something I need to tell you.'

'It's all right, Felix,' said Lucy, yawning. 'I know. Bryan Campbell has offered you a job at the glamorous Campbell's. I should take it if I were you.'

Felix gasped. 'Lucy, you witch! But actually, your detective skills must be exhausted, because that's *not* what I was going to tell you. For what it's worth, I turned Campbell down from the off. He doesn't like taking no for an answer.' He went a little pink. 'I'll have a drink with him, mind – he's frightfully attractive, isn't he?'

'He is.' Lucy stared at him, a smile beginning to spread across her face at the thought of not losing Felix. 'I'm glad you're not going anywhere. What did you want to tell me?'

Felix slid a sheet of paper across the table. 'End of year fiction sales. I thought you might like to take a look. Thanks to our salacious acquisition from abroad, they're looking a bit . . . healthier than expected.'

Lucy looked down at the paper and shrieked.

Chapter 39

wo days later, on a quiet Thursday night, Lucy met Bryan Campbell for lunch in a Parisian-themed brasserie in Soho, around the corner from his shop, all shining brass and red leather banquettes. Mr Campbell, in his elegant navy suit, looked more outsize and larger than life than usual. He rose and gave her his lazy grin.

'So, this is it,' he said. 'The great reckoning. Ready to lose, Miss Darkwether?'

'I'm prepared for the worst,' said Lucy, smiling at him. 'Shall we order some food first?'

They ordered sole and then crepe suzette and coffee. They discussed the arrest in the Egyptian mummy murder and Lucy told Mr Campbell the abridged version of what had not made it into the papers, which he listened to with gratifying interest, telling her repeatedly how plucky she was. As Lucy stirred her coffee, Mr Campbell drew out a sheet of paper from his breast pocket.

'Statement of accounts,' he said, setting it down. He laid his broad palm over the paper. 'Chessie was very fair about it. You won't find any cooking the books, I can tell you that.'

'I'm sure,' said Lucy. She picked up her bag and took out the sheet Felix had given her, covered in his neat figures. 'Here's mine and no cooking of books either. Shall we compare in silence for a moment? I hope you haven't beaten us by too dazzling a margin – my pride won't recover.'

'Sure,' he said amiably. 'Why don't I shift over and sit beside you, so we can take a good look.'

They laid the sheets side by side. Lucy could feel the warmth from his arm against hers. He smelled of something clean and fresh, outdoorsy and entirely out of keeping with the world of books and antiquities. Lucy carefully read the final line of the statement and composed herself while Mr Campbell did the same.

'Well!' he exclaimed at last. Lucy looked up into his rueful eyes. There was a pause in which humour and hurt pride warred visibly on Mr Campbell's face. Eventually, humour won. He burst out laughing. 'You beat me, Miss Darkwether, fair and square! By a whole two shillings, but even so. What is this title that has sent your sales through the roof?'

'A racy read, banned in England, but don't tell a soul,' Lucy warned him. 'I'll deny everything and all the evidence has been sold to the finest of high society, who will also deny it. It was Felix's idea, of course. We only meant to sell fifty copies but when we made that bet, I told Felix to go wild and order more. We charged the earth too.'

Bryan Campbell shook his head admiringly. 'I'll hire that man yet, mark my words.'

'Maybe,' said Lucy. 'He's shown himself surprisingly loyal so far. What do you think, Mr Campbell – will you and your sister agree to leave Cecil Court Books alone? Expand elsewhere? I'm sure equally charming and characterful sites exist.'

He nodded. 'I'm a man of my word, Miss Darkwether. You'll do your business, and I'll do mine. I'll tell your landlord I won't be pursuing the lease.'

'Shake on it?' said Lucy.

He held out his hand and they shook. His fingers on hers were warm and he held her hand a few seconds longer than necessary.

'Now that we're merely business rivals,' Bryan said, leaning closer, 'how about I take you out this evening? We can go dancing.

I've got to tell you, Chessie put me onto this scheme, but it's a relief to have it over with.'

Lucy hesitated. A night out with Bryan Campbell, free from the shadow of the mummy's curse, was exactly what she wanted. But right now, what she *needed*, she thought, was about a year's worth of sleep.

'Another time, perhaps,' she said, extricating her hand and ignoring the flutter in her stomach. 'It's been quite a week. And I'm due at my parents' for tea.'

* * *

In her parents' sitting room, John and Maggie pored over a pile of brochures and put wedding invitations into envelopes. Lamps were lit to fight back the late afternoon gloom. Maggie was wearing country tweeds and red lipstick, John was sitting with shirt sleeves rolled up. Her father was asleep in his armchair, his pipe in hand. The cosy scene did not, somehow, seem real after the lurid events of the last twenty-four hours.

Her mother handed her a slice of plum cake on a cracked plate. 'Lucy! You look awful! I can't believe everything that has happened to you! I wish you'd move home for a bit. Those reporters will leave you alone here – your father sent them packing.'

'And all along, it was your fusty old professor,' said John. 'You always were such a fan of his, Lucy. I confess I don't understand how this Eastley chap fits in. Or this Toby Calvert.'

'They were both just red herrings,' said Lucy, dropping into a chair. She took a mouthful of cake, luscious and sweet, cloyingly so, then put down her plate. 'Mr Eastley wanted to align himself with the case and he only lashed out when I cornered him. I don't think he ever meant to hurt anyone. And, as for Toby, he was just a scapegoat. Maggie, I meant to say – thank you for the business advice. I found my edge as the underdog, broke a few rules, and put Bryan Campbell and his sister in their place. I won the bet and Cecil Court Books remains in my hands for the foreseeable future.'

The triumph felt hollow. The girl who had taken out the lease on Cecil Court Books, fresh out of Oxford, full of dreams of starting a business with her adored tutor – that girl felt very far away.

'I always did have a head for business,' said Maggie complacently, licking a final stamp and tossing the envelope on the pile. 'I saved my daddy from a scrape more than once. Go on, then. Tell us what the papers can't, and the police won't, about the murders.'

'Another time,' Lucy said, wincing. 'It's all a bit raw.'

'All right, old thing,' said John. 'But you are mean; we've been waiting on tenterhooks for the full story. We'll have to go back to planning our honeymoon.' He picked up a glossy travel brochure at his elbow.

'Thinking of travelling abroad?' Lucy asked.

'I've had enough of this miserable climate,' said Maggie. She turned down the corner of a brochure with a ocean liner on the front. 'We're going to take ourselves somewhere hot. We're thinking of Egypt.'

* * *

As Lucy left her parents' house, her comfortable bed firmly in mind, she walked straight into a tall figure, walking quickly. Edward. He looked tense, she thought. His jaw was set and his usually neat hair wild.

'Lucy,' he exclaimed. 'That Felix chap said you weren't at the shop and then your maid said she wasn't sure where you were, but maybe with your parents. I came here to find you.'

'Well, you found me,' said Lucy warily.

'I saw that the mummy business was over. But this is more important.' Edward took a deep breath and seized her hands in his. 'I must tell you how I feel.'

'Edward!' Lucy took a step back and fought to repress a wave of hysterical laughter. *I'm too tired*, she thought. *This is what comes of staying awake for two days – I'm having some sort of halluci-nation, one where Edward proposes, yet again.* 'Edward, please, come to your senses. You're engaged, to Helen, who has a five-year plan for the ranch.'

His grip on her hands only tightened. 'I've tried to pretend, but I can't,' he said. 'Helen and I – we're friends, good friends, busi-ness partners, but we don't understand each other, not like you and I do Lucy. I could continue to make a life in the Argentine, but I'd want you by my side. You want to be independent – well, in South America, you can be what you want.' He fixed his eyes on her – pleading, dark eyes that she knew so well. 'What do you say – would you try it?'

Lucy stared at Edward and behind her eyes a picture took shape. Beautiful, open lands, lush forest, a ranch, horses galloping, dust rising up from their hooves. She could smell the earth and the trees. It *would* be exciting. But then, there rose in her mind another picture entirely. Cecil Court, piles of books, the smell of coffee and worn pages. Susan muttering over the accounts, Felix chatting to customers, Toby's head bent, carefully slicing paper (she would have to keep an eye on him around the till, she thought). And Mr Tollesbury – no Mr Tollesbury, of course.

He hadn't managed to ruin Cecil Court Books for her, she real-ised. It was still hers, it always had been.

Gently, she withdrew her hands from Edward's. 'I'm sorry, Edward,' she said. 'In my own way I love you and always shall, and I wish you all the luck in the world. But I don't think the Argentine is for me after all. You see, I have a bookshop to run.'

* * *

There was another tall figure waiting for her at her apartment, looking uncomfortable and out of place in her sitting room. All of a sudden, Lucy didn't feel tired at all. Instead, she felt an odd sense of anticipation.

'Inspector,' said Lucy. She felt, suddenly, overwhelmingly aware of him. 'How nice of you to drop by. And how unexpected. I thought our association was ended with the arrest. No more meddling, I promise.'

He gave a faint, reluctant smile. 'I thought I should come back and say thank you. For solving the case.'

Lucy's own smile faltered. 'Oh, the case. It – it was a team effort,' she said, but he held up his hand, stepping closer.

'If you hadn't kept on at me,' said Inspector Hayes, 'I would have been forced to let Sir Marcus run the investigation his way and Mr Eastley would probably be in jail now. Or worse, Toby Turner.' He took a step closer to Lucy and his fingers grazed her cheek, with the lightest possible touch. 'Is that a black eye Eastley gave you?'

'I think it's going to be a shiner,' said Lucy, with a touch of bravado. Her heart was beating fast, so fast that for a moment she was worried he could hear it, but when he took his fingers away, she felt sorry. 'And you told me detective work wasn't that exciting.'

'This is the first time I've come across an ancient curse,' he admitted. 'Or arrested three different suspects in forty-eight hours. Or had to work with such a frustrating – and persistent – witness as you, Miss Darkwether.'

'It's Lucy,' she said. 'Inspector Hayes. I think after all this I should know your first name.'

His expression softened. 'In that case, Lucy—'

'Excuse me,' said Mrs Thorpe, sticking her head round the door. 'But Lucy, that's Felix on the phone. Something about a new title you simply have to get the jump on.'

'That's my cue to leave,' said Inspector Hayes. 'Oh, and speaking of your enterprising bookseller – I would advise you to make the next order of novels from the continent your last. Some may be arguing it's art, but the Met are taking a different view. On one hand, I hope we don't meet again, Miss Darkwether – it spells trouble. But on the other . . .' His eyes locked with hers for a moment before he turned to go.

When the door closed behind him, Lucy stood quite still for a moment, hands on the back of the chair, waiting for her heart to steady. How strange that the quiet inspector should have made her feel this way.

Then she hurried into the bedroom to take the call.

*　*　*

Mrs Thorpe watched from the street as the officer walked, shoulders bent against the wind, saw him stop and turn and look up at the house. She heard Lucy hang up the phone, humming along with the gramophone, sounding happier than she had in weeks. Mrs Thorpe couldn't help but wonder a little . . .

DAILY MIRROR

Killer Brought to Justice In Mummy Curse Mystery.

After several false leads, a series of startling events resulted in the unlikely arrest of retired Oxford professor in the murders of the Ancient Egyptian Mummy, a case which has gripped and fascinated Londoners this past month. The curse, it seems, has ended, and a reign of terror cut short.

Sir Marcus Derwent announced that the evidence against the professor was overwhelming. He also confirmed that he would be retiring in the coming weeks, following the satisfying conclusion of the case. It seems there was no supernatural influence, only a human hand at work. In a separate statement, Sir Hector Derwent announced the dissolution of the famous Society whose ill-fated expedition saw the disturbance of the tomb and whose quest for financial gain brought the mummy to our shores – and untold terror to our streets.

Sir Marcus assures this paper that the atmosphere of superstition and dread that has gripped our city is truly at an end. There will be no more anonymous letters, presaging disaster and taunting our police, no more killings. Our city's streets are safe once more – or so the police would have us believe. This reporter always refuted the idea of a curse. And yet the past casts long and uncertain shadows . . . and some mysteries, it seems, are better left buried.

Acknowledgements

A heartfelt thank you to everyone involved with this book – to Melissa Cox for the opportunity to pay tribute to the Golden Age of detective stories; Caroline Hogg for the edit; Lily Cooper and Kate Norman for the editorial input; Saffron Stocker for a beautiful cover, Alyssa Ollivier-Tabukashvili for the copyedit, Annabel Maunder for the proofread. Thanks to Jane Finigan for everything and to Louise for the always invaluable feedback. A huge extra thank you to Alex and our network of friends for helping me juggle writing books alongside the day job. And to Flo and Theo for being so awesome – can't wait for you to discover the Golden Age of crime for yourselves.